BRAD HELD THE PHONE IN HIS HAND, AND FELT HIS ANGER RISING AT THE TONE OF MALLARD'S VOICE...

"So you think you might be the next victim, Mallard?" He tried to keep his voice even and free of irritation.

"What on earth do you mean?" Mallard's voice sounded strained. "Have you heard something about the deaths? What relationship would I have in all this?"

"Well," began Brad, "to begin with, you were a Knife, like the other two victims. And you were here in town during both killings. Shall I go on?"

"It seems to me, Brad, that those same random circumstances apply to you," Mallard said uneasily. "You could just as well be the next victim."

"Or the killer," Brad responded evenly....

TRIAD
OF KNIVES
TOM COOPER

A GOLD EAGLE BOOK

London · Toronto · New York · Sydney

*First published in Great Britain 1987
by Gold Eagle*

© William Thomas Cooper 1986

*Australian copyright 1986
Philippine copyright 1986
This edition 1987*

ISBN 0 373 97020 X

25/1187

*Printed and bound in Great Britain by
Cox & Wyman Ltd, Reading*

1

"YOU DON'T LOOK LIKE A SPY."

Nan Donahue watched her father straighten his silk tie in front of the ornate full-length mirror in the hallway of his apartment. He looked like millions of American businessmen preparing to leave for a day at the office. It was difficult for her to comprehend that for the entire thirty years of her life, Dan Donahue had been an official with the Central Intelligence Agency.

She moved closer to straighten the new silver tie tack she had just presented to him. Dan turned to her with an open, loving smile.

"Now tell me, Nancy. Just what does a spy look like?"

Nan tilted her head and ran her slender fingers through her long auburn hair. She appraised her father's neat, conservative suit, which cloaked his strong, muscular build. There was much more to him than his outward appearance would indicate.

Dan Donahue was a deceptive, intriguing man. His manner and appearance were almost professorial. He was not yet portly, for his routine physical workouts had arrested the creeping softness of his fifty-three years. At a second look, there was an understated elegance in the way he wore his silk tie and blue summer-weight wool suit.

A more studious observer could see his occasional cautious hesitations, his ever-moving, detail-consuming eyes, and the catlike tensing and relaxing of muscles in the changing of his stance. Nan reveled in the warmth of his smile. She reached up to touch and tame a lock of his reddish hair which, as usual, was in disarray across his forehead.

"You know. Sort of stooped over, in a dirty trench coat with the collar turned up, and an old slouch hat, with the brim turned down over the eyes."

Dan laughed out loud and gently clasped her shoulders as a proud father would, his mouth pulled into a mischievous grin. Despite a formality that lay between them, she felt the loving comfort that her visit had brought to them.

"Precious daughter, welcome to the age of computers and space satellites. I haven't worn a trench coat in years."

Nan knew his words were meant to soothe her. Through the years, she had learned something of his covert activities: his secret trips abroad, his multiple identities, and the gun he sometimes carried when extra caution demanded it. He was a complex man who lived and moved on several levels simultaneously. He was a careful observer, ever on the alert for the revelations of apparently insignificant details.

He was also her doting father, and she his impetuous daughter. By profession a secretive man, she knew he needed her affection and grand demonstrations of their father-daughter relationship on each of their infrequent meetings. In spite of his disapproval of her headstrong and quite often unpredictable behavior, she realized her presence gave him peace. Now, she would do her best to keep her life in order, at least temporarily, to show him how much she cared.

"Maybe that's why you're so successful. You look like a successful businessman."

"Well, I'm still alive, if that's any measure of success," he said in a more serious tone. "But enough of this spook talk," he said brightly. "What will you do with this fine spring morning?"

Her green eyes sparkled. "I'm going to finish packing and call some friends. I have to let my office know what time my flight arrives."

Dan took her slender hands in his rough and large ones, and looked into her eyes, his expression turning serious, his voice rich with feeling.

"Nancy, you've had a rough time of it, with your divorce. Not to mention your efforts at establishing a career in photography and modeling. But you've bounced back. The success of your fashion-design agency shows that, and I'm pleased and proud of you. You deserve the best."

"Thanks, Dad." Her voice quavered. "That means a lot to me."

The moments fled by in painful silence as a multitude of disorganized thoughts rushed through her head. Dan finally released a sigh, worry still registering in his eyes, a frown marking his brow.

"I'm sorry that I've been away for so much of the time that you needed someone close to you. If only your mother had lived," he added wistfully.

Nan recalled vividly the loneliness and pain of separation since her mother's illness and death twenty years ago. Her mind raced back over the years of CIA foreign assignments that kept her father overseas while she was enrolled in stateside boarding schools, exclusive colleges, and stop-and-go attempts at a career and marriage. She forced a smile for his benefit, quelling a pain in her heart.

"I know, Dad. You've done what you could, and I love you for it. But I would have had to do it my way, on my own, regardless of who was or wasn't there. I've had to accept some compromises and begin a new life. That other life is behind me now, and I've made the adjustment. At least, I hope I have. Sometimes..." She let her voice become inaudible.

"You're starting life anew, Pobrecita, and it will be painful at first."

She warmed to the endearment. *Poor little one.* He had called her that as far back as her memory could recall.

"Dad, I've been making an inventory of my personal assets, while trying to develop my business. My figure is too full now for me to be a model, and photography is out. I refuse to have my creativity constricted by the confines of a camera lens. So I simply must succeed with this design work."

"But Nancy, you're *suay mak*, very beautiful. You're strong enough to take on this design challenge. You'll be a success."

"Well, I've decided to devote all my energies and all my knowledge of upper-class life to my fashion design agency. I know I have the creative ability to make it work, if I can just come up with some new, exciting ideas."

"You will, darling. The secret is to unite your friends and spite your enemies."

She rolled her eyes. "Oh, I won't tell you what my enemies say about me! That's too painful to deal with right now. My friends say I'm beautiful and elegant, but not quite self-assured."

"You can handle it, Nancy. You handled those damned social butterflies once before."

She gave a painful shrug and meandered around the room, reluctantly recalling how she had been cruelly dominated physically and emotionally in her marriage, the painful breakup and divorce, and the other agonies of her tattered life.

Dan watched his daughter struggling with the torment of her memories. "What is it you're searching for?" he asked quietly.

Nan compressed her lips for a long moment, trying to mold the thoughts into words. When she spoke, the mellow softness in her voice surprised even her.

"I want a real man for a partner in life. A stable, but sensitive man that I can be open and honest with. Someone with feelings, someone I can share the small details of everyday life with, like waking up every morning in our own bed. Together." She glanced up at him shyly. "God, I've needed someone I trust to talk to. I don't know when I've talked to anyone like this." She looked away, but continued. "I suppose what I'm looking for is pretty idealistic."

Her face felt flushed, mirroring her feelings of vulnerability. Her father smiled and nodded approvingly.

"Hang on to your dreams, Nancy. Dreams tell you what you are, but they can also tell you what to aim for. Decide what you want and go after it. Just keep telling yourself: I want this—and getting it will be as easy as saying it."

"I'll remember that," she said, fighting back the tears that for some reason were filling her eyes.

"That's my girl."

"Dad, will you be there for me to lean on until some eager, unsuspecting, needful god stumbles over me?" she asked with a childlike smile on her face.

He walked over and put a hand on her shoulder. "Yes, I will," he said, softly, with love and pride. "After all, you're my favorite only daughter. We'll make things different for you now, Nancy. We'll talk things out together. This assignment I'm on now will probably lead to a desk job here in Washington, and I'll be able to spend more time with you, at last."

"Oh, Dad, I'm so happy to hear that. I'll try not to be a nuisance."

"A nuisance! You could never be anything but a delight. And as short as this visit has been, it's been a pleasure."

"I've loved it too. I hate to leave, but I need to get back to my work."

Dan nodded understandingly. "I have work to do too. I only regret that the phone call earlier is taking me away for your last morning here. I'll pick you up for lunch at Raphael's though, and then take you to National Airport from there, so please have all your bags ready."

Nan detected a subtle change in her father. As he talked, he turned and walked to his massive mahogany desk. Unlocking the center drawer, he removed a small black revolver. After checking it carefully, he tucked it deftly into a holster under his arm. The sight and the anticipated significance of the weapon brought Nan down to a more serious mood.

"Must be a difficult case. I've always wondered how often you actually have to use that gun."

"Oh, I could tell you some colorful stories, my dear. But then, much of my life is classified secret, and you, my innocent girl, have neither the security clearance nor the need to know."

"You mean, like the time you spent in Southeast Asia with the Knives? You've told me a lot about that."

"Yes, I can discuss a *skoshi* bit about those crazy helicopter pilots and the scrapes they got me out of. I owe them a lot. Many of those former crew members still keep in touch, especially Brad Gaelman. Unfortunately, there's so much more that I can't share with you."

Dan had started toward the door, but he paused again in the hallway.

"By the way, Nancy, if anything drastic should ever happen, tell me you'll go to Brad for whatever you might need. We've helped each other occasionally since Southeast Asia, and his success as a security consultant here in Washington has put him in a position to help you if you need it. I realize you two aren't close, but he's a good man and a fine friend. Get to know him better, and you'll like him. Just needs a little direction in his life from time to time," Dan concluded thoughtfully.

She gave him a perplexed look as he quickly changed moods and entered an area she wanted to avoid. She recalled that Brad had had his own share of problems these past few years. The last thing she needed was to get involved with a less-than-perfect friend of the family to complicate her life.

"Dad, I know you admire him, so if I do need anything," she paused, "while you're away overseas or something, I'll give Brad a call. But really, I'm becoming quite self-sufficient, you know."

They noticed their reflection in the mirror, and the resemblance between them struck a deep emotional chord in each. Dan put his arm around his daughter's waist.

"Yes, we Donahues have always found a way to bounce back. I knew that divorce wouldn't keep you down long."

Releasing her gently, he kissed her quickly on the forehead.

"I'm sorry, Nancy, but I must leave now. Please be ready with your luggage, in case I don't have much time at lunch."

"I'll be ready. I'm sorry about this visit being so short."

"We'll have to make them longer and more frequent."

"I'll try, Dad. I want to make up for all the lost time."

"I know your design agency will keep you busy, and the Agency is going to get every mile out of me that they can. But we'll both try to find time to make up for what we missed."

Nan brushed his lapels with her hands, and then on tiptoes, kissed her father on the cheek. Dan hugged her tightly.

"Take care, my Irish Princess. See you at lunch."

"I will. And you, too. Bye, Dad."

NAN LOCKED THE DOOR and turned back into the apartment. She loved the masculine look of it, the strong sandalwood scent, the rich earth-tone drapes and carpets, the plush rust-colored sofas and easy chairs, and the well-used fireplace with its gleaming brass fixtures. She brushed her hand across the inviting softness of a chair back as she walked slowly to the balcony doors.

The past three days here in the apartment with her father had been a refreshing change in her life. Her former troubles were put behind her. She felt strong, joyous emotions welling up within her. There was the excitement of starting anew, with new goals and new support from her father. She felt new energy flowing from him and from his apartment, and she had lost her habitual sense of foreboding. She twirled on her toes and danced across the room in joy.

A smile lingered on her face as she opened the french doors and stepped out onto the open balcony, clutching the light linen jacket of her suit to protect her against the cool spring morning. Brushing her hair aside, she stepped from the shade and welcomed the warmth of the sun on her face. Squinting her green eyes against the signal of another scorching afternoon, she watched her father stride across the Georgetown street below. Her slender fingers absently wiped the morning dew from the brass rail of the balcony. Nan noted her father's straight back and upright posture that she admired so much.

"Dan Donahue, I'm glad you're a cautious man," she whispered, as he slowly crossed the street and approached his car, parked at the curb where she had left it last night. Chewing on her thumbnail, Nan remembered his ingrained caution over the years: frequent glances over his shoulders while walking or driving, pauses in doorways before stepping into streets, and refusals to open packages that arrived through the mail. On their recent visit to a restaurant, he had avoided sitting in front of a window. He sat instead in a nook near an exit, facing the entrance, with his back against a wall. He usually kept his car parked in the tight security of the basement garage. Dan Donahue didn't leave much to chance.

She saw her father look his car over carefully, just as she had seen him check it many times in the past. She smiled, feeling reassured by his precautions. Nan saw him select the car key from the new keyholder she had given him last night, one she had proudly designed herself. He turned and waved up to her as he placed the key in the door lock. Even at this distance, she could see the warm smile on his broad, ruddy features.

The concussion from the blast tore her breath away, knocking her back through the open doors into the apartment. Groggily, she scrambled to her feet and lurched in panic and confusion back to the brass rail. She flinched from the oppressive wave of heat which radiated upward from the burning inferno below. Peering in apprehension over the balcony's edge, she shielded her eyes and saw a raging fire that sent long tongues of flame and thick, black smoke billowing into the stillness of the shattered morning.

As she mentally withdrew from the jolting reality of the shocking scene below, she felt as though she were watching her detached body from a distance. Her ears ached, and her knees felt like jelly. A continuous piercing shriek filled her ears as she desperately sought to find her father in the chaos below. She was afraid that she would see him, terrified that she would not. Then blackness dimmed her vision, and she felt herself spinning dizzily out of control, falling to the floor. As she blacked out, she realized the piercing screams were her own.

2

"Captain Bradford Wellington Gaelman, if you survive this takeoff, it'll be another miracle!"

Having properly admonished himself, Brad steeled himself to perform the miracle. With one hand, he nervously wiped away the sweat that ran profusely from beneath his flight helmet into his eyes. He then repositioned the stray strands of brown hair that stuck to his forehead. With his other hand, he resolutely gripped the cyclic control stick near his knees. It was his link to the enormous helicopter that vibrated in metallic protest beneath and around him while it squatted in an undersized jungle clearing.

Overhead, the spinning rotor blades were creating a furious blast of turbulent air, shoving the thick foliage to and fro in turmoil around the confining edges of the claustrophobic clearing. Sitting at the center of this maelstrom, Brad knew there was no room for miscalculation or sloppy technique in the upcoming takeoff.

From every direction, small Oriental people streamed toward the waiting aircraft. They all wore black clothing trimmed with bright colors, and desperate faces with wild, frightened eyes. Each one—man, woman, and child—carried a weapon and either a box, basket, or sack. This assortment of containers held all the worldly possessions they could quickly gather when the tribal headquarters was suddenly overrun by the enemy.

General Tran Vinh Lin, "the Golden Dragon," military commander of the Lawn Chin base, and virtual ruler of Xiang Province—had himself been caught in the surprise attack. Now he stood at the top of the open rear ramp of the chopper, calmly and efficiently directing his staff's efforts. With dignity and authority, he was personally controlling the boarding and stowage of frightened people and bulky goods coming up the ramp.

A sudden, staccato burst of automatic weapon gunfire nearby added to the confusion and din, and brought Brad instantly upright and alert in his pilot's seat. All the helicopter's intercom microphones were turned on, and the increased panic was obvious in the heightened screams and shouts of the terrorized people being packed into the aircraft.

Tree branches splintered and fell just a few feet in front of Brad as an unseen enemy's gunfire cut them down. He felt his breath catch and sweat popped out on him anew as a fresh surge of adrenaline rushed through his already taut body. He grabbed a portable radio hanging near his side, and controlling the lump in his throat, yelled uneasily into it.

"Alpha Three, this is Knife two-one. What the hell's going on out there? We're drawing fire here!" he railed with a rising urgency in his voice.

The response came back between gasps and panting breaths.

"Not to . . . worry, Cowboy. We're bringing in . . . the last of them. I'm at . . . your five . . . closing fast," the halting voice responded.

Brad swiveled to look back over his right shoulder through the Plexiglas windscreen. He saw Alpha Three break from the swaying brush like a wave dashing on rocks, a small child under one arm, a radio and rifle under the other. He was a tall, powerfully built man who moved with intent and authority. Despite his heavy breathing, he walked swiftly and deliberately toward the helicopter. His hat had long since given up on trying to keep up, and was left behind in the jungle.

The small child was hanging on and watching the big man in awe. Even at this distance, a drying rivulet of blood could be seen running down the man's face from a slight wound at the edge of his reddish hair. His combat fatigues were soaked with sweat, his boots were caked with mud, and a torn flap in the sleeve of his shirt waved as he moved.

Brad turned and leaned to his left to look back over the teeming mass of people in the rear of the helicopter. He saw Alpha Three reach the side of the open ramp and thrust the child up to a woman on board. The big man then turned his attention to a commotion made by three of General Lin's staff, who were pushing and pulling a water buffalo up the ramp, completely blocking the loading efforts.

Alpha Three grabbed the lead rope and pulled the animal to the side of the entry. He fired several shots into it and pushed the carcass over the side with his foot.

"At ease, men," came a crew member's voice over the intercom in response to the shots. "Alpha Three is just butchering the general's beef."

With a fierce determination marking his ruddy features, Alpha Three quickly turned his weapon on the former owner of the animal, who was babbling furiously and taking aim at him.

The big American yelled, "Put the gun down and get the people on board! Now!" In a greater wrath, he repeated the command in the Asian dialect.

Shouting above the chaos, General Lin stepped between his officer and Alpha Three to end the confrontation. The American turned from the general and quickly pushed four more tribesmen into the space vacated by the water buffalo. This filled the chopper to its ultimate capacity.

General Lin barked instructions to his bodyguards, and they turned their weapons on a huddled clump of people at the bottom of the ramp. With short bursts of gunfire, they quickly shot down the stragglers.

"My God! Stop them!" Brad screamed desperately into the intercom. "They're killing them!"

Alpha Three charged bodily into the general's firing guards, knocking them over other tribesmen now crouched in the helicopter. General Lin grabbed Alpha Three's arm and pulled him upright, then took the American's portable radio in his hand. In clear English, he said, "Relax, Cowboy. They were all traitors."

From his seat in the cockpit, Brad could see that the emotional strain evident in the general's voice showed in his expression and posture. As the pilot turned to face forward, his mind was filled with anguish and confused thoughts. The brutish killing brought bile into his throat, almost causing him to vomit. As he wiped a hand across his sweaty face for the hundredth time today, tears filled his eyes over the shock of the needless deaths, and he fought to control his emotions.

A dark movement among the swaying branches to his right caught his eye. A cold shiver shook him as he found himself looking directly into the barrel of an AK-47 assault rifle. It was held expertly by a young girl in black pajamas some forty feet away. He could see the determination in her sloped almond eyes as she sighted over the barrel at him. Ducking down, he yelled hoarsely into the intercom through a fear-contorted mouth.

"Bum! Fire at two o'clock level now!"

"Gotcha, Cowboy!" yelled Sergeant Bum Shandy, the crew chief and gunner.

The intercom headphones suddenly filled with the whine and roar of the multi-barreled machine gun positioned in the right door of the chopper. The young girl's arms and legs splayed as she was brutally knocked into the brush by a dozen slugs. Brad stared in shock and relief as his heartbeat slowed to a less-rapid racing. Even when he closed his eyes, he saw the afterimage of the bore of the AK-47 barrel as an eye of death.

"Taking some fire at nine o'clock," Captain Ed Richards announced calmly, punctuating his comment with shots from a rifle he fired out the left window from his copilot's seat.

"Heavy action at three o'clock," Bum yelled hoarsely over the new firing of his machine gun. "Let's haul ass outta here!"

"Get the ramp up!" Brad shouted decisively. "Ed, let's take her up!"

Brad anxiously gathered the power, lift, and control of the aircraft in his skilled hands. The sounds of engines and rotor blades intensified as he increased power for a climb straight up from the clearing. The whapping blades punctuated the muggy air. Tracer bullets burned streaked patterns across in front of him, and he had to force his concentration back on his flying efforts. The smell of cordite from the burned gunpowder mingled with the odors of sweat and fear to saturate the air.

"Kingbird, this is Knife two-one, over," Brad called roughly into the helicopter radio to the airborne command post aircraft that flew overhead. From high above, their lifeline responded.

"Knife two-one, this is Kingbird. Go ahead. Over," came the melodic reply from the aircraft controlling their rescue mission.

"Roger, Kingbird. We're attempting liftoff from the firebase with surviving tribesmen. Golden Dragon is on board. Over."

"Uhh, roger, Knife two-one," came the voice of another controller. "Better push it. We're…ahh…getting strong indications of large troop movements...with heavy weapons at your location. Over."

Feeling the chopper sluggishly break ground, Brad responded with relief, "Roger, we're lifting off now. Over."

Above the roar of the engines, the whapping rotor blades, and din of yelling from the rear of the helicopter, Brad heard, or felt, a hollow thump, like a mailing tube being opened too fast.

"Mortar!"

"Incoming!"

The blast of the shell at impact knocked down a tree at the edge of the clearing. The copter slipped sideways as Brad fought stubbornly to control it. There was apparently no severe damage to the aircraft, as he quickly brought it and his heaving stomach under control.

"Easy, Cowboy," Ed crooned, his face drawn, and his usual calm voice tinged with tension and anxiety.

With gritted teeth, Brad willed the overloaded helicopter upward through the trees to the open sky.

"Knife two-one, this is Kingbird...How do you copy?...Do you read, Knife two-one?"

As Brad deftly stroked the controls with both hands, Ed's smooth drawl answered the call.

"Roger, Kingbird. Read you five-by-five. We're a little busy right now. Taking mortar fire—"

Ed's words were interrupted as tracer rounds crashed through the Plexiglas around them. Fragments ricocheted off Brad's helmet and stung his chin and neck. Despite his shock, he remembered that there were several deadly lead stingers between each tracer round. He glanced at Ed and saw blood on his copilot's arm.

"Knife Two-one, Kingbird. Get out of there!"

"Kingbird, we've been hit. Still climbing," Ed said into the radio through clenched teeth.

Brad pulled the chopper up toward the swaying tops of the trees. The swirling branches seemed to close around them. Several thuds indicated more hits on the aircraft, and the screams in the rear of the chopper increased. His heartbeat and breathing also increased, but seemed less effective.

Alpha Three broke in on the intercom. "Go, Cowboy. Get us out. Now or never," he urged anxiously.

"Kingbird, get us help in here! We're overloaded!" Brad yelled into his radio. His entire body felt the strain of his efforts.

The trees seemed to grow and expand over them as Brad inched the copter higher and higher, slowly and sluggishly. Engines and blades protested with groans and high whines. Dials strained, lights blinked. A wave of dizziness swept over him. He felt his every muscle urging the awkward aircraft upward. Tracers cut patterns all around. He could feel the impact of the bullets thudding into the bottom and sides of his heavy bird, as though they were hitting him. He sensed his cries growing louder as his body grew more tensed and strained.

"Kingbird, help us! Help us! Help us! Help! Help!"

BRAD SAT UPRIGHT in his bed, disentangling himself from the bedcovers, awake at once, but still feeling the drowsiness of troubled sleep. His hands and arms were taut and trembling, his body covered with sweat. His heart was pounding, and he was breathing heavily. His cartwheeling mind began to sort out the overload of mental inputs. He fought to reach the surface of reality.

The recurring dream. The flashback. One of half a dozen that had stayed with him, haunting his nights endlessly over the years since he fought in Southeast Asia. He could still smell the cordite from the gunfire, and the engine fumes, and the odor of sweat and blood of all the people jammed into the chopper. It was still too real. There was no forgetting.

He shakily rubbed his hands over his face and blinked his eyes to clear them. Swallowing hard, he looked deliberately around the familiar bedroom, trying to establish himself firmly in the present. He reminded himself that he was a forty-year-old security consultant in Washington, D.C. That he was in a plush condominium apartment in Crystal City, in northern Virginia, making a six-figure annual income. That he was no longer an Air Force captain and helicopter pilot in Southeast Asia.

"God, a flight like that would kill me now," he muttered. "Why do I feel so old?"

He wiped the sweat from his forehead. He was tired of waking up every morning with an aching back, a sore elbow, and a headache. He stared blankly at the wall of the bookshelves in the gathering light of the morning. Focusing on the familiar titles sometimes helped bring him back to reality.

The aftermath of the flashback dreams always left him with a mixture of horror and yearning. Did he really wish he were still back there fighting a tangible and openly hostile enemy? That would be preferable to what he did now: advising diplomatic Washington on protection against unseen, unheard, and often unbelieved terrorist threats.

Propping himself up against the oversized pillows, he wearily rubbed his bloodshot eyes. He wasn't looking forward to another boring day at the office that would turn out to be just like all the ones last week, last month... He released a long sigh. Is this what he had survived the war to become? Is this what middle-aged meant?

He had never felt so alive as during his days in Southeast Asia working in special operations. Nothing else seemed to compare with that constant adrenaline high that comes with exciting action. When had his world become a dull morass of shapeless faces and problems? He grimaced.

It probably began when he received his divorce from Lora. The loneliness that followed the parting was a blow. He had tried to make up for the loss by putting in still more hours to build his business. And for a while, that approach had worked. Until recently.

Like last week: three routine embassy inspections, two routine residential security estimates, two long dreary consultations with security agencies, and a talk at a symposium on counter-terrorism at the State Department. What had once been a challenging, interesting consultation practice had become something to do while waiting for the next phase of a drifting, aimless life.

But he had no big appointments yet this week. Staring him in the face were invitations to boring business meetings, two quiet luncheons with new clients, a sedate diplomatic reception, and two staid parties, all in the name of public relations.

The loud ringing of the telephone intensified his headache. He wasn't used to getting early morning phone calls, and the interruption irritated him. He wished he'd left his phone-answering machine on.

"Hello," he growled.

"Good morning, Brad. This is Rafe."

Police Sergent Rafe Johnson, a black, hard-nosed, capable cop, was a close friend and business associate. Brad's outlook brightened at the call, even as his curiosity was piqued.

"Good morning, Rafe. What's happening?"

"Sorry to bother you so early."

Brad could hear a strain in Rafe's voice.

"Hey, no problem. In my business I'm always glad to get your heads-up notices on what's going down around town. And if I can do something for you in return, so much the better. I owe you a few," he added in sincerity.

Rafe hesitated, then sighed again. "I'm afraid this is bad news."

Trying to swallow the metallic taste still in his mouth, Brad sleepily responded, "Okay, let's have it."

"It's Dan Donahue. Someone took him out with a car bomb in Georgetown this morning."

Brad was instantly alert, adrenaline pumping support through the aching muscles of his awakening body. Taking deep breaths, he cleared his head, and his eyes blinked instantly into a sharp focus. The sound of whapping helicopter blades ran through his head as he sorted out the visual images of jungles and running people going through his mind.

"My God! Not Dan," he blurted, his voice breaking.

"Easy, Brad," was Rafe's soft response.

Dan Donahue. Alpha Three. The CIA agent with the third highest authority in Xiang Province just a few years ago. Only the ambassador and station chief were more powerful. But no one was more capable or had more impact.

"You know how sorry I am," Rafe intoned compassionately. "I wasn't over there with you, but he was my friend, too."

"God. How?" Brad questioned through his anguish and grief. "He was so good at his work, so careful."

And he was a good friend. In fact, in the restricted, secretive worlds in which the three each operated, they were one another's best friends. They each understood the need for secrecy, for confidentiality and trust. With Rafe, the three of them had fitted their lives over the years into a close comradeship.

"What about Nan? She was in town. Was she with him?"

"No. Nancy was watching from a balcony. She's been taken to George Washington Hospital in shock, but she had no outward injuries."

"Thank God for that much," Brad whispered. He struggled to sort out the details of the killing. He tried to systematically file away the information, even as his mind raced ahead. "What do you have on it so far?"

"It was a professional hit. We don't have a clue. No bomb fragments, no suspicious loiterers, no witnesses, no leads." Rafe said, the frustration evident in his voice.

"Stay with it, and let me know what you learn."

"We'll give it more than the usual look. But you know the possibilities are just too much."

"I know it'll be tough. Dan had a long career, and he made some enemies. But he was too good a man to let his murder go into the books unsolved. Find the bastards!"

After a pause, Rafe said quietly, "You're losing your professional perspective. You don't usually get so emotional."

Taking a deep breath and releasing it slowly, Brad said in a hushed tone, "I know, but this one hits pretty close."

"I feel it, man. Listen, you ought to go see Nancy. She needs a friend close by about now. The doctor told me she's really withdrawn. She knows you, and maybe you can reach her. I'd like to make sure she'll be okay."

"Yeah, I'll let you know after I've seen her."

"Thanks, Brad. Keep in touch. See ya, Cowboy."

The nickname plunged Brad back into the past, into the smells of rotting vegetation and JP-4 aviation fuel, and the droning sounds of helicopters. He hung up the phone without a response and slumped into the pillows, again losing contact with the comfortable surroundings of the bedroom.

As he slipped into the half-dream, he realized that Rafe would understand the abrupt ending of the phone call. They were close friends. Here in the Washington security environment Rafe, Dan, and he had shared a professional relationship that had grown into a deep friendship. The police sergeant had not been with them in Southeast Asia, but he had heard the names "Cowboy" and "Alpha Three" from all the war stories they had shared over drinks.

Brad's searching mind took him back to his introduction to Dan Donahue in a jungle clearing in Southeast Asia long before the Lawn Chin evacuation. As an Air Force captain and helicopter pilot in an elite special operations unit, Brad had flown classified missions under the call sign "Knife." As one of the unit members, called "Knives," he flew one of these missions to a prearranged pickup point in enemy territory to meet an agent called Alpha Three. Upon landing, Brad stared in disbelief out the helicopter window as Dan fought the wind blast of the rotor blades to lead an old woman, a beautiful young girl, and a large water buffalo to the open rear ramp of the aircraft.

Memories of the swirling greenery, the jungle smells, the loud bellowing of the protesting animal, and the anxiety of the aircrew all pulled him back into the past. Dan was dressed in muddy, sweat-soaked camouflage fatigues, with no insignia but the *U.S.* which was embroidered on each collar. He was a large and imposing man, but he looked harried and hurried. He assisted the woman and girl into the chopper and pulled the animal on board, tying it to the bulkhead by the knotted lead rope.

Sergeant Bum Shandy, the crew chief, buckled in the two passengers and raised the ramp. As Bum tried to secure the animal in place, Dan adroitly donned an intercom headset and plugged it in as he came forward in the chopper giving a thumbs-up signal. A look of relief was evident on his ruddy features.

"Should we ask this guy for an identification?" Brad uneasily asked his copilot, Captain Ed Richards.

"I'm not sure we can afford the answers, Cowboy, so why ask the questions?"

Dan had heard the exchange on the intercom. Cutting into the conversation, he interjected, "Cowboy, is it? Well, thanks for the ride, Cowboy. This is Madame Lin, mother of General Tranh Vinh Lin, the Golden Dragon. And this is Noy, the general's favorite daughter. That very illustrious four-legged passenger is his prize breeding bull. Would you believe moving them out of here is going to help the good guys defend this province?" Dan chuckled.

Brad was both amazed and amused. "All right, spook. We'll get you out of here. Let's go, Ed."

A rattle of gunfire gave evidence of just how close Dan's pursuers had approached. The crew quickly lifted the helicopter out of the clearing and out of range of the gunfire, to the delighted squeals of the woman and girl, and the protesting bellows of the water buffalo.

Brad was still chasing the wisps of memory when the insistent ring of the telephone catapulted him into the present. He pushed back the weight of the past and slowly reached for the receiver.

"Brad? It's Ed. Have you heard?"

The reassuring voice of his former copilot calmed him.

"About Dan? Yes, the police called. Rafe Johnson told me," he said with difficulty.

"I can't believe anyone got to him!" Ed snapped with an uncharacteristic emotional emphasis. "It just doesn't sound like Dan. Even in the old days, he was always the careful Knife."

"How did you get the word?"

"As editor-on-duty, I got a call from our police reporter. He got there before the fire was out. He saw them take Nan away. How is she?"

Brad felt an inner urge to get to Nan and talk with her. He knew her well enough to understand her pain. But what could he say to her?

"She's being treated for shock in George Washington Hospital. Ed. She saw it happen," Brad said softly.

"I know. I talked to the CIA official who checked out the apartment right after the hit. He's also making the arrangements. The funeral will be Wednesday. I'll be out of town until then, but I need to talk to you about all this."

"What do you mean—the arrangements or the explosion? How did you know who's checking things out and handling details?"

"Brad," Ed's impatient voice responded, "I'm a newspaper editor at a desk now, but I still have my investigative reporter contacts. I had been talking with Dan now and then."

"You know something about the bomb?" Brad asked, sensing a wariness and conspiratorial tone in Ed's voice.

"Maybe. It all seems a little farfetched on the surface. But it's big. I can feel it," Ed said, his voice rising.

"Ed, don't pump this out of proportion. I don't want Nan to get hurt any more." He hesitated to organize his thoughts. "Dan blew the whistle on a lot of people who could wire a bomb to a car, and who would do it on a personal grudge."

"This is bigger than that," Ed responded vehemently. "I know it. I was trying to get something out of Dan to corroborate some leads I got from others in the old bunch."

"You've been in touch with the Knives on this?"

"Yeah. In fact, it's funny, but most of them are in town right now. You know after we rotated back to the States, Dan was reassigned to other sensitive CIA operations in Latin America and the Middle East, then back to Southeast Asia. But he considered himself a Knife and kept in touch with the rest of us right up to the end." There was a thickness in his voice.

Brad filled the void in the conversation that followed.

"I know General Lin also considered himself to be a Knife after all the operations we helped him with. He was flown to the States after the evacuation of Lawn Chin, and he became a successful cattle rancher in Colorado."

"Yes, he's in town this week, testifying before Congress," Ed added. "And Luke Bonner, another honorary Knife, left the Green Beret outfit and advanced through the ranks to become an army general. He's now assigned here."

"I know. I see him often."

"As for other former crew members, Thaddeus Ralston is a U.S. Congressman, and it's his Committee on Americans Missing in Action that Lin is testifying before. Dan was tied to that somehow."

"Go on," Brad said in anticipation of clues about Dan's work. But Ed moved on to other Knives.

"Denton Mallard is president of his own electronics company, and he's in town at a business convention. Quincy Sennet is a district judge in Colorado, and he's here to consult on a court ruling. George Windham is an official at the State Department, but he's out of town on a vacation. Bum Shandy has lived up to his nickname. He's just one sad story after another. He's around town now, too, down and out, as usual."

"What's the significance of their presence here now?"

"Well, if I've come close to what's going on, any one or all of them could have been tied to Dan's work. I should know more when I see you at the funeral. They'll probably all be there."

"Sounds like the old gang is all present or accounted for. And all doing well, except for Bum. And Dan." He stopped, unsure of how to explain his feelings.

"Well, I hear tell that you've become top dog as a security consultant and counter-terrorist expert. Everywhere I go, I run into diplomats or other bureaucrats who say they're impressed with what you've done as a researcher, lecturer, or consultant. By golly, you've been such a success, I may have to assign someone to do a feature story on you." Ed chuckled.

"Successful if you leave out a divorce caused by too much work and too little communication. Or a series of more recent unfortunate love affairs, or erotic interludes, whichever you prefer," he added, with bitterness.

"Look, we've talked through all those times. You're not still hammering yourself on that divorce, are you? That was years ago, Brad, and you've done so well lately."

Wanting to avoid a discussion of his boredom with his work, Brad quickly changed the direction of the conversation.

"Look who's talking about success. I'd say a chopper jockey who writes a book on *The Secret War in Southeast Asia* that stays on the best-seller lists here and abroad for thirty-six weeks has to be considered a success. That little gem of yours is still used as a textbook at a lot of colleges. I guess that's what made you semirich and got you your cushy newspaper job."

"Hold it a minute, Brad." Ed partially covered the mouthpiece of his phone to talk with someone who had interrupted him. After a moment, he continued in an irritated tone. "Brad, I've gotta make a deadline now, but we'll talk later. And Cowboy. . . take extra care."

"Roger, Ed. Message received. I guess all reporters are just naturally suspicious."

"I wish I were still a reporter. Sometimes I wish I were still flying choppers. But I'm an editor now, and my readers await. Give Nan my love."

"I will. I'll probably see her this afternoon or tomorrow."

"Over and out, Cowboy."

"So long, Ed."

NAN LAY IN an uncomfortable hospital bed, struggling to regain her composure. She was still drowsy from the effects of sedatives administered by what seemed to be an endless stream of nurses. Out of a fog of dizziness, she looked through the sterile venetian blinds covering the window of her room. The red ball of sun was sinking slowly into the twilight haze outside. Slatted shadows raced across the walls. A rosy glow filled the room, coloring the backless, but confining hospital gown that had somehow bunched up around her shoulders and neck.

She remembered little of what had happened this morning after the intense fire that followed the explosion. But her mind still carried the sounds of her own screaming, and she could still feel the heat on her face and the pressure in her ears. Was that a minute ago? An hour? Her throat was raw and arid, making swallowing as difficult as remembering.

She didn't want to remember. Flashes of her father's face smiling up at her from the street taunted her, cutting through the oppressive ringing torment in her head. She recalled looking over the rail of the balcony for her father. The thick, black smoke boiled up again.

Anger suddenly slashed through her delirium and dizziness. She dug her fingernails convulsively into the hospital mattress, pressing her head back against the lumpy pillow. A low keening sound rose in her throat and escaped through her parched lips. "And it's *my* fault . . . *my* fault!"

Had she spoken aloud, or had she slipped back into fitful dreams in disturbed sleep? She struggled to control her emotions, her thoughts.

"*My* fault! I left the car out last night! *I* caused it!"

She tensed her body in misery, turning on her side, forcing her face into the pillow, pounding her fist on the bed. Again she visualized her father smiling and waving just before he put the key.... The vivid memories were just too much, and she sobbed, unable to regain control of her shredded emotions. Her taut body shook in mental anguish.

A nurse appeared beside the bed, clucking like a mother hen, hands fluttering about, to the patient's irritation. After patting Nan's shoulder, the nurse systematically rearranged the sheets of the rumpled bed and fluffed the pillow. Nan felt disquieted by this intrusion into her grief.

"How are you feeling this evening, Miss Donahue? Are you comfortable?" The voice sounded muffled and distant through her aching ears.

"Yes. No! I didn't mean to!" Nan croaked hoarsely. She tucked her lower lip between her teeth, fighting her inner turmoil to gain control.

"Now, now, Miss Donahue," the nurse crooned, her voice soothing. "Try to relax. Everything will be all right."

Those simple comforting words temporarily distracted Nan, freeing her from the spasms of grief. For a moment she felt the beginning of a wave of calmness and clarity. She tried to speak again, choking on the cottony feeling and taste in her throat and mouth.

"Here's some water."

Nan accepted the straw and drank heavily. Through cracked lips, she said, "Thanks. I'm much better now. I'll be okay."

"Feel up to a visitor?"

Stiffly, Nan sat up against the pillows, supporting her head with one hand to fight off the dizziness. "A visitor?" With effort, she wondered who it could be.

"A Mr. Gaelman. He's called several times to inquire about your condition. He's waiting now to see you. Do you feel up to talking to him?"

Nan's mind reeled in confused emotions. Brad Gaelman. She recalled her dad's last request: *If anything drastic should ever happen, tell me you'll go to Brad for whatever you might need.* Whenever she had visited her father, Brad had been around somewhere. *We've helped each other occasionally...* Brad was always helpful to her. ... *since southeast Asia...* All those war stories they had lived together. ... *and his success... has put him in a position to help you if you need it.* He was so confident and capable. *I realize you two aren't close....* All those divorce problems he had. ... *but he's a good man and a fine friend.* Always friendly. *You'll like him.* Always kind. He was her dad's best friend, and he could be her friend now when she needed someone.

But how could she face him? How could she handle her guilt in front of him? It was all her fault!

"Not now," Nan told the nurse softly.

She realized that she had straightened the disheveled hospital gown and had pushed her hair off her face. She found herself wishing for a mirror, then she was glad she didn't have one. Reflex actions?

"What am I doing?" she asked softly. "Why do I feel so foolish? Why now, when Dad is—?"

Tears welled up in her green eyes, streaking down her pale, drawn cheeks. Unwilling sobs tore loose, wracking her body. She leaned forward, burying her face in her hands.

"Now, now, Miss Donahue. He can wait until later. Why don't you just get some sleep? Lie back and relax, my dear. Things will look better tomorrow."

Nan allowed her head to sink into the newly fluffed but still lumpy pillow. She closed her eyes tightly. Thick black smoke swirled out of the corner of her mind once again. The heat of the flames grew. She was trying to see over the brass rail, and . . . she slipped into fitful sleep.

"GOOD MORNING, Miss Donahue."

Another nurse was by the bed as Nan woke up, this one less animated and without a sedative.

"Would you like some breakfast?"

"Yes, thank you," Nan muttered sluggishly. Though she felt better, she wasn't sure she wanted to . . . that she deserved to feel better. She felt guilty. She was still fighting to control her emotions—the anguish, the guilt, the anger, and a tinge of fear that still haunted her.

"The doctor said you had only a mild concussion, and your ears should be better by this morning. You can leave the hospital by lunchtime."

Nan drew in a deep breath and exhaled slowly, feeling a mixture of relief and humility. But she wasn't certain that she was ready to face the world again yet.

"Your Mr. Gaelman called again this morning. He wants to come by and take you home."

A kaleidoscope of emotions rushed through her. Her father's request, her refusal to become dependent on anyone else, the way she had been brutally dominated in her marriage. She hadn't even called her office yet. How could she face Brad and handle what she had done without breaking down again? But her dad had asked. She decided.

"I'll see him . . . if he comes," she murmured hesitantly. But she would leave by herself when the time came, she added to herself.

The nurse nodded and left.

Tears of distress surged up in Nan's eyes. She clenched her fists and breathed deeply in an attempt to restrain the crying. Some bastard had killed her father! She sobbed uncontrollably. Her stiff, sore fingers trembled badly as she shakily sat up and tried to dry her cheeks.

The nurse returned with a breakfast tray. Nan picked disinterestedly at the fare, swallowing tasteless bits of food. As she ate, she fought to organize her thoughts, to find a place to start putting things together. Her so-called "old friends" couldn't help, for most of those ties had been severed after her distasteful divorce. But she knew she would need help to do what family duty required. Thoughts of guilt and revenge alternated in her mind.

Slamming the fork on the tray, she crossed her arms. Why did she feel so uncomfortable about accepting help from Brad Gaelman? Because she was afraid of his accusations about her carelessness in leaving the car out and causing her father's death. She sat slumped against the pillows sorting out her feelings, poignantly recalling her times with her father, until a nurse entered the room.

"Mr. Gaelman is here now. Do you want to get dressed before he comes in? He's offered to take you home."

"No," Nan answered emphatically. "I have nothing to wear."

"Oh, a woman brought some clothes here for you. She said they were in your bags. This is such a nice summer dress."

Nan recognized her favorite summer traveling dress, and she was puzzled about how it got there. Who had been in her bags? Maybe someone from her father's office. Probably.

"Never mind," she said, waving the nurse away. "Thank you, but I'll dress later."

The nurse smiled as she hung the dress in the closet. Then she approached the bed with a comb, some pins, a brush and a mirror. "I thought you might want to use these before anyone comes in."

Nan warmed and smiled at the offer. "Yes, thanks," she said gratefully. She drew the brush through her auburn tresses until her hair flowed about her shoulders. Then, after studying the attractive effect in the mirror, she pressed her lips into a tight line, not satisfied that she wanted that impression. She twisted her hair into a neat, formal chignon at the nape of her neck.

The nurse waited patiently, then asked, "Ready now?"

"Yes, I think so," Nan said with resolve. She braced herself up against the pillows, wishing only to get the confrontation over with.

Brad entered the room slowly, quietly. She remembered her dad had called him a cougar prowling without a sound. He stopped inside the door, then walked over to the bed. His features were closed to her, and she desperately searched his face for some sign of what he was feeling. He was carrying a large bouquet which he awkwardly placed across her lap. She closed her hands protectively over the blood-red roses.

Brad's heart wrenched in his chest as he saw the play of emotions across her face. She looked in desperate need of help. So vulnerable. No makeup, swollen eyes, cracked lips. But God, she looked beautiful! A natural beauty marked her high cheekbones and the delicately shaped features of her face. The lines of her long, graceful neck carried his eyes down to where her full breasts swelled against the hospital gown. He had remembered her mostly as a thin, but pretty girl. When had she grown into such an incredibly attractive woman?

"How are you, Nan?" he asked, his eyes finding and never leaving her pale face, her soft green eyes.

"They're beautiful, Brad," she said, turning a rose in her fingers, avoiding the answer to his question. She hadn't expected flowers.

"So thoughtful," she mused. "Blood-red roses. They were Dad's favorite as well as mine. I wonder how many there will be at the funeral." Though she squeezed her eyes shut tightly, the tears nevertheless came through and ran down·her cheeks.

"Let me put those in water for you," the nurse interrupted, gathering the roses and leaving the room.

"Are you okay?" he asked, the frown on his features showing he was moved by the tears on her cheeks.

"I feel much better, actually. I'm going to be all right." Suddenly feeling defensive, she sat upright and added with rising emotion, "There's really nothing wrong with me, you know." She couldn't meet his suddenly compassionate gaze. It was as if he dropped those impenetrable walls from around him, and let his natural warmth come through. Her dad had been able to do that, too.

"They told me you could go home any time now. I have my car parked at the entrance downstairs." He grimaced, then forced a smile he didn't feel. "Hope I don't get a ticket," he observed wryly, and then wished he hadn't said it. It sounded like a complaint, when he hadn't meant it to be.

She compressed her full lips, her uneasiness holding back her normally polite social banter. She wondered why he didn't go ahead and say something about her carelessness in leaving the car out. In anguish, she swallowed to clear the lump from her throat.

"I don't want to trouble you, Brad. Or to take you away from your work. I'll just check out later and take a taxi to . . . to. . . ." She halted lamely, unable to complete the sentence. It hurt to say "Dad's apartment," the place that had so recently given her such strength, where she had caused his death with her careless actions. She had been in such a hurry to meet him at the apartment, and someone had used her carelessness to kill him!

Brad felt taken aback by her unexpected decision. "I've arranged things at my office so that I'll have some time off for the next few days. I'll have plenty of time to help you."

Nan pressed her fingers to the bridge of her nose, attempting to control her irritation at his persistence. "Brad, I have certain obligations myself. Like my agency."

"Oh, I meant to tell you. I called your office and explained the situation. They were worried about you, but said they would manage everything at that end."

She stared at him in exasperation. Why was he pushing his help on her? Just because of her dad? She didn't feel close to Brad. He was like a stranger. In frustration, she said in clipped words, "I appreciate your thoughtfulness, but I think I can take care of myself. I intend to try."

Brad walked to the window and stood there looking out, sensing that his gaze had been making her uncomfortable. He felt shut out, and he didn't understand why she was being so damned stubborn at a time like this.

"Nan, I don't want to be a bother, or to get in your way." He paused, searching through his confusion for words, then said, "I'll be nearby if you need me, but I won't press you. I know you're an independent lady, and you've taken care of yourself for some time now. I consider myself a friend, and I just want to help," he concluded thoughtfully. He wondered where his words had come from.

Nan recognized that she desperately needed someone to lean on. Her father had provided most of that emotional support since her divorce.

"You're a good friend," she whispered, unable to attempt eye contact. "I feel I have to make this adjustment myself. Please try to understand."

Pulling up the corner of his mouth in a rueful smile, Brad said quietly, "Always the self-sufficient woman. Your father's daughter."

He walked back to the side of the bed and reached out to grip her cool, slender fingers. There was a hint of admiration in his voice as he said, "You're a lot like him, you know."

Nan squeezed his large, strong hand. It felt warm to her touch. She suddenly felt secure for the first time since the explosion. She gazed up at him, awed by the open warmth in his eyes, the look of strength in his broad shoulders, the tall, trim body that was so like her dad's. Her dry, cracked lips parted in response. "Thank you."

Then, feeling confusion at the emotions washing over her, she retrieved her hand and absently smoothed out the sheet on the bed.

Brad again shifted his gaze away toward the window, searching for what he should say next.

Breaking the awkward silence, she asked, "Brad, what about the arrangements?"

"The CIA is handling all that, just like this room. They claimed the ... body ... and set the funeral for tomorrow. They searched the apartment yesterday morning. I guess that's routine. They left it pretty neat, though. A woman agent brought you some clothes to wear." He broke off his chatter, seeing her grow tense again.

"Please, Brad." Her voice broke.

"I'm, sorry, Nan. I guess this is difficult for both of us."

"I know," she returned, looking away. She asked herself if this uncomfortable feeling was what life would be like from now on. Tears filled her eyes and ran over her cheeks as anger and guilt came flooding back in clouds of thick, black smoke.

Seeing her distress, Brad turned to leave. He stopped at the door and said, "I'll see you at the funeral. The CIA will send a car for you. Ask to see some identification before you open the door to anyone. And please let me know what I can do to help."

"Brad . . . the coffin?"

"It will be closed," he answered quietly.

As Nan sobbed aloud, he felt an urge to help her somehow, to tell her that he hurt inside, too. But his presence seemed to irritate her, so he closed the door softly and walked slowly down the corridor. He couldn't remember when he had felt so unsettled or alone.

Watching him close the door without a sound, Nan felt more isolated than ever. "Men!" She was determined to fulfill her family responsibility, her obligation to her father. She felt a need to find independence, to avoid relationships that would lead to the mental and physical mistreatment and loss of self-esteem she had experienced in her marriage. She felt a deep guilt that gripped her unmercifully. If she could not find help, she would do it herself. She was Dan Donahue's daughter, and she would find out who killed him!

NAN PACED IMPATIENTLY in the waiting room of the police station. It reminded her of her hospital room without the bed. The walls were almost the same hideous shade of green. Where her hospital room window had opened onto a view of the sunset, this room had a motivational poster urging citizens to report crime promptly.

This was not an environment in which she could ever feel comfortable. She had never been in a police station before. Even in this closed room, the noise level was high, with the buzzing of activity, the hum of fluorescent lights, the clacking of typewriters and Teletype machines, and the constant chatter on the police radio: "Car thirty-one, see the man at...." None of this was helping her. This was not the atmosphere in which she would feel confident in pressing Rafe into action.

She had taken a taxi here directly from the hospital, determined to get things moving, to find some way to mitigate her feelings of guilt. There had been the usual administrative delay with the hospital registrar and cashier before her departure, and this had only added to her irritation and impatience.

Her access to the police station had been much easier. She merely presented the card Rafe had given her some time ago. On the side opposite his name, rank, and telephone number, he had scrawled, "Bring this lady directly to me and interrupt whatever I am doing. She is a special lady." Nan had kept the card as a memento, but she never dreamed that she would ever use it. At least it got her a visitor's badge and entry into this room while the clerk checked the authenticity of the note.

But now her progress seemed stalled, and the waiting was beginning to wear her down. She took a deep breath to relieve the pressure building in her chest and the dizziness lingering in her head. Her knees were weak and her back tired.

She was deciding which of the uncomfortable-looking chairs to sit in when the door burst open and Sergeant Rafe Johnson stepped into the room. He moved almost gracefully for such a big man. His expressive face showed agitation and the small scars of years of street experience. He ran his huge hand over his close-cropped hair as he gently closed the door.

"Nancy, I'm sorry about the wait. I didn't know you were out of the hospital. I thought Brad would take you either to the airport or to Dan's apartment." He paused a moment, smiled broadly, and asked, "What can I do for you?"

"I think I need to sit down for a while first," she responded as another wave of dizziness swept over her.

"Sure, come with me," he said, taking her arm and leading her out of the room. They went a short distance down the hall to an office that looked slightly more habitable. At least there was a padded chair beside a cluttered desk. "Have a seat. You look pale. Would you like a glass of water?"

"No, thank you. Rafe, have you learned anything in your investigation? Do you know who…did it yet?" she asked as she sat on the edge of the chair.

The police sergeant's face suddenly grew very serious. Nan saw a drastic change in his posture and mannerisms that reflected his change in attitude. He walked toward her, his arms folded, his thick lips pressed tightly together. Nan clasped her hands and sat forward, head down, looking at the ring her dad had brought her from Thailand. A feeling of expectancy grew within her as she anticipated news of her father's killer.

"I'm afraid there's not much to tell you," he said, stopping beside her chair.

"Why not?" she asked peevishly, a feeling of apprehension and anger welling up within her.

"We just don't know much," Rafe said, tugging at his ear. The expressive face mirrored his frustration and disappointment. "It was a clean, professional job. No witnesses to the installation of the explosives. No clues left behind. There's not much hope, Nancy."

She winced visibly as the words pelted her hopes. A sob broke loose before she could control it, and pent-up tears followed. She leaned forward again, burying her face in her hands.

Leaning over, Rafe put his hands gently on her shoulders with comforting pressure. "I'm sorry. I don't know what else to say, except that Dan had a lot of friends down here. We're all disappointed."

"Disappointed!" she snapped, sitting up abruptly, her face a picture of suffering. "Disappointed? I want action, not platitudes! I want answers! I want to know who murdered my father!"

"Nancy, Nancy, please calm down," Rafe pleaded. "I know you're upset, but please, be reasonable. I want

Dan's killer as much as anyone. We just don't have anything to go on.''

Sitting upright in her chair, Nan wiped away the tears on her cheeks. She shook with rage. "You were Dad's friend. You're a police officer. You have the means to find Dad's killer. Just what do you intend to do about it?" she asked in a tight, clipped voice.

Arms folded again, Rafe thrust out his chin defensively. "I intend to check out every lead we can dig up. I'm looking at every record of a similar modus operandi. I'm asking who might be in town that could've done this type of job. I've checked the national wire and several other police departments. I have a dozen commitments to help find suspects. I'm talking to the CIA and the FBI. I've contacted some of Dan's friends." He paused, placing his hands on his hips, looking up at the ceiling. "Nancy, there aren't any leads or clues turning up."

She stood and faced him, feeling her guilt and anger intensify. She clenched her fists and looked directly up into Rafe's dark eyes.

"And what are you going to do next?"

"Officially, there's nothing more that I can do. However, unofficially, I intend to pursue the investigation on my own through personal channels until we can turn up something for the official case. That's all I can hope for, Nancy. I'm sorry. Really sorry."

Rafe's stern look told Nan that she had pursued her questions about as far as she could hope. Despite her continued stare, he didn't blink. Yielding, she lowered her head and spoke softly, but with determination.

"Thank you for your time, Sergeant. I'm sure you think I'm totally out of line. I know you feel you've done what you can. But I've got to have some answers," she said with vehemence. "I intend to pursue this myself. I want the killer to get what he deserves."

"Nancy, I'm telling you, you're in no position to get into this. I can't assign anyone to help you. And you'd need it."

"I'll do it on my own then. And don't remind me that I'm only a woman!" she snapped indignantly.

"You don't understand. If you become involved, and you *do* find out anything, you'll become a target yourself. Dan is...was a professional, an expert. You're not. You'll need protection, and I can't guarantee your safety if you start nosing around in Dan's business. The CIA and FBI won't like it either."

"I guess I'll just have to take my chances."

"Nancy," he started, then hesitated, changing his expression to a softer one. He held his palms up in silent frustration. Then he took her hands in his and squeezed gently. He smiled and said softly, "Nancy, Brad and I were Dan's closest friends. We consider ourselves your friends, too. You're a super lady. We don't want you to get hurt. We want to help where we can. Both of us. Let us."

"I know," she sighed. "Brad came to see me at the hospital. I'm afraid I wasn't very nice to him, either. I do appreciate your offers. But there are some things I must do, and I'm not sure you can help me. This is a family obligation."

"I admire your spirit, but be careful. And don't be disappointed if nothing turns up. We can't solve every crime."

"Thank you for your concern, but don't patronize me. I'll be okay. I will come to you if I learn anything—or if I need help I can't get elsewhere."

"Where will you be staying?"

"I'll be working out of Dad's apartment," she answered assuredly, saying it without difficulty this time.

"I'll have someone stop by to check on your safety. But don't open the door, even on the chain, unless you're sure who is outside. I'll see you at the funeral. In the meantime, let me know if anything suspicious happens."

"Dad was the target, not me. I'll be okay. the CIA will get me to the funeral." She started to the door, suddenly feeling more composed, more determined. Turning back, she said quietly, "Thanks again."

"You take care, Nancy. And keep in touch."

"Bye, Rafe."

"Bye, Nancy."

Walking out to catch a taxi, she held her shoulders up straight, gathering her confidence in her posture. She felt ill-equipped mentally and emotionally. But she had Donahue determination. Her dad had called it hereditary intestinal fortitude. She would give it her best shot. It was better than drowning in guilt and anger. So she would swim, swim for her life. And she would get Brad Gaelman to help her find the killer.

3

THE BRIGHT, SUNNY MORNING was beginning to feel uncomfortably hot by the time Brad arrived at the funeral home. Brad parked in the spacious lot behind a cluster of late-model foreign cars with diplomatic license plates. He plodded pensively across the hot asphalt to the small but impressive building. At one side, near the parking area, a small crowd was gathering on a covered walkway leading up to the entrance of the modest chapel where the ceremonies would take place.

Brad saw General Luke Bonner in his green army uniform talking to his aide near the walkway. He walked directly to Bonner's side and nodded uncomfortably before shaking the general's hand. Running his finger around his sweat-soaked collar, Brad said quietly, "I guess it's appropriate that this day is as hot as any you and Dan ever saw in Xiang Province, Luke."

Showing a wry smile on his thin lips, Luke said dramatically, "Knives never complain, Brad. How are you otherwise?"

"Mostly frustrated. Hurt. Mad as hell. Otherwise, I'm the same old lovable Knife who carted you around beneath those damn noisy windmills years ago." It felt better to say the words to an old friend who would understand.

"You're looking fit, for a civilian," Luke chortled. His bushy white eyebrows jerked above the character lines around his steel-blue eyes as he talked. Lean and robust, his physical appearance was little different than it had been as a Green Beret team commander years ago. His rigid military bearing reinforced his image of taut strength and peak physical conditioning.

"You still running five miles a day?" Brad asked, impressed and envious, and much aware of how out of condition he felt.

"On weekdays. Ten a day on weekends."

"Still flying, too?

"Every chance I get. Since you got me started in helicopters I've put over twelve-hundred hours in the book and some more unofficially that the Army wouldn't want to log."

"You mean your spooky stuff? I heard you'll fly anywhere."

A wry smile again danced across Luke's face. "You always could guess more about what I did than I could tell you. But in this case, I want to tell you some things that may relate to—" He hesitated and looked furtively over his shoulder. "Not here."

"Just tell me where and when, sir."

"Let's have lunch tomorrow at the Fort Meyer Officers' Club. I'll be spending much of today and tomorrow in the Nassif Building and the Criminal Records Center in Baltimore. I'll have Captain Tim Blackwell, my aide here, set up a room for our meeting and secure it. That okay with you?"

"Sure, I'll be there," he responded, stifling his curiosity. Turning to shake hands with Blackwell, he said, "Glad to meet you, Captain. Just give me a call with the room number. Nassif Building—isn't that CID, General?"

"Right. Army Criminal Investigation Division. Special project with General Crime Division in their Operations Directorate. By the way," Luke said, changing the subject quickly with a wave of his knotty hand, "isn't that the priest who served as a chaplain when Dan was a Navy intelligence lieutenant?"

"Yes," Brad said, turning. "And that's Admiral Bob Dyson in dress whites he's talking to. He was Dan's roommate back then. Dan's Navy tour is the reason for the military funeral ceremonies here at the chapel and later at the cemetery."

Luke turned to observe others in the growing group waiting outside the chapel.

"There are several interesting mourners in this company. I recognize some of the CIA administrative staff people that I've seen in meetings, and a couple of agents Dan worked with."

"I see them," Brad responded, trying not to be obvious in his surveillance. "There are some FBI officials moving through the crowd, too. But I can't tell if it's for security, surveillance, or mourning."

"Brad, isn't that Bruno Borashilov from the Soviet Embassy?"

"You're right. And I see other security people I've worked with from several other embassies: Thai, French, German, British, and half a dozen Latin American countries. Several have armed bodyguards."

"There's Tanya Garsukov, the defector Dan brought out. She has three bodyguards," Luke observed. "You getting all this down, Blackwell?"

"Yes, sir," the captain answered, busily taking notes.

Brad said thoughtfully, "Dan had a long reach, and a grasp to go with it, Luke."

"Brad, I'll explain all this later, but keep your eyes open. Dan's killer will probably be at these services."

Brad stood dumbstruck. Luke Bonner abruptly turned and entered the chapel, followed closely by Captain Blackwell, who was writing furiously. Brad wondered if the general was guessing, or if he knew something crucial about Dan's murder. The hair on the back of his neck stood up, and he turned to survey the throng again, a feeling of apprehension washing over him.

"Brad, you look distressed. What's wrong?"

He turned to face Judge Quincy Sennet, who had a hand extended to shake Brad's. Brad made an effort to mask his apprehension.

"Hello, your honor. It's nothing, really. Guess this hit me pretty close. Dan's death, that is. How are you? Haven't seen you in a couple of years."

"I'm staying busy in the circuit court in Colorado. I love it. I enjoy the kick of a high-powered rifle, and the hunting is great. The climate and outdoor activity agree with me." The judge thrust out his chest and flexed his biceps. His full head of silver hair gave him a distinguished appearance.

"You look great, Judge. Better than when you were working throttles in the choppers."

"Well, we've all come a long way since then. Despite your low-profile activities, I hear you're the anti-terrorist expert to know these days."

"I'm a security consultant. I give a lot of advice, when people ask for it. They decide how to use it. How did you hear of my work?"

"I keep up with the old trade, mostly out of curiosity. You've done well. It's made you one of the more successful of the old bunch from the Knives."

Brad shuffled his feet and winced in his embarrassment. "That's really an overstatement, especially with a Congressman, a judge, and a corporate president as alumni. They all turned out pretty well."

"Except that Bum Shandy. He's been up before judges three times in recent years. I disqualified myself from the cases, of course. Once on probation, and twice incarcerated."

"Bum's had his share of bad luck, and then some."

"Actually, he's always been a bad fellow. I don't see how you endured him as a gunner. Always disorderly and underhanded."

"He was a great gunner and he knew helicopters."

"And explosives as well. You know he and Dan never got along well. Dan saw right through him. And said so."

Rafe Johnson stepped up to place his hand on the judge's shoulder. "Careful, your honor, you might prejudice our case," the police sergeant said with a grin.

"Case? What are you two talking about?" Brad asked the judge anxiously.

"I simply expressed my suspicions about Bum Shandy when we met earlier today. There's not a better suspect in Dan's murder than Shandy."

Brad felt his stomach churn and his adrenaline start pumping as he faced the two men, aghast. "You can't mean that! Bum is no saint, but he's not a killer!"

"He did rather well firing out the door of your helicopter," the judge said sarcastically.

"That was war, and we each did our share of it," he said with emotion in his low voice. "But you know Dan's death is entirely different."

"I understand he's an expert with explosives, and he had a motive and the opportunity. He had a run-in with Dan last week, and he was seen here in Washington the day of the murder," Rafe summed it up officiously.

"Circumstantial!" Brad growled.

"Circumstantial?" asked Denton Mallard, approaching the group. "You must be discussing Dan's unfortunate demise. How is the investigation going, Sergeant Johnson?" he asked, shaking hands all around.

"You've met?" Brad asked, looking from Mallard to Rafe.

"Yes, I checked with most of Dan's associates, past and present," Rafe replied evenly. "Several are here in town now. I tried to talk to George Windham, but he's out of the country on vacation from the State

Department. Denton Mallard here also mentioned Shandy as the most likely suspect.''

"Well, Drake, I commend you," the judge interjected. "Your judgment has improved considerably over the years since you landed that helicopter on the water."

"No one has called me Drake in years," Mallard said with a sheepish look on his face. "But recalling that I was flat out of airspeed and altitude, any place I could set down looked good to me."

"Lucky for you, Drake, that water was only a couple of feet deep," Judge Sennet said with a smirk. "As I remember, Shandy was your gunner that day."

"Yes, I borrowed him from Brad for that flight," Mallard recalled. "He seemed more interested in protecting his personal possessions than getting the passengers off. Dan suspected him of moving contraband. I never trusted Bum." He turned to Rafe. "You should check him out, Sergeant."

Brad was about to protest again when General Tran Vinh Lin approached the group with a large bodyguard close on his heels. "Cowboy, despite the circumstances, I'm very pleased to see you again. *Kuhn Sabai Dee, Lur?*"

"I'm fine, General. *Dee Mak*, thank you."

"Call me Tran, Cowboy. That's my Americanized name. I don't publicize my former military rank these days. I also keep this strong man close by at all times. But in your business you know about these precautions."

Lin was a small wiry man who moved like a coiled spring. He had the ageless face of the Asians, but his hair

was graying at the temples. Brad saw from the bulge beneath Lin's jacket that he was armed just as the bodyguard was. To carry a weapon to a funeral, particularly
with so many security people around, seemed tasteless
and unlike the image of the refined Golden Dragon of
earlier years.

As if reading Brad's thoughts, Lin continued, "One
of life's most important rules, Cowboy, is never to trust
anyone."

Brad recalled the long discussions he had shared with
Lin back in Xiang Province. Lin had given an informal
list of rules of life that summed up his personal philosophy:

Don't trust anyone.
Do unto others before they do unto you.
All power corrupts; enjoy it while you can.
Live for today; tomorrow and yesterday don't ex-
ist.
We're already dead, so don't worry about any-
thing.
No human life is worth more than your own.
Anything can be bought and sold.
Let no good deed go unpunished.
There is good in every bad deed.
Harshness is in the eye of the recipient.
Expect nothing; accept what comes without com-
plaint.
Kindness is the worst cruelty; death is the best.

Unable to accept the philosophy or the words, Brad had argued cautiously against the behavior that they caused, but Lin was immovable in his thoughts and actions.

"Do the Oriental rules apply in American society as well?" Brad asked softly, his brow furrowed.

"I'm very much an American now. In Colorado I have low profit margins with my ranch, the coyotes and cougars continually take out my stock, my taxes are driving me nuts, and I'm not exactly fully accepted in the local social circles. But I'm going to make it."

"Sounds like you've got your hands full," Brad observed, noting Lin's complete lack of Oriental accent and his cool, easy mannerisms.

"I'm using the technology you Knives taught me when you made me one of you. I have electronic listening and surveillance equipment better than that used on the Ho Chi Minh Trail. And I have booby traps and automatic weapons."

"Who armed the animals?"

Lin paused, then said deliberately, "They're silent and crafty, and so am I. And I fly my own helicopter and light plane now. I'm my own air force."

"Still fighting the war, huh?"

"In my own way, Cowboy, in my own way. And the Oriental rules still apply."

As Brad wondered silently what dragon was driving Lin, he was distracted by a long, black limousine that pulled up to the covered walkway. An aide opened the door, and Congressman Thaddeus Ralston stepped out. His hawklike nose in the air, he surveyed the crowd quickly, then thrust his hand forward and followed it into the crowd, shaking hands as if it were voting day back in his home district. A counterfeit smile was pasted on his thin features.

Ralston was followed by Bess Bradshaw, his beautiful top administrative assistant. Her prominence on the staff was demonstrated by the aide's attention in assisting her from the car. Brad had heard rumors about an intimate relationship between her and the congressman. He felt a twinge of envy upon glimpsing a flash of thigh as she swung her shapely legs out the door. Her curvaceous body and radiant smile completed the picture of an attractive and competent woman.

"What does she see in him?" Rafe asked, stepping up behind Brad.

"Power and prestige," answered Lin, with traces of envy. "And she wears them exceptionally well."

Ralston spotted Brad, and he made his way over in a slow and stately manner, greeting everyone somberly along the way.

"Brad, I know how close you and Dan were. Please accept my sincere condolences."

"Thanks, Congressman. I'm glad you could make it today. I understand your committee has been pretty busy."

"Yes, that's right. General Lin here has just done us the honor of testifying before us on the missing-in-action Americans in Southeast Asia. How are you, General?" he inquired, shaking his hand.

"Fine, Congressman Ralston. Glad to help. Anything for a fellow Knife."

"Ah, yes. That experience has turned into a valuable political asset. I see we have other alumni here. Hello, Judge Sennet," he said, clasping Sennet's hand effusively.

"Good morning, Thaddeus. You look very political today," the judge said wryly.

Ralston turned his back on Sennet to greet Denton Mallard. "Well, let me shake the hand of the next ambassador to Malway."

"Please, Congressman. Not so loud," Mallard said self-consciously, looking warily over his shoulder. "That nomination hasn't been announced yet. No need to get the opposition agitated prematurely."

"Sounds like you're finally going to make the big social circles," Lin interjected sardonically. "All those big political contributions really paid off."

"Well, Lin," said the judge, "you of all people should know how money talks. Right, Drake?"

Mallard looked from one speaker to the other uneasily and muttered, "I guess so." His furtive eyes met Brad's, and he diverted them quickly.

Brad was puzzling over Mallard's curious behavior when he sensed a stir in the crowd behind him. Ralston grasped Brad's elbow and turned him to face Bess Bradshaw.

"Brad, my boy, I don't think you've met Miss Bradshaw, my assistant. Bess, this is Bradford Gaelman, a former Knife, and currently the terror of terrorists in Washington."

Bess offered her slender, graceful hand, a demure smile on her full lips. "I'm very glad to meet you, Brad," she purred smoothly, her voice soft and full-bodied. "Your name has come up many times in my rounds about the District. It seems your services are a valuable commodity these days."

"You two excuse me, please," Ralston said quickly as he hurried off. "I see someone I must speak to."

Brad surveyed the assistant's strawberry blond hair, her upthrust breasts and slender waist in one sweep of his eyes. He felt stirred by the sensuous tone of her prologue. Bells inside him were ringing a caution to his reeling senses. He forced a smile onto his features that he hoped would hide his uncertainty and prevent his suddenly susceptible body from revealing his aroused interest.

"It's a pleasure to meet you, Miss Bradshaw. I admire anyone who can keep that irascible old politician in office and out of trouble." He said with a grin.

"Make it Bess, Brad. I see you know Thaddeus very well, and you're one of the few who will speak his mind frankly on the subject. We'll have to have lunch sometime to discuss the real Thaddeus Ralston."

"I guess you're in a position to know him better than anyone," Brad said hesitantly.

"Not as intimately as the stories around Capitol Hill might lead you to believe," she murmured, taking his arm in both her possessive hands, her long, slender fingers exploring the solid biceps. "I do have a life of my own, believe it or not. But I've learned here in Washington that I have to be assertive to keep that freedom," she said with a sparkle in her eyes.

Her energetic grip on his arm and her almost over-whelming assault on his reclusive attitude gave Brad a feeling of being washed out to sea by a tidal undertow. His senses reeled, his heartbeat hurried, his eyes were becoming addicted to the taut material stretched between the prominent points of her breasts. Her soft voice and eyes were mesmerizing.

The arrival of the CIA car carrying Nan was his life-buoy. He snapped his jumbled mind back into perspective, telling himself that he came here to honor Dan's memory, not to be flattered by some fawning political aide.

Nan stepped from the car directly in front of Brad and Bess, assisted by a tall, muscular man in dark glasses and a short haircut. Through a black net veil, she showed little more recognition than a slight nod in Brad's direction. He uncomfortably removed Bess's fingers from his arm and said icily, "Excuse me."

"Sure, Brad. If you don't call me, I'll be calling you about that lunch."

"Sure. Later."

When Brad turned back to Nan, she had been whisked into the chapel by the agents from the car. Denton Mallard was talking to her as they went through the door. The crowd began to follow and cut off his access to her. He would have to talk to her after the services. Discomfort gripped his throat, drying it, but he couldn't decide why. Was it a reaction to Bess's advances, or to Nan's arrival?

Rafe was again beside Brad, a frown on his dark face, his hands jammed into the formal suit that seemed to struggle to contain the large, dynamic body. He reached up and pulled at his ear as he talked softly to Brad.

"Nancy came by the station yesterday afternoon to ask about the investigation. I tried to be easy on her and not get her hopes up, but she got pretty upset and it turned into a pretty heated discussion. She's not at all satisfied with what I've done or the lack of leads, and she's being obstinate."

"If she came directly there from the hospital, I can see why. She has some adjusting to do, and I'm not sure she'll accept any help from us, based on our conversation at the hospital. I tried to call her last night, but I guess she had the phone disconnected. I'd like to help, but I'm not sure what we can do."

"Talk to her again, Brad. Make her understand that we care."

"I'll do what I can after the funeral, if she'll talk to me."

"Thanks, Cowboy," Rafe said, as he turned and followed the group into the chapel.

Ed Richards walked hurriedly to the door, meeting Brad as he entered.

"Ed, glad you made it. I was wondering...."

"Yeah, sorry, Brad. I need to talk to you later, maybe after the services. Some gathering, huh?"

They took seats at the back. Brad's eyes went immediately to Nan's rich auburn hair, tucked tightly to her head above the collar of a simple black dress. Her bowed head bobbed with an occasional sob. But she was a brave, strong woman, holding up as well as could be expected. She was Dan's daughter, and so much like him. For the memory of Dan, he would be a friend to her now, if he could find a way.

Brad's mind went back to the jungles and karst hills, the whapping of rotor blades echoing through his memories, obscuring the chapel surroundings and the droning eulogy.

'Knife two-one, this is Alpha Three. Do you copy? Come in, Cowboy.'

OF ALL THOSE in attendance, Nan felt only the presence of Brad. She sensed his eyes watching her. Was it because he was her father's closest friend, or because she felt a need for his help? Or did she dread his accusations about her role in causing her father's death?

She struggled to hold back the tears, to clear them from her swollen eyes. Dabbing at them with a linen handkerchief her father had given her years ago, she fought to grasp each speaker's words. She sat still and pale, trying not to remember the look on his face as he turned and waved. The boiling black smoke churned thickly in her mind, bringing with it guilt and anger.

She snapped herself back into the service as an admiral was speaking about her father's patriotism and faithful service to his country, with no mention of his profession. Words like "good father" and "honorable man" penetrated her fog of memories and images she was placing between her and the pain.

She raised her eyes to sweep across the assemblage of flower arrangements made up of groups of his favorite blood red roses. Her blurry vision crossed an A3 shaped of roses, designating the Alpha Three title her father had honored so much. Beside it her eyes settled on the shape of a dragon fashioned from yellow flowers that stood out among the crimson. The dense black clouds churned up again, obscuring her conscious thoughts, bringing the guilt, anger and pain.

The gentle grasp of an agent's hand on her arm brought her thoughts back to the chapel, and she realized that the services had ended. Loneliness closed in about her as though all support was gone. She was led slowly up the aisle past where Brad was standing, his eyes watching her with open sympathy. Seized by a sudden impulse, she stopped at Brad's pew, looking at him calmly.

"Brad, ride with me," she said softly. "Please."

"Of course."

Rafe said quietly over Brad's shoulder, "I'll get your car out there."

Surprised at her sudden request, Brad was, however, pleased with it, for he wanted to be with her, to help her somehow. He fished out his car keys and gave them to Rafe. Nodding to the agent, he fell into step behind Nan.

Helping her into the car, he saw that she looked exhausted and vulnerable. She settled back into the seat as he took his place beside her. Beneath the veil, her closed eyes looked bruised and swollen. He watched the slow rising and falling of her breathing, her pulse beating at the base of her throat. He wanted to reach out and take her hand, or better yet, to take her in his arms and comfort her. But he was reluctant to intrude.

Nan felt washed out emotionally, but her anger at the cruel injustice of her father's killing was growing again and becoming a consuming obsession in her mind. She submerged her guilt in her fixation on retribution. Clenching her fists in the folds of her dress, she swore silently that she would pull out of this and somehow find her father's murderer.

Beside her in the car, Brad noted Nan's change in posture as she sat more erect, her fists visibly clenched, her mobile facial expression going from soft and fragile to stern and hard, her jaw set. She seemed to stiffen herself and show a new determination, perhaps to get through the burial without breaking down. He could understand how she might want to put this past her and return to living her own life. His heart went out to her in sympathy, but he sat still and silent in respect.

When they arrived at Arlington Cemetery, she emerged from the car on her own and walked deliberately to the grave site without help from Brad. He stood behind her as the ceremony began. She again appeared exhausted, her shoulders slumped and her head down. When the rites were completed, the Navy honor guard carefully and precisely folded the American flag which had been draped over the coffin.

Stepping sharply up to Nan, Admiral Dyson presented the trifold of the flag and said formally, "On behalf of the President of the United States and the Department of the Navy, I present this flag in memory of the honorable service to his country performed by Daniel Murphy Donahue."

"Thank you, Bob," she responded, almost inaudibly, pride and grief gripping her simultaneously.

The firing team commander gave crisp orders, and the seven riflemen fired their precision volleys. Nan flinched with each explosive report.

Out of the corner of his eye, Brad saw a quick movement up on the hill away from the burial site. He recognized the stance and movements of Bum Shandy, who was watching stealthily from a distance.

As the bugler played the first plaintive notes of "Taps," Nan sobbed and swayed backward. Brad quietly stepped up to support her as she leaned against him, trembling. She seemed to accept his arm and his grasp gratefully, without speaking. He could feel her uneven breathing and the sobs that shook her. When he looked back up the hill, Bum had disappeared.

Nan had felt the strength flow out of her as the mournful music was played. Her knees had jellied, her arms went limp, and she gave herself over completely to the comforting support of Brad's arms.

AFTER THE SERVICE, Brad followed Nan to a nearby bench beneath the branches of a tall oak tree. She walked with her head up, shoulders proudly held high, and her back ramrod straight. It was as if he were watching Dan walk. It reminded him again of how much she was like her father. Yet, despite her carriage, she looked incredibly fragile. Her cheeks, once ruddy with health, were now pale beneath her veil, and she appeared almost gaunt, as if she hadn't eaten in a week. But Dan had died only two days ago. Brad inhaled deeply, a frown furrowing his brow as he sat down beside her.

Nan knotted the damp linen handkerchief that lay between her fingers. She bowed her head, the veil sheltering the tears that continued to roll down her cheeks. He felt awkward with her again. He longed to put his arm around her slumped shoulders. But another part of him warned that she didn't want to be touched or held right now. He allowed his instincts to make the decision. He remained quietly at her side, waiting for her to want to speak. She lifted the veil over her lowered forehead.

"Brad," she began, her voice hoarse with tears. "Dad trusted you." She pursed her lips, as if to halt another sob. The words came out in a strangled torrent. "Every time we were together, he always had something good to say about you. About the times in Southeast Asia. His eyes would light up, and I'd sit there watching his hand gestures. He told me some of the things you went through together. It was as though you were a brother to him." She lifted her head, gazing gravely up at him, her lips wet and trembling. "A brother," she repeated.

The sun peeked through the swaying branches of the large oak, and moving patterns of light dappled the already mobile features of her expressive face.

Brad felt his throat tighten. No one had ever been able to tap into his emotions this easily. Maybe it was Dan's death. Maybe it was Nan's grief touching him. He couldn't decide. He placed his arm across the back of the bench, his hand resting lightly against her back. He wanted to hold her.

"We may not have been relatives, Nan," he began, searching in her eyes for her reaction, seeking the right words. "But we were closer than most friends."

Now, more than ever, he wanted to choose the right words, to make her understand his feelings for Dan and for her. He could see the impact his voice was having in her incredibly transparent face. She became so damned easy to read, and what he read stirred him deeply. Every emotion was mirrored in those wide emerald eyes.

He wanted to be responsible for what he was going to say. He was circumspect in his usual daily communications, in his business. But right now, it wasn't business, it was very personal. The most personal kind of conversation, and he hadn't had many of those lately. Especially with someone as exquisite as Nan.

"Dan and I went through some good times and some rough times together. He saved my life more than once, and vice versa." He managed a slight smile, and saw it reflected in her expression. "In fact, we lost track of who owed whom what. Blood brothers. That's what we were."

"The very best at what you did," Nan agreed softly, her eyes searching his face.

He remained very still, aware that she was looking at him in some new, indefinable way. It puzzled him, but he quieted his curiosity. He had been drawn to her eyes, and for a second time today, he became aware of the strength and determination that he saw in their depths. They had always been the kind of flashing eyes that could make a man melt inwardly. But he had not seen this strength there before. There was much more to her than

he had seen previously. That was another way she had
become like Dan. She was more than what met the eye.
He was pleased for no particular reason he could name.

Nan focused those eyes on Brad and held his gaze with
her determined look. "Brad, I can't do this alone. Can
you help? I have no one else to ask."

"I'll be glad to help in any way I can," he said kindly,
with sincerity in his tone. "What do you need?"

"I want to find Dad's killer."

The intensity in her voice and her expression startled
him. His eyes narrowed speculatively as he searched her
face. She meant it.

"Do you realize what you're asking?"

Her green eyes became intense with defiant determination. She stood up, looking down at him in emotion-
laden silence, her face becoming more composed, more
resolved.

"Yes, I do."

"Nan," he continued, standing to face her, "we all
loved him, but he was no saint. He had his share of enemies. He dodged a lot of bullets over the years. The police don't even have a lead. It was a professional hit, a
bomb wired to the door lock. They didn't leave a clue.
There are just too many possibilities!"

She placed her hands on her hips, feeling her anger rise
again. Her jaw was set, and her eyes were narrowed, her
cheeks regaining some of their color.

Brad's mind whirled. He felt himself assaulted by her
sensual physical presence. He couldn't help reacting to
her beauty. He fought to reorganize his thoughts.

"Look," he said in frustration, "you know I'll do anything I can to help you. You know what I thought of Dan, and I hope you know something of what I feel for you. But be realistic!"

"Are you through now?" she asked in precisely enunciated words.

Brad stared at her in a confusion of amazement and deepening admiration. He realized that she had all of Dan's stubbornness and determination, and then some more of her own besides.

"Now see here!" he said hotly, his face revealing his growing irritation. "I'm a security consultant, not a private detective. I teach people how to protect themselves, not track down elusive killers. What can you expect us to do that the police couldn't do better?"

She gathered herself and leaned toward him, looking directly up into his face. Her words were crisp, measured.

"You knew him. You were close to him. You know how he lived, how he worked, where he went, who would like to see him dead. He said you know him better than anyone. *Knew* him," she corrected. She paused, a look of pain running momentarily across her face.

"Nan," he started.

Her emotions took complete charge. She was angry enough to overcome the grief. "I should've known!" she said loudly. "You're supposed to be his friend! You're just like Rafe Johnson! Just no help at all!" she said explosively, her rage finally rendering her speechless.

Brad's anger rose to meet hers. "I heard how you treated Rafe! There's no call for that! He's doing his job, and doing it right. You're going off half-cocked because of some personal crusade of yours, but Rafe is a professional. He's not letting his emotions get in the way of doing what has to be done!"

She lowered her chin, feeling her pride injured. She folded her arms, then looked up at him. "I suppose you're going to back out on me, too!" she said, but sounding weaker than before.

"He was your father, but he was my best friend," Brad said more calmly. "We fought together. He saved my life. I owe him. You couldn't know about that . . . about what it's like to survive death together, to share that bond of life as Dan and I did."

He stopped and bowed his head in a turmoil of emotion, as she silently stared at him. His thoughts ran like a rollercoaster across a spectrum of concerns.

The challenge to find Dan's killer made him feel more alive than he had in years. And he had seen in Nan's eyes a new determination, something beyond the easy times of her glittery social life. He liked this change in her. He wanted to see her responsible independence win out over the carefree, often irresponsible behavior he had known from her in years past.

Despite his grief over Dan's death, he felt drawn to her, charmed by her genuine beauty, attracted by her mettle, teased by the prospect of what might become an exciting experience shared with this new woman before him. He knew the odds were against any success, but....

Brad felt her piercing eyes on him. He shuffled his feet and shoved his hands deeply into his pockets. Looking away at the grave of his closest friend, he felt a twinge of guilt over his hesitating to try to help. His words to Rafe came rushing back: *He's too good a man to let his murder go into the books unsolved.*

He looked into Nan's eyes, seeing a vulnerability creeping into the determination her features had reflected. He felt a surge of warmth, a growing recognition that if he could help her find herself in this, maybe she could help him find himself, too. Maybe.

"All right, Nan. We'll give it a go. I'll try to find out what he was working on. Where can I get in touch with you?"

Nan took a deep breath and exhaled slowly, her chin dropping and her shoulders slumping forward. For a moment that seemed to last an eternity, she had feared that her hostility would drive Brad away. She couldn't allow that to happen.

It wasn't simply that she needed his help. She sensed a feeling of mutual need. The gamut of pained expressions she had just watched on Brad's face told her that he, too, was being tormented. She had a need for his strength and confidence. He no longer seemed intrusive, and she was becoming more comfortable with him, even after they had lost their tempers. She definitely didn't want to drive him away.

"Thank you," she said finally, showing the semblance of a weak smile. "I'll be staying at Dad's apartment for a while. And Brad . . ."

She hesitated, wanting somehow to comfort him, to let him know she understood.

"Don't wait too long to call me, Cowboy. I want to hear from you.

The sparkle in her eyes told him she was sincere. He experienced a strange giddiness that confused him. *Whoa, Cowboy,* he told himself. He smiled and took her hand in his. It felt warm and receptive as she gently squeezed his fingers.

"Okay. I'll call as soon as I check a few things. You go get some rest now," he said protectively.

She withdrew her hand slowly from his. Resisting an urge to sit again on the bench, she turned to the waiting CIA car, struggling to handle a new surge of emotion. The warmth in her flushed cheeks and her speeding pulse seemed too much reaction to be caused solely by Brad's promise of assistance. She wondered at this new feeling, and why it came here and now. On a sudden impulse, she turned and quickly kissed his cheek. "Thanks, Brad. We'll find whoever did it."

"Sure, Nan. I'll see you later."

As she walked toward the waiting car, he reached up and touched his face where her lips had caressed him. He watched her all the way to the car, seeing her in a different light.

He remembered how she had been in the days right after her divorce: a headstrong young woman without goals or values. She was always ready with a flippant remark. There was none of the maturity he saw in her now. He tried to label this new feeling for her, with hopes and doubts spinning in his mind.

Was he seeing only what he wanted to see? He questioned whether she was being honest with herself, or just playing on his emotions to assure his help. She did seem obsessed with finding the killer. He wondered what inner dragon was driving her so strongly toward that goal.

"She's some lady, huh, Cowboy?"

He whirled to see Ed Richards casually approaching. Brad felt off balance at the thought that Ed might have seen his confusion in the parting with Nan. He wiped his face absently with the back of his hand and asked, "You know her very well?"

"Well, some. I took her to lunch and dinner a few times after her separation . . . and a couple of times before," Ed drawled with a broad smile. "She's had some tough times, with that bastard of a would-be husband and with what she had to put up with trying to break into modeling and freelance photography. She has plenty of talent, but she got slapped down a lot trying to be nice to people she didn't understand."

"I didn't realize you two were seeing each other," Brad said, somewhat taken aback. He felt a new pressure inside.

"That was some time ago, when I was a reporter and had more control over how I spent my time. Dan wasn't around to help, and she'd given up on most of her former social circle. We had a lot of long, friendly talks, no more than that. She mentioned your name a few times. She always looked up to you."

"I knew her only through the time I spent with Dan," Brad said, rerunning his mental tapes of Nan's diffident behavior the times he saw her. "She always seemed too shy or too frivolous to notice me."

Ed grinned widely and said, "Well, Cowboy, she never looked at me like she was just looking at you."

Not wanting to explain his confrontation with Nan or to reveal his agreement, Brad hastily changed the subject.

"Do you know what Dan was working on?"

A serious expression formed on Ed's features and his stance changed to all-business as he moved closer to Brad.

"That's what I wanted to talk to you about. If the case he was on got him killed, there may be more to it than I had thought."

"What do you mean?"

"I'm not sure, but I think Dan was working on something called 'Yellow River.' That's probably not an official name, for it's really a hush-hush classified project. Something to do with using drug dealers in Southeast Asia to find information on American MIAs."

"You're kidding!"

"I know it sounds weird. It's a risky political situation. But I pieced this together from things I learned from Bess Bradshaw, Ralston's aide. I got some more from General Luke Bonner, and from George Windham at the State Department."

"And they said Dan was working with drug dealers?" Brad interrupted.

"It looks that way. They're all working on cases in that same area we used to fly into, I think. I tried to get Dan to talk about it before his last trip, but he wouldn't. He only said it was too close to home to discuss. With all the political emphasis on drug enforcement now, you can't really blame him. But with the other sources added in, you've got to believe that all these independent approaches going in the same direction are leading to something big."

"How much does Nan know about this? Or about the old unit?"

"Dan told her some stories, mostly about the crazy things you and Dan pulled. He said very little about the rough stuff. Nan asked me about some of your adventures a few times, and I tried to make you sound heroic," he said with his characteristic broad grin. "She told me Dan thought highly of you and he talked often of your times over there. But no security stuff was compromised."

Brad nodded thoughtfully, his mind wandering back to the way Nan looked walking to the car. He sought to move the conversation along quickly.

"You mentioned Thaddeus Ralston and Luke Bonner. As former Knives, could they know anything about who Dan was working with?"

"Congressman Ralston is on a highly publicized select committee to obtain information on MIAs. There's still a public demand for it, and knowledge is power. Publicity can be political power. He's been to Southeast Asia twice to check things out. And he got plenty of publicity."

"I've read about the trips. He hasn't said much about results."

"I can't get anything out of him besides political posturing. Now, his assistant is a different matter. Bess Bradshaw is a lot of woman, and she's a sucker for soft candlelight and warm wine."

"You mean chilled wine."

"It was usually warm by the time we got to it. Anyhow, she doesn't have access to some of the inside stuff. Some of it is so sensitive that very few people have access."

"If the topic is so sensitive, why are you looking for a story?"

"Our publisher wants it badly. He sees it as a political opportunity. But there's more. Smells like a cover-up of some official wrongdoing. General Bonner has been working with the Army's CID on drug dealers. He's tracking today's dealers back to where they were during the war. His investigation has apparently ended up right back in the same area we know so well. He wouldn't lay the whole story on me, but he's found something wrong there, something big and bad. I know it."

"And Dan knew about this?"

"Dan was apparently pulling leads from both Bonner and Ralston, and from George Windham at the State Department, too. George has been looking into drug traffic patterns all over the world. You know, it's funny that our old bunch is turning up in this thing, and it's taking them right back to our old stomping grounds."

"I haven't seen George in some time. Another successful Knife alumnus. They've all done pretty well."

"Oh, I don't know about that. George is a prominent statesman these days, but his personal life sucks. He's still a handsome dog, and he's married to the homeliest-looking wealthy woman I know. There's talk he still has a mistress somewhere, and that's why he takes long vacations out of the country without his wife. He's on one right now.''

"I guess George may be an exception."

"Well, let's see," Ed continued, ticking the names off on his fingers. "Quincy Sennet is still passing judgment on everyone. Now he's a politically ambitious circuit court judge in Colorado and chafing at the bit. Since his wife passed away two years ago, he's lost a great deal of drive, and a lot of political support.''

"Go on."

"Thaddeus Ralston is getting plenty of national attention with his committee, but his alleged relationship with Bess Bradshaw is giving him some publicity, too. His home district constituency is moving to the sun belt, eroding his political power.''

"I've heard that."

"Denton Mallard is a successful electronics corporation president, but he still hasn't found the social acceptance he's always craved. He's been nominated as ambassador to Malway because of some heavy campaign contributions, and he seems obsessed with being confirmed for it. He sees it as his entry into the social circles that have thus far shunned him.''

"Who else?"

"Tran Lin is also still trying to fit in and be a 'real' American. He's having mixed success with his ranch, but he always seems to come up with the financing he needs. He's a lonely, devious man, and he has little social acceptance."

"Sounds like all the old bunch have shadows in their background."

"General Luke Bonner is another lonely man. And a crusader. His wife, daughter, and son-in-law were killed in a head-on collision with a hopped-up junkie soldier. The soldier lived, and Luke used him to get the pusher, his supplier, and the overseas connection. He's been tracking drug dealing as a hobby ever since. Luke's an expert on drug routes out of Southeast Asia. The Army puts him on special assignments with CID from time to time because of his expertise in history."

"He told me he's on assignment right now. You seem to know what everyone's up to, what about Bum Shandy?"

"You know, he was always sneaking around with something illegal, even as our gunner. Everyone sort of overlooked all the extra gold jewelry he wore back from some of our missions, though I know you never got into any of that. Since then he's failed with two wives and half a dozen jobs. He's been in jail twice."

"What's he doing now?"

"I've had him doing some legwork on this Yellow River story. In fact, he had some sort of run-in with Dan just last week while trying to get some information. I had to tell Rafe Johnson about it when he asked. Now Bum knows he's a suspect, and he's lying low somewhere."

"Well, all Knives present or accounted for. What sad things can you say about the rest of us?" Brad asked curiously.

"Us? Well, I left out Dan. You know he was a lonely and overworked man. He stayed worried about Nan and felt guilty about not spending more time with her. And Brad Gaelman? He's tired of his job and going through a mid-life identity crisis. He needs a fresh challenge to give him direction. And a woman to give him motivation."

"Touché. And what about Ed Richards?" Brad asked with a grin to match Ed's.

After a thoughtful pause, Ed continued. "Old Ed is feeling a bit burned out after a lot of overexposure and national attention over some really enjoyable investigative reporting. But he's still looking for that big story to come along, mostly for the personal satisfaction. This just may be it, Brad."

"So where do you turn next?"

"To Luke Bonner. I have an appointment with him in the morning."

"He told me he thought the killer might be at Dan's funeral."

Ed's forehead furrowed in thought. Then he smiled and said, "Just think, you might have seen the killer in the chapel. That is, if you ever took your eyes off of Nan."

Brad's face flushed as he thought of how well Ed knew him, how observant Ed was, and how right he was about Nan.

Ed savored Brad's uneasiness for a moment, then broke into another grin. "You remember what a hellion Dan was in the old days? Remember the time he broke the eggs in Luke Bonner's green beret?"

"Oh, yeah. That was the flight when Thad Ralston got wounded by George Windham's Asian girlfriend."

"Yeah. Congressman Ralston now claims it as a heroic war wound."

"Did I hear my name being bandied about?"

Brad turned to receive the outstretched hand of Thaddeus Ralston. "Hello, Congressman. Yes, your name came up."

"I find this frivolity totally out of place at a funeral for an old and dear friend," the congressman said scornfully. "Especially when my unblemished record is being disputed."

"On the contrary, Congressman," Ed said, bristling. "Dan wouldn't expect long, dour faces on his cronies. And as I recall, you were never his close friend. As for your record—"

Ralston raised one hand defensively and jammed the other into his pocket, his face becoming even harder under a heavy frown. He turned to look over at Dan's grave, which was now being filled by groundskeepers.

"It's true that Dan and I had our basic differences, just as you and I have, Ed. Cowboy, I guess you're recognized as the only one of us who could entirely understand Dan," he said with a nod at Brad. He gave a big sigh and said abruptly, "I find this conversation in a graveyard morbid and depressing. Shall we adjourn to my club for a drink to honor Dan and old times?"

"Not me. I have a story to work on," Ed said, the muscles visibly tightening in his jaw. He nodded to Brad and turned to leave.

Brad recognized the old frictions that frequently cropped up between Ralston and Ed, and Ralston and Dan, and Ralston and most of the other Knives. There was something irritating about his imperious manner. Brad surmised that this characteristic may have prompted the voters back home to send him to Washington.

"I'll be glad to bring you up to date on my MIA hearings, Ed. You know, Tran Lin gave a great testimony."

"I'd like to hear about it, but not today," Ed said as he walked away. Stopping, he turned to Brad. "I'll call you tomorrow. Maybe I'll have more for you then. And Cowboy. . . watch your six."

The six o'clock position was directly behind a pilot. It was the direction he had to be most careful about, for it was from here that an attack was most likely to come. "I'll take care, Ed. And you, too."

"Problems, Brad?" the curious congressman asked.

"Nothing we can't deal with," Brad answered guardedly.

"Well, will you join me for that drink?" the congressman tried again.

"Sorry, Thaddeus, but I promised Nan I'd look into a couple of things for her today."

"Ah, yes, she's such a dear lady and she's been so abused. So unlike her father."

"I don't think so," Brad returned defensively. "I think they're remarkably alike."

"Well, God knows you'd be the one to judge that. I suppose you're as close to her as you were to Dan."

"We're becoming good friends," Brad replied cautiously.

"She is rather attractive. And much in need of some intimate support about now, I would think. If it weren't for my jealous wife and suspicious constituency. . ." he said lustily, a smirk on his thin face.

"I'll let you know if I find any way you can assist her," Brad snapped, trying to keep the irritation out of his voice. But the congressman was caught up in his fantasies, and missed the inflection entirely.

"Don't bother. I have enough problems as it is. Between me and you, politically, this MIA thing is turning into much more than I had bargained for," he intimated wearily.

"You want to explain that?" Brad questioned, hoping to draw Ralston out on the subject.

"Yes, perhaps it would be to our mutual advantage if we discussed the data we've uncovered. Let's get together for dinner soon."

Brad saw Bess Bradshaw, captivating as ever, walking briskly toward them.

"Congressman Ralston, Senator Belker on the car phone. He says it's urgent."

"Thank you, my dear. Well, Brad, duty calls once again. Excuse me for a moment, please."

"Certainly," Brad replied, crossing his arms and trying not to stare at Bess.

As Ralston hurried to his nearby limousine, Bess stepped closer to Brad. Her hands were clasped behind her, thrusting her full breasts forward. Her lips were pursed, her eyes measuring him speculatively.

"You look tired, Brad," she drawled softly, putting her whole body into the words.

The fragrance of her perfume and the sensuality of her presence were almost overwhelming. "I guess I am, Bess."

"You need to relax more. Relaxing can be most enjoyable," she whispered suggestively, her hand now tugging at his elbow. "You need to learn how to squeeze that extra something out of life."

Brad's pulse quickened, and he felt a giddiness that sent his senses into a whirlpool of bewilderment. "Frankly, I feel pretty squeezed already."

"Why don't you just let me take you home and help you recapture your vital essence and enjoy some gratifying diversion?"

Her erotic tone dazed Brad. He felt suddenly vulnerable. Her hands were again on his arm, prying him from his reclusiveness. He felt as if awakened from a drugged sleep. He also felt exhausted. He sighed heavily.

"Bess, I don't know when I've ever met anyone quite as glamorous and seductive as you. And I'm truly flattered by your attention. But I'm also emotionally depleted. Right now I'm not quite up to an adventure as thrilling as what you offer. How about a raincheck?"

In her high-heeled shoes, on the unlevel ground, she could almost look at him at eye level. Her blue eyes sparkled and a mischievous smile crept to her lips.

"You've got it, Brad. But I'll choose the time and place."

Ralston's approach interrupted them, and she disengaged her grip on his arm reluctantly.

"Bess, we must go. Brad, sorry I have to rush off. It's a political emergency."

"That's quite all right, Thaddeus."

"I'll call you and we'll have lunch. Or dinner," the congressman said while taking Bess's arm and walking quickly to his waiting car.

Over her shoulder, Bess crooned, "Brad, try to get some rest. Get a lot of it. I'll call you soon."

He merely nodded his head in wonder as they departed. Then he shook his head in amazement.

"So help me, Dan, I didn't expect this," he said aloud softly. "Forgive me this intrusion." Thinking again of their times together, he made his way pensively to where Rafe's patrolman had parked his car.

Knife two-one, this is Alpha Three. Stand by for a controlled transmission. Poppa, kilo, four, four, three, seven, Zulu. Do you copy?

WHEN BRAD CLOSED the door back at his condo, he leaned against it in relief. He was ready to call it a day, having spent much of the afternoon driving on the interstate beltway that surrounded the capital.

He had driven by Dan's apartment, but declined to intrude upon Nan's sorrow so soon after the funeral. So he had sat looking at the scorched spot where Dan's car had been parked. He tried to imagine the killer approaching the car. Placing the charge. Wiring the trigger.

No one had seen him. Her. Or them. The killer was definitely a pro, someone experienced at killing. Maybe someone desperate enough to risk working in the open.

Someone who knew Dan's schedule, or someone who had the apartment or Dan under surveillance, and knew the car had been left on the street unprotected.

Had the killer watched Nan park the car? The thought of her took his eyes up to the balcony of Dan's apartment. He realized how close she had been to the death and destruction on the street. His heart had raced to think of her. But he hadn't been able to bring himself to go up to the apartment. Not yet.

Here, back in familiar surroundings, he wished he had seen Nan, had talked with her. Hoping she might have called him, he went over to check his answering machine. Its red light was blinking, indicating that it held recorded calls. He turned the switch to *play* and settled into his favorite lounging chair as the recorder delivered its messages.

Beep. "Mister Gaelman, this is Terry, your faithful secretary. Just wanted you to know everything is fine. No problems. But please keep in touch. Bye now."

Beep. "Brad, old chap. About that inspection of our facilities. Not to worry, my boy. We fully understand. We'll be in touch later. Cheerio."

Dub Breckenridge. No problem there.

Beep. "Brad, this is Luke Bonner. I'll be out of town tomorrow, so let's make that lunch Friday. Tim Blackwell will be in touch. Sorry."

Friday. He wondered what had come up.

Beep. "*Guten tag*, Brad. This is Hilda. Sorry I missed you. And I do, you know. Please call me, and we'll have lunch . . . or something."

Hilda. The big-bosomed security assistant. He made a mental note to call her later.

Beep. "Hi, Brad. This is that sexy strawberry blonde. Sorry I missed you. Hope you're resting. I'd say something erotic, but I don't know who else you have there listening. Think of me now and then. I'll be thinking of you. Of us. I'll call you soon."

Despite his down mood, he couldn't help smiling and marveling at this incredible woman. Sooner or later, he would have to sort out his feelings about Bess.

Beep. "Brad, this is Nan . . . I hope you've learned something. I waited for you to call. Please call me, Brad."

He was puzzled by her message and the touch of hysteria in her voice. He turned to the phone to call her.

Beep. "Hello, Cowboy. Bum here. Watch your six, good buddy. You know too much. You were there on those flights, too. You had to know what was going on. I'm gonna protect myself any way I can. Just like in the old days. You and that Donahue broad watch out, Cowboy."

Brad sat back in stunned silence. He wondered why Bum would call him, and with such a cryptic message. He would have to pass it to Rafe. But it would add to the accusations against Bum. Could it have been some admission of guilt? What was Bum up to? What had he meant?

As the recorder clicked off, Brad sat thinking of Bum Shandy. He had always tried to give Bum the benefit of doubt when accusations arose. Bum was unpredictable, mischievous, often unreliable. But Brad didn't think

Bum was capable of unprovoked violence. The former sergeant never got along well with Dan, but Brad didn't believe Bum would kill him. Would he?

His thinking took him to a mental impasse again. He decided to put away his questions temporarily to call Nan. She answered on the second ring.

"Hello?" She sounded tired. Her voice quavered and came weakly through the line.

"Nan, it's Brad. Are you all right?"

"Oh, yes, Brad," she said more brightly. "I'm fine now."

"You sound exhausted. Did you sleep any?"

"Some. Did you find out anything?"

"You are in a hurry, aren't you?" asked Brad, a bit peevishly.

She paused. "Well, what do you expect? Have you done anything? Are you going to do anything?"

"I said I would, didn't I?" he asked defensively, feeling irritated by the intensity of her questions.

"Look," she stormed, "I wouldn't have asked for help if you hadn't been so close to Dad. And if it's too much to ask, I'll just find a way to do it myself!"

"Whoa, Nan. Slow down and cool off. Give me a chance to say something."

"Well...?"

"I had a long talk with Ed Richards, and I know what Dan was working on. At least I think I do. By the way, I know that you and Ed are very close. He told me he took you out a lot."

"Ed was very good to me at a time I really needed help, and don't you make too much of that!" she declared, wondering herself at the defensiveness in her voice. "He's been very sweet, and never demanding, and he's a good friend."

"You don't have to tell me what a great guy he is," he said, cutting off her explanation.

"I just don't want you to misunderstand. I mean, he's a good friend, but don't get the wrong idea."

"You don't have to explain anything to me."

"I know, so I don't know why I'm trying to. But I don't want you to think—I mean, I don't want to make it more difficult for you to help me. That is, I don't know why it has become so difficult to talk to you again!"

Brad hesitated before continuing. "Nan, I have some leads. I'm meeting Friday with General Bonner, and Ed will tell me more tomorrow. And Bum Shandy left a message on my phone machine, so it isn't as if nothing is happening."

"Bum called you? What did he say? At the funeral Denton Mallard called Bum a prime suspect."

"Circumstantial mistake. Bum left a pretty cryptic message. But he said that you and I should be careful."

"I'll bet! Did it sound like a threat?"

Brad again felt uneasy. "I don't think it was a threat."

"Mallard was right. You just refuse to see it, don't you? You can make me so angry!"

"I don't understand your obsession with finding the killer so quickly. I call with news of progress, and you get angry. What have I done wrong?"

"Oh, you! You really get to me!" She paused, and he heard a deep sigh over the phone. "Brad, I'm sorry. It's just so difficult to talk with you like this on the phone. I mean, I don't mean to be difficult. I just get so . . . so frustrated! Oh, I'm so tired I just can't think straight tonight.''

"I apologize if I upset you. I'm worn out myself. Why don't we talk tomorrow? We'll get together . . . maybe for lunch.''

"Okay, Brad. Call me in the morning. Maybe I'll be able to think more clearly.''

"Get some rest. Call me if you need anything.''

"Good night. And Brad, thanks for being there, Cowboy.''

"Sure, Nan. Sleep well.''

4

BRAD FELT THE SHOT that knocked the life out of his huge helicopter. It came as they were wallowing along above a tall triple canopy of jungle which seethed with thick, boiling vapor currents. As they had skimmed in and out of the highest of the three levels of vegetation below, tracer bullets cut patterns around them in a hail of gunfire.

Ed could be heard through the intercom, enthusiastically humming snatches of the *New World* Symphony, one of his favorites. Between musical phrases, he was calling out locations of enemy fire and looking for openings in the treetops into which they could safely maneuver the whirling blades. They were joyously playing hide and seek through ephemeral clouds of mist and soft, playful treetops.

Soaked with perspiration and wound as tightly as his nerves and muscles would allow, Brad was nevertheless enjoying the rollercoaster ride through the thick greenery. He was high on his own adrenaline, which replenished its surplus in his rushing bloodstream each time the rotor tips clipped leafy branches, or a tracer pattern appeared too near the Plexiglas canopy surrounding him.

His chopper was performing beautifully, and his own flying skills added to the thrill and satisfaction. Since escaping from the jungle clearing behind them, he had pushed the machine and himself to the limit in weaving in and out of the broken patterns of lush foliage and hot gunfire.

The fatal hit on his brave bird came as one of several dull thuds against his seat as he climbed above the branches. It was followed by a dissonance in the turbine engines, a discord from the dying chopper that ground down to a relative silence as the power to the rotor blades quit.

"Okay, gang, we're going autorotate!" Brad yelled into the intercom. "Secure what you can!"

Following a mental checklist ingrained by hours of training, he quickly went through the procedures for their autorotation. This process of using the lift provided by the free-spinning rotor blades would take the helicopter into the thick brush below in a controlled crash landing. He knew the rapid forward momentum he had just gained through his climb would help carry them ahead. The slowly turning blades would now help slow the descent of the aircraft.

Ed flipped switches and rushed through hurried emergency procedures. Brad quickly turned the helicopter into the wind to gain maximum lift efficiency. Fortunately, there was a series of openings down through the triple tier of foliage in the direction from which the light wind was blowing the misty vapors.

Brad lowered the collective control to full bottom, taking the throttle off, allowing the blades to become freewheeling. The angle of attack of the aircraft into the wind became critical. Too high or too low an angle would send them out of control, crashing through the dense jungle. Every raw nerve in his body was attuned to the instruments.

While Brad was wrestling the controls, Ed was calmly making an emergency radio call to the airborne command post that flew high above monitoring the operation in protective radio silence.

"Mayday, Mayday, Mayday. Kingbird, this is Knife two-one. Mayday. We've been hit. We're autorotate through triple canopy under fire. Mayday, Mayday, Mayday. Knife two-one is going down."

"Ed, cross-check our airspeed," Brad yelled.

"One hundred. Get a better glide angle."

Brad heard the wind whistling by. The trees rushed up at them. It seemed as though time were suspended, as though he were living his entire life in those few seconds, from the ups and downs of carefree flight through the treetops, to the quick, dodging dash down to a certain finality.

His fist white-knuckled. He used the cyclic controls to change the pitch on the blades. He swallowed hard to vanquish the harsh metallic taste in his mouth. The fun was gone now. With the control stick near his legs, he worked the rotor blades desperately, his eyes flicking from instruments to controls to the suddenly hostile growth of trees closing in on them.

"Eighty knots. Trees coming up," Ed droned, but with an edge of concern in his usually calming voice. An unbroken wall of foliage stood directly in their flight path.

Brad tipped up the nose of the chopper, turning it aside from the wall of trees, losing forward speed. The sickening drop took them through a narrow opening. The blade tips chopped through tender treetops, sending a shudder through the aircraft. Screams of warning came over the intercom. A hail of branches flew by, but there was no noticeable disabling damage to the helicopter.

"Get the nose down a little!" Ed shouted hoarsely. "Decrease collective!" The huge chopper was still losing forward airspeed. It began to glide ahead faster as Brad tipped it forward.

"Coming up on trees!" Brad warned through gritted teeth. The blade tips exploded into fragments as they struck something too solid to break through. But miraculously they were still autorotating rapidly through the trees.

"Sixty knots. We need to flare into these next trees!"

Increasing vibrations shook the chopper, rattling their teeth and shaking items loose from panels. Brad prepared to pitch up the nose even further to slow and soften the coming impact.

"I've got a spot to flare!" Brad yelled. "Hang on!"

"Stand by to flare. Hit it! Now!"

Taking a deep breath, Brad braced himself against his seat. He jerked the nose up by yanking the cyclic stick back into his lap. He made one pull up on the collective to increase the lift in the blades.

The chopper shuddered and rose briefly just above the dense ground foliage. It skidded sideways drunkenly into the nearby trees. Heavy branches exploded through the canopy on the right side. A hail of shattered Plexiglas and broken branches flew across the cockpit. Several severe blows struck Brad's helmet, and his arms were knocked from the flight controls.

"Ed, you got it! Take it! Help! Help!" he screamed hoarsely.

Brad lunged upward, and was sitting rigidly in his bed, his arms flailing, yelling for help. The flashbacks came and went as he fought through his semi-consciousness. He heard Ed say, "I've got it!" as the chopper slammed heavily into the dense brush. He felt his heart pounding as he heard a cacophony of harsh, jarring sounds, loud noises of Plexiglas popping and shattering, of metal bending and breaking, of people screaming on the intercom.

The dream yielded slowly, reluctantly, and he could smell the JP-4 fuel and the fear of his crew. His head was dizzy and aching, just as it had been back then when he had been struck and dazed. His heart was pounding and his breathing was too quick and too shallow. He felt as though he were fighting to get to the surface from under water.

Brad took deep breaths, slowly and deliberately. Shakily he reached across to turn on the bedside lamp, struggling to pull himself firmly into the present. Wiping sweat from his eyes with the sheet, he tried to establish himself in the familiar, friendly surroundings of his bedroom. He turned on his radio, seeking some sounds other than those of the crash. The soothing voice of his favorite female vocalist reached out to him with soft, seductive words.

He thought of Bess and her sleek, catlike body and sensuous voice. He thought of Nan, of her inner strength, her provocative beauty. He recalled the vision of her walking to the car, hips swaying gracefully above long, shapely legs. He felt a great need to be with her right now, to hear her voice. As he reached for the phone to call her, it rang.

Sitting on the edge of the bed, looking at the phone in confusion, his mind filled with memories of Rafe's call about Dan. Finally, he picked up the receiver and muttered hoarsely into it.

"Hello?"

"Brad? This is Rafe. Sorry to wake you," he said with concern in his deep voice. "Are you okay?" he probed carefully.

"Yeah. Just another dream. What's the matter? What time is it?" Brad asked, his voice rising and falling in his dry throat as he sought to gain his equilibrium.

"I'm afraid it's more bad news." The policeman's voice was full of unspoken feelings.

Brad felt a chill run through his stressed body. It suddenly sharpened his senses and focused his mind on a growing dread.

"Nan? Is Nan okay? Tell me, man!" he demanded in rising emotion.

"No, not Nan. It's…it's Ed," he stammered, the tone of his voice edged with sorrow.

"Ed? What happened?"

"A hit-and-run in southeast Washington about day-break this morning. He died instantly." Rafe uttered the words in a flat tone, like the reading of a routine police report. All feeling was gone from his voice, as though his usual inflection had been stretched tight by the pain of loss.

In silence, Brad faltered, absorbing the cruel blow, the aftershocks of the flashback still battering his mind.

"Brad, you okay?"

"Yeah, Rafe," he responded sluggishly, feeling his spirit flowing out. "How? What happened? Why?" he stumbled, feeling a growing anger as the shock wore off.

"It looks like it was intentional. The driver went out of his way to hit Ed. There was a witness."

"A witness? At that time of the morning? What was Ed doing in the southeast part of D.C. at that time of the morning?"

"Whoa! Slow down, Cowboy," Rafe pleaded softly. "We don't know why he was there. The witness was a hooker whose boyfriend had just given her a new camera. She walked outside and saw Ed step off the curb, and the car came after him. It was too dark to see much, but the driver was a man and the hooker got a photo of the car that may show the license plate. We're processing it now."

"Did she know Ed? That sounds a little too coincidental."

"Agreed. But we've already checked her out. We talked to the guy who gave her the camera. They walked out of the building and saw Ed standing there on the curb like he was waiting for someone. The dude left, and the hooker saw Ed step into the street like he was crossing it. She didn't see where the car came from.''

"And she got a picture?" Brad asked, trying to put it all together in a haze of confusion.

"She saw the car swerve and hit Ed, and she just jerked the camera up and snapped it twice. It was a fixed-focus camera with a flash, so maybe it'll come out okay."

"First Dan, and now this. Any connection, Rafe?" he asked, realizing that it was probably too early to know.

"I wouldn't want to guess right now, Cowboy," he answered in his officious tone again. "Just a minute...."

Brad heard a conversation going on over the sounds of a police radio in the background, then Rafe returned.

"I've got to give a report, so I'll have to get back to you later. Can you come down to the station?"

"Yeah, I'll stop by later. God! I've got to get to Nan before she hears about it on the radio or something! They were pretty close."

"Don't call her, Brad. If she knew him, you ought to go tell her," the sergeant said thoughtfully.

"You're right, as usual. I'll get right over there. She'll probably want to come by the station later."

"Fine. We can try to put some of this together then. But don't feel obliged to get involved. It's a police matter, you know."

"Dan was my friend and her father. Ed was my friend and hers too. You really think you can keep her out of this? Good luck!"

"In that case I'd rather talk with her here so I'll know what she intends to do. I'm still concerned about her safety, and I know you are, too."

"Roger that, Sergeant. We'll be there in a little while. She may need some time to adjust."

"I understand, Cowboy. Give her my condolences, too. And watch out. I don't need to lose any more parts of my life like this."

BRAD SHOWERED and shaved before leaving for Nan's apartment. He was caught between hurrying to reach her before she heard about Ed's death on the radio, and delaying to think of some way to break the news to her. He had told Ed that he didn't want Nan hurt any more. Now he had to hurt her again.

Brad wanted to escape from the grief, to think about upbeat things. But he felt guilty whenever he did. He kept remembering things Ed had said and done, tunes he had whistled, hummed and sung into the intercom. He remembered Ed's calming, supporting voice, his sympathy during the rough times of the separation and divorce, the double dates they had shared since then.

It was so final. So blunt. So total. He wanted to turn away from the pain. He needed relief from the agonizing reminders of unfulfilled promises he had made to Ed, things he meant to do with him, thoughts he wished he'd shared. Brad knew he needed a diversion. He needed something or someone to help him through his sorrow. He remembered Ed's words at the cemetery. Ed had told him he needed a woman to give him motivation and a fresh challenge to give him direction.

Well, he had plenty of challenge now. He had to get through this depression and get straight so he could help Rafe find the killer or killers. And he would find the bastards if he had to do it alone. And then, well, he'd decide that when the time came.

He went over a hundred options while driving to the apartment. Between memories of times with Ed, he rehearsed a dozen ways to tell Nan, and discarded each of them. On an impulse, he stopped at a pay phone on a street corner next to Dan's apartment building. At least he would wake her before arriving at her door. The phone rang three times before it was answered.

"Hullo?" a scratchy, sleepy voice murmured.

"Nan?" he asked, not certain that he had dialed the right number.

"This is Nancy Donahue. Who is this?"

"Nan, this is Brad. Sorry to wake you," he said tentatively.

"Brad? Brad!" she said, as though suddenly awakening. "Is anything wrong? Are you all right?" The concern came heavily through the huskiness of her voice.

"Nan, I need to talk to you. May I come up to your apartment?

"Yes, please do. I mean, what time is it? Where are you?"

"I'm at the corner phone booth. I can be up in five minutes, if that's okay."

"Is everything okay? Are you all right?" she asked, still not quite awake.

"Yes, Nan. I'm okay," he hedged. "But I need to see you. Is it okay?"

"Of course. Come right up."

NAN HUNG UP the phone and rubbed her sleepy eyes with her knuckles. She yawned widely, and wondered what could bring Brad over at this hour of the morning to see her. See her! Five minutes! She leaped from the bed and ran to the bathroom, grabbing her hairbrush along the way.

BRAD LEFT HIS CAR parked near the corner and sauntered toward the apartment. His light jacket felt good against the early spring morning chill, though it would be hot later. Then he saw the scorched curb where Dan's car had been parked. He felt a chill the jacket could not ward off. On both sides of the street were boarded-up windows that had been knocked out by the blast.

As he approached the door to the apartment building, Brad was surprised to see a doorman on duty. An attractive young woman in jogging clothes was entering the door. Brad heard her say in between panting breaths, "Good morning, Gerald."

"Good morning, Miss Snyder," the guard replied as he held the door for the young lady. Then, turning to meet Brad's approach with a conspiratorial smile, he added under his breath, "Quite a dish, isn't she?"

"You've got that right. I'm Brad Gaelman, here to see Ms Donahue," Brad said evenly. "She's expecting me."

"Oh, yes, good morning, Mr. Gaelman. When I returned from sick leave, Miss Donahue told me that I should send you right up anytime you showed up at the door."

With a friendly flourish, the older man winked and tipped his hat. Smiling the smile of fools and lovers, he held the door open wide. Brad thanked him and entered the lobby, where he saw the young woman holding the elevator door open.

"Going up?" she asked with a grin.

"Yes, thank you," he answered, hurrying to the door.

The woman pushed the button for Nan's floor and peered at Brad from beneath the headphones of a portable radio. "Thanks. Same floor," he responded.

After studying him openly for a few seconds, she retreated to coy glances. Then Brad took his turn, looking her over quickly with skilled analysis. Watching this woman was a welcome diversion from thinking about the task he faced with Nan.

She was a shapely young blonde in expensive jogging clothes that were fitted and revealing, rather than baggy and comfortable. Over the point of her left breast was a monogram: *Sue*. The doorman had called her "Miss Snyder." The glow of perspiration on her exposed body said that she had been exercising. She wore no rings.

He found the musky aroma of her sensuously arousing. But he was in no mood for sensuality or romance. Or was he? Any relief from the heavy load of sadness would help. He needed to ease the pain within him, and to avoid thinking of it.

She had a small portable radio at her slender waist, and it was turned up so loud that he could hear the music coming through the earphones. It was the same song of springtime and new love that he had heard earlier this morning. It took him back briefly to the aftermath of the flashback, and the feelings for Nan that he had then. It reminded him that he must face Nan. He was glad when they quickly reached the right floor.

"Have a good workout?" he asked in a friendly tone as he held the elevator door for her while she removed her headset.

"You bet," she flipped back at him over her shoulder, prancing over to the door of the other apartment on that floor.

"I could use some jogging myself," he admitted, releasing the elevator.

"You'll do," she said saucily over her shoulder as she entered the apartment.

He shook his head and chuckled to himself as he walked to Nan's door. Then he steeled himself for his task, his stomach tightening up, and his mouth suddenly feeling very dry. He cleared his throat and pushed the buzzer by the door. It opened to the length of the security chain, and Nan's sleepy green eyes appeared at the crack.

"Brad? Come on in," she said softly, closing the door to release the chain, then opening it wide. He entered quietly, and she closed the door behind him, absently replacing the chain. Realizing what she had done, she started to remove it again, but thought it would look odd to unfasten it now. So she was chained in with him, for whatever that might mean.

She wondered why he was here, and what she could do to wake up. The cold water she had splashed on her face hadn't helped much, and the hairbrush only seemed to tangle her long hair. His appearance was so neat. But he seemed tired and worried.

"Can I get you some coffee?" she asked, running her fingers through her hair to try to tame it.

"Not right now. Let's talk first."

He regretted sounding so eager to talk. He was put off balance even more by the fact that she was dressed in a soft silken robe that revealed more than it hid. The color of the thin, smooth robe matched the green of her eyes. Her hair seemed tousled, and she had on no makeup. But she looked absolutely lovely. As she walked, the folds of the robe followed the alluring lines of her body, making his breathing suddenly become difficult.

"Okay, please sit down," she said, indicating the couch. Noticing his studied gaze at her, she said apologetically, "I'm sorry, I didn't take time to dress." She had thought of him as just a friend dropping by. Now she felt slightly uneasy, but thrilled by his stare.

"You look terrific, Nan. I guess I didn't give you much warning."

He watched her sit on the couch beside him and draw her feet up under her. The clinging robe followed her shapely form, emphasizing her hips and long thighs. The garment was revealing enough that he realized that she had nothing on under it. He had trouble taking his eyes off her beauty, and he had to force himself to think about an explanation to her.

"Well, you said you wanted to see me, and you're sure doing that. Was there some talk to go with this, I hope, or do I just sit here and enjoy being visually ravished?" she asked with a smile.

"I'm sorry, Nan. I just don't know how to begin . . . how to say it," he stammered in embarrassment.

"Why don't you just jump right in, before my curiosity gets the best of me and I start prompting you? I'm not used to having handsome men show up on my doorstep at this hour with such soul-wrenching looks," she teased, trying to make him feel more comfortable. Then, more seriously, "Is it about Dad?"

She waited for his words with feelings of guilt and pain.

Taking a deep breath, he started into it, dreading the effect. His grief came washing back over him, eroding his confidence and poise.

"Nan, it's Ed." He hesitated, searching again.

"You didn't come over here just because of what I said about Ed, did you?" she said loudly, sitting up. "I told you, he's just a good friend. That has nothing to do with finding Dad's murderer."

Her frown showed irritation and impatience, and hid her relief that Brad was not accusing her of negligence, or worse.

He looked at her in pain, searching her face for sympathy to ease what he had to say. He could see no understanding there. She wasn't going to make it easy.

"I hope you know I would never say anything to hurt you."

"You're jealous?"

"Nan, Ed is dead. He was killed in a hit-and-run this morning. It looks like it was intentional," he said through his torment.

She sat back, her eyes widening with shock. "No, no, not Ed!"

"Easy, Nan," he said thickly.

Her hands went to her throat, where an aching constriction gripped her. A moan grew from deep within her as the meaning of the words twisted her insides. She looked at Brad, and saw her pain already reflected in his face. With a loud choking cry, she buried her face in her hands.

As great sobs erupted from within her, Brad gently drew Nan into his arms, rocking her in his embrace. With her head on his chest, she felt him shudder with emotion. As he rested his head against her hair, they shared the loss.

They sat holding one another for a long while, each thinking about Ed and what he meant to them. But they did so in silence, except for an occasional sob or sigh. Finally, she leaned back slightly and looked at him through tear-filled eyes.

"How did you find out? How did it happen?"

"Rafe called me. He said there was a witness who took a picture of the car. She saw it swerve and hit Ed as he stepped off the curb. She couldn't see the driver. It wasn't a part of town you'd expect to see Ed in at daybreak. I wanted to tell you before you heard it on the radio."

She started sobbing again, and moaned, "No, not again!"

"Easy, Nan," he said softly, taking her shoulders in his hands.

"He was a great friend. He was so kind and under-standing, especially when I needed someone close. I think he loved me, and I never even let him...."

"You don't have to explain anything, Nan. He was my friend, too. We fought together. We were very close for a long time. He told me he thought a lot of you."

"I think he knew I didn't love him. But I never showed him I cared, never even gave him the thanks he deserved."

"He knew how you felt. Ed was good with words, but he never needed a lot of them for himself."

"Brad, I feel so confused. I thought you were coming here to tell me something else. I never expected.... Oh, I acted so foolishly. You must really think I'm some kind of self-centered, conceited snob!"

"I wish I had myself put together enough to tell you just how deeply I feel. We're both overextended emo-tionally. All the way over here I was thinking about Ed's death, and Dan's, and about finding their killers."

Feeling her old guilt creeping up on her, she wanted action to relieve the pressure. "We've got to do some-thing! Do you think the two deaths are connected?" she asked excitedly, standing up to look at him. She wor-ried that she might have started a chain of events with her careless action.

"I'm not sure we can ever find out, but I'm going to try." He stood and held her arms gently.

"Oh, Brad. Did I kill Ed too?" she wailed, pressing her head against his chest. She desperately wanted a re-lease from the tight grasp of her shocked emotions. His arms were a comfort, and his strong body was reassuring.

The anguish in her voice ripped into his heart.

"No, Nan. God, no. You didn't kill anybody," he said, hugging her taut body closer. He ran his fingers through the thick hair at the base of her neck. "Easy now, just relax," he whispered in her ear. He resisted a rippling of desire, chased by a need for relief from the horrible impact of his grief.

But her softness and warmth were inviting, eroding his reserve. He wanted to ease her anguish, to erase her pain. He kissed her tentatively, soft, brushing kisses across her cheek to caress away her tenseness. He heard her sharp intake of breath, and she grabbed his arms, pushing away slightly, her emotional chaos showing in her eyes and mouth. Their eyes locked in intimate pleading and turmoil. He ran his seeking hands across her back, feeling the softness of the silken robe and the muscled softness beneath it.

The impulsiveness confused Nan, but sent a buzzing thrill through her. The light covering of the robe felt even thinner to her under the warm touch of his hands. Sensing how the clinging material outlined every curve of her body, she felt naked and vulnerable, desirable and uneasy in his arms. But there was a delicious wave of excitement now swirling between them. She wanted his touch, his kiss, and the comfort and escape they could bring her.

He raised her chin and placed his lips softly, fully against hers. She tensed even more at the touch of his lips, but he felt himself caught up in a building emotion, and held her even tighter. He stopped thinking.

Nan felt a sensation of floating free of her cares, from her grief, her brutalized emotions and her bruised mind. She yielded totally to his lips. He was lifting her from all of her responsibility, and she came willingly, then eagerly.

They moved apart, seeking air, their eyes locked.

"Brad, help me forget."

Brad saw her lips, parted and moist, turned up expectantly to him.

"Brad, I'm so—"

"Hush, now."

She again put her mouth to his. She felt herself sinking beyond any control or concern for what she knew was coming. The last fleeting caution was running naked through her mind when the ringing phone jolted her senses.

Nan turned toward the phone.

"Let it ring," Brad whispered, trying to kiss her again.

"Wait, Brad. It may be..." she urged in a rising inflection.

"Not now. They'll call back if it's important," he insisted, pulling her back to him.

The phone kept jangling persistently, bringing thick, boiling clouds of black smoke into Nan's troubled mind. A gnawing grew inside her.

"Brad, no," she said pushing away deliberately, feeling suddenly tense and uncomfortably out of place.

"It can wait," he said stubbornly over the ringing of the phone.

"No, we can wait," she said decisively, pulling away from him. She walked to the phone, picked it up, and said in a stern voice, "Hello."

Brad watched the sensual movements of her hips as she paced. He tried to put aside a residual desire which tugged at him. He hadn't meant this to happen. Where could it lead? She looked over the phone at him with concern.

"Just a minute, sir. I'll get him." She held out the phone to him. "It's General Bonner for you."

While Brad talked, Nan hurried to her bedroom. She removed the robe, tossing it on the bed. She looked at herself in the mirror and was surprised to see that except for a flushed face, she looked perfectly normal. She felt otherwise.

Her body still tingled with the excitement she had felt in his arms. She closed her eyes, breathed in deeply, and tried to still her racing emotions. His hands and mouth had created a raw hunger she hadn't known for too long a time, and she had responded eagerly in a way she couldn't control.

She quickly pulled on a soft, comfortable pair of shorts and her favorite faded T-shirt. As she rearranged her hair, she worried about how Brad's eyes could touch inside her, creating the pulsing and throbbing effects that she had not yet completely quenched.

She checked her appearance in the mirror and saw that her face was still flushed. She had to get herself under control. This kind of animal response on her part was what had set her up for problems in her marriage. It had too often led to humiliation and pain.

Well, she had wanted commitment and involvement from Brad. But his impulsiveness had caught her off guard. She wasn't sure she was ready. It seemed too casual. In fact, she really didn't even know Brad very well. How could she let him get to her like that? She would have to be more careful about her reactions if she wanted to keep their relationship reasonable. She wanted him to work beside her and find the killer. And perhaps more.

"BRAD? RAFE CALLED me about Ed. Caught me as I was going out the door to leave town. He said you'd tell Nan. What do you make of this?"

"Luke, I'm not really thinking very clearly right now. The loss of Ed is quite a blow."

"I agree. But these things never come easy."

There was a moment of silence that Brad attributed to Luke's unspoken memories of the loss of his family.

"At least we have more to go on this time," Brad said into the continued silence.

"You think the two deaths are connected?" the general asked.

"There's not enough evidence yet."

"Well I think they are connected," Luke said deliberately. "But I'd rather not discuss why on the phone."

"I was hoping you might have turned up something more," Brad said in relief. "Ed said you had been busy."

"Please say no more right now. If what I'm saying is true, I may be the next target," the general said fatalistically.

"You've got something that hot?"

"Like I said, I'd rather discuss it in person than on the phone. Besides, I've got to leave now to catch a plane."

Brad was thinking that it was foolish for Luke to worry about security of the telephone, unless his own was tapped. Since Dan had been with the CIA, surely there was no problem on this end.

"Don't let me make you late. I'll talk to Rafe and get an update on his investigation before I see you tomorrow," Brad said, distracted by Nan's appearance in a T-shirt and shorts as she crossed the room to the kitchen.

"Very good. I'll see you for lunch tomorrow. Just check with Blackwell on the arrangements. He's a good man. All Army."

"Fine. Have a good flight, General. And watch your six."

"Thanks, Cowboy. And you, too. Goodbye."

"Bye, now."

Brad hung up the phone and stood thinking of the implications of Luke's statements. If he knew enough to be a threat to the killer, the investigating general could well become a target. Luke was an old hand at defense. But so was Dan. And Ed was no easy mark.

What would the connection be? A CIA official, an editor, and possibly an Army general next? Or years ago when they were a CIA official, an Air force copilot, and a Green Beret? Was there a tie, or was it all sheer coincidence?

While contemplating the possibilities, his eyes came to rest on the light coming through open curtains at the french doors to the balcony. It must be painful for her to use those doors now, he thought. Why does she stay here where all the painful reminders are?

Then his searching mind gave him the answer. The apartment was a comfortable reflection of Dan. The familiar surroundings gave her strength and identity, just as the bookshelves in his own bedroom helped him re-establish his identity after the dreams and flashbacks.

Nan walked into the room with a platter of cheese and fresh fruit. The tight fit and frayed edges of her shorts indicated that they once might have been blue jeans that she had worn out. The blue T-shirt, softened in color and texture by many washings, clung to her like a second skin. The obvious outline of her firm breasts showed him that there was no bra beneath the thin shirt.

"You've certainly been busy," he said with a smile.

"You're right. Keeps my mind on more important things. You want to come to the dining table and help me eat this?"

"What's wrong with here?"

"On the floor?"

"I like it right here," he said sitting on the floor. "It's a nice carpet."

"Well, okay. That's where I usually sit. But you behave."

He didn't respond to that. He was too busy watching as she crossed her legs and lowered herself into a sitting position, placing the platter between them. Then she gracefully stretched out on one elbow, her bare legs reaching long and shapely before him, her firm breasts filling the T-shirt, and her head tilted with her hair falling attractively about her shoulders. He felt both intimidated and attracted.

"No hard feelings?" he asked quietly, picking at the fresh pineapple on the tray.

"None at all," she responded in a similiar tone.

After eating some of the sliced fruit in the silence that filled the room, he questioned, "Any regrets?"

"Not yet. But I think it's time to get serious. I have something to show you."

"You're getting my hopes up again," he said with a smile, only half joking. He picked up pieces of papaya and cheese from the platter to match the ones she was picking at.

"Behave. I found this note in one of Dad's coat pockets," she said, fishing out a folded paper that was tucked in the low waistline of her shorts, revealing a flash of bare flesh over her hip bone in the process.

He forced his attention back to the paper under the scrutiny of her smiling face and flashing eyes. She had withdrawn earlier, but not too far. And she wasn't angry. He couldn't pull together his thoughts to sort out what he was feeling, except that he knew he wanted to watch her beautiful body move, to be near her and to get back to where they were earlier this morning.

He took the note and unfolded it carefully. The handwriting was clearly Dan's; he wrote most of his notes in this distinct, precise printing of all capital letters. He had written the words *See the Mandrake* on a piece of note paper and put it in his coat pocket. It was obviously a reminder of a meeting or a contact of some sort. Or had he intended it as a message to someone else? Had an appointment been kept based on this note?

"I wonder how the Feds missed this," he said in curiosity.

"You mean the CIA and FBI? There were plenty of signs of a search. This had slipped through a hole in the pocket into the lining."

"Any idea what Dan meant?"

"I looked it up. A mandrake is a poisonous plant from the Mediterranean area. You think it could be a code name for an Italian spy?"

"I'm not aware that Dan was working anything in that area. But it's a possibility, I guess. We'll have to show this to Rafe. Maybe he has a clue as to what it means."

"I wish I had more confidence in the police."

She leaned back on both elbows with one lissome leg drawn up. She felt his eyes boring into her, giving an indication that despite her efforts to divert him, his thoughts still matched the residual desire that was fluttering around inside her.

An almost tangible tension hung between them. Nan's breasts betrayed her inner unrest. Protruding against the soft material of the T-shirt, they revealed more than she wanted him to know about her feelings.

"Must you ogle me like some love-sick schoolboy?" she asked defensively, sitting up and huddling to hide her arousal. But she could feel that he was still watching her.

"You've got to admit, you look pretty damned delicious in that T-shirt. And those cutoffs don't make it easy for me to get my mind off how good you felt a little while ago."

She threw her head back and looked at the ceiling, her slender neck stretched in a way that he thought attractively vulnerable.

"I apologize for making it tough on you. This is what I usually wear when I'm trying to relax around the apartment. I didn't mean to tease you. I meant well, honestly."

"Hey, I think it looks great. I'm glad you can feel comfortable enough to wear whatever you want to. I like that. But you'd look great no matter what you were or weren't wearing."

She put her head down, resting it on her drawn-up knees, which she gripped in crossed arms. She felt a conflict of emotions struggling within her, wanting his touch, but fearing what it might lead to, fearing that she might not be able to control her response. A collection of myriad memories of her marriage problems ran through her thoughts.

"Brad, please don't take this wrong. There's so much pulling at me. Please try to understand. I can't explain how I feel right now."

Brad sensed her inner turmoil. He also felt confusion in his feelings. He reached out to stroke her arm, and she pulled away slightly before settling back to his touch, lowering her head and keeping her eyes from his. She raised her head and looked at him with soft, moist eyes.

"Brad, maybe I should change clothes and go with you to see Rafe at the station. Maybe we can talk later," she said softly.

"Sure, Nan. I didn't mean to push. I just wanted you to know I think you look great. I don't understand all of this, and I don't know where we're going. I don't want how we feel to interfere with getting some answers about Dan and Ed. And I don't want to lose whatever it was that we felt a few minutes ago."

"Let's discuss that at a better time," she said, getting up slowly, her eyes still wet with unshed tears. "I'll be right back."

He again picked over the fruit and cheese on the tray while thinking of how his sensitivities for Nan had changed, had grown and deepened. He tried to define his feelings while he picked up the leftovers and carried them to the refrigerator in the kitchen. He couldn't decide precisely what emotion attracted him to her, lust or love. He had known and ignored several beautiful women like her. And several independent and capable ones.

Who was he kidding? All the women he had met lately were young and naive, or older and frivolous! He had never known a woman quite like Nan. Somehow he had missed the changes that had taken place in her.

She had become strong-willed and high-spirited, audacious and insistent. He felt a strong but indefinable link to her, perhaps because of his friendship for Dan and the trait she shared with him.

She was the most exquisite, desirable woman he had ever met. Whatever the reason, he felt a demanding need for her presence, her touch, and more. Despite her independence and continued abrupt withdrawal, he felt a growing need for her love.

But how could he express that to her? She would recoil from the pressure and turn away even further. He wanted her to know, but he didn't want to come on too strong. He might lose her altogether. And he couldn't let that happen. Not after the way she made him feel this morning. He felt like a man again, and she was a woman like no other.

As he walked out of the kitchen, Nan entered the room from the other side. She was wearing a spring outfit with a white blouse and a pastel green skirt that buttoned up the front. She looked like a photo from a fashion magazine. She was going to make it fun to notice what women wore again. With her beauty and proud spirit, she was bringing his dormant senses back to life.

"Pretty lady, I hope you don't mind if I say you look absolutely terrific."

"I'm beginning to think you're a little prejudiced, or a little insane, but you're great for my morale."

"I may be guilty on both counts."

They both laughed as she offered her arm. He took it carefully and escorted her out the door. He placed his hand on her waist as he closed the door behind them. The touch and pressure put her uncomfortably on guard.

"Brad," she said, freezing at his touch. She pulled away and turned on him, a frown on her brow and her shoulders drawn up defensively. Then she saw the little-boy look of obvious affection, marked by hurt because of her action. She relaxed her shoulders, smiling in spite of herself, and said, "Thanks for being here with me." Taking his hand, she started for the elevator.

Brad looked at her in wonder and confusion over her quick change in expressions. If he were going to understand her, he would have to watch her closely.

5

WHEN NAN AND BRAD arrived at the police station, she walked briskly ahead of him, opened the door for herself, and confidently approached the desk. She again showed the card Rafe had given back to her during her last visit, but since there was a new worker at the desk, again she had to await verification of the note on the card.

Brad was impressed with Nan's spirit and confidence. The presentation of the card was a novelty for him, and he made a mental note to ask Rafe for similar credentials for his own use.

He noticed that Nan's striking appearance did not go unnoticed by the policemen they passed, most of whom craned their necks to get a better look at the effect of Nan's blouse and skirt. It was not likely that they would see a woman looking as captivating during the rest of their day. Or week for that matter. He was proud to be with her, and by the looks the people were giving him, it probably showed in his face. He felt she looked absolutely devastating.

By the time they were directed to the waiting room to wait for Rafe, Nan was beginning to feel uncomfortable under all the scrutiny. She folded her arms protectively over rigid breasts, and shortened her step in the revealing skirt. Brad noticed her change in demeanor, and he very deliberately put his arm protectively around her and gave her a squeeze and a smile that needed no words.

The constant hubbub of the radios and typewriters reminded her of the last visit. She still felt that this was not a place she could be comfortable in under any circumstances.

"Wait until you see this waiting room," she muttered to Brad. "It's like a morgue waiting for bodies."

Brad chuckled and squeezed her arm again, realizing that she was uncomfortable for more than her bold appearance. He felt very close to her, and regretted releasing her when they entered the waiting room.

Nan resumed her pacing where she had left off during her earlier wait. But this time was totally different. She felt more at ease with Brad here, despite their encounter this morning in the apartment, and despite her reservations about getting emotionally involved with him.

During the drive to the station, she had felt his eyes on her at every break in the traffic. She had returned the glances several times, until their eyes met in electric contact and they each turned away. She could feel his interest, and the thrill it created. She didn't want to lose this feeling, for there was only emptiness to replace it.

It was wonderful to be caught up in something so exciting, but at the same time she didn't feel completely untroubled. She wasn't ready to make a commitment to Brad, and what almost happened this morning felt too much like the casual sex that she had avoided for so long.

But still, there was an almost tangible tie that pulled them together.

They had hardly spoken in the car, and yet a bonding was somehow communicated between them. With silence and smiles, they seemed to have made a tacit agreement to proceed carefully together. They would have to discuss it openly eventually, but she thought neither of them was ready to put it into words yet. Now a linkage held them together, one that neither fully understood.

She turned to look at him across the dismal room, and catching his eye, she matched his smile and said, "Don't you love this place? Their decorator must have been blind!"

He chuckled and replied, "It was probably a disturbed inmate. But think of the taxpayer money they're saving."

He warmed at the sight of her broad smile, as she resumed her pacing. She had been the same kind of distraction while he drove here. He remembered how she had caught him staring at her when he stopped at a traffic light. He had feared that she would overreact again and withdraw her light mood, but instead she had just smiled and looked away without speaking. The second time it happened, she reached over and squeezed his arm and said softly, "Try to watch the traffic, too, huh?"

He liked it. He liked the feel of it. It was comfortable, but more. It was very satisfying, but nevertheless exciting. Not that they fully understood it. Nor did he think she fully accepted that something special was happening here. But he could feel a togetherness growing, and it felt good.

Rafe entered the room apologizing.

"I'm sorry. I told those people you were coming, and they still made you wait. You look terrific, Nan. I think they just wanted to keep you where they could see you. I don't know what the excuse was for you, Cowboy."

"I'm with her," he responded laughingly.

"We should all be so lucky. Well, come on into my office. I have a stack of photos to show you.

"That's what we're here for," Nan chimed in.

"I'm sorry we have to keep meeting under these unfortunate circumstances," he said, escorting them into his office. "Have a seat."

"We understand. We just want to help," Nan said softly.

The use of *we* made Rafe look smiling at her and then at Brad. He chuckled approvingly, and said, "Looks like law enforcement has a new team to help out."

"Wherever we can," Brad said seriously, slipping his arm around Nan's waist. She moved into the circling touch and smiled up at him. They were still smiling at each other as they sat down. The mutual support felt good.

"Looks like we have more to go on this time," the police sergeant said, trying to regain their eye contact. He took a group of photos out of a folder on his desk and spread them for his guests to peruse.

"Take a look at these skid marks," he continued, using a chewed pencil to point at the picture. "They leave no doubt that the assailant accelerated sharply from this point up the street." He indicated the tire marks in the photo.

Brad and Nan stood and moved closer to the desk to get a better view of the photos. These were apparently made by a police photographer as evidence. The tire marks were but black streaks in a lightened area of the picture. A closer look where Rafe's pencil point was positioned showed Brad the slight sideways skidding that took place in the rapid acceleration of the tires on the smooth asphalt.

"Then, upon arriving at this point, he swerved sharply enough to skid again just before the point of impact," Rafe continued. He pointed out the tire marks in two other photos to make his point. Displaying two different photos, he droned on. "This debris is from the broken headlight and a piece of the trim. And these tire tracks show the accelerated getaway."

"What about the witness photo?" Brad questioned.

"There are two of them. Here, we got a partial license number in one photo, but no luck on the driver in either picture. You can see in this one that the camera strobe light reflected off the window and obscured the driver."

Brad picked up the new photo to look at it more closely. Nan leaned closer to him, and the softness of her breast pushed gently against his arm. He fought to concentrate on the exhibits, but he could not ignore her unintentionally demanding sensual presence.

The witness photo showed that the left front fender of the car was very noticeably crumpled and sparkling bits of the broken headlight were frozen as they tumbled in midair, reflecting the flash from the camera. At the bottom of the print, a man's shoulder and back could be seen near the curb.

"Oh, my God! Is that?" Nan cried, her hand going to her mouth, and her shoulders drawing forward as if to ward off the pain of realization.

"Yes, I'm afraid so," Rafe said quietly, a grim tightness around his mouth. "That shot shows some of Ed's body before the car pulled away. As you can see, the light on the window obscures the view of the assailant."

Nan turned away sharply, her eyes filling with tears beneath the cover of her hands. She struggled to control her emotions.

Brad rested his hand lightly on her arm, but he kept his attention turned to Rafe.

"You said there was another witness in a photo?" he asked, handing his handkerchief to Nan.

"Yes," Rafe mumbled, diverting his attention from Nan's tears. "Here's the same photo enlarged and printed with different lighting to emphasize the pedestrian on the other side of the car. He could've seen the driver, if the flash didn't blind him. If only we knew who it was!" the sergeant said, slapping his fist into his palm. "No one in the area remembers seeing him."

When Brad looked at the photo, the hair went up on the back of his neck. As he inspected it closer, he felt a sinking weight in the pit of his stomach.

He closed his eyes tightly, blinked them open and looked again. He examined the shape of the nose, the off-balanced posture, the dip of the shoulder and twisting tilt of the head. He had seen that same alerted, spring-loaded stance too many times not to recognize it. The dim details of the facial features fell into place with the overall appearance. There was no doubt. The figure should have a rifle in his hands.

"Rafe," he said evenly, "it's Bum Shandy."

"What?" Nan squawked, leaning back over the picture.

"Are you sure?" Rafe questioned, moving to Brad's other shoulder and scouring the photo with wide, incredulous eyes.

"I've seen him like that too many times. He's just gone on full alert. See how he's drawing himself in defensively? He must have been crossing the street, and he just saw the car hit Ed."

"What makes you say that" Nan inquired.

"He's too close to be on the other curb. He's obviously pulling back to get away from the car. See how he's turned? If he hadn't been crossing the street, the light wouldn't have reached him. Maybe he was running to Ed."

Rafe turned and yelled to someone in the outer office.

"Bronsky! Get Shandy's file in here! And make it quick!"

"Are you certain it's Shandy? I don't know his appearance that well," Nan interjected.

"I'm sure. Bum was there and he saw the hit. Maybe Ed was going to meet him. Bum had been working for Ed."

"Nevertheless, he could've been involved with the hit-and-run. I'm putting out an all-points bulletin on

Shandy,'' Rafe announced, picking up the phone and speaking rapidly and precisely into it.

As Rafe gave the instructions, Nan took Brad's arm in her hands and looked up at him tenderly.

"I'm sorry, Brad. I know how you must feel being the one to identify Bum."

"It doesn't mean he's guilty of anything. Just that he might be able to help us find the killer."

Her smile became unsteady and she dropped her chin.

"Oh, Brad. You may have to face up to the obvious answer sooner or later. I know it'll hurt if Bum was involved. Please believe I'm sorry."

"I think you're wrong, Nan."

"The order to pick up Shandy is being distributed now," Rafe said, hanging up the phone.

Brad pursed his lips, a frown marking his brow.

"Just in case you're wrong about Bum, are you going to continue follow-ups on other suspects?"

"Who, for example?"

"Someone who was affected by both victims. Like another Knife, for example."

"You can't be serious!" Nan said, a sharp, quizzical look reinforcing her exclamation.

"What about it, Rafe?"

"Okay. I thought of that. I've tried to keep tabs—informally, of course—on the Knives who were in town at the time of the deaths. George Windham is the only one of your old sidekicks who hasn't been seen. The others are staying in town for the funeral this weekend. You're right about that. They each had an opportunity—including you."

"Rafe! How can you say that?" Nan cried aloud, her hands clutching Brad's arm tightly.

"Relax, Nan. The police sergeant is making a point. So what if they were all here? What's the motive? We're still spinning in circles."

"But maybe one of those circles is a spiral, Cowboy. If these deaths are related, the correlations have got to turn something up that will spin us right into the solution. We have to just keep matching up coincidences until something falls into place."

"Speaking of coincidences, there's a doorman named Gerald at Dan's apartment. Have you checked on where he was when Dan got hit?"

"He was sick with flu symptoms and severe stomach cramps, and his scheduled replacement from the employment agency didn't show up that day. The alibi's legit. The FBI checked it out. They talked to the doctor who treated him. Some nonspecific viral infection, but he was definitely in pain."

"And the replacement?"

"Never found him. Apparently left town. There's no trace of him, not even in the employment agency's files."

"Who arranged the replacement?"

"Dan's employers. It's their building."

"I thought so. Any tie to the bomb?"

"*Quién sabe?* Who can tell? There's no apparent link, but the pattern fits if it was a professional hit."

"It had to be. It's too clean."

"What are you two talking about?" Nan asked, coming out of deep thoughts about the Knives. She had only half heard the questions and answers. "Gerald has been doorman there for years. He's absolutely reliable, and you're making it sound like he might've been involved with Dad's murder.''

"Nancy, he could've been suckered away," Rafe explained impatiently. "Someone could've made him sick. I tried to explain to you before. This can be dangerous business."

Brad listened with mixed feelings. Rafe still thought of Nan as a girl. He hadn't adjusted to her name change to Nan any more than to her change in maturity. She had matured considerably in just the last few days.

"Rafe, what about a young woman named Sue Snyder?" Brad asked.

"She checks out, too. Questioning verified she was in her apartment during the set-up and the blast. The feds checked her out, as well. She lives alone, has been there fourteen months, works part time at a nearby spa."

"She looks it. I met her on the elevator," Brad explained.

"You must have enjoyed checking out that lead." Nan smirked.

"To be honest, I enjoyed questioning her myself," Rafe said. "She's a tough lady, built for strength as well as beauty. Seems nice enough."

"I don't know," Brad mused aloud. "Somehow I had a funny feeling about her. I just can't put my finger on it yet. How about checking a little deeper?"

"I won't touch that straight line!" Nan said, folding her arms and turning away.

"Well you can both relax. The feds gave her a clean bill of health."

"Just the same."

"Okay by me, Cowboy. What do you want besides her phone number and measurements?" Rafe asked, grinning broadly.

"Why don't you see if you can check her contacts without going through the feds?"

Rafe changed his stance and put a serious expression on his face.

"I get you, Brad. I'll do that."

"What are you two up to now?" Nan queried. "You're leaving me out of something. I know it."

"You're not getting a little jealous, are you?" Brad countered.

Nan's face flushed a deep red, right down to her neckline. Brad could see that he had obviously hit a nerve, so he didn't press it. He was thankful for the diversion, which would keep Nan out of details that could complicate her life. And threaten it.

"Of course not!" she sputtered. "If you two are through with your gossip, I think we should go now!"

"Okay, take it easy, Nan. We'll see you later, Rafe."

"Sure thing, Cowboy. Listen, I know you two may need protection, but here's just a warning: it's illegal to carry a concealed weapon in the District without a license. Just be careful. Stay in touch. And stay out of trouble."

BRAD WAS SURPRISED how late it was when they left the station. In the car, Nan was quiet again. He regretted embarrassing her, but she was just being too sensitive.

She seemed to be in a fickle mood he couldn't quite understand.

Nan sat in confusion, trying to assess her own mood. She had never been really jealous of anyone. Was that what had taken her by surprise? Was she really jealous of this girl that neither of them really knew?

She sat still, trying to keep her bare knees covered. But he wasn't watching her knees now. He was solemnly studying her face. And he looked upset. Had she embarrassed him in front of Rafe? She felt the need to get away from him for a while, to ease a tension that had grown between them.

Brad decided to break the impasse with the new impulsiveness he had suddenly acquired since being around her so much.

"How about going to dinner with me tonight? You can pick the place."

"No," she said quickly, and then tried to soften her response. "I've been gaining too much weight lately."

"You don't look like you have any worries."

"Well, I used to model, you know. Now I'm not exercising enough, and I've drifted away from my diet. Fashion designer or not, I don't want to grow out of all my clothes. You'd never guess how much I really weigh."

Brad sensed that she was making excuses. As he pulled to the entrance to her apartment building, he shut off the ignition and turned to face her.

"Oh, I don't know. I'd say about five-foot-eight, and one hundred twenty-five pounds," he said as he looked her over carefully with twinkling eyes and a broadening smile.

She felt her face warming with a blush again, and a tingling ran over her skin as though she could feel his eyes measuring her.

"Say, that's pretty good. I'm impressed!"

"Well, I've been watching you a lot lately."

"You're getting that look in your eye again. I hope you'll understand if I don't ask you upstairs."

"Why don't I walk you to your door? I'd feel even better if I could see you safely inside."

"Sounds like a convenient excuse," she said, grinning. "Okay, if you want to. But I won't ask you in. Not tonight . . . I mean, today. Please understand."

"I can wait," he said weakly as he stepped from the car.

The doorman had remained at a discreet distance until the door opened.

"Gerald, can I just leave the car here a minute while I walk Ms Donahue upstairs?"

"Sure Mr. Gaelman. I'll keep an eye on it for you."

Gerald helped Nan from the car, and Brad escorted her to the elevator. As they entered it, she felt his now familiar hand at her waist. But this time, it felt comforting. Perhaps too comforting for the doubts growing in her mind. This scene at the door could be a problem for her. She was feeling vulnerable again.

As they stepped out of the elevator on her floor, an attractive young blonde walked by them to enter the elevator.

"Hi, Sue," Brad said effusively. "Going for a jog?"

"Sure thing. Want to join me?"

"No, thanks. See ya."

"You bet!" she said with a tilted head and coy smile.

As the elevator doors closed, Nan asked tersely, "Who was that?"

"That was your neighbor, Sue Snyder. The one I met on the elevator. Cute, huh?"

"You bet!" Nan returned curtly.

"She certainly looks healthy. Especially around the—"

"Okay! Enough! You want to go catch her?" she asked, heat rising to her face, as she paused in opening her door.

Brad wasn't certain how far he could carry a joke with her right now, or why he was even pressing it, so he retreated a bit.

"Me, catch a jogger? No chance. Besides, I'd rather stick with red-haired fashion designers."

"Probably healthier," she responded with a smirk. "Or at least more relaxing." She opened the door.

"If you say so," he said without conviction.

They both smiled as their eyes locked onto one another.

"Well, aren't you going to ask to come in and relax?" she ventured.

"I'll have to go move the car."

"You're right. Never mind," she said quickly, the spell now broken by the reality. "Probably not a good idea at that."

"Then why did you mention it?" he asked.

She took a couple of deep breaths, organizing her thoughts before answering.

"Because I feel confused and jealous. And I'm not used to either feeling. I like being with you. I liked the way you made me feel this morning, when you kissed me, and I'm not sure I'm ready for that yet. But I sure don't want you chasing any tight-assed little jogger around because I turned you away at the door!"

Her heated words brought his heart to a momentary halt. He regarded her in silence for another moment, feeling his heart gaining momentum, but feeling a warmth about what she had said. It took some caring on her part to make that confession. He offered her a gentle smile, and then reached out to her and touched her troubled face. He decided.

"Nan, why don't I just kiss you good night at the door and call you in the morning?"

"No kiss. Just a hug. And don't get carried away. Come out of the hall," she said, stepping into the doorway.

"Okay," he said, but he hesitated outside the door. "I probably couldn't catch her anyhow."

They both smiled again.

"You're horrible!" she said, smiling even more. "But I'm awfully glad to have you around—when you behave yourself." She reached up to hug him.

"You feel really nice. Been doing any jogging lately?"

"Oh, you! Kiss me. But be—"

He silenced her by kissing her fully, warmly on the mouth.

As she pulled away, Brad murmured softly, "You're really something."

"I ought to go in now."

"As you wish. I'll be thinking of you."

"Be thinking about leads."

"Just as soon as I get through," he inflected decisively.

"Get through what?"

"Jogging. See ya later."

"You're hopeless! Good night, Brad. And thanks."

WHEN BRAD ARRIVED back at his condo, he saw the red light of his phone machine blinking. He walked over and touched the controls, then slumped in his favorite chair to listen.

Beep. "Hi handsome. Tonight's the night. I told you I'd pick the time and the place, and this is it. I expect to see your eager face in my apartment tonight. I want to see your expression when you see what I'm wearing. Call me soon, and I'll give you the time and directions."

Bess was making her move.

Beep. "I've been waiting for your call, handsome. I've got the sterling candlelabra polished and the champagne iced. Now I'm going to soak my eager body in a hot tub until you call. Don't wait too long."

Since the machine had no timer, he couldn't tell how long ago she had called. He had to think of what to tell her.

Beep. "Well, Brad, I'm standing here fresh out of the tub, with water dripping off my nose and nipples, waiting for that call. I wish you were here to dry my back and...the rest of me. Hmmm. This towel feels so good, but I'd rather feel your touch. Call me."

He felt both aroused by her banter and uncomfortable under the confusing pressure her words created.

Beep. "It's a good thing this food doesn't have to be eaten right after it's cooked. I've planned a delectable snack so we can get down to the real pleasure. I have several surprises for you, honey. Please call soon."

In addition to the increased intensity of her voice, Brad detected slurred indications that she might already have opened the champagne.

He sat pondering a few moments before picking up the phone and dialing her number. This just didn't give him a good feeling. He felt intimidated by the calls.

"Hullo?" a soft, low, slightly intoxicated voice answered.

"Bess? This is Brad Gaelman."

"Finally! I've been calling all afternoon! I canceled out of a senator's party to be here with you tonight!"

"I've been with Rafe Johnson and Nan Donahue going over the details of Ed Richards's death."

"Oh, Brad, you should let the police do that. And let the dead bury the dead."

"I don't see it that way," he responded, feeling his irritation growing. "This investigation is an important part of my life right now."

"Please don't be cross with me, Brad. I was hoping you could join me for dinner here this evening," she coaxed with pleading in her voice. "I kept waiting for your call."

"I'm sorry I couldn't call you earlier so you could change your plans. You sound as if you started without me."

"I got so hungry thinking about you that—ooooh! I'm drinking some champagne I opened for us, and I just spilled some between my boobs! It's all cool and bubbly, and it feels like little tongues licking my skin there. I wish you could see it. And taste it."

"Sounds like fun," he admitted.

"It would be, with you here. The candles I lit for us are all burned down to a puddle of warm wax, just like I am. If you were here, you could take me in your hands and shape me into whatever you wanted, and then just melt me down and start all over again."

"Bess, I. . . ."

"I want to please you," she interrupted. "I've brushed my hair out till it shines in the candlelight. I've changed from a robe to a gown, to a camisole to a negligée—just trying to match what I'm wearing to my mood while waiting for you. It's black silk . . . soft and flowing, thin enough that it clings . . . in all the right places. The black lace is so open you can see the edges of my . . . curves, and the open, lacy texture is just rough enough to feel exciting against my nipples. I feel like I'm going to poke them right through the holes in it just talking to you like this."

Her pulsating, quivering words went from soothing and melodious to trembling and exciting, punctuated with profound ravines of silence that yielded slowly to soft, deep breaths.

"This soft light makes my bare skin glow...or maybe it's all the heat I'm radiating...just thinking about you. Oh, and I'm wearing my favorite evening perfume: a heavy, spicy, musky fragrance. It makes me feel all tingly and . . . wet, if you know what I mean."

"I think I've got the message."

"Hmmm. Hearing your voice makes me shiver all over, like a feather brushing lightly all over my nakedness. I have a feather right here just waiting for you, and my whole body is just quivering in anticipation. Wouldn't you like that?"

"Of course I'd like it," he said, her sensuality overcoming his resolve. "But I'm just not sure how to handle you. You make me feel like a kid in a candy shop."

"Is that a rush of blood I hear?" she teased. "Could it be that your body is craving the same pulsating feeling that mine is? Can it be that my voice has touched you where you need to be stroked? Can't I do more for you?"

"Frankly, you sound a little overwhelming. What you offer sounds wonderful, but a bit casual for my taste."

He could hear the soft rustle of clothing through the phone as she sighed, "Well...I'm taking off these black stockings, since you won't come and do it for me. And I'll just put this lacy garter belt away for another night. Hmmm...can you guess where my hands are now? Don't you want to help a girl out?"

"Not tonight, Bess. I'm sorry."

"Oh, you!" she said in agitation. "I am so frustrated, I feel like someone is rubbing sandpaper over all my nerve endings! I'll probably lie here all night like this, just thinking of what we could've done together."

"I don't mean to disappoint you, but somehow I don't feel comfortable about it this way right now."

"Well, it's your choice, darling. I know, I'll be swaying my horny ass in front of you again, hoping you'll follow me home. But just for tonight, I think you're a mean son of a bitch for leaving me aroused and alone like this."

"Bess, please try to understand . . ."

Clunk!

He sat holding the receiver for several seconds, his eardrum ringing from the slam-dunk on the other end. He hung it up and sat looking at it, still dazed at the experience. Decisively he picked up the phone again and dialed the seven numbers that would connect him with a more stable reality that he could handle—the one that had been nagging at him throughout Bess's call.

A repetitive, aggravating busy signal came through the line. Nan was talking to someone. He put the phone down quickly in frustration. He felt like an idiot. Why should he think that she would be sitting around waiting for his call?

Brad watched the news on television, wanting to call again, but afraid she would still be talking to someone else. He became obsessed with talking to her. He couldn't think clearly or get her out of his mind.

When the news was over, he realized he had absorbed very little of it. He picked up the phone and dialed her number again.

"Hello?" came the sweet, sleepy response.

"Nan? It's Brad. Sorry to call you so late," he mumbled apologetically.

"It's all right, and you know it, Brad. You sound funny. Are you okay?" she asked sincerely.

"Yeah, I just couldn't sleep, and I guess I wanted to hear your voice. Do you mind?"

"Don't be silly. Of course not. I've been thinking about you," she said coyly. She was more glad to hear from him than she should be. She felt vulnerable again, and needed to be closer to him. Close enough to touch.

"No regrets, I hope. Or sudden decisions about how I acted today?"

"How could I? It was a very good day. A little surprising now and then. But all in all, I'm very happy with it, I think. I hope that's not what was keeping you awake."

"I guess I have a lot to think about."

"I realized tonight how much you were giving up to help me. I mean with your consulting and all. I do appreciate it. I talked with my agency tonight. I guess I should feel badly that, despite their working overtime, they're doing great without me."

So that's who she was talking to. He felt a weight lifted from his chest.

"My office can get along fine for a while. I've got a good secretary there who thinks she runs the place anyhow."

They laughed together, sharing an insight to their similiar feelings about work. It felt good to know someone that well.

"I know what you mean. I was thinking about Dad and Ed, and feeling pretty low when my assistant at the office called."

"Maybe, like me, he just likes to hear that pretty voice."

"I doubt that. Brad, when are we going to discuss the killings? We've both been avoiding it. And what we'll do."

After hesitating to think of how opening up those feelings might affect their ability to work together, he asked, "When do you want to?"

Nan thought again of the questions that had been running through her mind all evening. Questions about who they were, and her reservations. And her driving need to find out who killed her dad and her friend. And why.

"You're right. I'm probably not ready yet. What can we do anyway. I mean, without the information from Ed?"

"We'll talk to Rafe some more. Maybe Ed kept a notebook, or a journal. And I'll check the newspaper files."

"Would he have put anything in writing? Wouldn't that have been risky?" she asked with excitement rising in her voice.

"Maybe it *was* too risky. But Ed was methodical as a copilot, always planning ahead. I'll have to give that some thought."

"I'm sure you will come up with something to get us going."

"I'll see General Bonner tomorrow. He can string all this together. He was in touch with Dan and Ed."

"What do you think it's all about?"

"Nan, I could only give a wild guess at this point. If the deaths are connected, they may be related to the operation they were working on—something about the Knives. I'm not sure how much you need to know. I don't want you to become a target."

"Don't start with me! You'll really get me mad!" she flared heatedly. "I'm in this all the way. What you learn, I want to know. Wherever you go, so do I. I'll eat, sleep and drink with you until we find the answers."

"Sounds cozy. Especially the sleeping and drinking part."

They both laughed at her slip of the tongue.

"You know what I mean. Don't take advantage of me when I'm upset."

"Then don't get upset, Nan. We've each got to keep cool heads if we're going to work together and get anywhere with this case."

Nan welcomed the chance to steer the conversation away from their relationship and onto the case.

"Now that sounds more like it. We work together and we each keep a cool head. Now, what can I do next?"

"That's tough to say without productive leads. Think about it, Nan. Try to remember things Dan discussed."

"Well, I do remember one comment he made. It was one time when I was kidding him about getting out more. He said something about getting friendly with the girl next door. I know she's a lot younger, but maybe Dad knew Sue Snyder. Would that mean anything?"

Even as she said it, she wondered if her suspicious feelings were tied to her jealousy about the girl's attention to Brad.

"Well, she is convenient and attractive enough. Maybe Dan did look for a companion in Sue. He never mentioned her to me, so I can't say. He was very secretive about some things."

"Did she say anything about Dad?"

"No, but then I didn't ask her."

"She lives by herself, too. I just thought that if she knew him, she might have seen something that would help."

"Good thought. I'll check. Two people living alone next door to one another might get well acquainted. I've been alone so long it should've occurred to me. I don't like living by myself, but I guess I've accepted it."

"Sometimes I like the freedom of choice and movement that living alone gives me. But maybe that's because I haven't met anyone that I want to be with." She stopped abruptly, realizing that she was off guard and saying too much about her inner feelings.

"I understand that," Brad continued the thought. "Sometimes it hurts not to have someone special to lie down beside me, to be a part of my life and to be there when I wake up from bad dreams."

"I've had those feelings, too. It was one of the last things Dad and I discussed. I was just beginning to see the world in a new light."

"Maybe we can get that feeling back for you. My emotions have been washed out and spun dry by admitting all this. You make me feel I'm walking outside on a morning after a good rain has cleared the air, and everything is bright and crisp.''

"I didn't know security consultants were such poets."

"Just this security consultant," he said smiling. "Besides it's my job to notice everything. It's part of the job. Like how little you weigh, so I can pick you up and carry you to safety if necessary."

"If you carried me, I have a feeling it wouldn't exactly be to safety," she said teasingly.

"Would you believe relative safety? We may need some practice."

"The offer sounds quite provocative, and I'll give it some thought, if you'll promise not to drop me," she said.

"Only on the bed."

"You're awful," she said with a laugh. "And I love it."

"Nice laugh."

"Yes, it was, wasn't it? Thanks for making me laugh."

"Yes, but at my expense."

"Don't pout. You can afford it. You have enough confidence to take a joke. And you're a pretty nice guy."

"Convince me."

"That shouldn't be difficult. But for now, just take a cold shower and have sweet dreams. Think about putting some leads together, Sherlock. We'll save the rewards for later."

"That's the best incentive this consultant ever got to finish a job," he said lightheartedly. "Now, try and get some rest. I'll call you tomorrow."

"Good night, Brad. And thanks."

6

BRAD KNEW THAT HIS LEGS were still entangled in the twisted wreckage of his downed helicopter. The broken pieces of bulkhead and panels that had collapsed around him when the chopper crashed held his legs firmly. He had twisted his painful back to look down, to make certain that his legs were still there. The nerves had stopped sending painful messages some time ago, before his copilot had died beside him.

Brad tried to shift his aching hips to extract his arm and shoulder from the hot metal that pressed against him. He gritted his teeth with the effort and found that his jaw had also been injured. He fought down the panic for the hundredth time and tried to think through what had happened, searching for hope, for faith that he would be rescued.

It had been only the third flight of this second tour with the Knives. His crew was to pick up a reconnaissance team that had been inserted deep within enemy territory. The mission had ended when the ground team in the pickup area had been ambushed by a large enemy force just as the chopper landed.

Brad recalled that a second bird had held high while he took Knife two-one in for the pickup. The successful escape of that helicopter, which was low on fuel, was his only hope for a rescue. All around him enemy troops lurked in the foliage.

Heavy enemy fire killed the reconnaissance team as they ran to the landing chopper. More fire had cut the helicopter into shreds as Brad and his new copilot had attempted to lift clear of the area. Bob Foley, the gunner, had been killed immediately, and copilot Ray Benchley, on only his third flight in Southeast Asia, had been severely wounded. While Brad was able to keep the chopper from going off the edge of the narrow plateau or rolling over when it hit, he had been battered severely by the impact, and the torn metal ripped by the crash had entangled his legs so that he could move very little.

He heard a movement nearby. A subtle snap of a twig or dried vine signaled the approach of another *gomer*, the name applied to the irregular foot soldiers of the various groups who opposed them. Brad rested his shorty Armalite rifle on the edge of the metal canopy frame above him and fired three rounds in the direction of the noise.

By twisting painfully, he could see that he had added another body to the eight that were scattered around the chopper. Ray had killed two of the enemy before he died. Since then, Brad had used up the remaining ammunition in both their .38 caliber pistols and one of their rifles. By his count, there were twelve rounds left in the remaining rifles, but he didn't dare remove the clip to count them with the enemy so near. He realized they would soon figure out that he was low on ammunition by his infrequent and carefully measured fire.

He had decided that they could kill him easily without even approaching the chopper, but instead, they had sent several gomers sneaking through the heavy brush near the downed aircraft. He thought they must be trying to determine whether he was using his radio to summon help. Then they would ambush the rescue team, as was their standard procedure.

He knew they would be monitoring the radio frequencies, but nevertheless, he yelled into his dead radio periodically with the standard mayday request for rescue assistance. He would try to keep them guessing as long as he could remain conscious. As another wave of dizziness swept over him, he knew he couldn't last much longer.

Brad wished he had some way to signal for aircraft to stay away. He had heard the gomers moving equipment into the area, and he guessed that there would be even more anti-aircraft artillery, or triple-A as it was called by the Knives. If the guns weren't detected, the gomers could easily massacre his rescue force.

Fighting to clear his head, he inventoried the equipment he could reach. The infrared beacon wasn't much use until darkness fell. Or could they detect it in the daylight? Why was it so hard to remember? The flares and signal mirror were near his hip, but his elbow hurt too much to pick them up.

He had no water, and his thirst was the greatest immediate problem, though he also worried about his numbed legs. The area in front of the chopper out to the edge of the plateau was clear of brush, and the sun had been beating down unmercifully on him for some time.

He tried to remember if he should eat without water to wash it down, or save the food until he could get some water. He had to think straight!

Were there classified papers to be destroyed? He couldn't burn them because of the fuel fumes that filled the cockpit area. And he didn't know where they were anyhow. And the codes would be routinely changed. The sweat ran into his eyes again and burned the cut on his head. The pain was good. At least he knew that part of him was working.

Was that another movement? He knew they were out there, behind their guns, waiting for his buddies to arrive. The gomers wouldn't risk coming for him, for that might warn off the rescuers and spoil their ambush. If only he could warn away the aircraft.

He knew he was beginning to hallucinate. He could hear the droning of a chopper making a turn nearby. The throbbing sounds became louder, then softer, coming and going away again, in and out of his consciousness. He twisted up to scan the skies, but they were cloudless and empty. He heard the sounds again—muffled, echoing, surreal.

Suddenly there were other sounds nearby. He heard talking, then yelling in agitated Oriental voices. Were they coming for him? He heard the droning-pulsing again, but with the echoes around the valley, it was impossible to determine what direction the sounds came from. But they were real!

Suddenly, explosions erupted all around and shuddering jolts rocked the wrecked helicopter. The smell of smoke and granulated earth and shredded foliage filled

Brad's nostrils. Human screams were drowned out by the growling engine of an A-1 Super Spad roaring low overhead with guns and rockets still blazing.

A heavy whump was followed by a shock wave and heavy blanket of heat carrying the sweet-smelling odor of napalm. His broken chopper was immediately rocked again by nearby explosions of more rockets as a second rescue fighter made its pass. More heat and heavy napalm odor flooded over him. Through it all, he could hear the chatter and crack of the anti-aircraft artillery, and tracers ripped through the smoke in a kaleidoscope of fire and confusion.

Brad curled up, protecting his body as much as possible in his trapped position. He pulled his visor down over his face for added protection. The fighters roared over again, obviously in teams to take out the ambush force and triple-A guns nearest the chopper first, while others worked out from there. Brad felt his adrenaline surging, and he ignored the pain to raise up and see what destruction was not masked by the heavy clouds of smoke. The next wave of explosions was further down the valley, where low, fast, pinpoint strikes were eliminating opposition.

He was sitting up looking through the shattered canopy toward the plateau edge, when he noticed a strange whirling pattern in the smoke from the napalm and rocket strikes. Unable to believe his eyes, he flipped up his visor and strained to see through the haze. A huge doughnut of boiling smoke was forming at the plateau's edge.

First the rotating blades appeared, driving the smoke into a maelstrom down toward the valley. Then the engine area, and the fuselage of a big, beautiful helicopter rose out of the valley below and appeared over the edge of the cliff. The huge chopper waddled up across the precipice, moving slowly toward his downed helicopter, much as a large bird might carefully approach a fallen bird of its own kind.

It had been this helicopter that he heard, and so had the gomers around him. They had become excited and had revealed their positions, and the big A-1s had smashed them. The fighters and helicopters had sneaked up from the valley below, flying at treetop level, staying behind ridges out of sight.

As the chopper moved forward with guns blazing bright tracers out of every opening, Brad saw through the swirling smoke that it was not a Jolly Green Giant rescue aircraft, but a chopper from his own unit. That meant instead of a pararescue team, there would be an assault squad on board to fight its way to him. As he watched, a backup helicopter rose out of the smoke behind the first, its progress marked by tracers blazing from its doors. It was an eerie, chilling, beautiful, exciting sight for Brad, and he felt heavy tears running through the grime on his face.

He shook himself out of the fascinating spell and waved his arms vigorously to show them he was alive, but trapped in the wreckage. As the first chopper touched down in the clearing, people spilled out of it. Brad recognized a muscular movement beneath a jaunty green beret, as Luke Bonner in a flak vest approached the wrecked aircraft.

Brad saw his friend from an earlier tour dodging, ducking, and running with determination toward where Brad waved with aching arms. Small arms fire raked the rescuers, knocking several to the ground, and larger weapons started dropping shells into the area. As Brad ducked down for protection in the wreckage, he saw Luke fall, or get knocked to the ground. The soldier rose slowly and came on, only to be struck down again.

The A-1 fighters returned again to growl overhead and strafe the nearby enemy positions. In the added smoke and confusion, Brad lost sight of Luke and the others of the assault team. As he strained to see through the chaos, he realized he could now move his legs. The broken seat beneath him seemed much softer, and a row of books appeared where the shattered canopy had been. He wiped the sweat from his eyes with his sleeve, which became a sheet in his apartment bed. The loud noise from the explosions faded into the sound of a horn in the street traffic below.

Brad shuddered as wisps of tortured memories washed over him, confusing his thoughts, trading him from a karst plateau in the midst of battle to a comfortable bedroom in northern Virginia. He flexed his elbow to find that it no longer gave him excruciating pain. He slipped back into the dreaminess and remembered how Luke had emerged from the smoke bleeding and grinning to peer over the edge of the broken canopy. Another assault team member appeared, firing over the chopper ruins.

"You gonna spend the rest of your career sitting around this resort, or you wanna come with us?" Luke questioned with his characteristic sarcasm.

"If you can get this metal shoe off me and carry me to that luxury liner whirlybird over there, I'll gladly be your fourth for bridge," Brad quipped.

He recalled how Luke had ignored his own pain to pry the wreckage away and carry him to the waiting rescue chopper. The first thing Luke did after securing him on board was to hand him a cool can of beer. Brad remembered how his hands were shaking, and he turned the beer up to drink so fast that some of it spilled to mix with the tears of gratitude that washed over his face.

Brad relived giving the thumbs up sign to Captain Denton Mallard, the pilot of the rescue chopper. As he did so, he again found himself in his condo bedroom. The thirst remained with him, and he thought of the juices he had placed in his refrigerator last night. He switched on the bedside radio to complete the transition to the present.

He was assisted in the transition by the loud ringing of his bedside telephone. The sound brought a shudder of foreboding over him. He recoiled in anticipation of another death notice. The phone that had been such an integral part of his daily work and social life had become an instrument of morning terror. He hesitated, huddling in his bed, knees drawn up protectively, staring at the harmless-looking receiver that held such potential for anguish.

The phone kept ringing, and Brad sat stupefied, staring at it with a heavy dread that rolled around in his stomach. Finally, he picked up the receiver, but he could not bring himself to speak.

"Brad? Brad, are you there?"

The voice was strange at first. He knew it, but could not place who it was.

"This is Brad Gaelman," he muttered hoarsely.

"Brad, this is Denton Mallard. Sorry if I've awakened you too early."

"Denton. No, that's all right. I didn't recognize your voice."

"Well, I guess we don't talk on the phone much at that. But I'm flying out of town for the day, and I wanted to touch base with you before I left. Are you sure you're okay?"

"To be honest, I thought it might be another call from Rafe—Sergeant Johnson—notifying me of another death."

"Oh, my God. I'm terribly sorry. I didn't think of that. I guess you've had more than your share of death notices lately. Almost like the old days, huh?"

"Sometimes lately it's seemed that way. What can I do for you?"

"Actually, I told Sergeant Johnson I'd keep in touch with him. I wanted to let him know I'm leaving town on business, and I won't be back until Ed's funeral tomorrow. But the sergeant wasn't in, so I had to leave a message."

"Well I'm certain his staff will notify him where you are. I wouldn't worry about it," Brad said sleepily.

"I was sort of hoping I could get an update on the investigation. Have you heard anything of George Windham?"

"I thought you were after Bum. Changed your mind, Denton?"

"Absolutely not! Bum's still the prime suspect. I just thought you'd heard something by now from Windham. He's out on some island with that dragon bitch of his!"

"We haven't heard what he's doing. I'm sure he'll be in touch," Brad said irately.

"Sergeant Johnson told me of Ed's death and the clues that led to the pickup order for Bum Shandy. I'm certain I was right after all. I'll feel a lot better when he's behind bars."

Brad felt his anger rising at Mallard's insinuations. He was more alert now, and he couldn't resist turning the words back on the accuser.

"Why is that, Denton? You think you might be the next victim?" He tried to keep his voice even.

"What on earth do you mean?" His voice sounded strained. "I'm aware that you and the Donahue woman are casting about in all this. Have you heard something about the deaths?"

"I was just wondering why you seemed so concerned about Bum," he said, ignoring the question. "Do you have some reason to suppose you're in danger?"

"Why would you think that? What relationship would I have to all this?"

"Well, to begin with, you were a Knife, like the other two victims. And you flew with Bum sometimes. And you were here in town during both killings. Shall I go on?"

"It seems to me, Brad, that those same random circumstances apply to you," Mallard said uneasily. "You could just as easily be the next victim."

"Or the killer," Brad responded evenly.

"I wouldn't joke like that until all this is cleared up, if I were you. The wrong people might hear you, and you'd have a lot of explaining to do. You'd be better off protecting yourself."

"I'm keeping one eye on my six. You'd better do likewise, or maybe you'll never be the ambassador to anywhere."

"Don't joke about that appointment, Brad. That means more to me than anything, and I intend to have it. I appreciate your little insights, but I really must catch my flight. I'd like to discuss this more when I return."

"I didn't mean to worry you. It's just that I still think Bum is innocent. And I don't appreciate unfounded accusations being thrown around."

"I understand your loyalty to your former crew, Cowboy, but Southeast Asia is ancient history. Soon you'll have to face reality. There's not a better suspect than Bum Shandy."

"Don't protest too much, Denton. The wrong people might hear you."

"We'll continue this little chat later. I'll call you when I get back."

"Watch your six, Denton," Brad said testily, hanging up the phone.

Brad sat on the edge of the rumpled bed stilling his anger. Denton Mallard was a social climber and a pain in the ass. He never talked like that before he became a corporate official. He must have been practicing for the diplomatic circles. He seemed dead serious about getting that post.

The phone rang again, startling Brad for the second time. He again lifted the receiver uneasily, with a feeling of dread.

"Hi, handsome. Care to take a red-haired fashion designer to lunch? I promise I won't bite or make you jog." Nan's voice was upbeat and cheery. It was a welcome breath of fresh air to replace the apprehension.

"Well, you're certainly right to the point this morning, lady," he responded.

"Right to the stomach. The way to a man's heart, I've been told. Want to test the theory?"

As tired and sleepy as he felt, he could nevertheless feel his body responding to her lilting voice.

"You sound feisty enough to test something. Think I'm safe?" he jested, recalling their conversation from the night before.

"Come on, take a chance!"

"Sounds like a challenge I'll have to accept. But I've got to call Luke Bonner first. I'm scheduled to meet him for lunch, and the conversation may get very interesting. He mentioned meeting in a secure room, but I'd like to ask him if you can join us."

"Sounds great. Why don't you ask—hell, you don't have to salute any more. Why don't you *tell* the general and let me know what time to join you."

"I'll get right back to you."

"Don't keep me waiting. I'm hungry. Bye."

As Brad looked up Luke's number and dialed it, he thought about the difference between Nan's invitation to a good-humored lunch and Bess's summons to a seductive love-feast. In many ways, they were equally tempting.

The phone rang several times before someone picked it up.

"General Bonner's quarters," said a hoarse, muffled voice. Brad thought he recognized the man who answered, but he sounded strange somehow.

"Captain Blackwell, is that you? This is Brad Gaelman. I was trying to reach the general. Did he get back this morning?

There was a hesitation on the line. "Mr. Gaelman." Another pause. "I'm sorry, sir." Then a silence.

"Captain Blackwell?"

"Yes, sir. I'm sorry, sir, but there's been an accident."

Brad felt the pressure of the words in his ears, and the heavy weight of dread filled his stomach again. He couldn't bring himself to ask the question. He knew he couldn't afford the answer, didn't want to hear it. But even if he hung up now, it wouldn't go away.

"Go ahead, captain," he said with a strain in his voice.

"General Bonner was flying down from National Airport to Fort Belvoir in an Army helicopter early this morning. It crashed short of the runway, killing all on board," the captain said, wringing the words from torn emotions.

"My God," Brad uttered. Luke was an expert pilot. Brad had introduced him to choppers. They had been through so many dangerous flights together. Why here? Why now?

"There's more," the captain added. "There was obvious tampering with the helicopter. It was sabotaged."

"Are you certain?" Brad asked intensely.

"Without question. It was done by someone who knew about helicopters. But the crash didn't burn or destroy the altered parts. Someone killed the general."

Brad sat considering these answers to questions he was only now forming in his mind. Luke had foretold his own death. He had said he might be next—if there were a connection between murders of Dan and Ed.

"Captain Blackwell, I'm very sorry. I know you were close to him."

"Sir, you're military—or were. You can understand how I feel. He was my sponsor. We were almost family. He treated me like a son, and my wife like a daughter. He was a strong, very righteous man, and deservedly so. I may resign my commission to carry on his fight against drugs."

"Don't do that," Brad interrupted. "Instead, continue his work in the Army. He was more than an anti-drug crusader. He was Army. And so are you. He told me so, only yesterday. Now you should have the right motivation, too."

"Thank you, sir," he said with a quiver in his voice.

"Talk to someone. You know General Donaldson?"

"In the Pentagon? Yes, sir. I've met him."

"I'm going to contact him and ask him to talk with you. Will you?"

"Yes, sir. And thanks. I guess I needed to hear that."

"Your wife will need some consoling too, judging by what you said about Luke's feelings toward her. Take some time now to go to her and hold her."

"Yes, sir. I'll do that. I've been making the arrangements. The funeral will be Sunday. I hope to see you then. And sir . . . thanks again."

"Any time I can help. Keep in touch."

"You, too, sir. Let me know if there's anything I can do for you."

"Take care."

"Good day, sir."

Brad realized as he was giving the comforting words that it was as much to relieve his own anguish as to help the captain. As he placed the receiver in the cradle, the grief rolled over him in great crashing waves. He kept seeing Luke's smile beneath the immaculately clean green beret. No matter what the conditions were, that cap was always as clean as the smile beneath it.

He felt the waves of dreamy thoughts sapping his resolve, pulling him back. He had to call Nan. Now. She answered on the first ring.

"That certainly took a while," her cheery voice answered before he even spoke. "You must have had to twist the general's arm."

"Nan," he started, but lost the words in his mind-numbing daze.

"Brad? That is you, isn't it?"

"Nan, they got him. They got Luke, just like he said."

"Brad? What's that? What do you mean?"

"Someone trashed his chopper. He died in the crash. Just like that chopper almost did to me the day Luke saved me."

Nan felt an anguish as the meaning of the words came through. Brad sounded stunned, confused. She had not been close to the general like Brad, but she felt some of his grief. Brad was obviously hit very hard by Luke's death.

"Brad, just stay where you are. I'll come to you. I have your address. I'll get there as soon as I can. Just take it easy. Brad?"

"What? Oh, thanks, Nan. I'll be here."

AS HE HUNG UP the phone, he fought to maintain contact with reality. He again saw Luke running through the smoke toward him, dodging and falling, getting up despite his wounds. Coming to save his life.

Nan was coming now, and he had to dress. He looked over the clothes in the open closet, and his eyes settled on a faded pair of jeans. He leaned against the door to pull them on, struggling to maintain his equilibrium.

The flashbacks had mostly come during his waking from sleep. The doctors had long ago said that they would not be a problem unless they began to occur with frequency during waking hours. Unless his physical behavior matched the mental turmoil of the memories. This would come only with severe stress and lack of emotional focus.

He had learned to avoid emotional involvement that could lead to such stress. Now, with the deaths of his closest friends, the flashbacks had become more frequent. His dormant senses had been reawakened, and he was emerging from his self-imposed reclusiveness, only to find the past crowding in. And he felt himself yielding to the persistent tug back into oblivion. He sank to the bed, into dreamy mists, falling into the past.

The jungle trail he followed was narrow, forcing him to place one booted foot directly in front of the other. His eyes followed a deliberate routine, scanning the brush to the right side, watching his steps on the path, measuring the distance to the back of Luke Bonner's neck five steps ahead of him, and then back to sweep the right side of the trail, just as Luke watched the left.

As a spare crew member on this mission, he had volunteered to go out with Luke to locate a reconnaissance team that had missed a rendezvous. They hadn't intended to come this far, but the information the team held was vital.

The grass that fringed the narrow track was thick with pungi stakes, the bamboo sticks sharpened to the cutting edge of a knife and fire-hardened before being smeared with human excrement and butted point-up into the ground. The points would easily slice through the side of a leather boot, and the canvas of their jungle boots was not nearly a match for the cutting edges. To leave the trail meant leaping over the stakes at the edge, hoping that a second row did not lurk beyond them in the brush.

Sweat dripped off Brad's nose, but no sudden movement was allowed that might catch the eye of a trail-watcher. His hands were both wrapped loosely around the Soviet AK-47 assault rifle that he carried in the combat-ready position. The heavier slug of its cartridge would penetrate the brush around them with more assurance than that of the M-16 issued to them. And ammunition for the AK-47 could be taken from the bodies of any enemy they met.

He glanced quickly past Luke to where Chen, a Nung guide, led the point some twenty yards ahead of them, and then looked over his shoulder to see Chop, another Nung mercenary, bringing up the rear twenty yards behind. They had done this together before, and they were a well-disciplined team deep in enemy territory. Luke had trained the Nungs, and they were the best Brad had seen.

The hair on the back of Brad's neck rose as a chill went through his sweating body. Something was wrong. But what? Then he realized that he smelled something not quite right. As a non-smoker, his sense of smell was better than the other three with him. He stopped, and quietly tapped the stop signal on his gun butt. He gave an almost imperceptible hand signal to Chop behind him, and the Nung froze in mid-stride. As Chen made his routine check over his shoulder, he saw Luke's signal and he slowly dropped in place on the trail. Luke turned to look at Brad as he slowly crouched, gun at the ready. Brad's finger to his nose told Luke all he needed to know to go on even greater alert.

In the noisy quiet of the jungle, Brad now heard something that shouldn't be there. But he couldn't quite sort it out. He tested the direction of the slight breeze, but there was nothing to help. Then he perceived a snap on one side of the trail, a rustle on the other. Luke's face told him he had caught it too, and he signaled to the Nungs, pointing to his ear and indicating both sides of the trail.

That odor again! Brad searched the ground for signs. He looked in the brush for the flash of new-cut vegetation.

Nothing.

Was that a movement ahead? Chen was pointing off to the right, his cautious move so deliberate that he looked like a slow-motion ballet dancer.

Brad longed to relieve the strain in his leg. To scratch his nose. But his hard-earned discipline won out, and he remained frozen.

Two odors now! Open earth and urine! No breeze now, but movement on the left! A quick movement of a branch on the right! Luke caught it, too, and he gave the hurry-up signal. Ambush!

Back out carefully. Watch for trip wires, booby traps. Chen checking left, Chop checking right. Forget the front, check the rear.

Had they closed the door behind them? Could they smell his sweat? Could they smell his fear?

Watch that branch!

Leave no trace!

Make no sound!

No sudden movement!

Odors are weaker now. No noises. They were out of the mouth of the ambush. Brad forced himself to breathe, but very silently.

Chop pointed to another trail, almost unnoticeable as a slight break in the brush leading downhill off the main trace. He had sweat dripping from his nose and chin, saturating his fatigues. As they followed him down the hill, Brad's eyes were burning from the sweat running into them. Though they were now out of the teeth of the trap, he would not remove his hand from the AK-47 to wipe away the sweat.

Chen had just cleared the main trail when Luke gave the take cover signal. They quietly slid beneath concealing branches. Then Brad heard the sounds, too. Above them the point man for another patrol passed not too quietly. Right behind him was a large group of heavily armed gomers moving quickly, giving up stealth for speed. They were headed right into the ambush.

In sign language, Brad quietly questioned Luke as to who the group was. Luke smiled as he signed back they were the enemy.

The jungle hillside was rocked by the explosion of a Claymore mine, followed by another, and a constant rattle and chop of automatic weapons fire. Luke gave the signal to move out quickly, and they stumbled down the hill hurriedly, their noisy progress covered by the battle above.

Brad thought of the effect of the Claymores on the gomers moving on the narrow trace. There would be human limbs and blood scattered across the brush that he had just been hovering beneath. There would be wounded bodies thrown across the hidden sharp pungi stakes. The thought of the carnage almost turned his stomach. Some gomer leader had sacrificed caution for speed once too often. This group didn't have the leadership and sharp combat insights of Luke Bonner.

Brad felt a wave of dizziness, a ringing in his ears, and he was back on his rumpled bed in his condo. There was a persistent pounding, like artillery fire. Muffled shouts. But they weren't back there on the trail. They were here and now. Gradually he realized the pounding was someone at his apartment door, and the muffled calls were his name. It was Nan at the door.

He made his way on unsteady legs to the door, threw the bolt, and opened it slowly. Nan stood there, fists clenched and red from the pounding, little tendrils of auburn hair falling across her brow. She looked apprehensive, and beautiful. He felt his heart leap. It was okay now. She was here.

"Brad! You didn't answer the doorbell. I was so worried that you might be . . ."

"Come in, Nan. I'm sorry if I upset you. I guess this hit me pretty hard."

"Brad, you don't have to explain," she said, coming through the door and wrapping her arms tightly, protectively around him. She felt the taut muscles of his bare back, her face pressed against his firm shoulder, and she felt a sensual jolt surge through her. She had worried, not knowing why, but now she had him near again. And this arms going around her were so manly, so reassuring. They embraced warmly, without further words, for several moments.

Then she pulled away slightly and said softly, "I'm sorry, Brad. I know you were close to Luke. I want to help you any way I can."

He wiped the sweat of mental stress from his forehead and turned to cross the room.

"I could sure use something to drink."

Nan watched his back as he walked toward the kitchen. She felt butterflies of passion flitting softly in her belly.

"Brad, why don't you shower and finish dressing while I whip up something for us to eat. I presume you have a moderately stocked pantry in there somewhere." She smiled for effect, but her emotions were churning. He looked so vulnerable, so very attractive, so like someone whose head she wanted resting in her lap. But right now, she was equally vulnerable.

"Thanks, Nan. You should find everything you need in the kitchen." He smiled weakly and turned to enter the bedroom.

She paused to watch his hands rubbing the chest she was still aching to touch. His naked torso was muscular, his chest brushed with soft curls. Even from here, she could see scars that told of combat duty. She wanted to follow him into the bedroom. But she feared that if she entered that bedroom now, she would never want to leave. She turned abruptly and entered Brad's bachelor kitchen.

She was impressed with what she found there. The cabinets and counters, even the food in the pantry and refrigerator, were all neat and clean, arranged with military precision. She quickly realized she was in the kitchen of a gourmet cook, or at the least, a man who loved to prepare and eat fine foods. She wasn't even certain what all the equipment was for.

While preparing a brunch of bacon and omelets, she thought about the man of the house. Brad was forty years old and clearly set in his ways. She wondered what his favorite foods were. How much sleep did he need? What TV shows does he watch? His hobbies? His fashion in clothing? Her agency was in Chicago. His work was here. Could either give up their work? Could they be satisfied with a life of commuting?

What was she talking about? He hadn't even said he loved her! He may have other girls. She was jealous, and she didn't even know of another woman. Except perhaps Sue Snyder, and she was too young. But that Bess Bradshaw—she could be a formidable opponent.

Nan realized that she had not told Brad of her feelings for him either. She had been holding him at a distance. Too much. Too long. Now she needed to get closer to him. And she would. But right now, he needed her protection, her comforting for the loss of Luke. And they had a killer to find: the murderer of Knives.

BRAD STOOD in the shower, letting the hot water wash away the tension. He felt numb from grief. And he felt the flashback hovering over and around him. Soft images and sensations ebbed and flowed through his consciousness. The vapors from the spray and the spicy smell of the soap pulled at him, seducing him back into the jungle.

He was watching the monsoon rainwater run off Luke's foul weather gear. They were crouched in the Oriental position of waiting, but Brad couldn't remember what they awaited. They were just squatting in the mud, as patiently as gomers. The intense monsoon shower washed over them as if the tears of all of Asia were being shed over this little corner of the war.

The pelting rain became the shower spray again, bringing Brad to the present. He increased the cold water in an attempt to stay alert and in charge of his thinking. The flashbacks were coming more frequently and while he was awake, just as the doctors had said they might. It was the stress of three personal losses, he knew. If he could control his emotions, he could handle the flashbacks. He needed an outlet for the stress, some goal, something he could control. He had to harden to the losses, just as they had done in combat. He had to get his feelings straight about Nan.

As he toweled off and dressed, he considered how unshuttering his emotions had taken a toll. At first he had felt only a growing physical desire for her. When his emotions had erupted in her apartment, she had responded like she might want him, too.

But when they were abruptly interrupted, he felt more than a physical loss. He felt a sensation of being bonded to her in some deeper way. It was not a feeling he had experienced before. Not even in his early marriage. A closeness, a sharing of need and understanding, despite all the loss and confusion they were experiencing. A sort of love.

But love hadn't been in his plans. He had carefully avoided any emotional involvement that might create enough stress to bring back the flashbacks. And now he suspected he was falling in love with Nan. How would that affect his emotional turmoil in dealing with the flashback stress?

Dressed in jeans and a pullover, he walked to the kitchen door and stood quietly watching the lady in question. She looked at home in designer jeans and a silk blouse. Tiny beads of perspiration glistened on her brow and upper lip as she turned to smile at him. Her eyes were absolutely sparkling. She looked like a mother and a friend and a lover all rolled in one.

"Well, you look a lot better now. How are you feeling?" she asked as she picked up the two full plates and headed for the table. "Come on, let's eat this while it's hot." She sat and patted the chair pulled close beside her, looking at him with appraising eyes but a warm smile.

How did he feel? He wasn't sure he had an answer to her question, so he ignored it. So did she.

"You fix an impressive brunch." He sat beside her, placing his hand lightly on her arm. "You could get to be habit-forming."

Nan placed her hand over his. Being together and touching like this felt right. It was a habit she could gladly accept. She needed this handsome, complicated man. She felt a stirring within, a feeling of possessiveness emerging with every blink of his rich brown eyes.

"Just don't quit cold-turkey on me, Cowboy. Give things a chance to work out. Let's face this thing head-on. Together," she said, squeezing his hand lightly.

"Don't worry. I'm in for the duration," he answered with a grin.

As she turned back to her food, he couldn't avoid dropping his eyes to the curve of her breasts beneath the blouse. She was a total woman. Sexy, caring, but strong, independent, capable, intelligent. She could make a good partner in life.

"I know you and Luke were very close. I saw the pictures of you two on the wall there, along with all the medals. Did you win them together?"

"The medals are from all three of my tours over there. The pictures mean more to me. I met Dan and Luke on the first tour. Ed became my copilot after I lost mine early in my second tour. We were all together the last time around, just before we pulled out. We did everything together."

She wanted to soothe away the lines of pain on his forehead, to hold him tightly against her as he had held her after Ed's death. But she feared their bodies and their passions would betray them now as they had then.

"I know Luke's death has hit you hard. I'm here to help. I want to be with you."

Brad watched her as they ate. She looked strong, assertive. He recalled how she had looked at Dan's funeral, so frail and vulnerable. She had come a long way since then. They both had. She looked ready to take on a division of killers to protect him.

"Thanks, Nan. It's hard to know how much to mourn when friends die so close to each other."

She recognized his struggle with his emotions, for it matched hers. They shared an understanding that would remove guilt and hesitation about their feelings for one another, and allow them to share the joy of discovery amid the pain and grief.

"Mourning hardens us, Brad, makes us stronger. And we look for something else to put our minds into, something to make us feel better. The grief will still be there. But we can't let it control us. We'll move on. Together now."

Brad sat quietly, considering what she said. She seemed strong, and he needed her strength. He was definitely falling in love with her. He wrapped this sudden realization around him like a protective cloak to hide his new vulnerability.

AFTER THEY had finished eating, they decided to go to see Rafe concerning Luke's death. When they arrived at the police station, Nan and Brad were directed immediately to Rafe's office. A buzzing flurry of activity assaulted them along the way. Typewriters and telephones, loud voices and radio calls assailed their ears. A police radio monitor loudly announced, "Unit twenty-three, see the man Holowitz at Seventh and Massachusetts. Unit seventeen, proceed to armed robbery in progress near Eighth and Delaware. See the man at that intersection."

Nan felt uncomfortable in this environment. Something in the radio calls seemed familiar, but she couldn't quite identify it.

Rafe met them at the door of his office.

"Well, how's our newest crime-fighting team?" He grasped Brad's arm. "Sorry to hear about Luke. I know how much he meant to you, Brad."

Nan saw the comfort Rafe's words gave Brad. She considered the contrast in the two welcoming statements. Warm and friendly, then sober and supportive. Rafe knew how to deal with personal losses. His and others. It was a lesson she and Brad would have to learn.

"Thanks, Rafe," Brad returned softly, shaking Rafe's large hand. "This is getting away from us. We're falling too far behind it all. It's got to be stopped, and I can't seem to get a handle on it."

"I know your feeling," the police sergeant said as they took their seats. "We're checking with all the investigators, the Army, the airport police, the FBI. So far there are no witnesses to any activity around the helicopter. The maintenance guys were old friends of Luke's. They're taking the loss pretty hard, and blaming themselves for letting it happen."

"I hope you're checking them out anyhow," Nan interjected with feeling.

"We will, Nancy. The Army is being very cooperative. The word about tampering leaked out, and the press is having a field day with it."

"Are they connecting the three hits?" Brad asked.

"Not yet. Not many people see a connection. They don't know yet that all three were Knives, or that they were all involved in investigating the same type of activity in the same area."

"Do you know that for a fact?" Nan asked, her inflection showing her hope for a solid connection they could work on.

"We know now that they were all looking into drug smuggling, and digging around in the records of the Knives' activities in Southeast Asia years ago. What the connection is, we haven't yet determined."

"What else have you learned?" Nan was sitting on the edge of her chair, all energy directed into her question.

"The doorman Gerald checks out okay. He was legitimately sick and in his apartment in your building." Rafe was thumbing through a worn notebook as he brought them up to date. "The jogger, Sue Snyder, is apparently living beyond her means. We're still looking into that. I'll probably take on that follow-up myself," he said with a grin, looking from Brad to Nan.

"Go on," she prompted with sarcastic inflection.

Rafe sobered as he answered his persistent phone. After a few muttered comments, he hung up and continued.

"The car that hit Ed was a rental. We found it eight blocks away with the body of a dead Hispanic in it. His throat was cut."

"What?" Brad and Nan asked together.

"A study of the blood splatter pattern shows he wasn't killed in the car. A label in his suit was from Bogotá, so he was probably Colombian. Expensive suit, too."

"But there was nothing in the paper or on the radio about him," Nan said.

"We're keeping it under wraps. We haven't identified him or placed him in the case yet. We traced the rental vehicle to a dude who had been hired by an unknown party to check out the car and leave it in an alley. He can't help us beyond that. No one in the area saw the driver or Bum Shandy. Still no word on the all-points bulletin for Shandy." Rafe closed his book as Brad interrupted.

"Rafe, don't bank too much on that. If you keep the pressure on Bum, he may never show up again. He's a survivor."

"I know your concern for Bum. But there are four agencies that want to talk to him."

"What about Luke?" Nan asked, reaching out to put her hand on Brad's arm.

"His plane into National was delayed. The chopper sat on the ground for three hours. Whoever got to it knew what he was doing and knew how to elude security. Maybe someone who flies or works on helicopters. The evidence of tampering should've been destroyed in the crash, but Luke was flying, and he was a damned good pilot. He almost got it in anyhow."

The three sat in silence, pondering the information. Finally Brad spoke.

"Did Ed have a notebook on him? He usually kept one with him.

"Yes, we've had someone going over it for hours, but nothing in it seems relevant."

"Can I take a look through it?"

"Sure," Rafe said, already picking the phone up to dial the evidence room.

As the sergeant gave instructions, Nan leaned to put her arm around Brad.

"What do you expect to find?" she asked.

"I'll know that when I see it."

An officer brought in the small green book, and before the door closed, the radio monitor blared again, "Unit twenty, see the man at Twelfth and Pennsylvania..."

"That's it!" Nan said, jumping from her chair. Her face was alive with discovery, her eyes shining and her features animated.

"What?"

"What is it, Nancy?"

"That radio call. I knew it meant something when I came in, but I couldn't put my finger on it. Remember Dad's note?" She was almost breathless.

"Yes, I have it right here. It says *See the Mandrake.* Why?"

"What if it meant, See the man, *Drake?*"

"Hmmm. Could be," Rafe mused. "Puts a whole new light on it."

Brad winked at Nan, feeling pride in her insight, and warmth for the excitement her discovery gave her. She was a valuable partner, and it was a good lead.

As she and Rafe engaged in discussing the note and then in reminiscing about times with Dan, Brad thumbed through the book. The hurried scrawl on the small pages gave Brad's emotions a real blow as it catapulted him back to the many reports Ed had prepared for him years ago. It was all in Ed's unique script and notation, a sort of personal shorthand that only those who worked with him would understand. But there was nothing there that looked of interest . . . until the last page.

"Nan, look at this."

As Rafe and Nan stood on either side of him, Brad read the annotation aloud: "Talk to Drako."

"What is that? Someone you know?" Rafe asked.

"Is that an *e* or an *o* on the end?" Nan asked.

"Looks like an *o* to me," Rafe said.

"I'd have to agree. But it's on the last page, and it may be who he was meeting that morning he got hit."

"I still say it's an *e*!" Nan insisted. "That matches it to Dad's note!"

"I don't know," the sergeant drawled. "I wouldn't stretch things to fit what we want them to say, Nancy."

"But she may be right. It is a possibility, Rafe."

"But where does it take us? We're still circling around any firm leads. This is just supplemental, not supportive. Look, I don't want to dampen your enthusiasm. But don't jump to any conclusions. Take it slowly and be meticulous. We do."

"I guess you're right," Nan said dejectedly. "It may not mean anything, and if it does, we still don't know where to go from here. I just feel so frustrated!"

"Hang in there, Nancy. We'll work all this out . . . and together. Thanks for the clues."

"Thanks, Rafe," she said with a smile lighting her face.

"Why don't we go somewhere and ponder this?" Brad asked.

"If you're dumb enough to be including me in that invitation, I'm afraid I can't get away right now," Rafe said with a big grin.

"On the other hand, I'm available," Nan said. "Since I fixed your lunch, why don't we go get dressed so you can take me out to dinner?" She held his arm tightly.

"Now how can I resist an offer like that? See you later, Rafe."

"Sure, Cowboy. You two take care, now."

As THEY ENTERED his apartment, Brad thought of the difference between this and the last time he had stood at this door with Nan. Their lives were moving quickly, up and down like an emotional rollercoaster.

Nan had driven them to the condominium by a circuitous route, enjoying the outing together. They had joked and laughed, letting the stress escape, making much of their image as a crime fighting team while avoiding any direct reference to the emotional team they were becoming.

When Nan stepped into the cool apartment, she had a feeling of satisfaction, of enjoying being alive, of being in control of her emotions. It lasted until Brad turned and wrapped his arms around her. His eyes were much too close and too expressive, and she seemed to be falling under a disturbing, bewildering spell. It made her unexpectedly cautious, for she had looked forward to this very moment.

Pushing back from him a little, she shook her head and said, "I could sure use something cool to drink."

"Okay, lady. I didn't mean to rush you," he said, releasing her slowly and leading her to the kitchen. "Why don't you fix a couple of drinks while I grab a quick shower and dress for dinner?"

"I'll do that. But don't take too long. I'll miss you, and besides, the ice will melt."

"How romantic," he said sarcastically, stopping to play back his recorded phone messages on the way to the bedroom.

Beep. "Hi, boss. This is Terry. I miss your handsome body around here. But things have been quiet, and it's finally Friday. Give me a call if you need someone to talk to."

"Well, well," Nan said dramatically. "Looks like your office may need more attention."

Brad winked at her and grinned. "She can get along fine without me."

Beep. "Dear Brad, this is your Hilda. I am still missing our lunch together. Please call me when you can."

Nan didn't say anything this time. She merely raised an eyebrow and looked at him skeptically.

"Security client," Brad muttered. "Would you believe I've only seen her once, and I've never been out with her?" Why was this so uncomfortable? He felt the distance between them growing.

Nan leaned against the door to the kitchen, her arms folded and her blood rushing. She felt like an intruder into his personal life, and she didn't like what she found there. She was being possessive and jealous. She felt very uncomfortable now.

Beep. "Brad, this is your strawberry blonde again. How about giving me another chance? I have on the same lacy garter belt and sexy black stockings as before, and I didn't get a head start on the champagne this time. Please call."

As the recorder clicked off, Brad felt a hot flush creeping over him. He was too embarrassed to look at Nan, and when he did, he kicked himself mentally for playing back the calls. How could he possibly make her understand?

"Bess Bradshaw, I presume?" she asked through the menacing glare that was like an electric current between them.

"Yes, Nan. But it's not like it sounds. I didn't go there. She just called about it."

"Well, don't let me stand in your way, lover boy! You have three ladies already waiting for you!"

"Nan, listen to reason. I had no control over this."

"Why should I listen? What am I doing here, anyhow? I don't need to hear this. I've got other things to do." She couldn't think straight, and she had to get out of there. She started for the door.

Crossing the room quickly, he tried to beat her to the door.

"Just stop a moment and listen. I don't want you to go."

"You don't want! What about what I don't want?" Nothing that was happening was making any sense. She stormed out the door and slammed it.

Brad leaned against the door, aching to go after her, but confused about what had happened. She hadn't even given him a chance. She just assumed the worst. By the time he decided to follow her, he realized she would be in her car and gone.

He fell into his chair and held his head in his hands. Images ran through his mind, tugging him from reality. And the foremost of the images was Nan's face with her shattered emotions playing across it.

BY THE TIME Nan drove away, tears were running freely down her cheeks. But he hadn't seen her cry. She had been so embarrassed by the calls, and then by her own reaction. She had never felt this possessive or this jealous about anyone or anything. She didn't like what she felt. She hadn't meant to hurt Brad, but how could he be so thoughtless to play back his personal messages in front of her? Didn't he know how much she loved him?

She had to have time alone to think about this. How could she face him again? There was too much emotional debris piling up between them. Her guilt about her father's death. Her memories of being abused in her marriage. Her independence. And now, her jealousy. She sobbed deeply as she recalled how sexy he had looked without his shirt, and how nice he had been to her all day. Couldn't anything good come of all this?

BESS ANSWERED on the fifth ring of Brad's call. She sounded as vivacious and charming as ever.

"Why, Brad, honey. I'm glad you called so early this time."

"You had no right to do that." His emotions were bunched in each word.

"What? To do what?" Her voice became tightened, weaker.

"To leave a call like that. What made you think no one else would hear it?"

"Why, Brad, don't get angry. I didn't know you were going to play my message for your guests." After a pause, she added, "I hope it didn't embarrass anyone. I meant it to please you."

He sat quietly for a second, feeling his misdirected anger fade away. It was himself he should be blaming for the whole thing.

"Brad? I hope you're not too mad at me. Was it someone special?"

"Yes. Very special. But you're right, I should've waited to play back the messages. I'm sorry for jumping on you."

"Honey, you can jump on me any time."

"Bess, don't start again. Not now." He felt frustrated and empty, his head hurting, his breathing difficult. And he couldn't get his mind off Nan.

After a few seconds of silence, she continued.

"I know you're upset, and this might not be a good time to get together. So when? You tell me what you want."

"I'd like to have dinner with you and Thaddeus Ralston on Monday night to talk about the work he was doing with Dan, Ed, and Luke." He had blurted it without thinking. But it really was what he wanted and needed.

"Somehow, that wasn't exactly what I had in mind. Does Thaddeus have to be along?"

"Yes. You asked what I wanted." He waited expectantly.

After a moment, she continued.

"Well, if you say so. There's a little place in Georgetown he likes to go to, called Renoir's."

"Can you get him to discuss the work?"

"Oh, sure, for you, he'll probably spill all the beans. You're a pretty easy guy to talk to, and he thinks the world of you. But he'd deny it if anyone asked."

"Okay then. I'll meet you there Monday night. Are you going to the funerals?"

"Look, I'm not a part of these killings, and I don't intend to get involved. I only want to be involved with you, Brad. And I intend to have you all to myself."

After bidding her good night, he wondered who was using whom. But he had to talk to Ralston, and Bess could help him get what he needed. He would work out the rest later. Right now he had to straighten out things with Nan. He could take her to the two funerals. They would need each other for that.

He dialed Nan's number, and when she answered, she sounded as if she had been crying.

"Nan, listen, I'm sorry. I—"

Clunk!

He hadn't counted on her hanging up. He had to talk to her, to explain. She answered on the first ring of the next call.

"Nan, I want to take you to the funerals this—"

Clunk!

Well, he could be as stubborn as she could, if it took all night! She answered again on the first ring.

"Nan, please listen...."

"Don't say a word about that woman! About any of them! If you want to take me to the funerals, you can pick me up an hour before they start! I don't want to talk to you tonight. And thanks for the invitation."

She hung up more softly this time. Her voice had broken and softened with the words of thanks. Maybe by morning things would be better.

7

NAN ROLLED OVER sleepily in the bed, and there was Brad. He was standing naked over her. She was lying on her back, naked, but unafraid, watching him between her drawn-up knees. He was smiling that little-boy smile, but she could see desire twinkling in his eyes and dancing around the corners of his mouth. She knew he wanted her, but he was still just standing there, arms folded, watching her, waiting.

Suddenly she wanted him, all of him, now and forever. She held out her arms to him, and he came to her, slowly and tenderly, caressing with loving murmurs. He kissed her mouth, and as she felt a glorious ecstasy rush through her body, she cried out with joy.

She awakened with a start, hearing her own cries. Her back was still tense with the strain of arching it. She found herself out of breath and covered with sweat, the traces of the dream running through her mind. The fluttering pleasure still flowed through her lower body.

She couldn't believe it was just a dream. She had never dreamed so vividly, so very intensely. She had just encountered something almost as intense as her experience with Brad yesterday in the apartment. And that was a sensation she thought she had forgotten forever.

She drifted into dreamy thoughts of the past, dozing and waking. Suddenly, she heard a noise in the bathroom. The shower was running. She got up from the bed and walked into the warm steamy room. She could hear him murmuring softly in the shower, but the glass door was covered with fog and he couldn't see her. So she would surprise him.

She slid back the shower door slowly and looked directly into the eyes of a voluptuous young blonde. The girl had an empty look on her face of someone spaced out on drugs, and she hardly noticed the intrusion. She was bent over with her hands tightly gripping the towel bar. And her husband stood closely behind her, in her, his arms wrapped around her full young body, his hands gripping her breasts.

"Close the door, stupid! You're letting the warm air out!"

The words cut into her heart, and she slammed the shower door and the bathroom door quickly as he had ordered.

She sat up, fully awake, rubbing her eyes, trying to wipe away the images. She wanted to reach inside and forever erase the hurt. She could drive down the memories while she was awake, but in sleep the bitter thoughts crept back.

But the dream of Brad was different. It was full of pleasure and promise. If only she could bring herself to accept him fully. Looking at the clock, she saw that it was still early morning. She would have several more hours of dreams before she dressed for Brad to pick her up for Ed's funeral. She lay back, sobbing softly, letting the mixture of emotions wash over her.

"KINGBIRD, GET US SOME HELP in here! We need help! Help!"

Brad awakened from his dream with the usual clawing to the surface of reality. It had been the recurring nightmare: the evacuation of the tribal headquarters, the desperation of struggling against odds in a traumatic upheaval. It was a sense of accomplishment in the face of a personal challenge.

He reached automatically for the bedside radio and the lamp switch, and his eyes swept the familiar rows of books. The raucous music that filled the room was not to his liking, but it helped to establish him firmly in his present life.

Some life! Another in a series of funeral days. Another mourning for a close friend. A rejection by Nan, a woman who had gotten to him, one he was beginning to want beside him much more than he wanted to admit. And the constant teasing of Bess, a sensual, lustful woman pulling at his senses, breaking down his caution—dragging him from his seclusion into the promise of a world of physical pleasure.

He vaulted from the bed in an attempt to abandon the wisps of the past that fluttered around inside his head. His usual thirst for something to eliminate the metallic taste of battle from his mouth led him to the kitchen. He paused at the door, peering into the morning light from the window, remembering how Nan had looked standing at the stove, the tiny beads of sweat on her face, the warm smile above the firm breasts in the silk blouse. He could almost see her there now. He switched on the light, and the image vanished.

Looking at the clock, he realized he had slept through the alarm again. He would have to hurry or they wouldn't make it to the funeral before it started.

BRAD FOUND a parking place right in front of Nan's apartment building. As he left his car, the doorman waved and smiled, then put his hands behind him in a casual, at-ease position. Even in this uniform, he looked military, with close-cropped hair and rigid, erect posture. He seemed a product of long hours at this type of duty.

"Good morning, Gerald. Permission to come aboard?"

"Aye, aye, sir," he answered sharply, popping a smart salute.

"Were you Navy, Gerald?"

"No, sir. Retired from the Marines. Still proud of it, too."

"You were an old friend of Dan's, weren't you?" A guess.

"Yes, why?"

"Meet him while you were on embassy duty?" Another guess.

"As a matter of fact, I did. Why do you ask?"

"Just curious. He was an old friend of mine, too." Take a stab at it. "You still in government work, Gerald?"

A cautious look came over the doorman's face, narrowing his eyes, confirming Brad's suspicion.

"Like I said, I'm retired from the Marines."

"And Sue Snyder?"

Gerald's shoulders raised reflexively, his chin thrusting forward and his eyes seeking a spot across the street to focus on. His reaction said Sue Snyder had to be with the agency, too.

"I don't discuss the tenants with anyone, Mr. Gaelman."

"Just curious, Gerald. Speak to no one, except in the line of duty. That's a good policy. One of the general orders for guard duty, as I recall."

"Like I said, Mr. Gaelman, I'm just a retired Marine working as a doorman."

"Sure, gunny. Keep up the good work."

Brad could feel the man's eyes on his back as he entered the building. Gerald was another loyal employee of Dan's "Company." He was probably incorruptible, and any lapse of security on his part would be caused by some action completely beyond his control. The security of the building was faulted when Gerald was ill and no replacement arrived. Was Sue Snyder his backup? Was she a trainee, or an agent? Was she also incorruptible? Had an attachment to Dan blinded her caution? Could they have a lead that would identify the killer?"

The door to Nan's apartment opened as Brad was knocking.

"You're late!" She brushed past him and walked abruptly to the elevator, a scowl marking her face under a black veiled hat.

"Sorry. I had a rough night." Closing the door and turning to follow her, he felt every tortuous moment of the night again as her brusque tone and behavior cut through him.

"Didn't we all!" She said it softly, but vehemently, her eyes holding on the elevator light, avoiding him entirely.

It was going to be a tough day.

She looked agitated, more than just impatient at his tardiness. Beneath the black net, her eyes were swollen. Had she already been crying? Or had she not slept? As the elevator door opened, he reached for her arm.

"Nan, let's don't make this any harder than it already is. Forgive me for whatever difficulty my problems have caused you. We're going to need each other today."

Stepping into the elevator, she turned and looked up at him, her eyes moistening, her mouth pulled down at the corners.

"Then bear with me as well. You aren't the only one with needs and problems."

As the elevator door closed, she put her arm in his. But she stood slightly away from him, keeping a distance. She felt all the soul-wrenching sentiments of the night before enfolding her, pulling her emotions in a dozen directions. His arm was warm against hers. He was trying to be so sweet, and she wanted to trust him, to turn to him and feel his arms wrapped around her. She was lost in a forest of dark emotions, of grief, of loneliness, of need. She needed to be held. But she didn't trust him—or herself.

The doorman quietly held the door for them as they left the building. Though he didn't speak, Brad could feel his suspicious eyes on them as he helped Nan into the car. The world seemed to be made of suspicious people today, and it seemed everyone was watching Brad. But then, he was suspicious as well.

THE SERVICES were starting as they arrived. An usher escorted them to the seats reserved for them. There was a large showing of newspaper people as well as most of the contingent of Knives. Mallard was apparently late in returning from his trip, for he was not there.

As the ceremonies began, Brad fought to keep from sinking completely into the past. It was so much more comfortable to let his mind wander among the good times he had spent with Ed. But he thought too of Ed's murderer, and these thoughts demanded that his mind remain in the present.

At a sniffling beside him, he offered Nan his handkerchief. She took it with a quiet thanks, brushing his hand with her fingers. Then she grasped his hand firmly and held it for the rest of the service.

At the grave site at Arlington Cemetery, he stood close behind Nan, near Ed's elderly parents, who had flown in from Kansas City for the funeral. The words of the minister were about another Ed, one that Brad hardly recognized. There was little in the prayers to hold his attention here amid the mundane.

Across the casket from them were a number of newspaper executives, and behind them were the Knives: the rancher, the corporate president, the judge, and the congressman. George Windham's absence was conspicuous, as was Bum's.

Beside Thaddeus Ralston was Bess, in a simple black dress that looked sensuously engaging on her. She caught Brad's eye, tilted her head, and winked slowly. Brad looked quickly away, disturbed by the inappropriate flirting. He wondered if Thaddeus had changed her mind about attending. Or was it her memory of time spent with Ed?

Brad's eyes searched the fringes of the large crowd and the hills and trees nearby. He recognized a couple of plainclothes police officers standing away from the group, but there was no sign of Bum Shandy.

Nan leaned back into Brad's hands as the precision Air Force ceremonial team fired their volleys and played taps. The flag was folded and presented to Ed's mother. And then, too quickly, it was over, leaving Brad and Nan standing beside the grave. They spoke quietly with Ed's parents, then started back to the car. The slamming of car doors sounded an unwelcome finality.

The movements of a well-dressed elderly man in the middle of the departing crowd of mourners caught Brad's eye. A familiar manner in the old man's almost comic shuffle touched a memory. His security experience told him that a handicapped person might attract attention, but even searching officials dislike looking into the eyes of a cripple. It was a well-disguised Bum Shandy.

"Excuse me a moment, Nan." He stepped into the crowd and started toward Bum. Suddenly, he felt a restraining hand on his arm, and Denton Mallard stepped in front of him.

"Brad, how are things going?"

"Hello, Denton. Looks like you made it back okay." As he spoke, Brad looked past Denton to see Bum accepting a ride with some newspaper people. No one else had recognized him. Brad turned back to Mallard, who was pulling at his arm, demanding his attention.

"I mentioned that I wanted to discuss your progress in the investigations."

"Well, Mr. Ambassador, we don't have any solid leads yet. But we're working on it."

"Don't joke about that appointment, Brad. I don't intend to let that slip away. Now tell me what you've found."

"We found a note from Dad and a memo from Ed," Nan said, approaching them.

"Oh, hello, Miss Donahue. And what was the apparent significance of these clues?"

"We're still considering that," Brad broke in. He felt uneasy about discussing the matter with Mallard, or with anyone, for that matter.

"Well, I certainly hope you'll keep me informed, Cowboy." Mallard's eyes were narrow as he stared at Brad.

"We'll do that," Nan said, as Brad took her arm and moved her toward the car. "I don't like that man," she whispered.

"I always knew you had good instincts," Brad said softly.

THE DOORMAN was not there to let them in to Nan's
building and she had to use her key. Brad accompanied
her to her door, trying to decide what to say if she asked
him in. She did.

"Why don't we talk things over? I mean, we can discuss the investigation, can't we?"

"If you think it's okay," he said stepping inside. "I
don't want to intrude." He was lying. He wanted to intrude. He wanted her in his arms.

She turned and walked across the room, placing her
purse and hat on a table. Then she turned suddenly and
faced him, feeling confusion reeling through her, feeling uncomfortable and upset with herself for treating
him as she had.

"Brad, I don't like walking on eggs all the time when
we're together."

He approached her slowly, reached out for her, and she
moved into his arms. She felt taut and very nervous. Her
hands ran across his shoulders and clasped at his neck.
He kissed her fully on the lips, pouring all his pent-up
feelings into the contact.

Nan had welcomed the feel of his arms and his body
against hers. As she had turned up to tell him, she met
his lips. His kiss felt surprisingly violent, and his arms
held her tightly. She hadn't intended to resist, but she
had a sense of being captured, and she found herself
struggling against him. She was swept into an overwhelming storm of sensual reactions, and she felt tears
spring to her eyes.

"Brad, wait."

"I want you now, Nan." He whispered into her ear.

Still holding her tightly, he coaxed her trembling chin higher with one finger, forcing her to look into his eyes. With a wavering finger, he traced the outline of her full, pouting lips, causing her to quiver all over.

"Brad, please don't."

She turned away, resisting his touch. But with an insistent finger on her chin, he brought her eyes back to him and kissed each one softly. Because he had moved his hands to hold her face, she felt locked into him.

"Lady, you're like a fluttering bird. Be still and relax. If you can't come to me, then just let it happen to us."

Feeling trapped, she tensed suddenly, shoulders drawn up, trying to drop her chin. But when he pressed his mouth more firmly, her lips parted and her tongue met his just inside her lips. A low moaning sound stirred from deep within her, and her body moved firmly and completely against his. Then suddenly she jerked back and broke away from him.

"Brad, please. Don't do this to me! Please, I can't control myself! Don't . . . use me . . . like this!"

Brad backed off, releasing his tight grasp. He was confused, full of desire. But he also feared he might drive her away.

"Am I supposed to be sorry, or glad that you lost control?"

"Neither. Just let me think.

"Suppose I don't touch you. What will we do? Can we talk?"

"Just sit over there. I need to sit alone and talk with you. Please understand, Brad. I'm just not ready for anything else right now."

He slumped into a chair, and he watched her face as she struggled with her inner turmoil.

Nan sat with her hands clasped in her lap, her head down, and her eyes closed. She had almost let go, almost given in. She was still aroused by his physical presence, but her fears of his complete domination of her, physically, emotionally, and sexually, caused her to back off.

"Nan, what is it?"

She was touched by the pleading in his eyes. His voice touched something deep inside her.

"I can't do it this way. You're too much. It doesn't feel right."

The words echoed harshly in her heart, and she regretted saying them. But before she could speak to soften them, she saw the pain in his face.

Brad was hurt that she wouldn't accept or trust him. But he couldn't turn away from it, from her.

"Nan, please listen. I admit I want you terribly. You're a lovely, desirable woman. I need you physically, but there's more. I want to help you in whatever way I can. Please let me."

"You're a threat to me, Brad. I know you wouldn't harm me intentionally. But if I give in.... Please, let's talk about something else."

He tried to read her face. But he couldn't figure why he frightened her. Under his gaze, he saw her shiver and suddenly divert her eyes.

"Nan, I don't know what to say to you, except that remaining separate won't help either of us. We need each other, but we're basically two strong people. Strong enough to survive each other. I think we should try."

His words touched her deeply. She wanted his smile, his nearness, his touch. But his need seemed so great that it might totally overwhelm her. She wanted to be dependent without being submerged in his need. She didn't want to be suffocated. She had had more than enough of that for a lifetime. When she spoke, her voice was husky with feeling.

"Brad, please. I'm too vulnerable. I'm not sure I can keep control right now. Don't take advantage of me."

She couldn't meet the look on his face. She closed her eyes and tried to forget the naked need in those soft brown eyes of his.

Brad became conscious of how he had moved to the edge of the chair to get closer to her. He sat back and tried to relax.

"What shall we discuss?" He kept the words guarded and free of the passion he felt for her.

She opened her eyes and looked at him searchingly. He seemed less tense, more open and receptive, the need tucked away for another time, perhaps.

"Who do you think the killer is? Why hasn't George Windham shown up?" She paused. "And what part does Bess Bradshaw play in the killings?"

He sat forward again, elbows on his knees.

"Well, first, it could be someone who knows the Knives well. But I'm afraid one of the Knives is the killer. I can't decide who. I can't bring myself to believe it's

Bum. Maybe George Windham isn't out of the country. Maybe he's here in town, engineering all of this. Any one of them could be guilty, but I don't really know why. I feel sure Bess had no part in the killing.''

"Even if she's innocent, I think we should give serious thought to framing her!''

Brad looked at her sharply, but she was avoiding his eyes. Nan was now telling him about some of her inner conflict. She was jealous of Bess, but she couldn't bring herself to admit it to him.

"You're in a vindictive mood.''

"She's like fingernails on a blackboard.''

"She's not a threat. She's harmless.''

"Nobody's harmless,'' she whispered. "Nobody.''

"Jealousy goes beyond loving possessiveness, Nan. It's a petty, childish emotion.''

"Don't lecture me!''

They looked away from one another, each caught up in a turmoil of doubts.

"Are you going to hurt me, Brad?'' The lines of her face showed her doubts and fears.

"I hope to hell not.'' His features said far more than his words. "I never wanted to hurt you.''

How could he explain that he was falling in love with her? That he was already there? Would it be too much for her? How would she react?

"Talk to me,'' he pleaded. "Whatever else we become, I'll always be your friend. I'm an *intimate* friend, remember?''

"Indeed I do. I also remember that hot little message on your recorder from Capitol Hill. Which impulse do I believe?"

"I thought I explained that. It wasn't my idea. She's a friend."

"With friends like her. . . ."

"I tell you, she's harmless."

"You've already said that."

"I occasionally repeat myself for emphasis."

He saw her look at him with searching eyes, and a look of determination came over her. She shifted to the edge of her chair and leaned toward him. He couldn't keep his eyes off the curves of her body.

"This conversation may be awkward as hell, but we're going to manage it, Cowboy."

"Well I've got a lot riding on the outcome of this little conversation. Please help a former recluse draw some lines in defining our expected behavior."

"Brad, passion's a dangerous thing. You never know when it's going to run wild, or with whom. Relationships don't always evolve as planned, even when people know exactly what they want. I don't want any lines drawn. I just need time to let things happen. I'm not trying to drive you away. I just can't let go like you want me to. I want to, but I can't do it yet."

"That leaves us with an excruciating dilemma. I'm just not sure I know where it will lead."

"Would falling in love make it any clearer, Cowboy?"

"Less and less. I don't think I understand this kind of love. I can't tell whether I'm winning or losing. Or even what the game is."

"Brad, my marriage drove me inside myself. I've been looking inside so long that I don't have anyone to talk to about you, about how I'm trying to decide how I feel. I'm very uncertain about too many things. I find your touch both desirable and intimidating."

Standing, he walked to her, and she stood, cautiously. He took her hands in his and kissed them, and she flushed with the warmth of the gesture. There was still a doubt there between them, but his touch on her hands aroused her feelings again.

"Why don't you let me help?"

"Would you get that involved? You'd do that for me?"

"For us, I would. Whatever it takes."

"Oh, Brad, let me think about what help I can handle."

"How about physical therapy?" His face was an impish grin.

"You're terrible! Go take another cold shower."

He kissed her softly on her waiting lips.

"Lady, you're running up my water bill tremendously."

WHEN BRAD reached the lobby, a large man in a dark business suit blocked his departure through the front door. He could've been a wrestler or a barroom bouncer by the look of his build and his scarred face. He looked ominously like someone who was doing an official job and didn't want to be bothered.

"Who are you?" The grunted question came from behind a huge, ham-sized left palm held up as a stop sign. His narrow eyes also said stop and identify.

"Brad Gaelman. Visiting upstairs. Where's Gerald?"

"Sick. I'm his replacement. Got identification?"

"Sure. Do I need it to get out, too?"

His answer was to wave the large ham in a give-me motion. His right hand crept toward a bulge beneath his coat.

Brad cautiously removed his wallet and showed him a driver's license.

"Now let's see yours." As the large man hesitated, Brad tried, unsuccessfully, to improve upon his six-foot stance. Even without the gun, the huge man had him beat by six inches in height and chest size, and at least sixty pounds.

While they stood there eyeing one another, a small, perky blonde bundle jogged to the door. Sue Snyder in another tight, stylishly revealing running outfit. The logo of the nearby spa decorated the protrusion of the sweatshirt over her full breasts.

"Hi there. He's okay, Victor. Goes with the redhead beauty upstairs." She spoke between breaths. "I see you've met the new doorman, Mr. Gaelman."

"Where's Gerald?"

"Sick again. Got a replacement this time."

"From the same agency?"

"He'll do. Sorry about your friends."

"Thanks. Nice of you to keep up. Good run?"

"You bet. Gotta shower now. See ya."

She gave Victor a long look before ambling over to the elevator. Brad watched her tight, shapely rear all the way. She flashed a smile over her shoulder as the elevator doors closed behind her.

Brad almost followed to ask the questions about Dan and her that were pestering him. But the imposing presence of Victor was a new input to be considered. Another time would be better.

"So long, Victor."

"Take care, Mr. Gaelman." He almost sounded civil through the grimace that lined his pug face.

Brad felt better about the security at the door. Victor had to be from the CIA, probably another ex-Marine. But there was still a nagging in the back of his mind that there was yet another question to be answered.

8

NAN REGAINED CONSCIOUSNESS slowly, drowsily, in a listless but satisfying fog. She could feel the debilitating effect of the drugs. She hadn't meant to take them again, but they took away the fears and the cares, and made her feel so good. They gave her an escape from the callousness and cruelty that defined the rude borders of her life.

She was sprawled on the large couch. A cool dampness told her the bikini pants were gone and her dress was pulled up, but she couldn't make her arms move to pull it down. It didn't seem to matter, despite all the men in the room.

She forced her eyes to scan the room for her husband, but she couldn't find him. She remembered why her dress was in disarray. Her husband had pulled it up. Then the men had touched her. And kissed her. And made her feel so good she could hardly stand it. The drugs kept her from participating actively, but they also released her inhibitions and made it feel better and better.

Now the men were standing around her again. Their faces were blurred, but she felt an apprehension about them. Where was her husband? There. Arms folded. Smiling at her. She could hear them talking, but she couldn't make out the words. They were laughing now. There were more of them than before. Now they were pulling her clothes away, tearing them. She felt the pain vividly as they treated her body roughly. They were pulling her onto the floor. Her head hit the carpet, and a psychedelic scattering of stars flashed with the dull pain.

Her legs were being held high in the air, pulled apart. She felt a pleasurable wave, and then a pain that quickly became too much. She writhed on the floor, trying to pull away, and the voices became louder, sharper. The shock of the event and the pain swept over her, gripping her tightly, suffocating her senses, humiliating her. She wanted to die. Then there came a blessed blackness, washing away all pain.

She woke suddenly, tossing back and forth, grasping for something to hold onto, gasping for breath. Then she sobbed loudly, deeply, realizing it was a dream that wouldn't go away. It would be back to haunt her when she was sleeping and couldn't keep it out. It was a part of her past that she couldn't escape. It was the wild, sensual circus of her miserable marriage. It was her life gone berserk, ravaged, reckless, debauched, under the complete control of others.

She ran her hands over her body, measuring her arousal. It was still there, for whatever pain there was in the dreams, there was also the feral passion and great pleasure that drew her back. Even then when it happened, the pleasure was always there, teasing her, beckoning to her. And when she gave in to it, the pain and humiliation always followed, supplied liberally by her husband, his family, or his friends.

She buried her head in her pillow to wipe away the tears and to try to push away the images. She drifted back into troubled sleep, as always wanting the sensations of pleasure—and fearing what the pain would do to her.

BRAD AWAKENED Sunday morning with the metallic taste of battle in his mouth. He had been fighting all night alongside Luke Bonner. And today they would go out to bury the soldier. Having survived the war, Luke didn't make it through the peace.

Brad went to the window and looked out on a dismal morning. Weeping clouds hung heavily, spilling their tears of deep sorrow on the streets and buildings below. He remembered the cold Asian tears of the monsoon rains he and Luke had shared on better days. Or were they better? They were for Luke.

He went through the kitchen for his usual glass of orange juice, and he walked along the wall of mementos as he drank. This was what was left of those better days. The medals, the silver star, distinguished flying crosses, bronze stars, air medals, and a host of foreign awards shone from their display cases. They all said that he had done a good job, that his performance was excellent.

With the decorations were the photos of the Knives. These meant something. They were a close-knit group. They lived together, fought together, ate together, and whored together. The smiling faces from the past reached out to him in fellowship and common accomplishment. Here was a thing of substance, something worthwhile, something worth remembering, worth going back to, if only in dreams.

But his dreams were rapidly becoming the only way to summon these people. Three of them were dead now. A triad of heroes. Perhaps killed by someone else on that same wall. He searched out the survivors from among the figures in the photos. Mallard, Ralston, Lin, Windham, Shandy, Sennet . . . and himself. Seeing a photo of Dan with a cute teenager in a short skirt, Brad added Nan as another possible. They were all targets, except maybe one—who was a killer.

This was a lot like the war they had shared. They were never certain just who their friends were among the battlefield Asians. A friendly group one day might turn hostile the next. The deadly Claymore directional mines were placed accordingly, some facing out, and some facing in. The threat could come from anywhere. And now the threat was probably from within the group of these veterans.

And what was the motive? Something that had happened back then must be reaching into the present to threaten someone and drive them to murder. But what could be so terrible? What dragon was chasing the murderer? Maybe someone who couldn't have his past exposed. Who among those brave heroes was afraid of the past?

He straightened a picture of the hawklike face of a Knife now turned congressman. Here was a real survivor, both then and now. All of the investigations had focused on Thaddeus Ralston's hearings. Had something come up there that threatened his blossoming political career? He had made trips back to the old area of war operations. Had he stumbled on something there? If he weren't the killer, he was the best possibility as the next victim. No one alive knew more about what had really happened in their group back in Southeast Asia. Brad realized he couldn't wait until Monday evening. Maybe a word of warning could be given at Luke's funeral today.

But that would probably mean seeing Bess, and up close. She was a threat to his vulnerability. She was so damned tempting! It would be so easy to throw off everything and just sink into the voluptuous, sensual life she promised. It would be an easy way to forget all the conflict, the bad memories and dreams, the responsibilities of today, like working out the difficulties with Nan. But he didn't want to forget those responsibilities. And he could not forget Nan and what she had come to mean.

He stopped again in front of the picture of Dan and the young Nan. She was so much of what he wanted. Not because she was Dan's daughter. Not because they both wanted to find a killer. But because she was someone of value.

His life seemed out of his control. It was being reshaped by the unseen hand of a killer and two very visible women. He couldn't tolerate losing control of his life.

It was too much like the old days in Southeast Asia. Always driven by some outside influence. Haul ass, suck it up, tuck it in, swallow hard or spit it out, duck your head but keep your chin up, keep 'em flying and happy landings. Get the job done, but if this bastard is going to earn all his medals on this flight, you can set me down at the next clearing. At least over there you could fight back. Hit someone. Shoot someone. Get some feeling of satisfaction out of hitting back. But not now.

Now he had to get dressed to pick up Nan and go to a funeral. A funeral for one of the best soldiers who ever fired a shot for the U.S. of A. A hero's hero. A shepherd among sheep, an eagle among doves, and a crusader among peasants. Luke Bonner was a helluva Green Beret.

WHEN BRAD PARKED in front of Nan's apartment building, the gargantuan guard was still on duty. Victor's tent-like raincoat made him look even more enormous. Otherwise, his stance and manner were similar to Gerald's, with echoes of similar military experience. But this one didn't have Gerald's finesse. Victor wasn't one to trade tricky talk with. He looked like he was one to brutally correct his mistakes, including verbal slips and any misplaced facial expressions.

"Good morning, Victor. Okay if I park here?"

"Good morning, Mr. Gaelman. Your car's okay there. The lady should be ready by now. Miss Snyder says so."

They were certainly keeping better tabs now. Maybe now Sue Snyder was the lead and the doorman the backup.

"Thank you, Victor," he said, checking to see if the hinges were holding up as the massive doorman held the suddenly flimsy-looking door for him.

"Nobody's gonna bother your car, Mr. Gaelman."

"Thanks."

Upon stepping out of the elevator, he met Sue Snyder, again in a sexy running outfit. He wondered if she owned any other clothes. Would Dan fall for a female jock? This one, maybe yes.

"Good morning, Sue."

"Good morning, Brad."

First names. Just like that.

"You working on Sunday, or just running around the nearby neighborhood?"

Her cautious look remained as she held the elevator door.

"Gotta keep an eye on things. I like to keep things in shape." She said it with a smile.

"Nice outfit. Fits . . . just right. Are those special leg weights bulging around your ankles, or standard issue Smith and Wesson?"

Her look of surprise was rapidly replaced by a wide, knowing smile.

"Those soft brown eyes are sharper than most. I'm glad we're on the same side." Her facial expression said she meant it.

"Remember that if you ever need anything."

"Same here, Brad."

"I'd like to talk sometime about Dan."

"I thought you would get to that eventually. But not now. I have a tour to run. You know how important timing is. See ya."

"Let me know if you see anyone I should know."

"I will. We'll talk soon."

The elevator doors closed on her bright smile. Yes, the security looked a lot better around here now.

DESPITE THE RAIN and traffic, they got to the funeral in plenty of time. The gathering was a hodgepodge of raincoats and umbrellas. An officious Army chaplain led off the eulogies for General Luke Bonner. Captain Tim Blackwell was one of the speakers, and his small son, Luke Bonner Blackwell, participated as well. Aside from these observations, Brad again found little to hold his concentration.

Nan watched Brad's detached behavior, and wondered what images were flashing behind those soft, moist brown eyes. His stare was vacant and unblinking, as though he were far away. He looked more than sad. He looked as if he were hurting inside, just as she had seen him at Ed's funeral, and she suspected, as he had looked at her dad's services.

She leaned against his shoulder and hooked her arm in his, holding his larger hand tightly.

"I know, Brad. But it's okay. I'm here with you," she whispered. She hoped her smile would show him the reassurance she felt for him. The boiling black clouds of guilt were not with her today. She was feeling only a fulfillment of being with Brad and supporting him.

He squeezed her hand softly and smiled lightly before slipping back into his bereaved trance.

THE RAIN FELL heavily at Arlington. The traffic was backed up, slowing the procession. The large crowd of mourners was drenched by the rain and wind before the services were half over. Brad again stood close behind Nan, and found himself once again looking across a grave at the surviving Knives, minus Bum and George Windham. There was a large contingent of Army senior officers within the crowd, and an Army honor guard.

Since Luke had no surviving relatives, the folded flag was presented to Grace Blackwell. She in turn presented it to her small son, Luke Bonner Blackwell. He held the flag tightly beneath his arm, wiped away tears with his other hand, and again grasped his mother's hand. Tim blinked his moist eyes as he held Grace's other hand. They were an Army family. Luke's family.

Brad scanned the hills and the edges of the crowd for Bum Shandy. The hills were empty except for the raincoat-clad plainclothes men and some Army military police spaced at intervals around the mourners. There was no sign of the well-dressed comic cripple. There were too many people crowded in under the nearby trees to single out Bum in this rain. But Brad felt that Bum was here. Rafe would have to be told. Tomorrow, maybe.

Tran Lin approached Brad and Nan as they finished speaking with Tim and Grace Blackwell and their son. Lin's wide western hat was pushed rakishly to the back of his head. His expensive raincoat was unbuttoned and held back by a hand at his waist, a posture Brad had observed during the services. Lin's suit coat was also unbuttoned, and the edge of a large shoulder holster showed under his coat. The large bodyguard in a tent of a raincoat stood two paces behind Lin and appeared to be ready for anything. Lin was a cautious man.

"Hello, Nan, Brad. Again we meet under less than pleasant circumstances. But it is always good to see old friends. How are you two doing?"

"Hello, Tran."

"Hello, General Lin. We're fine, thank you."

"Make it Tran, please, Nan. I was referring to your own investigation. You haven't given up on finding the killer, have you?"

"Not at all," Brad answered evenly. "We're still at it."

"Are you making any progress? The police seem to be up against a stone wall, from what Sergeant Johnson tells me."

"We're working with Rafe," Nan said with confidence. "We've been able to turn up a couple of leads for him, but we're not at liberty to discuss them."

Brad looked at her with wonderment and pride. Had she somehow picked up on his earlier discomfort in discussing the case with others, or had she decided on her own to hold the information closely?

"Well, surely you can tell me if you have a suspect, even if it's me." An inscrutable Oriental look accompanied the statement, followed by a smile that would charm a mongoose. "You know, I am very interested in the progress of this case. I mean, being an honorary Knife, and a possible target myself, of course."

"Your Oriental rules apply, Tran. But if we do turn up anything you should know, we'll be in touch. I guess now you'll be going back to the ranch with your private army."

"Yes, I have trails there to walk, as you could guess. The ranching business never lets up."

"Wouldn't want the other predators to get ahead."

Lin looked at him sternly, started to speak, then smiled broadly at Nan.

"You have a dangerous way about you, Cowboy. May you be cursed with an interesting life. But may your sharing of it be gentle and kind, Miss Donahue. Happy hunting."

"Watch your six, Tran."

Lin stalked away in his characteristic short, choppy steps, his bodyguard swiveling his head to and fro watchfully as he walked closely behind.

"I know he's a general and an honorary Knife and all, but somehow, I don't like him, either," Nan whispered as they walked toward the car close under Brad's umbrella. "I guess I don't really understand him half the time. I mean, his accent's very Americanized, but he always seems to talk in Oriental parables."

"Your instincts are holding right on course. Lin's a very dangerous man. One to be on the watch for."

"Brad, you think he's our killer?"

"Could be. He has a helicopter, so he knows them well. He's an expert with explosives, too. I can't see an obvious connection with the three deaths, except that Tran knew them all, and worked with them back then. But that condition holds true for most of the survivors. He's a definite suspect, though."

"He seems to realize that being a Knife makes him a target," Nan said. Then she sneezed twice, searching for her handkerchief until Brad handed his to her.

"Let's get you in out of this rain. How about some Irish coffee?"

"You're asking the right person. I'll do the honors, if you want to risk another scene in my apartment."

"You've got it, lady."

BRAD LET NAN out in front of her building and parked the car. As he walked up to the door, he was surprised to hear Victor talking jovially with Nan.

"Yep, you look as wet as Miss Snyder did when she came in." What could be a smile crinkled his lumpy face. As Brad approached, the doorman turned his warmth on him as well.

"You're soaked, too, Mr. Gaelman. Better get inside and out of those wet things."

Nan and Brad grinned at each other at the suggestion, and thanking Victor, they hurried through the door. As they entered the elevator, Brad took her arm and pulled her close, smiling down at her mischievously.

"You know, that Victor's a very understanding fellow after all. Nice of him to worry about our health, and to make such nice suggestions, don't you think?"

"I think you'd use any excuse to get these wet clothes off me. But if you push that idea too hard, I'm going to steam them dry before the first zipper is unzipped."

He pulled her to him for a kiss, but she turned quickly and sneezed again. She backed away and searched her pockets for his handkerchief as the elevator door opened. Walking quickly to her door, she fished her keys out. By the time he was again beside her, she was inside and closing the door behind them. As he reached for her, she sneezed again.

They laughed, despite themselves. He took her wet shoulders in his hands and looked deeply into her eyes.

"You need to get warmed up, lady."

"And you, too. Look, there's one of Dad's robes in the spare bedroom closet. Why don't you take a hot shower and get into it while I change and make the Irish coffee?"

"Wouldn't you like to warm up in the shower with me?" He was only half joking.

"Better make that a cold shower, Cowboy. I'll use the shower off my bedroom, if you don't mind. Now get moving."

"Yes, ma'am," he said obediently.

When Brad returned to the kitchen, Nan was there with the coffee almost ready. Her hair was pinned up, and dry and shining. She was simply lovely. He realized for the first time that she looked as good without make-up as with it.

She was in a heavy, floor-length robe, less enticing than the last one he had seen her wear. But the front of it bulged with the firm fullness of her breasts and made it just as easy to look at. He could feel his heart leap.

"Come wrap your hands around one of these, Cowboy."

"My pleasure, ma'am," he said as he started for her.

"I mean the coffee mugs, silly. Now behave. Please, Brad."

The last words came almost as a soft and pleading lament, and her face reflected the turmoil stirring just below the surface of her emotions. He was moved by it, and torn between taking her in his arms to tell her it would all be okay and standing off to take the coffee. He took a deep breath and reached for the coffee, seeing her relax as he did so. They took seats on opposite sides of the table.

He searched her face for a hint of passion. Every feeling of loving warmth that he could muster went into his gaze. He was rewarded with a lusty look from her, eyes wide and glowing, tongue licking her lips, head tilted, and finger running down her neck. She laughed a throaty laugh, and leaned back, tossing her auburn hair.

"Brad, don't look at me that way! I can feel your eyes touching me inside this robe!"

"So can I. Why don't you just make it easier on both of us and get out of the robe? Then I can let my fingers do the looking."

"Brad! Stop talking like that!" She flushed from her face down to where her hands gripped the collar of the robe.

He felt their feet touch under the table, and an electric shock ran through him. He felt a surge of hot blood. He ran his foot up her smooth leg and felt her foot exploring in return.

"You are a horny bastard, aren't you?"

"Nan! I can't get you out of my mind! I'm thinking of you constantly. I want you more than any woman I've known." He reached into the pocket of the robe and brought out a small package. "Maybe now is the time to give you this. Open it."

She hesitated, looking at the gift wrapping, and then tore into it quickly to reveal a small bottle of perfume. Reading the label, she laughed softly.

"Kiss at Dawn?" She set it on the table and looked into his smiling eyes. "Is that what you're after, Cowboy?"

"I can always hope. Put some on. I think you'll like it."

She picked up the bottle and turned it in her hand, giving thought to the meaning of the gift, the significance of wearing a scent he gave her.

He leaned toward her with his warm smile.

"If you're trying to think of where to wear it, I have a couple of suggestions."

"Oh, you!" she said laughing. She opened the tiny bottle and dabbed a bit behind each ear. The musky scent quickly enveloped them, creating a more sensuous atmosphere.

"Now that's more like it. That fragrance will always make me think of you."

"Brad, I don't like this. I can feel myself yielding to you. I'm falling in love with you, and I'm beginning to want you too much. I know if we don't stop now, I'll lose what I am. I know it. That's how it happens."

"Nan, I've told you I love you. Let me show you. If you love me, too, then show me what you feel, or at least tell me why you can't."

"I can't. I can't even tell you. Especially you. You mean too much to me now."

"It can't be that bad. But let me decide. Show me what you feel. Touch me. Let me touch you."

"Brad, you're making me feel so...."

"Do you need me, Nan? Do you?"

"Yes."

"Do you want me?"

"Yes, Brad. Yes! You know I do."

"Then take my hand. Here."

"I can't, Brad!"

She got up abruptly, and turning sharply, left the table, moving unsteadily toward the counter.

Brad rose quickly to follow. He moved up behind her, and with soft, caressing hands, began to knead her shoulders and neck.

"Easy, Nan. Just relax."

He pressed his lips against her hair, smelling her perfume. Moving the robe, he kissed the bare, hot skin of her shoulder.

After an internal struggle, her words came tumbling out breathlessly.

"I can't let it happen again. I'm not a kid this time. I'm thirty years old. And I promised myself it wouldn't happen again."

He ran his hands across her shoulders and down the robe to her firm breasts. Through the robe, he cupped each one gently, squeezing them as they rose to meet his palms. He wanted to comfort her, to arouse her, to make it easy for her to meet him halfway.

Nan was caught in swirling emotions. She felt her body respond as he opened her robe and caressed her bare breasts. She could feel the firmness of his arousal against her bottom. Her whole being was torn between giving herself to him or tearing away. She jerked herself free and turned to him, her eyes tear-filled, and her voice shaky.

"Brad, you're not being fair."

He took her again in his arms, and looked down at her, his mouth inches from her lips.

"Nan, you've got to let go. There's nothing you can't tell me. If we love one another, what else matters?"

"Oh, Brad, you don't know what I've been, what I've done!"

"I know I love you, and that's enough."

He pressed his mouth fully on hers, squeezing her body to him, pressing against her thighs and lower belly. Her arms went around his neck, but the intensity of his desire alarmed her. Again she struggled, resisting without wanting to, feeling trapped in the snare of his arms.

Desperately, she dug her fingers into his hair and pulled without any result. There was a tingling in the back of her legs as her thighs tightened and her blood rushed to where he pressed against the center of her pleasure. Her body was out of her control. The muscles of her bottom contracted, and her hips and pelvis thrust against him with no effort on her part.

He felt the change in her body and her actions. His hands went beneath the robe and around her body, kneading her softness, and dropping to her hips.

Then the feeling of his hands grasping her hips, pulling her upon him where they stood, registered in her innermost cautions. She felt the ecstasy fall quickly away, and a sense of peril and fear replaced it. She fought back again and pulled away from him, now breathless and panting. His warm lips went to her throat and lingered softly on her pulsing neck, tugging at her passion, and pulling her back to him.

He whispered assurances to her, feeling her drawing away, not understanding her actions. Then she felt almost lifeless in his arms. He drew back and looked at her incredulously, seeing her face empty of passion or need.

"Nan, what is it? What happened?"

"It's no use, Brad. I just can't."

She turned and walked slowly away, closing and tying her robe. A sob erupted from deep within her.

Their fragile relationship was again threatened by her silence and withdrawal.

"Nan, talk to me! Tell me what's wrong!"

"I can't! I just can't talk about it with you."

She turned away, covering her face with trembling hands, sobbing deeply.

He grabbed her shoulders and turned her to face him. His heart knotted at what he saw in her eyes. He leaned forward, gripping her arms and pulling her insistently to him.

"Lady, there's nothing you can't say to me."

She felt his fingers burning into her arms. She felt an agonizing confusion and frustration, and she grew angrier at his persistence. She shook loose and took a step back away from him. She jerked her chin up, glaring at him.

"Don't touch me!"

"Nan," he said pleading, reaching again for her arms.

Her nostrils flared, her lips thinned and drew back over her teeth in furious anger.

"You just leave me alone!" she said viciously.

Brad was startled by her intensity. He stepped back, hurt and confused, wanting her, but sensing the pain he was causing. He turned, uncertain and sorrowful, and muttered softly, "Okay, Nan."

He started to the spare bedroom to get his clothes.

"Brad! Wait!" She cried out the words, a sob ripping from deep within her.

He hesitated with the door half opened, but couldn't look back.

"Please, Brad. Don't go away." She pleaded in moans, her voice barely audible.

He turned to look at her, not understanding, not believing what he heard. She was standing with her hands over her face. As she shook her head from side to side, the pins flew from her hair, and the auburn curls tumbled over her shoulders. His heart was pounding in his ears, his nerves raw with tension.

"Brad. I need you. Please forgive me. Please help me. Hold me."

He closed the door and crossed to her slowly and very deliberately, not knowing what to expect. Reaching hesitatingly for her shoulders, he gripped her softly, pulling her quivering body next to his.

She fell against him, sobbing helplessly, her arms seeking the firm strength of his shoulders. His hands were warm and comforting as they slid across her back. She loved his touch, and her body was already craving more, but there was no strength to seek what they wanted now.

Brad rested his cheek against her untamed hair.

"Easy, Nan," he muttered comfortingly.

"I am so unsure about myself . . . about us." He could barely hear her.

"I know, honey. I'm sorry I pushed so hard for you to get it out, to talk to me. But I need to know how I can help free you from whatever fear that is holding you prisoner."

She looked up at him like a frightened child. Her eyes were brimming with large tears. He leaned to kiss away the tears, softly, tenderly.

"Please, be patient with me, Brad." She spoke softly, haltingly. "Please give me time. But don't ever leave me alone. Don't ever let me be like that again. Alone and afraid of everything."

"I'll be here. Just put up with my impatience. And my need for you. And my wanting to share life with you. We need each other, Nan. We can help each other, I know it."

He reached down, and with an arm under her knees, swept her into his arms. He felt her body go taut, a gasp coming from her lips, her arms pushing away slightly. He stepped quickly to the couch and sat down, holding her in his lap, placing her head on his shoulder. She relaxed in his arms, snuggling to make them comfortable. She looked up at him with a slight smile.

"Brad Gaelman, I love you. For this. For trying to understand. For being you."

"And I love you for all that and more. Just don't send me away. And I'll put my passions on hold for now. You're worth the wait, for however long it might take."

"Just hold me right now. Let me feel your strength flowing to me like this. I'll be okay in a minute. Just promise me you won't do anything."

"I promise, Nan. I'll just hold you for now."

They spent a long time locked in the intimate embrace of outspoken eyes, declaring in silence what they could not find words to say.

Nan reveled in the warmth and comfort of his embrace. She loved the feel of him, the presence of him. Where her father was formal and her husband was callous and unfeeling, Brad was sensitive and full of tenderness and compassion. He could openly show his feelings. And he could make her face up to herself, and make her laugh when she needed it. It seemed too good to be true.

"Brad, I'm afraid." She spoke softly, her head on his shoulder, her lips near his ear.

"I'm here. You're okay."

"I mean . . . afraid of us."

"Why? What is it?"

"I'm not sure I'm ready."

"You mean you're afraid of me?"

"I'm afraid . . . of what you'll make me."

"I'm trying to understand you."

"Men haven't always been good to me. I've been . . . treated badly."

"By whom?"

"By my former husband—and his friends."

"Nan, are you sure you want to talk about it?"

"They dominated me completely. In every way. Often. Cruelly."

"You mean, you were raped?"

"In several ways. Rape isn't just sexual, you know. Not really. The main thing about it is a man's domination of a woman, to humiliate and degrade her. Making her a sexual victim comes after making her a victim of his domination."

"Your husband did this?"

"Yes. And he helped others. He got me into drugs. I didn't resist. It was a way to forget that I had lost my self-respect. They made me perform acts I didn't know much about. And I did them willingly at first. Maybe I enjoyed it at the time, or maybe it was the drugs. But later, I couldn't stand to think about how they made me do those things, how they treated me. Some of the bruises lasted a long time. The mind bruises easily, and heals slowly."

"Then why did you marry him? Or stay with him?"

"He was so handsome and the life he offered was so glamorous. That is, at first. He gave me things I never knew I wanted. He made me feel things I never knew I needed. Gradually he changed. He became brutal. His little games became more and more unusual, and I was the one getting hurt. But I didn't have the strength and discipline to leave him. Then I realized none of the torment was worth it. I broke away, and I decided to never let myself be treated like that again. Ever."

"I'm sorry if I reminded you of something unpleasant."

"Don't you see, Brad? I've been living with it ever since. Keeping it inside, telling no one. If Dad had found out, I don't know what he would have done. I turned within myself, and let nothing outside get to me. Until you came along. You made me care again."

"I'm sorry I didn't know before. I always thought you were shy or frivolous, just a spoiled young woman. I didn't realize."

"I never wanted to be dominated in any way again. I never wanted any man to have any control over me . . . until now." She looked at him honestly, her face open and pleasant, but not quite smiling. "That's what scares me. I feel the same urges that got me into trouble before. And I'm afraid if I let go, I'll end up the same way."

"I could never intentionally hurt you, Nan." He took her hand to his mouth and kissed it softly. "I would never try to own you, but I think I might want to make you mine."

"Is that a proposition?"

"Want it to be?"

She raised her lips to his and kissed him with passion, exploring the inside of his mouth like a blind man exploring a piece of sculpture. And she searched his soul the same way. She finally leaned back on his shoulder, breathing deeply.

"Lovely lady, I never knew what courage it took to live your life."

"I never realized how much sensitivity you have."

"I've learned it the hard way. Had an insensitive partner."

"Your wife?"

"You got it."

"Want to tell me? I care too, you know."

He squeezed her in his arms, then took a deep breath and started.

"I guess it began the first time I was assigned to Southeast Asia. Things were tough over there sometimes. Sometimes the best times were when it got rough. I'm not sure I can really explain. In combat the constant pressure, the constant traumatic assault on the emotions, changes people. It makes them hard, so they can accept losses. You experience grief, and then quickly put it aside to get the job done."

"Dad used to tell me that. I think he was trying to help me get over losing Mom."

"Sometimes when you can't set aside the emotional stress, people revert to basic needs and survival becomes the most important thing. Pleasure is grabbed wherever it can be found, sexual needs are satisfied at whatever opportunity may arise and there's a demand for living totally in the present, living fully while it lasts, but assuring survival by whatever means may be necessary. It's hardly an aspect of polite society. It's a society based on fear and survival."

"Dad said you were expert at handling fear. He said you used it better than anyone he knew."

"Once you know and accept that you're scared, it's easier to deal with. It makes you desperate enough to ball up the fear and shove it aside and use the emotional momentum to do things you never thought you could. And next you begin to enjoy the feeling of pushing away the fear, and to enjoy living on a ragged edge of a high that gives great satisfaction."

"Sounds like what I used to feel on drugs."

"I think the adrenaline-pumping becomes habit forming, and the body begins to crave it. And you keep going back just for the thrill of the danger, and the feeling of strength it gives you to perform the acts of bravado you never dreamed you could handle so well. And your body's senses and reactions begin to attune to the rhythms. Later on, it becomes easier to return mentally to those times than to face the stress of current problems.''

"How do you mean?''

"Have you heard of flashbacks?''

"You mean delayed stress syndrome? Sure, I've read about it.''

"Don't lay any labels on me. I hate that! You're no doctor!''

"I didn't mean anything, Brad. It's just that I have dreams like that sometimes. I had an analyst back then after my divorce, and he said it was like DSS. That's all. Have you sought any professional help?''

"A long time ago. But, maybe I'm just getting what I deserve.''

"I don't understand.''

"Most people don't. You weren't there.''

"Dad was.''

"Bet your sweet ass he was. He was the best.''

"And your wife didn't understand this? Was that why you divorced?''

"That and the communication problems it led to. And she was growing in a different direction. A lot of time on her own while I spent three years over there. New people, new interests.''

"But we're growing in the same direction, aren't we?''

"It's beginning to look that way.''

"Brad, whether you want it or not, I'll be here to help."

"I can't think of anything I'd want more."

"Are you sure, Brad? Very sure?"

"I'm committed to it. Do you want me around?"

"Yes. Because you gave me help when I needed it."

"Maybe I have ulterior motives."

"I'll accept whatever you have to give me. I need it all."

"You've got it all, lady. I want you. I love you."

"Thanks for telling me about it. I know it wasn't easy to talk about. Dad had that problem, too."

"I could only tell you. No one else. You're special. You help me feel things, and I want to share them with you."

"Please just hold me. I feel exhausted. I need to be held by you."

"You just relax. I know this has been hard on you. I'll just hold you."

She put her head on his shoulder, feeling the texture of her father's robe against her face, and beneath it, the vibrant body of the man who loved her. A feeling of peacefulness crept over her for the first time in days, releasing her from her cares.

Brad watched her face relax, the lines disappearing, and the softness showing her happiness. After a few minutes she was sleeping deeply, and she did not awaken as he shifted his arms. He lifted her gently and carried her to her bedroom. Placing her carefully on the sheets, he removed the robe, his eyes sweeping blissfully over the lovely undulating swells and curves of her body.

"Another day, lady," he said softly, covering her with the sheet. "I'll be back, and you'll be mine. But another day, when we're both ready."

He kissed her lips softly and left her, glancing back once from her bedroom door. In the spare bedroom, he dressed again in his still moist clothes. Checking to make sure the door locked behind him, he let himself quietly out of the apartment.

9

NAN CAME AWAKE SLOWLY, amid vague wisps of dreams about Brad carrying her to bed, and then crawling in beside her to wrap her up in his desire. But her exhaustion had led her to sleep so heavily that she couldn't establish clearly in her muddled mind whether it was a dream or reality. It all seemed so real.

She ran her hands languidly down her naked body, thinking about Brad. Abruptly she sat up wide awake, realizing that she had slept in the nude as usual, but she couldn't quite remember undressing last night. Could it have been a dream, or had Brad actually come to bed with her?

She couldn't remember clearly just how the evening had ended. Deep inside she felt that maybe it wouldn't have been so bad if he had overcome her resistance and taken her to bed. But she had to know! If only she could recall precisely.

She reached for the phone and dialed the number that she had long ago memorized. Long ago. Only a week ago, Brad was still practically a stranger. Her father's friend. A friend of the family. Certainly not the man she loved above all others. Not then. Brad answered on the third ring, his voice tentative and raspy.

"Brad, this is Nan. Good morning." She wished she were as sure as she sounded.

"Hi. Is everything okay?" There was anticipation in his voice.

"I think so." She hesitated. It sounded so silly, not to remember what happened. She didn't want to hurt him if he had done anything. "I just have this little problem. I woke up naked this morning, and I don't remember undressing last night."

"Of course you didn't. You feel asleep in my arms. I put you to bed."

"Is there…anything else you might want to tell me?"

"Like what?" He sounded confused. "Oh, you mean did I…"

"Yes, anything I should know? Like *did* you?" She felt very foolish."

"As I recall, you made me promise not to take advantage of you yesterday." The tone of his voice was tentative, playful.

"And did you?" He's enjoying this too much, she thought.

"Well, maybe a little. When I took off your robe, my eyes got a little carried away. That's all. But I'm only human, you know. And you've got some fantastic looking body, lady."

She felt a mixture of relief and loss.

"Remind me to wake up before you go home next time." But there was a touch of light music in her voice. She wasn't really upset.

"I was hoping that next time I wouldn't have to go home."

"Don't push me, Brad. We made a lot of progress yesterday. Don't screw it up now."

"Yes, ma'am."

"I think I'll catch up on some of my agency work today. That is, if you don't have some pressing investigative work for us."

"I'm afraid not. I'll call Rafe and see how things are going. He should be at his office in a few minutes. I'll call you back when I find out."

"Okay. I'll be looking forward to your call."

"Fine. Talk to you later."

BRAD'S CALL to police headquarters came just as Rafe had arrived.

"My, Cowboy, but aren't you up early this morning. You're not back at your office, are you?"

"No, it's just the prompting of my dear colleague. She wants to know how your investigation is going."

"About like yours, I'm afraid. No new leads. No news on Bum or Windham. What do you plan next?

"I'll be meeting for dinner this evening with Thaddeus Ralston and Bess Bradshaw to discuss what they know about the work Dan, Ed and Luke were doing. Maybe they have something from the hearings that they don't realize is significant."

"Congressman Ralston is bad news. Tight as a clam when you want information and he can be a pompous ass to get along with otherwise. But Bess Bradshaw! That's really tough duty, but I guess someone has to do it." Rafe's sarcasm was obvious.

"I'll survive somehow. And I'll call you to let you know what I find."

"Sure, Brad. Have a nice day. And night."

Brad ignored Rafe's laughter as he hung up and dialed Nan's number again. She answered quickly.

"What? You didn't go back to bed?" he asked teasingly.

"No way! I'm up and dressed and ready. What did Rafe have to say?"

"No luck. Rafe has nothing new."

Nan could sense the dejection in his voice, and it was contagious. She suddenly wanted to be with him. Maybe tonight could be their night of celebration, the night she would be able to open herself up to him as they both wanted so much. After a pause to collect her thoughts, she made her appeal.

"Brad, I do have a dozen or so things to catch up on for my agency, but I do want to be with you later. These last two days have cleared up a lot of doubts for me. I trust you more than anyone I've been around for years. You've let me lean on you and talk to you, and now you're practically a part of me and my life. I want you to come over tonight and let me fix you a real dinner for two. I think I can make it worth your while. We need some intimate time together."

"Nan, I don't think you can know just how good that sounds. But I'm pursuing leads this evening. At seven I'm having dinner with Bess and Thaddeus at Renoir's in Georgetown. You know how tough it is to book time on his busy calendar. I could come over afterwards."

"Bess Bradshaw! Will she be wearing her black stockings and garter belt for you again? That'll give you a lot of hot leads!"

"Calm down, will you? It's not like that at all."

"Oh, yeah? Then why didn't you tell me about to-night? Why am I remembering her hot phone call so well?"

"Do you have to keep harping on that? I explained everything before. And I thought you understood."

"I thought so, too. I trusted you. I shared my inner-most feelings with you. And now you've betrayed me, running back to that alley cat! That really hurts deep. I wouldn't see you now for all the promises you could think of! I don't want to talk to you!"

She sounded on the verge of tears. This wasn't going right at all.

"You've got it all wrong. I've told you, you're the one I love. You're the one I chose to be with."

"I notice you didn't invite me to this cozy little din-ner party. Afraid I'd get in the way?"

"Well, frankly, yes. You've been so hostile about Bess that I didn't want to risk a confrontation that would cost us the very information we're trying to get. It looks like my instincts were right."

"Well, Cowboy, I hope you and your sex kitten have a fun night. And all of them from now on! I never want to see you or speak to you again."

Clunk!

Brad slammed his own phone down in frustration and spun out of the chair, kicking it in anger. The resulting pain caused him to sink back in the chair, rubbing his foot. It matched the pain he felt inside. He had really blown it with Nan, and now they were finished. A wave of grief washed over him, touching him with a pain of loss deep inside. He felt the tightening agony constrict his chest and cramp his stomach. Her last harsh words tormented him.

The droning, popping of helicopter blades slipped easily into his thoughts. As he slipped into dreaminess, his mind wandered from the pain of dealing with Nan back to another time, a better day.

It was hot in the jungle, and even his shorty rifle had grown heavy. But he felt the adrenaline high. There was danger out there, and he was threatened. But he could hit back. And he could handle the challenge, as though he were born to it. He was a man, and this he could do.

Brad was drawn from his perplexed thoughts by the persistent ringing of the phone. He slowly sat up and reached for the receiver. Then he realized. It could be Nan.

"Hello, Nan?"

"Hello? Brad, is that you?" A man's voice. "Brad, this is Thaddeus Ralston." Always formal, as if his thin, birdlike voice needed an introduction to someone who had been listening to it for twelve years.

"Good morning, Congressman. How are you?"

"Morning? Brad, you've got to get yourself together and get back to work! It's the middle of the afternoon!"

"Sorry, Thaddeus. I guess I got caught up in things and let the time get away from me."

"Well you're not going to find any killers that way. Hard work and persistence is what it takes." It was his best pedantic, patronizing tone. "How are you doing with that, anyhow?"

"That's what I wanted to talk to you about this evening. I was hoping you could tell me about your hearings. I thought maybe some aspect of the hearings might shed light on the deaths. Can you still make it?"

"Yes. I called to confirm that. And to answer your next question, Bess will be there, too, although somewhat late. How about meeting me at Renoir's about seven? We can have a few drinks while we're waiting for Bess."

"If Bess has a problem with being there tonight, there's no need to trouble her about it." Brad wasn't certain whether he wanted her there or not, despite the way Nan had reacted to it.

"Brad, I don't think there's a chance she'd miss it. She's out this afternoon buying a new dress and getting her hair done. I take it you two have made quite an impression on one another. It should be an interesting night—if you can keep up."

"I think I can handle it, Thaddeus. I'll see you at seven."

"Good. And for God's sake, bring some intelligent questions. Talking shop can be such a bore when handled sloppily."

"I'll try not to let you down."

Hanging up the phone, Brad began to put together the key questions he would present to Bess and Thaddeus. Remembering what Ed had said about plying Bess with warm wine to get answers, Brad thought for a moment about speaking to Bess privately after dinner. It would be so easy to do, for she was always willing to get together. But what else would it lead to, and would he be able to control it? Or did he really need to control it? What if they did play around a little? With the silly way Nan was acting, would that be so bad? Her cutting words still hurt him badly.

Nan was just being too obstinate in her jealousy. Brad would feel no guilt about using Bess to get information. And he was only human. If he had to get into Bess to get answers, why not? They weren't kids. Bess was a big girl, and she could handle herself. But he felt like a kid trying to sort out his fickle girl friends.

If only he could be sure that it was Bess's information and not her body he was after. She was sensual, voluptuous, voracious, and in some ways, sexier than Nan. And she was so available! It was pretty obvious now that he would get nowhere with Nan after tonight! This second break sounded permanent. And with her continued withdrawal from him, perhaps it should be.

WHEN BRAD arrived by taxi at the restaurant, he was told Congressman Ralston was already there. A pompous waiter led Brad across a brightly lit and sparsely peopled dining area to a darkened booth where a screen of large plants provided some privacy from the main area. The early diners paid him little attention as Brad made his way to the candlelit table where Ralston waited.

The decor of Renoir's was richly appointed in shades of burgundy, with plush chairs and rich tablecloths. Heavy velvet drapes and classic paintings adorned all the walls, but Brad's trained security eye told him by their

casual hanging and lack of any protection that the art-
works were copies.

Thaddeus Ralston slumped on the padded banquette
that curved around a dining table. Judging by the casual posture and the glazed look, the congressman had
arrived early and had been drinking steadily.

"Brad, my boy. Meet André, my favorite waiter. André, this gentleman would like a vodka martini, if I remember correctly."

"Right. On the rocks, with a twist. Thank you."

"Make that two, André. He has some catching up to
do."

"Of course, Congressman. And will Miss Bradshaw
be joining us tonight?"

"Yes, André. She'll be along later."

"Of course. We'll look forward to seeing her again tonight. Her presence always adds so much beauty, just as
you add prestige by honoring us with your visits."

"Thank you, André. Now just stand by for her grand
entry."

As the waiter strutted away, Brad marveled at the ex-
tensive orchestration of a simple dinner meeting. Bess
was simply window dressing for the politician. Ralston
wore her like jewelry, like an exquisite cufflink sparkling from his arm. She was his example of conspicuous
consumption, to be admired by others as a showy dem-
onstration of his good fortune and good taste. And perhaps frequently he did not take off this jewelry when he
went to bed. He wore her often and well.

Brad looked at Ralston with a mixture of scorn and
respect. This hawk could be a dangerous enemy or a

strong ally. Perhaps both at once. Ralston had learned his lessons well in Southeast Asia, and it made him a successful politician. But maybe the extra drinks in him now would loosen his tongue.

"Thaddeus, tell me about Yellow River."

"Well, you're right to the point. So you know about that, too."

"Enough to know that it might have led to the murder of three men I held in great esteem."

"You're probably right about that. Yellow River was the product of some desperate action officer's fertile imagination. It doesn't matter what the agency was. This is politically sensitive enough that they're all involved in one way or another. But no one was having much luck in getting to the roots of the rumors that Americans missing in action are still in Southeast Asia. Then someone realized that drugs coming into America from Southeast Asia had to have some organized movement to transport them."

"So naturally the agencies involved were willing to overlook the effect of the drug smuggling temporarily to gain access to information that was otherwise too difficult to ferret out."

"You seem to understand the methodology. But keep in mind that there was a great deal of political pressure, right down from the top. This effort was given top priority in order to find some MIAs quickly."

"So the old-timers in the ranks used their old contacts in Southeast Asia to find the present-day drug movers."

"Right again, Brad, my boy. And then they used the current drug runners to attempt to ascertain the whereabouts of the MIAs, if any."

"Were there any? I mean was all this in vain, and three good men died because they got involved?"

"I don't know. There were some new leads, but nothing of substance. I went over to check some leads out myself, but I didn't find anything. Of course, I could never admit that much publicly. It's too damned political, and I've gained too much advantage from it."

"So they died for nothing because they knew about it?"

"Your friends were more than bystanders. They knew the areas and the power players, and they were respected by friends and enemies there. Luke had researched the historical routes until he knew more than anyone about where to look for contacts. In fact, some observers have noted that he knew them so well that he might have used them himself when he was the chief military advisor. They were included so someone could keep an eye on them."

"You can't really believe that."

Ralston paused as André brought the drinks, then continued.

"Right now, I'm just repeating the rumors. Dan was active in the area very recently, and he too could have been involved in the traffic. After all, he was a powerful authority in that particular province some years ago, and he still has some good contacts in the Orient. Ed was pestering them, and me as well, I might add, for an exposé. It may have been his questioning that upset the apple cart."

"How is that?"

"I personally think he made someone too nervous about the past, and maybe the present. It was bad enough that all these agencies were digging into the muck, but to make it public in the newspapers could foul up someone's equilibrium. Enough to make them do something rash and violent."

"You mean like an ambitious Congressman?"

Ralston's hawklike face took on a sardonic smile.

"I will admit to being concerned about the possibilities of allegations that there were misdoings in my past. Those kinds of accusations are almost impossible to disprove or eliminate, once they're published. That can mean murder for a congressman."

"Is that a confession?"

"Brad, my boy, you're naive. I would not be sitting here with you if I had anything to do with those killings. In fact, you surely would have been the first one I would have eliminated."

He said it evenly and with a straight face. It sent a chill up Brad's spine, and put him on guard.

"And why is that, Thaddeus?"

"Because you're so dangerous. You're so damned naive and straight. You probably still haven't figured out that someone back in our Knives outfit was probably smuggling drugs, perhaps even on your helicopter."

"What? That's impossible!"

"You were too busy fighting the war to notice such things. While I'm sure you were ignorant of the fact, of course, most of us knew that Bum Shandy was smuggling gold regularly. In fact, Dan Donahue tried to put a stop to it through the Oriental sources, mostly to protect you. As the provincial commander, Lin had to know about it. But then, the amounts weren't significant, and we all thought it would keep Shandy out of worse trouble. Like smuggling larger amounts of drugs. I frankly think that he was smuggling drugs under our noses in spite of us."

"You wouldn't happen to have proof of that, would you?"

"No proof, but as much indication as three dead men had."

"What makes you so certain it was Bum?"

"If nothing else, by process of elimination. Lin was helping Dan track the drug routes. He would've hardly dug his own grave. George Windham was working with Luke, since he knows all the European drug routes through his State Department work. So he's out. Ed was working with Bum Shandy through some misdirected charitable motivation, and he probably confirmed Shandy's drug smuggling. Mallard knew Shandy was smuggling. He told me so himself."

"But what if it isn't Bum? What if it's a cover-up of some official operations, or someone trying to hide the past? Mallard didn't speak out on Bum back then, did he?"

"My dear boy, Denton Mallard is about to be named as an ambassador. Don't you think they would have looked deeply into his background before naming him?"

"Listen to what you're saying, Thaddeus. Wouldn't that be reason enough for murder if he had something to hide? He wants that ambassadorial appointment."

"I hardly think he would risk even more for murder. He doesn't seem the type. He was always shut out over there, too much of a loner. And smuggling requires help from others.

"But any one of several others could be smuggling today."

"Yes, Dan was traveling all over the world, just as Windham is, and Shandy has underworld contacts that make him the best suspect."

"And you, Congressman, have been back to Southeast Asia twice, and Lin is being very cooperative with your hearings."

"Which only shows that all this is getting us to no certain conclusion. Drink your drinks, Cowboy. We're getting nowhere."

"You mean just like your hearings?"

"Brad, you must learn to deal with political realities, with power and compromise. Knowledge is power, and revelation is compromise. And after all, we must not let our friends die in vain."

"Thaddeus, sometimes you make me sick. And I thought I was coming here to resolve something on the killings."

"Well, have you turned up anything of substance? You've certainly bothered everyone in our old bunch about it, haven't you?"

"We've got some leads, but nothing solid yet. Nothing ties together right. But I haven't talked to George Windham. That bothers me."

"Ahh, George Windham is a wimp. He's always chasing that Oriental mistress of his around the world somewhere. If Windham had the intestinal fortitude to kill anyone, his wife would be his first victim."

Brad could see that the drinks were having a pronounced effect on the congressman. His eyelids seemed to droop, and his words were becoming slurred.

"What do you know about his mistress?"

"She's the same *telak*, or lover, he had back in Southeast Asia. You saw her there. A lovely young thing. High, firm tits, a tight ass, luscious lips, and a mouth that could suck-start a Harley-Davidson. And she was always all over George like a mink in heat. Must have been all that passionate French colonial heritage. Her mother was a lovely lady of Paris, with Chinese and Lao lineage mixed into her French blood. She probably gave her daughter many of her attributes."

"You seem to have known her well."

"I knew the entire family before George got involved. Seems to me the girl tried to shoot Mallard one time."

"Wrong, Thaddeus. She tried to cut Mallard. You were the one she shot. Your war wound, remember?"

"Ah, yes. You do enjoy reminding me of that."

"What was that all about?"

"Oh, George caught me reminiscing about old times— with my hands up her dress. I laughed at his complaint, and he backed off. Then I said I was going to tell her father his little girl was screwing George's brains out.

That's when she shot me. But her aim was off, and the slug only grazed my thigh.''

"How old was she then?''

"Sixteen, I think. And incredibly beautiful for that age. A flower of the Orient, with the temper of a dragoness.''

That description again. Where had he heard it before?

"And George is still with her today?''

"Yes, he is. I'm sure he'd like to spend more time with her. He's just too timid to leave that horse-faced wife who provides his money and prestige. If he wants someone else, he should just leave his wife.''

"What about Cassia Ralston? Is the rule different for a congressman's wife?''

"Don't get so personal, Cowboy. But since you mentioned my dear Cassia, I'll say that she had excellent breeding, and she likes the visibility, the security, and the good life I provide. Cassia puts up with my whims and my ramblings because she knows she must do it to survive as she wishes to live. But dear Cassia and I have had no sex life for years, so it pays to have a full-bodied, lusty woman at hand.''

"And that's where Bess comes in?''

"Ah, dear Bess. She was wronged by a senate staffer right after she got to D.C. Been paying men back for it ever since. Especially me. It was a long time before I got into her pants again. In fact it was after I got elected and hired her as an assistant.''

"You did that, and she works for you?''

"Oh, she's a bit unruly at times. Likes to shop around and keep me guessing. But she's the best administrative assistant in town. She's a natural flirt, and she gets the job done for me on Capitol Hill. And when she needs her belly rubbed, she provides a necessary outlet for my sexual needs."

"And what about her needs?"

"Don't be taken in by those large, limpid eyes. She's a first-class tease. But she's no bimbo. She doesn't put out freely, or sleep around. Bess is poised, intelligent, gorgeous and practically untouchable. But she's also a power-hungry, scheming shrew who will tease you into a heated frenzy and then drop you coolly, just for the pure excitement of it. Ah, and speaking of the devil, here she is now."

Brad turned to look across the room, where he saw that Bess was indeed making her grand entry. She was parading a good six paces behind André, as he slowly made his way to their table. All eyes in Renoir's were on Bess.

She was wearing a flowing white dress that draped loosely across her tanned shoulders to caress each firm breast, clinging down to a slightly rounded belly and stretching tightly across shapely hips and buttocks, before falling gracefully to slender ankles. The effect was dazzling, and the feelings of envy and desire she created swept across the room like the bow wave of a beautiful ship.

At each step, her long slender legs kicked open the front of the dress in a taunting manner, showing her tan up to her thighs. A small golden purse in her graceful hand became a scepter as she lavished her glamorous princess smile on diners she knew, nodding right and left casually, with eyes sparkling brightly. Each new turn caused a shift in the soft fabric, revealing a new glimpse of a golden pendant bouncing in her ample cleavage. The lines of the dress left no doubt that she was naked beneath it.

"Now isn't that a dream walking?" Ralston asked softly as she approached the table.

Brad noticed that the congressman had sobered considerably at the sight of Bess. Ralston greeted her regally, then leaned very courteously over her hand and kissed it profusely, all in sight of the staring spectators in the main room. Then he drew her out of sight to the booth, where she brushed his cheek with her lips and made her way to Brad.

"You look like you need to sit down, Cowboy," she cooed, pressing down on his shoulders, and giving him the full benefit of that lovely goddess smile at close range.

She was spectacular. He felt still stunned by the entrance, and found himself sitting again in the booth. She leaned over to kiss him fully on the mouth, and her fragrance made him dizzy. Her wet kiss lingered while she waggled her rear at Ralston behind her. As she straightened, Brad saw that the pendant was a golden cheetah, jealously guarding the full breasts that peeked teasingly from the soft material. Then she abruptly crossed to Ralston's side of the table to slide into the booth and move around next to Brad. The contact of their knees beneath the table was like an electric shock.

"Bring the lady her usual drink, André, and then our meal. Then we would like some privacy."

"Of course, Congressman. I shall personally see to it."

"Well, Brad, looks like we're finally going to share that meal," Bess purred at him. "But I do wish you would relax and enjoy it more." Beneath the table, her leg rubbed against his, demanding attention.

"I guess I'm still taken back by that entrance. That was quite impressive. Dazzling, in fact."

She threw back her head and laughed heartily, showing her slender neck, and drawing the pendant from its lair.

"I love to do that," she said loudly, and then she leaned closely, her voice in a whisper only for him. "But the dress is just for you, Brad. And tonight, everything in it. Just for you."

Brad felt his head spinning at her words and the fragrance of her perfume. He saw Ralston leaning closer to hear.

"And now what are you two conspirators whispering about?"

"I was just about to ask you two gentlemen the same thing, but I can't seem to get Brad to talk. In fact, even to breathe." Her chuckle was low and guttural.

"Oh, I think he'll get over it, Bess. He just hasn't become accustomed to the rich living you enjoy. He'll come around just as soon as he see that you're real flesh and blood."

"Well, any time you want to pinch or feel to make sure I'm real, just help yourself, Cowboy."

Again the low chuckle, as her hand reached for his thigh beneath the table. This time Brad joined in the laughter, as his hand caught hers in his grasp before she moved too high.

"As a matter of fact, we were discussing the investigation that Brad and the young Donahue woman are pursuing. It seems that they aren't making the anticipated progress, and they would like to hear what we might have uncovered. Brad doesn't think the culprit is Bum Shandy."

"I agree," Bess said heartily, squeezing with her hand. "I think you know Shandy better than anyone, Brad. If you think he's innocent, I'll go along with that." The hand was moving, seeking again.

"Ah, my dear Bess, how can you be such an airhead?"

"Hold on, Thaddeus. You still haven't come up with anything but speculation. You have no proof," Brad put in.

"I guess you must cling to your past loyalties, Cowboy. But you'll have to change that if you intend to pursue the smuggling angle."

"You mean the smuggling routes from Mexico?" Bess asked with arching eyebrows.

"From Mexico?" Brad interjected. "Tell me more about that."

"Really, Bess. I wish you wouldn't be so free with such sensitive information. You really must learn to control those impulses." The congressman was peevish.

"Well if we're here to help Brad, why shouldn't he know? It came out at the hearings."

"You're stiff-arming me, Thaddeus. What's this all about?"

"Oh, all right. As a result of the hearings and other inquiries, we learned that Luke was tracking a current cocaine smuggling operation from Mexico. It apparently had its roots in an earlier heroin smuggling activity that originated in Xiang Province years ago. It is apparently quite active and profitable, and was somehow connected to a former Knife. We weren't able to determine who it as before Luke's demise."

"And you were holding this back? You bastard!"

"Give him hell, Cowboy." Her hand was creeping up his thigh again, making concentration difficult.

"As I said, knowledge is power, and revelation is compromise. I don't often compromise cheaply."

"Don't you see, Thaddeus? Since you know so much about it, you could become a prime target!"

"Oh, Brad, do you think so? Are we all in danger?" Turning to Ralston, she asked, "Is that why you didn't tell him?"

"Now, now, Bess. Don't take on so. I didn't mention it because I didn't want him meddling in our material. Besides, that's all we learned about it, and that much won't get you far. Ah, here's our meal. I took the liberty of ordering for us."

André poured the wine and served the rich French meal quickly. As they ate, Brad dissected the new information as Bess and Ralston began a discussion of congressional bills, political power plays, and prominent figures in the current scandals on Capitol Hill. Brad found his thoughts drifting to Nan, wanting to tell her the news. He was jerked from his deep thoughts painfully as Bess brought her high spike heel down sharply on his foot, covertly demanding his attention even while she was talking in earnest to Ralston.

He smiled at her, and reached under the table to pinch her bare thigh in return. She jumped, but didn't miss a beat in her discussion. From her purse, she brought out a folded newspaper clipping. She opened it to show Brad.

"See what the paper said about the funeral? We're in both photos."

As she passed the article to Brad, it slipped from her hand and fell to the floor under the table. As they both leaned down to get the paper, her loose neckline fell open. Her shapely breasts were swaying slightly as she moved. Her face was so near he could feel her warm breath. Her full lips were pursed, slightly opened. She was too close, too provocative. He became intoxicated by her fragrance, the sight of her breasts, and her smile.

"Do you see it, Cowboy? Can you reach it?" she asked too loudly. Then softer, "Just help yourself to what you see."

Brad retrieved the clipping and straightened quickly. He didn't like feeling so uncomfortable about a woman, as though she were using him for some unknown purpose. He saw that her nipples were even more evident through the soft fabric when she sat up straight. She licked her lips lustily and smiled warmly at him.

He felt his head spinning again, with the wine and the rich food and Bess. Ralston's words were fading in and out as he droned on about his life. Bess was squirming sensually on the seat of the booth as André appeared.

"I'm sorry to intrude, Congressman, but you have a telephone call from Senator Brampton's office. He said it's quite urgent."

"Thank you, André. Well, if you two can excuse me for a moment, the business of running the country calls." Ralston rose and made his way unsteadily toward the phone.

"Ahh, alone at last," Bess crooned, leaning to Brad and running her hands inside his unbuttoned coat. The front of her dress fell open again, exposing the tops of those lovely white breasts. Her scent floated out to him.

She shifted her rear closer to Brad and kissed him lightly behind the ear. She giggled at his discomfort, making the shimmering curls dangling in front of her ears bounce teasingly against his face. Somehow she had unbuttoned his shirt now, and was running one hand through the mat of hair on his chest. The other hand ran caressingly up his neck to tickle his ear.

Brad's mind kept going back to Nan's apartment, and the intimacies she shared with him there. It was good with her. This didn't feel right.

"Why is it that Thaddeus so conveniently leaves us alone like this so often? You wouldn't have anything to do with that, would you?"

"This time, I definitely did," she admitted. "It cost me a date with someone I despise, but it was worth it. Thaddeus is about to be called away for the night, leaving us to spend the rest of it together."

''That's funny. I don't remember that being discussed in the arrangements.''

She raised her fingers to his lips, silencing him.

''Oh, Brad. You can't refuse me tonight. You've got me all turned on and ready. Here, give me your hand under the table.''

''Bess,'' Brad held his hand away, trying to avoid the touch of commitment that he knew he could not reject. He looked up to see her eyes melting him, her nostrils flared in hot passion just inches from his. ''Bess, not now.''

''Not every man is lucky enough to have a hungry woman to adore him and indulge his every whim and fantasy. But I'm here and I'm ready for whatever you want of me.''

''Slow down, Bess. You'll overheat.''

''It could take you all night to calm me down, Cowboy.''

''Don't count on it.''

''You're a bigger flirt and tease than I am,'' she whispered hoarsely as Ralston returned to the table.

She formed her lips into a smile—and Brad tried to return her easy, affectionate, teasing manner, but it was no use. Looking away, he closed his eyes and wished he really were what she wanted him to be. But inside his eyelids he saw only Nan's face. And he felt a hopeless need to be with Nan now.

Ralston was smiling triumphantly from his telephone conquest.

''I hope you don't mind if we skip dessert. I have an urgent mini-caucus to attend that might take all night.

I'll have my car drop you off, Bess, and then run you home, Brad. Sorry if things didn't turn out like you wanted them."

Bess laughed out loud at the words, but Brad merely mumbled, "I understand, Thaddeus. I may not agree with you, but I do understand you."

Ralston paid the bill and led the way out of the restaurant, with Bess following close behind. Brad followed quietly in his confusion and uncertainty. Again, every eye in the restaurant was on Bess. She was an intimidating woman, and she made him feel trapped and used.

They went out the door of Renoir's in the same order, with Ralston calling and waving above the passing people for his car up the street. It was a warm night, one to enjoy. But Brad stepped outside with reservations about what it would lead to.

He suddenly felt the hair go up on the back of his neck, and he knew something was wrong. Over Bess's loud, chatty voice, he heard the soft rasping slide and chunk of metal on metal. The brick Georgetown sidewalk became a jungle trail in broad daylight as his training and instincts spoke: closed-bolt automatic weapon, above left and out of place in this environment.

He felt a surge of adrenaline warming him, getting him ready.

"Thad—" He saw Ralston's head turn to the left, his eyes looking upward, across the street. Ralston's body was tensed.

"Sniper!" Ralston barked, almost simultaneously with Brad's warning.

Though they each moved quickly, time seemed to stand still. Brad's hands were on Bess's shoulders pulling her back as a soft sputter whispered and the twanging whine of ricocheting bullets split the night. Ralston stumbled forward as Brad pulled Bess down beside him on the sidewalk.

Silencer! Still firing! The sputter led another noisy splattering of lead against the pavement and building as another burst of slugs was fired.

"Thad!" Bess screamed, as she jerked away from Brad and ran toward Ralston.

Another burst caught her in mid-stride, and Brad saw bright red flowers growing on the white dress at her shoulder and side. He leaped to a crouch and moved to catch her just before she hit the pavement.

Bystanders were crouching or lying on the ground, screaming and yelling, and cars were screeching to a halt in the street to avoid the running pedestrians. But no one else was hurt.

Suddenly it was very quiet. It was over, just like that. Brad was holding Bess in his arms, pressing a handkerchief against the blood on her shoulder. She seemed unconscious. Ralston appeared at his side.

"He's apparently gone. Stay with her. I'll get the police and an ambulance," the congressman mumbled, rubbing his knee where his trousers were torn. He handed Brad his handkerchief as he hurried away.

Brad saw that Ralston's face was even more drawn than usual. They were both shaken.

Bess stirred and opened her eyes to Brad as Ralston left. She moaned and twisted her shoulders, then cried out sharply.

"Easy, Bess. Just be still. We're getting help."

"That was a dumb thing for me to do. It hurts like hell, Brad. But I thought he was hurt. You saved my life, didn't you? Does that mean you own me and have to take care of my needs for the rest of my life?"

"Just hush. I don't think these are too bad, but you've got a couple of holes in you."

"About time you noticed." She tried to laugh, and cried out again. "It hurts, Brad. Don't leave me."

"You'll be all right. It's just the shock. You've lost some blood. Let me put you down and get your feet up."

"Don't let go of me. Hold me. I need you more than ever now."

"Be quiet, Bess," he whispered softly in her ear, dabbing at her side with Ralston's now-bloodied handkerchief. "I'll hold you. Just relax as much as you can." He carefully covered her bare thighs with the folds of her blood-splattered dress.

As he held her cautiously, Brad felt his adrenaline cutting back. For a moment, it had been as good as combat again, and his mind and body had responded with joy again. An unseen enemy had threatened him. But he had no gun to fight back with. And the trouble with combat always was that people got hurt. He wondered who had set them up and had hurt this pretty lady.

RAFE MET THEM at the hospital. After questioning Bess briefly, he met with Ralston and Brad in the waiting room.

"Relax, guys. The doctor says the wounds are superficial. They may leave a couple of interesting scars to go with her war stories, but she's a strong woman, and she'll be okay."

"I'm certain that you mean well, sergeant, but someone very important to me is in there hurting, and we don't have even the slightest idea who did it or why. Now when are you going to get to the heart of the matter and determine just who this maniac killer is?" The congressman was tense and troubled, and it showed plainly.

"I was hoping you two could help me with that. The firing patterns looked like an automatic weapon. How was it that he missed at that range if he was trying to kill you?"

"Rafe, we heard him first. That is, I heard him cock his weapon. Sounded like a closed-bolt automatic with a silencer. I yelled at Thaddeus and grabbed Bess just as he fired."

"Yes, I presume we both heard the bolt. I looked to the left, across the street and above us. I thought I saw a muzzle flash at the roof line, but he was obviously using a flash guard with the silencer, and I couldn't be certain. I'm afraid I sought cover rather quickly after that and didn't look up until it was over."

"Bess jumped up to run to Thaddeus. She thought he was hit. The next burst caught her halfway there. I jumped up and grabbed her, and got her behind the cars again. That's all there was to it."

"Didn't see the gunman, huh?"

They each shook their heads.

"I don't suppose you might have determined the whereabouts of Bum Shandy, have you?"

"Now hold on, Thaddeus. There you go again, leaping to conclusions without proof of any kind."

"Take it easy, Brad. We're looking at all suspects in this, including hired guns. Any Knife but you two is suspect. I only rule you out because I know how each of you feels about Miss Bradshaw, and I know neither of you would endanger her."

"Well, I must say I'm pleased to see you move out so quickly and seriously on this, Sergeant Johnson. And thank you for the extra guard at the door to her hospital room. Please do keep up the fine work."

"Well, it's not every evening that we get an assassination attempt on a U.S. congressman. We have to take advantage of the opportunity, you see."

A doctor approached quietly and, smiling, took the arm of the congressman.

"She's ready to see you now. She has a little pain, but she's in good spirits. She says she wants to talk to you first, Congressman Ralston."

"Of course. Excuse me, gentlemen."

"Of course," Rafe said precisely as Ralston departed.

"Easy, Rafe. He's under a strain."

"Aren't we all! Well, I guess this screwed up a great night for you, Cowboy. That is, unless you can talk the nurse into letting you share that private room with the patient."

"Lay off, Rafe. I was having enough trouble keeping things straight before this little one-sided firefight came up. I know this sounds crazy, but I keep thinking how glad I am that it wasn't Nan with me."

"I know what you mean, man. I thought the same thing, don't you know?"

"For God's sake, don't tell anyone I said that. I mean, Bess is a helluva woman. But she's not Nan."

"Then why was she with you instead of Nancy? You and Nancy having a little misunderstanding?"

"You are a good detective, aren't you? We had some harsh words over my going out with Bess and Thaddeus."

"Maybe it's a good thing she wasn't there. Someone set you up, Brad."

"Yes, but who? How?"

"Might have followed you. You come from Nancy's?"

"No, not today."

"Good. You might want to stay away tonight. Want me to run a patrol car through the neighborhood? Put an extra set of eyes there?"

"I'd appreciate it, Rafe. Tomorrow, I'll try to get Nan out of town for the day to keep her safe while you check things out. That is, if she'll speak to me again."

"Let me know if I can put in a good word, Cowboy. I'm a good friend of the family."

"Thanks, buddy. See ya later. I want to check with Bess before I leave."

WHEN BRAD was finally allowed past the policeman posted at the door to Bess's room, he found her arranging her reddish hair on the lumpy pillow. She looked pale but beautiful in the loose hospital gown. A nurse was leaving the room as he entered.

"Mr. Gaelman? She's been asking for you. But don't pay too much attention to anything she says. I think she's a little woozy from the sedatives. She's talking weird." The nurse wore a puzzled look on her face as she went out the door.

"Bess? You still awake?"

She opened her eyes and sat up with a grimace.

"Brad Gaelman, get your ass in here. How long are you gonna keep me waiting? You may be a hunk, but I can get over even you if I try hard." Her tone was tough, but her smile said she was glad to see him.

"I came in as soon as they would let me. You're getting a lot of attention. Must be a lot of horny doctors and nurses around here. Does it hurt much?"

"Naw, they gave me some local anesthetic. Get up here in the bed with me and I'll show you."

"Bess, you're a bawdy broad. Impossible. Incorrigible. Unbelievable."

"But you love me anyhow, right? I could tell by the way you grabbed me out there. I don't remember all of it, but I know you saved my life. Here, I want you to have this." She handed him the golden cheetah pendant.

"Bess, I couldn't...."

"Didn't your mama ever tell you not to argue with a sick woman? Now take it. You did so much for me. I need to give you something."

"Thanks, Bess."

"Don't mention it! You deserve a medal. Lord, I never knew there were so many unique ways to end an evening until I met you." Her soft laugh was cut short as she yawned widely. "God, I'm getting sleepy. Come kiss me, quick."

He took her gently in his arms and kissed her warmly.

"You really love him, don't you? That's why you ran over to him." Brad spoke softly, his lips near her ear.

"Thad? Yeah, I guess so. Didn't know it myself, I guess. Till now. Like you love that Donahue woman. I can tell by the way she looks at you."

"Now how do you know how she looks at me?"

"Because that's the way I'd look at you if you loved me." Another yawn.

Her logic escaped him, but he heard through her sedated haze that she knew he loved Nan, and not her.

"Get some sleep, pretty lady. I'll check with you later."

But she didn't hear him. She was asleep.

BRAD FELT EXHAUSTED when he got home. His neck was sore from looking over his shoulders. His whole body ached from tension. If it weren't for his pressing need to call Nan, he would gladly have fallen into his bed fully dressed. But he had to try to re-establish that lost, fragile relationship. Above all, he had to know that she was safe for tonight. Safe from an assassin who shot women.

For some reason, that thought triggered memories of the last evacuation from Lawn Chin. The girl in black pajamas was aiming down the barrel of an AK-47 assault rifle, and he was begging Bum Shandy to shoot her. And Bum did, ripping her slender body to shreds with the mini-gun of the helicopter.

As he sat by the phone, he realized that he had forgotten to turn on his recorder before leaving. Cursing himself again for his carelessness, he reached for the phone as it rang.

"Cowboy, listen quick. I don't want this call traced. I was following the wrong one. I heard about the hit on the radio. It was like that recon team ambush on the plateau when you were shot down. I would've warned you all if I had known it was goin' down tonight. But he's another one. Now I'm movin' in right on this bastard's six. It's about coke, Cowboy. Mex stuff. I'll have the proof this time tomorrow, and the judge will have to listen. Be talkin' to ya."

"Bum! Wait!"

But the line had gone dead.

Bum Shandy was running scared. His voice had reeked with the tenseness of someone pursued and pursuing. From the sound of the phone connection, it could have been a long-distance call. He was trying to keep the communication line open, just as he had when he was a gunner talking the pilot onto a target. Brad recognized the tone and pattern of the voice. Bum wasn't the gunman on the roof. And he was closing in on the killer.

The phone rang again, startling Brad from his thoughts.

"Mr. Brad Gaelman, please." A woman's voice with a British accent.

"This is Brad Gaelman."

"One moment, please."

Brad waited impatiently. It sounded like an overseas call, with all the noise in the background. Then the line cleared.

"Brad, this is George Windham. Are you there, Brad?"

Brad heard a raspy, strained voice. It was Windham, and he sounded upset, disturbed. And maybe a little drunk.

"George, where are you?"

"Brad, he killed her. I heard it. I saw it. Just like Dan."

"No, George. Bess was only wounded. She's at the hospital. I just left her a little while ago. They say she'll be all right.

"Brad, tell Rafe Johnson I'll be back Tuesday. We're going to find the bastard who killed her, and I'll finish him myself." The words were so slurred Brad had difficulty making them out.

"George?" The line was dead.

Windham's words haunted Brad. "Just like Dan," he had said. Was Nan all right?

Despite the numerous times he had called her, he had trouble dialing her number now. He got it right on the third try. She answered on the first ring.

"Brad? Is it you?"

"Yes, Nan. It's me. Please don't hang up."

"Oh, Brad! Are you okay? I heard it on the radio. They said Bess Bradshaw was shot. I've been calling for the last two hours. First there was no answer, then the line was busy. Brad, tell me you're all right." She felt the panic that was evident in her voice.

"Nan, I'm okay. Relax, lady. Take it easy."

"Oh, Brad. I was so scared. I treated you so badly, and I was so afraid you wouldn't come back. Then I heard it on the radio. They didn't mention you, but I knew you were there."

"Yes, I was there. And I'm glad you weren't."

"Brad, please come be with me now. I need you so much."

His mind reeled back to Rafe's words at the hospital. He could've been followed to Renoir's. Someone could follow him to Nan's. He could lead a killer to her, someone he could miss seeing in the dark. He had to keep her safe.

"Nan, as much as I'd like to, I don't think that's a good idea. Not tonight." He had to be careful not to frighten her even more.

"Please don't be angry with me. I'm so sorry I hurt you. I didn't mean to. I love you, Brad. I . . . I'll deliver you a full apology in person tonight if you'll come over." She felt fear creeping over her. Fear of rejection and fear of the unknown.

"Look, I'm not mad at you, Nan. I didn't act very smart this morning myself, so I have no room to criticize you. It's just that it's oh-dark-thirty in the morning now, and it's been a long, tough day, and I'm exhausted." He didn't want to worry her with the danger. "I love you, too. But tonight's not the time for us to get together."

"I'll come over there."

"Nan, no. You don't understand. I need you and I want to be with you, but not tonight. Please."

"I'm so scared. Please take me away from all this."

"Is Gerald at the door? Is Sue home?"

"Yes. I saw them both tonight. But it's you I need to be with."

"Okay, listen. There's a beautiful waterfall in the Blue Ridge Mountains, just a couple of hours from here. It's near Matthews Arm, just below Skyline Drive. Do you know about it?"

"No, but it sounds wonderful."

"Why don't I pick you up about six in the morning? We'll drive up there for the day, and get away from all this for some quiet time together. I think you'll like it. It's really beautiful up there."

"Oh, Brad, you're wonderful. It sounds delightful, and just what we need to get us together like we should be." She felt no doubts or reservations holding her back.

"That's just what I want. Time for us to be together and alone. I want to share that place with you . . . make it our special place for all time."

"Yes, Brad, yes. Anywhere with you will be special."

"Get some sleep, now. And bring a sweater in the morning. It'll be chilly. And wear some sensible shoes. I'll take care of everything else."

"Those are just the words I want to hear. Take me. Take care of me. I love you, so much, my darling Cowboy."

"Good night, my lady."

Nan kissed the receiver before hanging up, then lay back on her bed, stretching her awakened body in sheer pleasure. How could he expect her to sleep after that. Six o'clock was only a few hours away, and she was so excited now that she would never get calmed down enough for sleep.

Brad hung up his phone amid feelings of relief for her safety and overwhelming joy over their coming together again. Tomorrow at Matthews Arm, he would show her just how much she had come to mean to him. She would know that she never needed to be jealous again.

His weary mind tried to pull together the decisions he had finalized during the last twenty-four hours. Thoughts of Nan weaved together with the words of Bum's call, and Windham's. The resultant chaos led Brad into a deep sleep of exhaustion that allowed no dreams.

10

BRAD CHECKED HIS WATCH again to see that it was already a few minutes after six. He thought to himself: *extra care takes extra time*. And this was a time for extra care.

The Georgetown streets were quiet at this early hour of the morning. Brad was nevertheless still very watchful. He even made several diversionary turns en route to assure that he was not being followed. When he was satisfied that no one was tailing him, he parked on the street in front of Nan's building.

Gerald was not standing at the door when Brad got out of his car but appeared as Brad approached the building.

"Good morning, Mr. Gaelman. Kind of early to be out, isn't it?"

Brad noted that the big man's eyes were not on him, but systematically scanning the street and the buildings across the way.

"Good morning, Gerald. Not too early when I have a date with a lovely lady. You and Sue may be glad to know that we're leaving town for the day. Should be back late this afternoon."

"Before dark, I hope."

Realizing that his comment was out of place, Gerald dropped his face and his hand raised to cover his mouth.

"We're not trying to make problems. We should be back before dark. Was that Victor I saw in a car up the street?"

"You're a very observant man, Mr. Gaelman."

"Anyone that big is hard to hide. Have a nice day, Gerald."

"Thanks, Mr. Gaelman. You, too."

As he stepped out of the elevator upstairs, Brad thought he saw a slight movement of the door to Sue Snyder's apartment. He heard the door latch click slightly, and knew she had checked to see who was using the elevator. The building security was still intact.

As he walked the few steps to Nan's door, he recalled that Sue had agreed to talk with him about Dan. Somehow that seemed a long time ago. Now was not the time to get into it.

The door opened on the second knock, and Nan stood there in a bright red V-neck pullover.

"You're late again, Gaelman," her lips curving into a grin.

"Was I supposed to hurry just to be on time?" His smile was matching hers.

"Damned right you were!" she said exuberantly, throwing her arms around his neck and seeking his mouth with hungry lips.

Brad took it all in. Her searching full lips, the softness of her breasts against his chest, her hands at the back of his neck, and her pelvis pressing firmly against him. And the spicy scent of the perfume he had given her. He kicked the door shut behind him, and returned her onslaught in full.

Nan had been waiting by the door long enough that her whole body was humming in anticipation of his arrival. She delivered herself to him enthusiastically, without reserve. They were together again, and she wanted to keep them that way.

When they broke apart gasping for breath, their eyes met, and their smiles reached deep within them.

"We'd better go, before this gets totally out of hand."

"Hey, Mr. Gaelman. I expect your hands to keep up today."

"They'll do their best, ma'am," he said, leading her toward the door with an encircling arm. His hand came to rest on her rear, and she pulled away to tie up her flowing hair with a rolled scarf.

"You can be very distracting. You know that, Cowboy?"

"I was about to say the same about you. Let's get out of here before we change our minds."

"I want to see that waterfall," she said with determination. After staying awake thinking about it all night, it had come to represent a personal spilling-over from a barrier that had held back her passion too long.

Nan's sleepiness caught up with her during the drive, and she snuggled against the door and closed her eyes, yielding to her drowsiness. She wished the bucket seats and console of the sports car didn't keep them so separated, or her head would be in Brad's lap now. She drifted into restful sleep, assured by his presence, and the comforting feel of his hand on her thigh.

Brad had tried to hide his frequent checks for cars following them. He wanted her to feel relaxed, comfortable and safe with him. This was a time he had sought for much longer than he had known he was in love with this woman. This new, easy feeling of being together and a part of each other was something he had needed for most of his life.

The cars behind them had been there too long for comfort. He was approaching the fork in the road that separated the route to the upper end of Skyline Trail from the route that entered the trail further down at Thornton Gap. He waited until the last moment, then swerved to the turnoff to Thornton Gap. This would not be the expected route. None of the cars behind them followed him.

He looked over at Nan to see if the sudden movement had awakened her, and he found she had been watching him with a soft, lovely smile on her face.

"You can put your hand back now. I miss it already."

He smiled and slid his hand back to the softness of her thigh.

"Have a good nap?"

She sat up and put her hand on his shoulder.

"Yes, thank you. Probably better than I've slept in a week. Eight nights, to be precise."

"I know what you mean. Bad dreams?"

She snuggled against his shoulder. "Not this morning. I like your sweater. You fill it out so well." Feeling the fabric, she asked, "Would you let me wear it sometime?"

"No. You'd stretch it," he said with a grin.

She punched his arm, straightened her own sweater, and curled up against her door again.

"Wake me up when we get to the mountains. And don't move your hand unless you have to."

"Yes ma'am," he responded, smiling in the comfort of her presence, and the relief that there was no car in the rearview mirror.

BRAD AWAKENED NAN as they began the twisting drive that climbed the mountain above Sperryville. She stretched and yawned, and he had difficulty trading his eyes from the curves in the highway to the equally challenging curves in her sweater. She luxuriated in the warmth of his glances, and returned the gesture by leaning to kiss his ear on a hairpin turn.

"Nan, I think we'd both be safer if you buckled into that seat belt," he murmured with a smile.

"Yessir," she returned softly as she buckled up. "I can wait a little longer."

Until the waterfall, she thought. She pictured a torrent of water leaping over a rocky ledge to fall wherever nature took it. What a beautiful symbol of her total passion for him.

They entered the Skyline Drive at Thornton Gap and proceeded northward toward Matthews Arm. Nan was enthralled by the beauty of the trees and the views from the highway. Like a small child, she insisted on stopping at each turnout, even if they stayed in the car to look. It warmed Brad to know that she could get so excited about an area he had long ago come to love.

At Pass Mountain Overlook, he showed her the town of Luray between the Massanutten Mountain and the mouth of Kemp Hollow, and she made him promise to take her through the Luray Caverns there some day. Despite his explanation that trees now obscured the view at Beahms Gap, she insisted on stopping to look. After checking the panorama at Thornton Hollow Overlook, they stopped at Jeremys Run Overlook, where she insisted upon getting out of the car. Brad welcomed the chance to check once more for anyone showing an interest in them.

The spring morning was still chilly at this altitude. Brad drew her close for warmth as they walked arm-in-arm to the low wall at the edge of the parking area. He pointed out the various peaks and valleys that made up the marvelous landscape before them.

Brad looked to Nan's face and caught her watching him with a smile that overflowed with love.

"I love to hear you talk about things that move and stir you," she said, cuddling against him.

"Wait till I get you where I can start talking about you."

"You can't know how much I'm looking forward to that."

"Then why don't we go? We've got some walking ahead of us."

"I'm ready, Cowboy. God, am I ready!"

They returned quickly to the car and drove on up the highway to the Matthews Arm parking area. Leaving the car, Brad took a small trail pack from the trunk and slipped it across his shoulder.

"Munchies," he responded to her quizzical look. "Where did you get those boots? They're the same style as mine."

"Dad picked them out for me years ago. I've broken them in on hikes now and then, but they haven't had a chance to get worn much. I had left them at Dad's apartment."

"Well, they'll get a workout today. We'll walk down a fire trail for a little over a mile before we get to Overall Run Trail. It's up and down and rocky then, so you'll have to watch your step." After one last look confirmed that no one was watching them, he said, "Let's go."

THE WAY THROUGH the campground to the fire road was wide and easy, so she walked beside him, holding his hand, and chatting about the trees, small animals and campers. Her long, slender legs easily allowed her to match Brad's pace. When they reached the downhill slope of the rocky fire road, it was easier for her to fall in a few steps behind him as they picked the best footing and easiest going.

He kept a watch over his shoulder to assure that he didn't get too far ahead in the easy downhill walk. The descent was steady and winding, with a wall of leafy foliage obscuring distant views of the tree-smothered mountainside.

"Hey, Mr. Trail Guide. I thought you said we were going to have a workout. This is a stroll."

"Keep in mind that we have to return up this slope, so save some energy. If we're quiet enough, we won't scare away all the wildlife."

There was something peaceful about losing themselves in the harmony of nature among the trees. He pointed out various birds and small game that moved about them in the stillness. Then, freezing on the trail at a movement nearby, he quietly motioned for Nan to stop. A few yards ahead of them, two deer majestically walked across the trail and disappeared into the brush.

"Oh, Brad," she whispered. "This is so wonderful. It's so beautiful."

As she caught up to him, his arms encircled her. His mouth found hers and he kissed her with passion. When their lips parted, she giggled throatily, and kissed him again quickly.

"If we keep this up, we really will scare the animals. Where's that waterfall?" she asked, her pulse still pounding.

"Nan, that perfume is pretty enticing stuff. You shouldn't wear it on the trail like this. I could've picked up the scent a hundred yards downwind on the jungle trails I used to run."

"Good. Now I know you'll find me if I get lost."

"Come on, lady. I have so much more to show you."

As he walked ahead of her, she watched the muscular movement of his shoulders and hips, his swinging arms and pumping legs. He looked back over his shoulder at her every few minutes, and the look of desire was still in his smile.

"Hold up, Brad. I've gotta get out of this sweater. All this exercise is getting me hot."

He turned to see her pulling the sweater over her head to reveal a clinging red, deep-V knit shirt beneath it. The low-cut opening exposed the white edges of her firm breasts and the area between them.

Stuffing her sweater in his small pack, he asked, "Where did you get a sexy shirt like that?"

"Designed it myself. I'm in the business, remember?"

"I hope you sell a lot of them . . . and wear them frequently."

"You can count on it, Cowboy. Just for you."

They soon left the fire road for a narrow but well-worn path that led steeply down the mountainside in occasional switchbacks through a second-growth broadleaf forest. At a sharp turn, Brad left the trail to scramble across a rock and sit on its edge. When Nan joined him, she realized that the sound she had been hearing was not a breeze in the trees, but the rushing of water over the rocks below them. She crouched behind him with her arms around his neck and her cheek against his.

"So this is your waterfall," she said, looking below them. "It's beautiful!"

"This is only the preview. The real thing is several-hundred feet down the gorge. It falls about ninety feet. This is just to prepare you for what real beauty can be."

Nan held him tightly. She knew she had never wanted anyone or anything as much as she wanted to make love to him now.

"Brad, let's go on. Let's hurry."

BRAD MOVED QUICKLY but carefully down the steep trail, driven by the need he felt for Nan, and the urgency he sensed in her. He could see by the way she held herself and the dreamy look in her eyes that she was caught up in what she saw in him and the surroundings. But he didn't want it to happen too quickly. He had waited too long for this loving commitment, and he wanted it to be just right.

As they moved down the mountainside, Nan could hear the sound of falling water constantly on their left. The trees and rock formations masked the view, so she kept her eyes on the trail and Brad's back.

He stopped as the path broke out of the trees on the brink of the gorge. When she caught up to him, he took her hand and led her out on a rocky surface that opened onto a dramatic view of a broad hollow and the Shenandoah Valley beyond. She felt small and very insignificant.

She turned to see Brad's little boy look of obvious affection and pride in introducing her to this vastness. Then he took her hand again and led her to a small ledge that jutted out over the gorge. From there, she could see the majestic beauty of the source of falling water and the symbol she had been searching for.

A narrow band of glistening water plunged over the lip of a cliff to spill over breaks in the rock face and fell to the floor of the gorge some ninety feet below. A bright rainbow arched down from the stream of water into the brush that bordered the creek.

She was speechless. She turned toward Brad to see him sitting with his back against a large rock, while he poured hot tea from a thermos. She ran over to him and knelt between his knees, a grasping hand on each one. She kissed his waiting mouth firmly and fully.

"The view is just fantastic!" she whispered, still in awe.

"It certainly is," he whispered back.

But she saw he wasn't looking at the landscape. His eyes were searching her face.

Handing her a cup of the hot tea, he pulled her down to sit between his spread knees. He wrapped his arms around her. She pulled the scarf from her hair and shook it loose, tickling his face in the process. He gathered her tresses to the side with his hand and nuzzled her neck with wet kisses. He released her with a quick kiss on her cheek.

Brad poured his own tea and unwrapped two trail cakes, passing one to her. She took it and settled back to munch and sip quietly, trying to relate her feelings of joy to the rocks and trees around them. Suddenly, he pointed down the open hollow and whispered into her ear, "Look!"

She sat up, and following his direction, saw a large bird flying up the mountainside toward them, circling almost motionless and effortlessly above the slope below.

"It's an eagle," he breathed quietly. "It's riding the air thermals, and coming our way."

They watched until the eagle flew a few feet over them toward the mountainside above. Nan leaned back against Brad to see the bird soar overhead. She felt his lips on her ear. He had put down his cup, and his arms went around her, his hands cupping her breasts. She was quivering at the gentle touch of his hands, and his mouth on her neck. She turned her head to receive his kiss.

Brad placed a string of kisses up her elegant neck and sought her full lips. Her kiss was soft but quietly demanding. She broke away and turned to kneel before him, pulling the knit shirt over her head to make the fully aroused breasts sway slightly. She took his face in her hands and drew it to her.

His hands went to her hips, holding her firmly.

"You would decide to yield when you're wearing tight blue jeans!"

They laughed softly together, and she leaned to move the thermos out of their way. All at once they heard a buzz of whispering insect sounds just overhead, followed by a noisy spanging and humming.

"Get down!" he yelled, picking her up and pushing her aside abruptly.

"Brad!" She was confused and scared. More sharp sounds ripped the air around them.

"Sniper! In the trees above!" he shouted, trying to pull her behind a larger rock.

Nan raised up shrieking, not knowing what to do, and another burst slashed the brush and chipped the rocks around them. One slug tore the thermos from Nan's hand, and she stood up, screaming in panic.

Brad quickly lunged at her, driving her back and down. His tackle carried them over the lip of the cliff in a sickening drop into the gorge.

They fell through the needles and branches of a pine treetop, his arms straining with the weight of her still in his grasp. He turned, his back taking the force of a glancing blow as they slid off a loose rock slide and fell through a large bush. He grabbed a branch of the bush with one hand, desperately holding Nan to him with his other arm. Their weight pulled his grasp from the limb, and they rolled onto a small ledge beneath a rock over-hang.

She had landed with her bare back against the rock face, his arm still encircling her, and he found himself pressed tightly against her as a cascade of stones fell behind him. Shocked and stunned, they quietly lay there side by side, face to face, gasping for breath. She started to cry out in fear and pain, and he quickly and firmly covered her bruised lips with his hand.

"Quiet, Nan," he whispered hoarsely, his voice breaking as a pain shot through his ribs. "We've got to be absolutely quiet! This may not be over yet!"

He eased the pressure on her mouth to assure that she could breathe, and she emitted several soft involuntary sobs. She felt his gentle hand go over her face, and his lips brushed her dusty eyelashes as he whispered quietly, "Shhh. Shhh."

Through the panic, the fall, the pain, and with rocks still bouncing off his back, Brad felt the questions growing like a mushrooming cloud. Who was up there trying to kill them? How did he find them, and how long would he persist before leaving?

Nan clutched Brad tightly with the one arm that was not pinned beneath her. She fought to get herself under control, trying to stop the sobbing that wracked her body. Her back was stinging with scratches and her whole body was beginning to ache from the impact of the fall. It had all happened so fast, she could hardly think clearly.

Brad's mind raced. It was like combat again. Except he had no gun to fight back with. Weapons were illegal here in the park just as they were in the District. Without a weapon, they could only hide.

He put his hand behind Nan's head and pulled it to his aching shoulder as he considered their course of action. The gunman would probably come down to the edge of the cliff to look for their bodies. When he didn't see them, he would probably try to reach the floor of the gorge. He couldn't get down here without ropes, so he would have to follow Overall Run Trail down the mountain to where the climb down was easier. That should give them time to cross the creek and start up the other side under cover. They would hide now and run later.

Nan was shivering. The sun was not yet up over the mountain, and the rock was cold against her bare back. She knew that as much of her reaction was from fear as from the chill. She tried to snuggle even closer to Brad's comforting warmth, pulling her bare skin away from the rock face.

"Wait," Brad whispered. "Be still."

Above them, over the sounds of the waterfall and the creek, he sensed, or felt, or heard a scrunch of loose rock beneath steady footfalls. Was it the gunman, or some other observer?

His answer came by way of the crashing of a boulder as it bounced down the cliffside. A rattling of smaller loose stones followed, and then another large rock swished through the pine tree to bounce off the rock slide and fall into the creek below them. The gunman was trying to see if they were alive and could be scared from cover. When the rockslide ceased, they could hear only the waterfall and the rustling waters below.

After a few moments Brad started to lean back to see if he could hear anything. What he heard was the quiet sputter of the automatic weapon as it swept the gorge in three-round bursts, the slugs clipping branches and ricocheting off rocks around the banks of the stream. Then, except for the water sounds, there was silence again.

He waited until his cramped body and impatient mind would not let him endure inaction any longer. Pulling carefully away from Nan, he whispered, "Let's go. Be as quiet as possible."

He lowered himself from the ledge down the side of the rock, helping Nan as he went. He looked her over carefully, from her swollen lips, to the bruises and scratches on her bare back and sides. Her hair was full of pine needles. Her face was as pale as the white area across her breasts, but there were patches of red coloring on her cheeks. She looked scared, shaken, but she was also angry and determined, and he knew she would keep up as well as she could.

Staying beneath the cover of the trees, they moved silently but quickly down to the stream and along its bank, watching the hillside through openings in the trees. The rippling noise of the running water covered most of their movements. The going was rough, but it would be just as rough for their pursuer.

Nan felt pains with every step. The hand that had held the thermos was still numb. She tried to keep that arm protectively across her breasts as she held Brad's arm tightly with the other hand. She was still scared, but now her anger was overcoming the fear. And these emotions were stronger than the pain.

At a break between two large rocks, Brad suddenly scooped her up in his arms and waded into the stream. She wound her arms tightly about his neck, soaking in the heat of his body, feeling the coarseness of his sweater against her bare skin, and feeling the dampness of his sweat rub off against her face. She was too overwhelmed by the events and her emotions to tell him that she loved him more right now than life itself. She could only shiver with the excitement and terror of it all.

Behind a large rock on the other bank, Brad put her down gently, and felt her lean heavily against him. He hugged her tightly, then sat her against the rock. Peering over its edge, he saw that he could observe the lower approaches of the gorge without being seen. Taking a bandanna from his pocket, he wet it in the stream and applied it to Nan's body.

"Let's try this on those cuts," he murmured softly.

She couldn't decide which felt better—the coolness of the cloth on the scratches or the touch of his hand. Despite her feeling of being pursued, the combination of pleasant tactile sensations he offered roused her spirits, and she was able to return his caring smile with one of her own.

"I love you, Cowboy," she said softly, her eyes locked with his. She pressed her bruised lips softly against his, ignoring the pain. "God, I must look like hell," she murmured while taking the bandanna from his hand and applying it where she thought she needed it most.

"You look a little worse for the wear, but I'll settle for a durable, spirited lady like you any day. Here, put this on," he whispered, pulling his sweater over his head.

She took the sweater and clutched it to her breasts, watching the movement of his muscles as he straightened his shirt.

"You still think I'll stretch it?" she asked coyly.

"I'll have to take that chance. We've got to move quickly now."

His smile warmed her as much as the sweater as she pulled it over her head and smoothed it into place. She turned to show him and saw that he was straightening rocks they had stepped on, and removing any trace of their presence. A chill went up her spine as the seriousness of their situation clutched at her again.

With one last look around, he said firmly, "Let's go."

They started up the rise that marked the side of the gorge. It was less steep here, and they moved at a rapid pace from one covering bush or tree to another, crouching and scurrying like animals of prey ahead of a predator. Once over the gorge's rim, the going was easier, and she again fell in behind Brad. The whip of branches against the sweater made her glad for its protection.

Nan was again caught up in the beauty of the wooded hillside. She found herself having difficulty sorting out what had happened, and the threat that might be following in the midst of this paradise. Brad's anxious looks were a constant reminder of the danger.

Brad finally stepped onto a narrow trail, and they stopped for a breather. She slumped to the ground, breathing deeply.

"This is Beecher Ridge Trail," he said between deep breaths. "It will ultimately take us back to the parking lot."

"You seem to know this area very well."

"Yeah. Spent a lot of time getting to know it years ago when the things chasing me were all in my mind. Not like this. And not with someone who matters like you."

She offered her hand in affection, and when he took it he pulled her to her feet and into the brush across the trail.

"Let me know when you need to stop again. The going will be a little rugged for a while."

She nodded, but she was determined to keep up, to follow the steps of this wonderful man who had become the spirit and essence of her life.

They didn't stop for rest when they reached the car. As soon as Nan was seated, Brad was behind the wheel with the motor started, and they left with a squeal of tires. He pushed the speed limit all the way back to Thornton Gap and down the curving mountain highway. Brad saw no one following them.

Nan slumped in the bucket seat, sorting through her fears and needs. She wanted to get out from under the feeling of being pursued, to talk instead about a hopeful future.

"Brad, we need to get away from here for a few days. Just us, together. We need to put some of this behind us."

He studied her carefully, sensing her mood, and agreeing.

"Nan, you're a changed person from just a week ago."

"Maybe I am. If so, I owe it all to you."

"I'm just the guy who loves you and wants to spend his life with you."

She looked out the window with a frown marking her bruised brow.

"Brad, we have to find the killer before he tries again. Maybe next time he won't miss."

As he reached out to squeeze her thigh. Nan settled into the seat. She dozed off, but her fears caused her to wake periodically with a start, reaching out for his arm. She slept all the way back to Washington, the marks of terror showing against the softness of her elegant face and neck.

And all the way back, he pondered how someone could have found them on the cliff.

AT NAN'S APARTMENT building, Brad parked in front of the door and hurried Nan inside. Gerald met them halfway to the building and walked through the doorway with them.

"Well, I see you made it back early," he said jovially. Then, peering at the welts on Nan's face and neck, he asked, "Are you all right, Miss Donahue?"

"Yes, thank you, Gerald. Just took a nasty fall." She tried to relax her bruised body and avoid limping.

"On your toes, Gerald," Brad said tersely, echoing his concern in a stern look. "Keep a sharp eye."

"Yes, sir, Mr. Gaelman." Gerald hurried back to the doorway, his eyes searching up and down the street.

"All clear," he said, as Brad and Nan entered the elevator.

Upstairs, Brad took Nan's key and opened the apartment door. He stepped in and searched the room before allowing her to enter. After closing the door, he walked straight across the room to the telephone.

"Who are you calling? Rafe?"

"Not just yet. I've got a hunch."

He quickly unscrewed the receiver mouthpiece, and felt his anger overflow at what he found there.

"What are you doing?" she asked in a tired tone.

Nan heard him mumble softly but vehemently.

"What was that you said?" she asked curiously.

"I said damn it to hell!"

He removed a small, flat disk from the receiver and, touching only its edges, held it up for her to see. Looking around the room, his eyes settled on a nearby bookshelf. He walked quickly to it and began to remove the leather-bound volumes. Eventually, he held up a small box, and clicked a tiny switch on its side.

"Lady, we've been bugged! This listening device let someone hear every telephone conversation we've had!"

"For how long?" she asked, thinking of the personal nature of her recent calls.

"Long enough to hear me tell you where we were going today. And probably long enough to hear me tell you I was going to Renoir's with Thaddeus and Bess. This shouldn't have happened! It should've been checked!"

"Oh, Brad! When did they put it there?"

"I don't know yet, but I'll find out!"

He stormed across the room and out the hallway door of the apartment, leaving it open behind him. Nan stood watching for him for a moment, then went to her bedroom to remove her trail clothes.

Brad stopped in front of Sue Snyder's door, and pounded loudly, putting his anger into each blow.

He heard someone approach, then the chain was unfastened. Sue Snyder's big blue eyes peeked around the door, her fresh young face framed by wet tendrils of blond hair.

"Why, Brad. Hello there," she said brightly, while staring at the marks on his face. "I'm sorry if I didn't hear you knock before. I just got out of the shower."

On the portion of her not hidden by the door, he could see the filmy gown she wore.

"I want to talk to you," he said evenly, laboring to keep the anger out of his voice.

"Just give me a minute to throw something on."

"Now!" he said sharply, clutching the slender wrist that leaned on the door facing.

As she moved around the door, he drew her abruptly into the hallway and slammed her door behind them. He pulled her across the hall and through the open door to Nan's apartment, slamming that door as well.

"Brad, what is it? What happened to you?"

He whirled her around by her wrist, propelling her onto the couch. She sprawled there in an ungainly fashion, her shapely curves peeking through the filmy material of the soft gown. She lay still, looking up at him in confusion.

"Brad, what do you want?"

"Just give me some straight answers."

Nan, hearing the slamming doors, had paused in her dressing to put on her blue robe before reentering the room. "What's going on?"

"This young lady is going to provide us with the answers to some questions I should've asked long ago," Brad snapped.

"Brad, she's hardly dressed for a formal interrogation." Sue's feelings of discomfort were obvious in her look.

"She'll just have to endure it," he said, staring down at the woman, trying to ignore all but her expressive eyes. "Sue, when was the last time you swept this apartment?"

"What? I spent some time in here, but I'm not the maid."

"Don't give me that cover stuff. Someone almost killed us today, and we don't know how far behind he might be. You know precisely what I mean." With that statement, he reached to a nearby table and picked up the listening device and the companion transmitter box. He held them before her surprised face.

"Oh, God!" she said, coming half off the couch, her gown in disarray again. "Where did you get that?"

"From the phone here. You know, the one you're supposed to keep secure. Now, when was the last time you checked out this apartment?"

"Oh my God. Not since Dan...Mr. Donahue was killed. I guess I was too busy watching the streets after that happened. And I never thought anyone would wire it after he was gone."

"Will somebody tell me what's going on?" Nan asked, slumping limply into a chair.

"Correct me if I go astray, Sue. You see, Nan, your friendly neighbor's spa work and running are a cover. She's an operative for the Company Dan worked for, probably in training to become an agent. She represents the outside security of this building for the agency, which owns and maintains these apartments for its people. Until just recently, she was Gerald's backup."

He paused at Nan's querulous look. "Yes, he also works for the Company. But Sue took the lead when things started heating up around here. Which is amazing to me, since they should've been replaced when they fumbled the security and let someone get to Dan."

"Brad, that's enough," Nan said softly. "It wasn't her fault about Dad. I left the car out on the street instead of in the secure parking. It was my carelessness that got him killed."

Nan drew upon the new confidence and self-assurance that the recent events had hammered into her resolve. She removed her robe and put it around the shoulders of the whimpering woman on the couch. Then, ignoring Brad's dazed look at her bra and pants, she stalked out of the room to get another housecoat.

Brad was deeply touched by Nan's gesture. He moved to the couch and helped Sue get into the robe. Her arms went desperately to his shoulders, her troubled eyes searching his face earnestly for sympathy. She drew him down on the couch beside her.

"Brad, I loved Dan. We were lovers for months. No one knew. We both would've had trouble from the

Company because of it. We had to be especially careful while Nan was here. He had come to my apartment after she went to bed that night. He left me so tired I slept late the next morning. Gerald was sick, so no one was watching. And I lost him, Brad. I lost the only man I ever really loved.''

''I'm sorry, Sue. I shouldn't have been so hard on you.''

When Nan returned, Sue was sobbing softly in Brad's arms.

''Well, I should've known you could handle her okay alone, Cowboy,'' she said with a wry smile.

''Nan, thanks for your understanding,'' Sue said weakly. ''But don't punish yourself. Brad was right. It was my fault. And I let you down again when I allowed this bug in here.''

Brad hugged the young woman, and Nan sat beside her, holding her hand.

''Sue, I regret this,'' he said, ''but we've got to talk now. I don't know how much time we have before someone else gets hurt or killed.''

''What do you want to know?'' she asked, looking first at Nan, then to Brad, with a silent plea for mercy and discretion.

''Who out of the ordinary has been in the apartment since the last time you swept it for listening devices?'' Brad asked.

She sat pensively for a moment. ''I really can't think of anyone, except maybe the gas man.''

''Gas man? Tell us about that. What did he do?''

"Well, Gerald smelled gas in his apartment, and then I did, too. So we called for the gas company to send a man over. He went into all the apartments to check on a leak."

"And did someone stay with him all the time he was here?"

"Yes, I did. Oh, except when he asked me to go see if there was still a gas smell in my apartment," she said thoughtfully. "I was only gone a few seconds." A look of concern crept across her features, wrinkling her brow.

Brad leaned back and rubbed his eyes, not wanting Sue to see his frustration and disappointment.

"You think that was it, Brad?" Nan asked tactfully.

"I did blow it, didn't I?" Sue said more as a statement than a question. "And I wanted so much to be good at this."

"And when was he in here alone?" Brad finally asked.

"Well, it was twice, actually. Both times on weekends, as I recall. The first time was on Sunday, Nan. That was the day you and Dan—you and your father—went to the museum. It was the day before the explosion." She halted, staring straight ahead, her face creased in pain.

"And the second time?" Brad prompted, wanting to get through with this.

"It was on a Sunday, I think. No, it was Saturday. When you and Nan went to the editor's funeral. I remember because Gerald was . . . sick. Gerald was sick both times." She put her flushed face in her hands and began to breathe deeply.

Brad got up from the couch and started pacing. Nan's hands were tenaciously playing with a handkerchief she

had meant for Sue. Realizing she still held it, she offered it to the woman beside her. She then put her arms
around Sue as they shared the realization that Sue may
have seen the murderer.

"What did this guy look like?"

"Well, like a repairman. He was in coveralls, and the
name on the back matched the truck he came in. He had
a beard and a mustache, was just about your height and
build."

"That rules out Lin," Nan said quietly to Brad.

"Gerald looked in his equipment bag both times, but
those bugs are so tiny."

"I thought you said Gerald was sick both times," Nan
reminded her.

"Well, he was at the door when the gas man first came.
But then he got sick afterward."

"Gerald wasn't on the door when we returned from
Ed's funeral," Nan said quietly.

"That's right," Brad agreed. "Nor was he there when
someone planted the bomb." Brad resumed his pacing.
"Sue, tell me about the gas smell. What was it like?"

"It was like when you light a stove, or when a pilot
light goes out. Only stronger, especially the last time."

"Stronger? Where did it seem to come from?"

"Everywhere. It nearly made me sick after a while.
I aired out the apartment, but the odor stayed for
days."

"I didn't smell it over here," Nan said.

"And what did the gas man do about it?" Brad asked.

"He said it must be a leak downstairs, with gas coming up through the air conditioning. He didn't say what it was."

"Did you see him adjust anything, or turn any valves?"

"No, I don't think so."

"Did you see him leave anything behind?"

Sue thought about it for a moment.

"Only a cigarette he smoked in here. I had to bring him an ashtray from my apartment, and I threw the remains out and washed the dish after he left."

Nan broke in excitedly. "He was smoking around a gas leak? He was either crazy. Or a phony."

"I should've caught that," Sue said quietly.

"Unless he knew there was no danger," Brad said thoughtfully. "Sue, can you get me into the air conditioning room?"

"Yes, I have the keys in my apartment. And a flashlight."

"Nan, get dressed. We'll be right back."

Brad followed Sue into a utility room on the ground floor of the building. The room was dominated by a large air conditioning unit that serviced the entryway and Sue and Gerald's apartments, but not Nan's. Attached to the intake vents, he found two small tubes. After tracing them along the unit to the back of the machinery, he used Sue's flashlight to locate two aerosol cans, attached to a small electronic unit.

"Look at this, lady spook. One can is labeled mercaptan, the scent gas companies put into natural gas to give it a smell. The other is an organic chemical with a name I don't recognize. Someone wired these up to spray into the air conditioning system on demand, using this radio receiver.''

''He was only in here alone for a few minutes. I stayed outside because the utility room is so small and crowded. But he didn't have time to hook that up like that.''

Brad noticed a door across the room.

''That lead outside?''

''Yes, but it's locked from this side. And the hall door is locked, too. And yes, I do check it regularly.''

Brad took the keys from her and moved to the door, searching for signs of forced entry. There were none. He unlocked the door and looked carefully at the bolt. It was a spring latch, rather than a dead bolt. He found small bits of residual adhesive on the door plate.

''Lady, you've been taped. Watergate special.''

''What?''

''He put adhesive tape on the latch so it wouldn't lock. He came back later. You'd better change that to a dead bolt.''

''Oh, Brad! I feel so miserable! How could I be so dense? You walked right to it!''

''It comes with experience, Sue.''

''I may lose my job for this, if they don't throw me in jail!''

''Come on, let's go. I want Rafe to get someone to check out this chemical. And I want you to talk to a good police artist with a description of that gas man.''

"Brad, I want this guy as much as you do. You'll get an accurate portrait or there'll be a former police artist on unemployment with me!"

"Let's go, lady spook. We've got work to do."

RAFE MET THEM at the police station.

"Brad! Nancy! What in the hell happened to you two? You both look like you've been in a fight with a junk-yard dog!"

"Well, we can't really say. We never saw the guy who was shooting at us," Brad explained.

"What?"

"That's right, Rafe," Nan said with high emotion. "Someone was sniping at us up on Skyline Drive."

"And they came too close for comfort," Brad added.

"Well if he missed, how did you get so beat up?"

"We went over the edge of the cliff into the gorge."

"He saved my life, Rafe, and it nearly cost him his."

"You two come on back to my office. I want to hear this, but I've got something to tell you first," the sergeant said, heading for his room.

"Hold on, Rafe," Brad interrupted. "There's more. There was a tap on Nan's phone."

"A phone tap? How did that happen? But wait, let me—"

Nan interrupted the sergeant this time. "We think Sue Snyder saw the killer. He was disguised as a gas repair-man."

"Nancy. Brad. I ought to tell you about—"

Brad interrupted him again. "We've got to get a police artist over there to draw up Sue's description. And get someone to check this out." He handed Rafe the electronic bug and transmitter in a plastic bag.

Rafe entered his office and stood looking down at the small objects a moment before he spoke. His voice was soft and full of emotion.

"Please sit down a moment. I have something to tell you."

"But Rafe, this may clear Bum once and for all."

"There's no need, Brad. Bum's dead."

"He's what?" Brad asked incredulously.

"Oh, no!" Nan uttered.

Nan and Brad slowly sat while Rafe took his seat behind his desk. Nan reached for Brad's hand and squeezed it gently.

"Brad. I'm so sorry," Nan whispered in an anguished tone.

"How? When?" he asked Rafe quietly.

"The Colorado State Police reported it just a while ago. They say Bum broke into Lin's ranch house and killed his bodyguard. Somehow he missed Lin. Then Bum went after Judge Sennet and killed him with one of his own rifles. The police found Bum dead in the judge's house of an overdose of heroin. The needle was still in his left arm. They say he got high and went crazy."

"Wait a minute!" Brad's head jerked up suddenly, knowing it was all wrong.

"Take it easy, Brad," Nan said softly.

"Rafe, Bum was left-handed. The needle was in the wrong arm."

"Are you sure about that?" Rafe asked, his brow drawn into deep wrinkles of concern.

"He was my gunner. He was my friend. He was a lefty. Always."

"You mean he would've put the needle in his right arm with his left hand?" Nan asked.

"Right! And if they check, I'll bet there are no other needle marks anywhere on his body, and there would be if he were a user."

"I'll have that checked out right away."

"Oh, my God!" Nan interjected. "This means we have two killers!"

"I guess you're right, Nancy," Rafe said, his large hand running through his hair. "One was shooting at you while one was at work out in Colorado."

"I haven't had a chance to tell you, but Bum and George both called me last night. Bum said he was closing in on the killer. I couldn't tell where he was calling from."

"We'll try to get a line on that with the phone company. What about Windham?"

"He was pretty drunk."

"Try to remember what he said and write it down. It could be crucial."

"Doesn't it seem odd that Lin wasn't involved?" Brad asked.

"The State Police said they were looking for him for routine questioning. They're afraid Bum killed him and then hid the body. They have a stakeout at Lin's ranch to pick up anybody who looks suspicious.''

"I'd say he's a pretty good suspect, wouldn't you?'' Nan asked.

"It doesn't mean Bum didn't do some of the killing,'' Rafe said.

"You and Thaddeus won't be convinced of Bum's innocence until the real killers are found.'' Brad got up and started for the door. Nan rose to follow.

"Speaking of Ralston, he had quite a press conference this morning at the hospital.''

"Press conference?'' Nan and Brad asked together.

"Yes, he told all about how Bess Bradshaw saved his life in last night's shooting. Made her a real heroine. They got pretty chummy on camera. There are rumors that he may be leaving his wife.''

"I can't believe it. He's committing political suicide.''

"I can't believe he'd leave anyone for *her*,'' Nan quipped.

"Maybe I'll stop by the hospital after all. I want you to get some X rays, too,'' Brad said.

"Whatever you say, lover,'' she cooed. "You just keep your bedside manner as formal as you were with me when I was in a hospital bed.''

"Yes, Ma'am. Rafe, let us know what you learn about Bum, that bug, and Sue Snyder's description.''

"Wait a minute. You didn't finish telling me about that.''

"Please, Rafe," Nan said wearily. "It's been a long, tiring day, and we've got to stop by the hospital before we can settle down for any rest. Get Sue to tell you about it. We'll check with you in the morning." She followed Brad out the door. "Wait for me, Cowboy."

BRAD FINISHED with his X rays before Nan was through, so he decided to stop in and see Bess. Visiting hours at the hospital were over, but Rafe had told the guard at Bess's door to expect Brad. He found Bess watching a replay of Thaddeus's press conference on the eleven o'clock news.

"Can I come in?"

"Brad! Certainly. Oh, your face! Those marks look awful! Are you all right?"

"Nothing showed up in the X rays. Just some bruised ribs."

"What on earth happened?"

"Just got shot at again. And took a bad fall. Don't worry your pretty head about it. You okay?"

"Yes, the doctors say I'm healing fine," she said, centering her thoughts on herself again. "And all the important parts are still functional." Her face was a picture of temptation.

"Bess, you're really something. I would've thought you had settled down after what I heard about that press conference."

"Oh, you just missed it," she said, clicking off the set with a remote unit. "I'm afraid you didn't get much mention, but that's politics."

"I wasn't looking for any mention. I don't need that kind of visibility in my business. I was talking about how close you and Thaddeus apparently got on camera."

"Thad was just wonderful. He kept hugging me, saying how brave I was, and kissing me. He didn't mention how you saved me."

"Bess, where are you two going? This can't be good for his career."

"Thad says he's willing to give up politics for me if necessary. He says he loves me that much."

"What about his wife?"

"A mere technicality."

"A rather significant one, I should think."

"You're sweet, Cowboy. But the course of true love is relentless, and he's been after me since the first time I came to D.C. When I want loving, I can't settle for just a smidgen. He doesn't run away like you do."

Brad was searching for a response when the door opened behind him and Nan entered. Brad looked at her with a smile, then turned back to Bess. She was primly pulling her neckline over her half-exposed breasts.

"I thought I might find you here," Nan said easily. "How are you, Bess?"

"I'm very fine, thank you. I was just telling Brad how thoughtful he was to visit me."

Nan walked to Brad and put her arms possessively around him.

"Yes, I've found him to be a very thoughtful guy. And right now I'm going to return the courtesy by fixing him a supper at my apartment. Ready, darling?'' She was practically pulling him to the door.

"Sure, Nan. Bess, take care. And keep in touch."

"Certainly, Cowboy. You'll be hearing from me. For God's sake, get some rest. And take care of that handsome face!"

"How were your X rays?" he asked Nan as they walked into the hall.

"The doctor said they were okay. But I have a few places I'd like you to check out personally, if you don't mind."

"Just lead the way."

AT NAN'S APARTMENT, Brad took a hot shower while she fixed a light meal for them. Then he, in Dan's old robe, and she, in her blue favorite, shared wine and supper at her kitchen table.

"Tired?" she asked, breaking the silence of eating.

"God, yes. Bushed. Like I haven't slept in a week. I guess I'm not used to being chased. And maybe it's the wine and the stress and the bruises and the long day."

"I'm exhausted myself, and I got a nap in the car. But having you here makes it all okay." She reached for his scraped hand and touched it soothingly. Her face said more than words could.

He leaned over to kiss her, reaching beneath the robe to fondle her breasts. Her body tensed with her sharp intake of breath, and her hands went to his.

"Brad."

"Yes, my love."

"Before you get too far with that, the coffee's ready. Why don't we have it on the couch. It'll perk us up."

"Whatever you say, pretty lady." He felt too tired to argue.

He patted her fanny as he walked to the living room, where he collapsed full-length on the couch. When Nan brought in the coffee tray, she found him fast asleep, his body sprawled in exhaustion. Setting the tray down, she knelt beside him, taming the hair that fell in disarray across his scratched forehead.

She kissed his mouth lightly, and then again. He didn't even stir. Realizing how tired she was too, and how futile a loving encounter might be tonight, she pulled a light comforter from a closet shelf and spread it carefully over the body of the man she loved.

"Well, Cowboy, I guess turnabout is fair play," she whispered, her hands caressing him lightly.

II

WHEN THE URGENT RINGING of the telephone awakened Brad, he sleepily rolled over to reach for his bedside table. He came fully awake as he rolled off the couch and hit the floor. The phone stopped ringing, so he sat back against the couch and tried to figure out where he was and why.

As he recognized the room, the events of the night before came trickling back.

NAN FOUGHT OFF SLEEP as she reached for her bedroom extension of the phone.

"Hullo?"

"Nancy, it's Rafe. Let me speak to Brad."

"Rafe, he's not here. I mean, he's here, but not in my bed. He's sleeping on the couch."

"Then roust him out and get him down to the station. George Windham called and said he'd be here in an hour."

"We need to stop by Brad's place to get him some clean clothes."

"Well, make it snappy. We've got a lot of pieces to put together, and quick. See ya later."

Nan dashed to the bathroom, grabbing clothes and brush along the way. Now they were getting somewhere!

Brad was still sitting on the floor, rubbing his eyes, when she breezed into the room, tucking a shirt into her jeans. Her hair was up, and hastily applied makeup somewhat softened the marks of yesterday's violence on her face.

"Up and at 'em, Cowboy. Rafe wants us downtown in less than an hour, and we've got to go by your place for some clothes."

"Wait a minute. Slow down. I'm still trying to remember why I was sleeping out here on the couch, while you were snuggled up in your bed."

"By mutual agreement, lover. You were too tired to stay awake, and I was too tired to argue. Now get dressed."

"You're a tough first sergeant this morning." He rose and walked to where she was clearing last night's dishes. "No hard feelings about last night?"

She put the dishes down and turned to him, her arms going up around his neck, and a loving smile turned up to him.

"Last night was fine, Brad. We'll get our time together, eventually. But if we do what we want now, we'll never get to Rafe's office. And George Windham will be there in less than an hour. You think he's coming to confess?"

"George will be there?" he asked, disengaging from her slightly. "Why didn't you say so? I'll put yesterday's clothes on now, but we'll still need to stop by my apartment first. I'll be ready in a minute.''

"Yes, dear," she said, realizing he was still groggy and still recovering from his exhaustion of the day before.

Nan smiled lovingly at his attempts to wake up. She led him by the arm to the bathroom where he had left his clothes, and kissed him lightly before turning back to the kitchen. She thought how nice it would be to spend the rest of her life starting her days with him.

Brad was fully alert and functioning by the time they got to his car in the secure parking area. The drive to his condo was one of occasional quiet affectionate words and yawns and stretches as they each silently thought of what might lie ahead.

At his apartment building, Nan decided to wait in the car.

Hurrying into his condominium, he had second thoughts about leaving Nan alone in the car on the street. But by then he was almost in his apartment, so he decided to dress as quickly as possible.

Nan was in fashion jeans and a blouse, so Brad pulled out new jeans and a western shirt with snaps down the front. While he shaved, he pondered what the meaning of two killers might be. One was in Colorado, where two more Knives had been eliminated, along with Lin's bodyguard. Another was in the D.C. area, or was yesterday. And George Windham was back in town.

Before leaving the apartment, he quickly opened the double-locked steel door of a closet and made a brief inventory of the tools of his trade. Then he hurried downstairs.

Back in the car with Nan, his mind was divided between his driving, his contingency planning, and the way the bright sun was lighting up her auburn hair. Her beauty won out over all other thoughts. And he told her so.

"Thanks, fella. Flattery will get you wherever. You look pretty sharp yourself, Cowboy. How did you shave so fast without cutting your throat?"

"In the National Guard we used to shave in the field with a bar of soap and cold water from a steel helmet, using polarized sun glasses for a mirror. Anyone who survived that can shave himself in his sleep!"

She shared his laughter and leaned to run her fingers down his smooth cheek.

"Nice," she said, with a deep sigh. "I hope this short discussion with Windham doesn't lead to an all-day questioning or anything like that."

"Why, you have a date later?" he asked.

"No, but I'd like one."

NAN AND BRAD were escorted to Rafe's empty office at the station. They had just sat down when Rafe breezed in waving a sheet of paper in his huge hand.

"You two are getting well-known enough to get fan mail here. Take a look at this."

Brad took the paper and held it so that Nan could read it with him. It was a sheet of bond paper with cut-out letters of various sizes and type faces pasted on it to spell out a message. Nan read it aloud.

"Sergeant Johnson: Tell Gaelman and Donahue I'll get another chance at them, but they'll never know when. Then I'll get you too. I'll never give up."

Brad handed the paper back to Rafe. "I don't suppose there were any fingerprints."

"You got that right," Rafe said with frustration sounding in his voice. "Oh, come on in, George."

Nan and Brad turned to see George Windham enter the office.

"Brad! Nan! What happened to you?" Windham asked, his eyebrows raised.

"That can wait, George," Brad answered evenly. "We'd like to hear your story first."

"Go easy, Cowboy," Rafe interjected, his big hand raised in a gesture of caution. "He'll tell it in his own way."

Brad shook Windham's hand and Nan nodded politely as he took a seat before them. They saw a beleaguered man, with deep, dark circles in the puffy skin beneath bloodshot eyes. He slumped in the chair, as if he hadn't rested or slept in days.

"I'm sorry I was drunk when I called you, Brad. I guess I've been drinking a lot since the cremation. I tried to tell you that Noy was dead, but I wasn't certain you understood."

"Who was dead?" Nan asked.

"George, I'm sorry. I didn't realize," Brad started.

"How could you? I kept my life with Noy secret from almost everyone. At least I thought I did. We spent those last days on the island making love all the time. We were together Saturday night. She went out to the car Sunday morning when I was about to leave. I saw it blow up when she opened the door. In fact, my leg was injured slightly in the blast.''

"Just like Dan.''

"Yes. She was killed instantly. I had to stay and take care of the cremation. Then I got drunk and stayed that way until last night.''

"So you were with Noy all the time you were gone?'' Nan asked.

"Yes. We were trying to decide if I should finally leave my wife for good. But Noy said she was willing to go on as we had all these years.''

"Since Ralston introduced you in Southeast Asia,'' Brad said thoughtfully.

"Yes, that's right,'' Windham responded, his eyebrows characteristically arched. "Thaddeus knew her mother quite well. And, of course, we all knew her father.''

"Her father?'' Rafe asked.

"Yes, the Golden Dragon,'' Windham said, nodding.

"Of course!'' Brad uttered. "How could I have forgotten? Noy was Lin's daughter!''

"Yes, but he disowned her years ago, and cut her off from any financial support. They hadn't spoken in years. But he let me know he still cared for her. He always asked privately about her.''

"But who would've wanted to kill her, and why?'' Nan asked.

"They were probably after George,'' Rafe said quietly, his eyes on the floor.

"Our investigation must have been getting too close. She took a hit that was meant for me." Windham leaned over in his torment, his head in his hands.

"But who? Who knew where you were?" Brad asked him.

"I don't know, but I'm going to find out. I'm going to nail the bastard!"

"Did your investigation give you any clues? Could the State Department help?" Rafe asked.

"Oh, you know how those requests work through a bureaucracy. They're like water running off a drake's back."

The minor change in the old saying triggered both Brad and Nan, and they stood and spoke their thoughts simultaneously.

"Duck . . . drake . . . Mallard . . . Drake Mallard!"

"What? What are you two talking about?" Rafe asked.

"Denton Mallard's nickname! Drake Mallard! I had forgotten that," Brad said, almost shouting.

"The note in Dad's pocket! See the man, Drake. Drake Mallard!" Nan said with enthusiasm.

"And the notes in Ed's book and on Luke's desk."

"Hold on, you two," Rafe interrupted. "You're jumping to conclusions again."

"That's right," Windham interjected. "Besides, *drake* or *draco* also means *dragon*. Draco was Noy's nickname for her father."

Windham jerked back as Nan, Brad, and Rafe all sharply turned their scrutiny on him.

"Two murderers," Nan whispered, still staring. "Drake and Draco. Mallard and Lin."

"Now wait a minute!" Rafe said. "You're getting way ahead. Both of them were at the funeral that Sunday."

"The bomb could've been planted earlier. Mallard was out of town," Brad said.

"And we only saw him at the cemetery. He could've come in late," Nan added. "He could've put the gas in the apartments and bugged the telephone."

"We didn't use the car for three days before the explosion," Windham said softly.

"Now hold it!" Rafe said sharply. "All that stuff is just circumstantial!"

Brad smiled to hear someone else use the words for a change. Then his chest tightened as he thought of Bum's death.

"But it's a damn good start, Rafe. What about the bug? The artist's drawing? The chemical spray? What did you find?"

"Well, I've got to admit that the description Sue gave could be Mallard with a beard. The mysterious organic chemical was a substance that would affect someone's lungs like the flu, as it did both times with Gerald." Rafe paused uneasily.

"Go on, Rafe, tell us," Nan prompted.

"The listening device was made by Mallard's electronics plant."

"I can't believe he'd be so careless!" Brad said, sitting down heavily.

"I couldn't either. I thought someone was trying to frame him."

"You say Lin could be a murderer, too?" Windham asked.

Brad summed it up. "Well, he knew helicopters. He could've rigged Luke's. And Bum showed up at Lin's ranch and killed his bodyguard after he told me he was closing in on the killer."

"But there's no proof!" Rafe reminded them.

"But Brad's right," Windham said. "It's a good start. So let's check the airlines and the present location of these two," Windham suggested, rising and rubbing his palms together. "Want to join me, Brad?"

"He can't," Nan interrupted. "He's got a date."

Turning to Rafe, Brad said, "Let me know what you find."

"Yeah," the sergeant answered with a grin. "I'll know where to find you two."

WHEN BRAD closed the door behind them in Nan's apartment, she took his hand and led him directly to her bedroom. He followed willingly, his expectations rising with every step.

"Brad, I don't want anything to interrupt or get in the way this time," she said softly as she stopped inside the door. "I want us to have our time here and now."

She saw desire in his eyes long before he spoke of it, yearning to kiss her long before his motion came. They stood closely, their bodies restless with excitement.

She looked to him as though she had stepped from a classic, erotic painting. She was all grace and beauty, and her soft, rosy mouth was made for kissing. The fragrance of her perfume tugged at him.

"Nan, I love you, all of you, now and forever."

He took her into his arms, putting his words into actions.

She clung to him, as though the passion of their embrace welded them together, each seeking to relieve the long-denied desire for the other.

"I don't have the words to tell you how much I love you," he whispered in her ear.

"Words aren't needed, Brad. We know the words. We need the actions."

Running his hands down her back and across the curves of her rear, he pulled her tightly against him and said, "I want you more than anything in the world."

"Then come and get me, dammit, or I'll come after you!" She pulled away from him slightly, and tugged at his belt buckle and jeans until they were down around his ankles. While he stepped out of them, she quickly removed her own jeans.

Tossing the clothing aside, he took her again in his arms. She sensed the arousal spreading through her as he pressed his body against hers.

She was lost in the magic of the moment. She sent her hands exploring, hugging him. She held to him fiercely.

"Lady, you'd better be ready to take the results of all the hunger you've been building in me."

She turned sharply away from him, bewildered at her loss of control. She felt choked and breathless. But the truth was that she liked being this way with him. She loved it. She felt her last inhibitions split asunder by it.

He felt the same eagerness for her, and his passion as his eyes followed the lines of her body. Her belly was flat, her thighs taut, her bottom rounded and firm. The white, smooth texture of her hips contrasted with the filmy black bikini pants edged with lace. He watched with restraint as she turned to him, her breath fast, her breasts rising and falling rapidly under the softness of her blouse.

"Why don't we get out of the rest of these clothes?" she asked recklessly, while kicking off her shoes.

He watched her in awe as she moved to the bed and started taking off her garments. For her, the act was sexual beyond any words she could have spoken. She looked at him with an expression he had never seen before, then finished unbuttoning her blouse, removing it slowly and deliberately, and dropping it at her feet. She stood erect, shoulders back, taut breasts thrust against the lace of the black bra. A dark triangle marked the front of the sheer pants.

"Now, Cowboy. It's your turn." She beckoned with one slender finger. She wanted to intensify his need, to make him feel the excitement that she felt.

He moved to her as if mesmerized by her beauty and her actions. His body trembled as her fingers went to the snaps of his shirt. She impatiently jerked them all apart in one motion, pulling the shirt down from his bared shoulders abruptly, leaving him overcome by a desire that took his breath away.

He wanted to take her, to possess her, to drink in the aroma of every inch of her skin. He reached out to cup her breasts, pushing them up out of the bra, and causing a quick intake of breath and a soft moan from her.

Her hands rose to grasp his and hold them tightly before her.

"Brad, I want you to keep looking into my eyes like that, into my soul like that. Always." Her voice came to him mellow and loving.

He was amazed to see himself reflected in the soft, glowing liquid green of her eyes. He saw there too a wave of sexual excitement that was sweeping them into an unknown world where time and space meant nothing. He watched her breasts rise and fall rapidly, straining against her bra, the taut coral tips peeking over the edges of the filmy fabric, begging for release.

He bent and kissed her fervently, until they were breathless and flushed with arousal. Her lips parted, and he tasted the sweetness of her mouth.

She uttered her strange, happy little murmur of surrender, feeling it come from within her without effort. Her firm breasts heaved as she drew another breath, and again as he squeezed her closer. She felt her aching nipples freed from their bindings and grazing deliciously against the soft mat of hair on his muscled chest. A delicious warm tension ran up the insides of her legs, and created tiny little explosions low in her belly as if there were an awakening taking place.

He moaned softly, and with hands under her hips, lifted her up against him, feeling the points of her breasts on his chest.

She answered with a strident, lingering cry of sensuous joy. Ripples of pleasure ran up and down her spine, settling low in her body.

He felt her lips and tongue over his eyes and lips in quick little butterfly touches.

"On the bed," she whispered hoarsely.

She removed the bra as she turned, and slipped from the pants as she crawled onto the large bed. She was erotic poetry in motion, sensually flexing a well-contoured leg, her full breasts descending in gently swaying profile, the soft roundness of her shapely bottom inviting attention.

She turned and lay naked on her back, her breasts bold and bare. Her hands stroked her thighs, beckoning to him, opening herself to his eyes and his desire.

He quickly kicked off his shoes, removed his shorts and stretched out beside her on the bed. He was eager and longing for the ultimate consummation they could now achieve.

She was bright and responsive. She was insatiable, lovely and loving.

"Don't say anything, Cowboy," she said with a little giggle. "Just...."

He slipped deliciously into her. She was moist and ready, and she let out a shrill welcoming cry. They started moving together in a tempo that rose with the throbbing of their pulses. They were soon finding that sure and wondrous rhythm that brings lovers to fulfillment.

She had never felt anything like the feelings he was giving her. The room around her became a charmed shrine of tenderness and love, all the forests and meadows and beaches and glens she had ever dreamed of making love in. And the lovemaking surpassed any delight she had ever had or dreamed she could have. She found an overwhelming rapture as Brad played with her body, distilling the essence of her love down to one keen point in her being. Her soft cries and moans were echoes of his.

Brad was borne on an all-encompassing surge of end-lessly aching sweetness, an overwhelming sensation that became timeless and all-obliterating. He had never experienced anything so carnal and yet so pure. She was everywhere around him, clutching him, thrusting at him, crying out loudly in ecstasy as he matched her every move.

She closed off her mind to all expectations and opened herself to her thirsty senses. She smelled and tasted the manly sweat of his sexual effort, and heard his moans of pleasure. She felt the soft roughness of his skin moving against hers. She saw his strong and muscled body from one view, and then another as they moved about the king-size bed in their passion.

She was soon reacting instinctively, hungrily, in strong and urgent thrusts, feeling a throbbing tightness clutching at her every sensitized nerve. She became tensed and trembling, unable to catch a breath. Her drumming heart pounded in her ears, her pulse hammered throughout her body. Behind her closed eyelids, she saw only Brad's loving face.

She felt an urgency that drove her to become rowdier, with more abandon, until a point was reached from which it was impossible to turn back. The tension it built up made them both rigid with expectation. The compulsion broke over them in waves of pleasure.

A quick warning detonation in her lower belly brought them sharply together, then another. Pulsations ran along her body, then focused between her legs. The shocks grew stronger and built until they burst in a bright shower of sensual fireworks, and then spiraled down, on and on, in tiny, explosive reminders.

Brad experienced a similar buildup and release. The feel of her encouraging heels pressing at the base of his spine as her legs squeezed around him at the moment of her climax drove him wildly into his own surging fulfillment.

Their rigidity was replaced by a relaxation, a new sensation of being immersed in a soft, warm, liquid ecstasy that they floated in languidly.

Brad held her tightly in the afterglow of their lovemaking. He felt pleasantly exhausted as he lay upon her, supporting his weight. He began kissing her ears and the corners of her mouth.

Nan responded in kind, feeling a new desire rising within her. They were soon involved again in one another's bodies. She was over him, then he was over her, thrusting, sliding, filling and fulfilling. She was beside him, then he was behind her, clutched in loving embraces.

The climaxes exploded again and again, and she cried out joyfully each time. The pressure of passionate need within her body built and rebuilt to a screaming level, but what emerged from her with each climax was a long, low, muffled moan of all-consuming ecstasy.

Eventually they lay side by side, breathing deeply, touching and caressing in loving silence, and finally slipping easily into dreamy sleep.

IT WAS MID-AFTERNOON when Brad awakened. He opened his eyes sleepily, looking around without realizing at first where he was. Then he gazed across the bed and saw Nan sitting there, serenely watching him. She was naked and relaxed, leaning casually on one elbow.

"Hi there, nice lady."

"I didn't want to wake you. You were talking to me in your sleep, and trying to kiss me. I loved it."

"We'd both enjoy it more if I were awake."

"You look like a little boy when you're sleeping. Your face is all relaxed, and there are no lines. And you were smiling in your sleep, looking very pleased and satisfied. I hope I gave you that happiness."

"Oh, my Irish princess, you gave me more than just happiness. You gave me fulfillment, and yet left me with a sweet longing for you. God, you're so good! I've lost track of how many times...how much we did, but if I were younger, we'd do that all over again."

Her hands reached out for his body, her fingers seeking, squeezing, playing. He lay there, as she brought a new and unexpected surge of hot blood through him, pushing his need and response with an urgency.

She gazed into his eyes with a flirting little-girl look of teasing devilment and asked, "Just how young do you want to feel?"

Yielding to his desire, his arms went out to her loveliness, and she moved eagerly to him. With hands and mouths and bodies, they brought one another to a renewed readiness. In the mounting excitement of their passion, they experimented with each other's bodies and their newfound loving commitment.

And then they spent their desire all over again, finding between them a rhythm of mutual need and satisfaction. They forged a new physical commitment to match the solid emotional commitment they had perfected. In new and different ways, they found themselves feeling closer together, and younger and more vigorous than before.

WHEN NAN WOKE UP again, it was late afternoon. She lay cradled sleepily in Brad's arms, her legs entwined with his, and his fingers running softly through the silkiness of her hair. She looked up to see him watching her through eyes that smoldered with love.

"God, you're beautiful, lady. And more woman than I ever dreamed I'd know." His hand brushed her cheek and caressed the receptive skin of her neck and shoulder.

The phone rang before she could answer him, and being nearest it, she reluctantly rolled over to answer. Brad's hand slid across her back, coming to rest possessively on her bottom.

"Hello, Rafe." She smiled over the bareness of her shoulder and breast at Brad's grinning face.

"You been waiting for this call?" the sergeant chuckled.

"Not exactly, Rafe. But I thought it would be you. What's up?"

"Everything! You and Brad come on down here. Pronto!"

"We'll be right there," she said, and hung up the phone.

Turning to hug Brad, she said, "I guess everything's coming together."

"Think you can find the energy to get us downtown?"

"I may walk funny for a while, but I wouldn't miss this for the world! That is, unless you have a more pressing idea," she said, reaching for him.

"Lord, lady! Have mercy! Come on. Let's go see what they've put together."

THEY ARRIVED at Rafe's office just as George was entering. He dropped a stack of folders next to Rafe's paperwork, and turned to them with a smile of satisfaction.

"Well, how do you want it? Chronological by victim, or topical by area of investigation?" he asked with a flourish.

Brad could see the anguish behind George's eyes, and could identify with the effort George was making to put his grief behind him and immerse himself in the facts.

"It's your show," Brad answered. "Any way you can explain it quickly will do."

Rafe cut in. "Ah, but this could take a while. We've had help from a lot of agencies. We've got it all now. Go ahead, George."

"Well, to begin with, it's all about drugs, and it started back with the Knives in Southeast Asia. The coincidence of all the current investigations and the Congressional hearings brought it up to date.''

''Can we have a few details?'' Nan asked impatiently.

''I'm getting to that. I've done a quick correlation today of records at the State Department, the FBI, the Army, and the CIA. Your father was working with Luke to do a computer match-up of known illegal drug deliveries, dates, and routes that took place back when we were in Southeast Asia. They were matching them up with missions and flight plans of the Knives, and apparently, with some success, I might add.''

''What tipped them off?'' Brad asked.

''It probably started with the plan to use earlier drug smugglers to find information on the MIAs. Then during Ralston's hearings, an informant mentioned that his former partners were drug runners back in Southeast Asia, and that they were working cocaine now with their earlier contact. All he knew was that they delivered the drugs by air from Colombia to either Kansas or Colorado, and the contact's code name was something like Dragon. His ex-partners died in a crash while returning to Colombia from a delivery.''

''Sounds like one of our two boys was involved. Have you questioned the informant?''

''No such luck,'' Rafe said. ''On a hunch, I obtained the photo of the informant from the Congressional committee. It was the man we found in the car that was used to kill Ed a week ago. We've obtained a positive identification.''

''So the Colombian could've been killed because he informed,'' Brad said.

Nan broke in. "Maybe he was going to meet Ed. Or Bum."

"We'll probably never know," Rafe said. "But the circumstance was enough to justify showing photos of Lin and Mallard around in that murder scene neighborhood. Two people picked Lin's photo as a man seen near where Ed was killed and where the car was parked. We think Lin killed the Colombian and put him in the car."

"Not Mallard? But why would Lin kill Ed?" Brad asked.

George took up the explanation again. "Ed had somehow picked up on the story and the computer matching. The evidence was pretty clear that Lin was controlling drug routes through his province, but he didn't know a Knife was smuggling drugs. The dates and flights look like it was Mallard, or someone on his crew."

"And if Lin was the Colorado cocaine contact with the Colombians, he really couldn't let that knowledge get out," Nan said with a thrill in her voice.

"But what about Mallard?" Brad asked. "What about the phone tap and the police artist's drawing? Did that check out?"

"It wasn't necessary, but it helped," Rafe explained. "The drawing looked so much like Mallard that I had beards drawn on photos of each of the Knives, and Sue Snyder picked out Mallard right away. The phone tap was made at Mallard's electronics company. And by the way, that same company also makes a tiny electronic explosives detonator. I'm having drawings of it sent to the island police to check the debris again.''

"And with the ambassadorial confirmation coming up, Mallard couldn't have his past examined that closely with witnesses around," Brad said.

George cut in abruptly. "And speaking of photos, when the FBI showed photos to people at National Airport who were near Luke's helicopter, they limited their choices to pictures of Knives from their earlier military records. That meant Lin wasn't included. I supplied them with a photo of Lin made at Ralston's hearing, and members of the ground crew identified him as being near the helicopter with a tool bag.''

"That sounds pretty certain. So what now?" Brad asked.

"We checked the airline reservations and flight attendants, too," Rafe added. "Not only did we confirm that Mallard went to the island and back just before the funeral here, but we were able to trace Lin and Mallard to Colorado. Lin was back there in time to have killed Bum and Judge Sennet.''

"Are Lin and Mallard in this together?" Nan asked.

Brad answered, "I don't think it started that way. But if they ever were, the death of Lin's daughter will end that. Right now Mallard is probably tracking Lin just like he was tracking us on that mountain.''

"That's right," Rafe said. "Neither one can afford to have the other one around to talk. So it's probably kill or be killed for both of them when they get together. I've notified the state police out there to pick them up as soon as possible, and I'll try to go out there myself tomorrow.''

George spun around, a look of disgust on his face. "If I hadn't been hurt in that bomb blast that killed Noy, I'd go kill the bastard myself!"

"Hold on!" Rafe interjected. "Let's don't have any of that kind of talk. What we have is still a lot of good circumstantial evidence. We have no real proof. There may be enough to pick them up and get a grand jury called, but we'll need more than this to prove them guilty beyond a shadow of a doubt."

"You mean they might get away with it after all?" Nan asked incredulously.

Rafe looked perplexed, his huge hand running across his short hair. "Nancy, there's always that possibility. That is, unless one of them confesses, or we get an eyewitness or some other hard evidence."

"They're too careful for that," George said sullenly.

"Yes, they probably covered their tracks, just like they're trying to do now," Brad said thoughtfully. "It's kill or be killed, just like in the old days, except this time they're on opposite sides. They can run and wait for it to happen, or they can go at one another and get it over with."

Nan looked equally pensive. "If they kill each other before the police get to them, then we'll never be sure what happened."

Rafe got up and walked around the desk. "Now don't get so downhearted, Nancy. We'll just have to hope that we get to them and that they made a mistake somewhere. But right now, if you all will excuse me, I think

I'll go home to pack and get some sleep before that flight tomorrow. It's been a long, if productive day.''

"You know where Lin's ranch is?'' Brad asked casually.

"Yes. It's marked on that map on the desk. I have another copy with me.''

"Take care, Rafe. And thanks for the good work, George,'' Brad said as he and Nan shook hands with the men. He then escorted Nan out the door. As Brad practically pushed her ahead of him down the hallway, Nan pulled up and faced him with a questioning look.

"Wait a minute. Where are we hurrying to? Are you acting on your passionate impulses again?''

"Later, lady. Right now we've got places to go and things to do. So hurry along quietly and don't make a scene. I'll explain later.'' As she started to protest, he took her arm and smiled at her. "Trust me.''

She went along quietly to the car, and kept her silence as he drove quickly to a nearby service station, pulling up next to a phone booth.

"I'll be right back,'' he said, hurrying to the booth to make the phone calls he had planned at the police station.

She watched him make a call from a number on a card from his wallet, and then refer to a credit card while talking on the phone. Then she saw him make another call and refer to the map that had been on Rafe's desk. She thought to herself that he was too anxious to stand by while things were happening in Colorado. She hoped he wouldn't try to go alone.

When he re-entered the car, she said evenly, "You're going to Colorado." It was a statement, not a question.

"Nan, I can't stand by while they kill each other or get free. I know them, how they'll think, what they'll do. I've got to be there, for me and you, and for Dan, and Ed, and Luke, and Bum, and Quincy, and Noy."

"You could get killed out there!" she said as he drove into the street.

"Would you rather wait until the winner out there comes after us? You saw that letter. You want to look over your shoulder the rest of your life? I want a better life than that for us. So I intend to settle this now. I made a reservation for a flight tonight."

Stopping for a traffic light, he looked over to see her reaction. She was sitting tensely, her head down, chewing distractedly on her thumbnail. She didn't look at him when she finally spoke.

"I suppose you have a plan for this escapade."

"Yes," he said decisively, mustering his confidence. "One they'll understand. I'm going right at them. Fully armed. Then they'll have to stand and fight." He paused. "They won't get away," he said with resolve as he pulled into the traffic.

He felt her eyes on him. After a hesitation, she asked the question that had been hanging unspoken between them.

"And where do I fit into this macho menagerie?"

His answer was firm, with feeling.

"You can watch, if you do it from a safe place."

"Dan Donahue was my father," she said with spirit. "I'm going with you."

"I thought you'd say that," he said, smiling into her look of determination. "So I made a reservation for you, too."

He swerved the car erratically in the traffic as she reached across to hug and kiss him enthusiastically.

"Oh, you wonderful hunk! I love you so much!"

"Don't get the wrong idea. I want you safe. I just don't want you too far away from me. Not ever again."

"Oh, Brad. I'll have to wash my hair and pack some things."

"I have some rather specialized packing to do, too, so we'll stop by my place first. We have time, for the next flight is an overnight one that doesn't leave Dulles for a few hours. But remember, we're not going to a resort."

As Brad let them into his apartment, he squeezed Nan's arm and said, "Why don't you fix us a sandwich or something? This will take a few minutes."

"Whatever you say, lover. But leave me some time for a hot shower and shampoo," she said pertly. She watched Brad's careful preparations while she worked in the kitchen.

Brad pulled his large metal suitcase from a hall closet, and then opened the double-locked metal door of another storage area. From this he began to remove boxes and canvas bags, from which he took several leather cases. He opened them to inspect his equipment.

He quickly assembled a custom-built Mini-14 rifle with a folding stock and a telescopic sight, checked it, then disassembled it. Next he placed it in a metal case and into the large suitcase. Then he checked and added a night-vision scope, field glasses, an automatic pistol, some camouflage clothing, a long knife in a well-worn sheath, compass, ammunition, canteens and dried-food pouches.

Then Nan saw him disappear and return from the bedroom with more clothing and boots for the suitcase and slacks and a sport coat on a hanger. As he locked the big case, Nan noted that it was marked BOOKS— PLEASE HANDLE WITH CARE.

"Does that notice work?" she inquired.

"No one has asked me to open it yet. I'll change into these other clothes at your place. Is that food about ready?"

"Yes, it is. Can we eat in the car? I don't want to make us late."

"Sure. Hey, don't be so jittery. Relax," he said as he took her taut body in his arms. "We're going to take that trip you wanted. Pretend we're going to the Rockies to relax."

"I wish I could feel that comfortable about it. I just have this premonition that something bad is going to happen," she said with a shudder.

Brad squeezed her to him again. "We're going to catch up with them and make everything right, so don't worry about it. Now grab those sandwiches, and let's go."

Carrying the heavy suitcase, he followed her out the door. The hair standing up on the back of his neck made him wish he felt as casual as he was trying to sound for her.

LEAVING HIS SUITCASE in the car, in the secure parking area beneath Nan's apartment building, he followed her through the lobby and up to her apartment.

As she locked her door behind them, she started for her own bedroom, saying over her shoulder, "That sandwich made me thirsty. Why don't you pour us some wine while I wash my hair and get dressed? I hope I have time to dry it."

"Don't worry, we've got plenty of time."

Nan hurried to her bedroom and its adjacent bath, planning her packing as she went. She would need her trail boots, jeans and shirts and a jacket for the cool mountain weather, and a dress for the plane. But first, she needed a shampoo and a hot shower.

She removed her clothing quickly and adjusted the shower water, wishing she had time to soak in the tub for an hour or so. Closing the shower door behind her, she welcomed the hot, pelting water on her tired body. She applied a lotion, seeking a further healing of her bruised and dried skin, thinking of how nice it would be to have Brad doing the rubbing.

Wanting to look her best for him, she was determined to get her hair clean. While she was still rinsing the rich lather from her hair, she felt a coolness as the shower door opened behind her.

"Does Madame wish her wine served here?"

"Brad! You made me get soap in my eyes!"

"Then here, let me help."

She felt his naked body against hers, as his strong hands ran through her hair, freeing it of lather. A growing hardness was pressed against her bottom, telling her he had a more urgent need in his thoughts. It was such a sensual, sexy experience that she gave in freely to her own growing arousal.

Her mind went back to another shower scene, in a motel long ago, on what was intended to be a second honeymoon. The image of her husband and the blonde girl came and went quickly, her brief hesitation replaced by the loving warmth of the present.

Brad's hand caressed her body, seeking and teasing, touching and pleasing, bringing her to a state of tantalizing readiness for his body. His hardness slid between her legs, causing her hot throbbing there to intensify, and sending tingling sensations up and down her legs and spine.

"You feel so good," he said, his fingers and hands finding all the places she needed to be touched, and touching her within gave him a growing pleasure.

As he entered her, she had a quick thought that if anything happened to him tomorrow, this would be the last time they might make love, the last time she would feel him inside her. She put one hand behind him, holding his body to hers.

"Oh, my Brad, my Cowboy, you're such a terrific lover."

"With you, I can be anything. I love you, Nan."

He tried to put his feelings into his movements, thrusting slowly and deeply to fill her with the depths of his love. He felt her responding with matching emotions and movements.

"Ohhh, I love you so much," she moaned in a deep rich tone. "That's so good."

Feeling a humming vibration starting deep within her, she released a long, delighted sigh. Holding her face and breasts up to the hot, stinging spray of the water, she remembered again the cold waterfall leaping freely into the hollow from the cliff. She let her mind and body go with the growing rapture and began to thrust herself backward to meet his moves. She kept her legs and her squirming, mobile bottom in motion until the humming gave way to intensifying spasms that matched his thrusts. Soon the explosive shudders came, and they had each found their mutual fulfillment.

They stood together quietly in the warm shower spray, each breathing deeply, as he held her tightly in the afterglow. Then she turned to him and lovingly soaped every inch of his muscled body and kissed him here and there as she rinsed away the lather.

He rinsed her in return, and then took her face in his hands and kissed her gently on her eyes and nose.

"This time with you is precious, Nan. But we've got to get to that plane," he said, looking into her shining eyes. He turned off the shower and stepped from the tub with her.

"I know. I'll hurry," she said.

AT THE AIRPORT, Brad let Nan out at the terminal entrance with the bags while he took the car to the long-term parking. When he returned, he was pleased to see Captain Tim Blackwell standing beside her.

"Look who I ran into," Nan said cheerily.

"Hello, Tim. Did you get everything?"

"Yes, sir," he answered, handing Brad a folder. "There's a topographical map of the ranch area printed to a scale big enough for you to navigate as well as someone who's been over the area. There are some satellite photos to go with it." He was obviously pleased with the success of his efforts.

"Great. I hope this won't get you in trouble."

"No, sir. I had to use a few blue chips for them, but this mission is worth it. I want you to get one of those killers for General Luke Bonner."

"These will help me find them. Then we'll see what happens after we get there."

"I understand, sir. I made the reservation for the rental car, and there's another map of the general area and roads for you."

"You do good work, Captain. Thanks."

Nan, who had been looking on in curiosity, could hold back her questions no longer.

"Just what's going on here? I get the distinct feeling you two have been planning and working on this like a real military mission without even telling me. When did all this take place?"

Brad smiled at her and put his arm tightly around her waist, with his hand resting pleasantly on her hip.

"One of the calls I made this evening was to enlist Tim's help. I thought he might want to participate in some way, and he came through with his usual superior results. Tim, we really do appreciate this."

"Just nail the bastards, sir. Excuse me, ma'am," he said, looking down in his embarrassment at his language. Then he was serious and concerned again, looking directly into Brad's face. "And you take care, sir."

"You, too, Captain," Nan said earnestly.

"We'll talk to you when we get back," Brad added.

As Blackwell turned and walked away, Brad and Nan followed a porter and their bags into the terminal, arriving at the gate just as their flight was boarding.

Brad and Nan sat holding hands, looking out the window at the lights of the Washington area as the plane climbed to cruising altitude in the clear night air. Brad, sitting on the aisle, saw their reflections in the window. They looked good together, he thought, like two newlyweds on a honeymoon. But the apprehension he saw reflected in their faces now was caused not by wedding night anticipation, but by concern that if anything went wrong tomorrow, they might not ever have a honeymoon.

Nan turned to him, her expression a mixture of happiness and concern. She squeezed his hand and leaned to softly kiss his lips. He returned the light pressure, softly probing her lips with his tongue.

"Let's make it last a long time," she said softly. "See that you get through tomorrow safely."

"I promise. Now why don't you get some sleep while I study these maps and photos."

"Just don't go away without waking me first."

As she leaned her head against his shoulder, Brad adjusted the light and started studying the lay of the land of Lin's ranch. He found the trails, the canyons, the creeks, and the brush cover. His mind kept going back to the karst hills and jungles and trails where he had fought with instead of against Lin and Mallard.

In a way, he was stepping back into the past, to a time of survival by wit and instinct, to the definite possibility of killing or being killed by a sly and crafty enemy. Two enemies, in fact. They were a triad of Knives, each seeking the others, in a triangle of death.

He put the map aside and gazed at the beauty of Nan's lovely face and body. She was absolutely beautiful and vulnerable in the defenselessness of deep sleep. No one seeing that sweet face so calm and quiet in sleep would ever guess the insatiably sensual side of her nature that she had so recently shown him.

He would have to get her out of his mind tomorrow. He just couldn't afford the luxury of thinking of her when his life would depend upon his every thought and every move. He would see her safely away before he entered the killing zone. And he would then survive whatever happened to live out his life with her.

He turned back to his maps and photos, planning, remembering, preparing.

12

THE MORNING SUN was but a red glow in the eastern skies when Brad and Nan drove away from the Denver airport. It had been an uneventful flight, and even the baggage retrieval had gone smoothly. The car Tim Blackwell had arranged was waiting and the maps he provided were clear and helpful.

Nan had slept most of the flight and now she felt full of eagerness and anticipation, despite the early hour. She sat gazing at the man she loved at the wheel of the car, marveling at how quickly she had overcome her inhibitions and fears to accept the overwhelming love he offered. She was afraid that if she didn't think through each exciting and agonizing episode of the last ten days, that she would forget some precious moment that they had spent together. This time together was precious.

Brad was quiet and tense, his eyes on the road, but his thoughts obviously racing ahead. There was a tightness in his mouth, and lines of tension creased his brow. She felt guilty that she had slept while he stayed awake planning, for it was he, not she, who would be going into danger. She wondered how much sleep he had been able to find last night, and whether it had rested his taut and keyed-up body and mind. But his face now showed no emotion. He looked ready for anything.

After a while, she leaned and touched his thigh lightly. "How're you doing, Cowboy?"

"Just fine, lady, just fine. Sorry I'm not so talkative this morning. It's not the company. Just a lot on my mind." His smile rearranged the lines of his face, and he put his arm across the seat with his hand resting on the back of her neck. "I promise it'll be different when I wake up on a pillow beside you. Then you'll think I'm just a morning nuisance."

"Never," she said firmly, stifling the nagging thought that there would not be a morning like that if he didn't live through the day. "I'll probably be the one to wake you up with a sexy proposition. You're the bed partner I've been waiting for."

"Well, we'll see about who takes the initiative. Right now we've got to clean up a few details in our life and find the security that will let us sleep with both eyes closed. Then we can negotiate who'll do the waking and who'll be the nuisance."

"I think we should take turns," she said laughing and squeezing his leg.

"Just like a liberated woman, wanting it her way!" he said teasingly. "What is this cowboy getting into?"

She looked into his eyes sincerely. "Just remember that your love liberated me from whatever I was, Brad. You've helped me be what I am." Then with a smile she added, "And you can leave your spurs at the foot of the bed. This mustang is tamed and friendly."

"Shucks, ma'am, I thought we were gonna be a regular rodeo, wild horses and all."

"Maybe we will. That'll give you something to think about."

He pulled her closer and drove for a while with his arm around her, while she ran a loving hand up and down his thigh. Though the sun had come up, it was still cool at this altitude. They were in open country now, with few, if any houses. Soon he turned off the highway and found a side road into some low trees.

"Don't think I'm becoming a morning nuisance already, lady. We've got some repacking and dressing to do before we get to the ranch."

Brad took the large suitcase from the trunk of the car and started removing equipment to place it into a pack made of sturdy camouflage material. He attached the knife and several other items to a pistol belt and placed it on the floor in the back seat and put the pack in beside it. Then he assembled and checked the rifle and telescopic sight, placing it on the back seat under his sport coat.

He was changing from his dress shirt and slacks to his tough camouflage trail clothes and boots when he saw Nan in panties and bra on the other side of the car. Her skin was like gooseflesh in the chilly mountain air as she hurriedly changed her clothes.

Brad zipped up his last piece of clothing and moved around the car to take her in his arms, running his hands over the bare skin of her back and shoulders beneath her open blouse.

"You wearing that perfume again?" he asked in a teasing accusation.

"I was, but I won't put on any more."

"You drive from here," he said softly in her ear. Then with his arm around her, he walked her to the driver's side of the car and opened the door for her. He paused

to study the look of anxiety on her face and the tenseness of her body.

"You are pretty worried about this, aren't you?" he
asked in a troubled tone.

His cold fingers on her bare skin sent a new, different
chill through her. She looked up at him, their eyes just
inches apart.

"I'd be a fool not to be worried, Brad, and I'm nobody's fool. I know the chance you're taking by going
into that ranch to find two killers. I understand why
you're doing it, and I agree with you. And I know you're
good at what you're doing. But you've become my whole
life, my whole reason for living. So I can't help being
worried."

He kissed her warmly, fully on her eager lips, his
mouth capturing her fears, stealing her doubts, soothing her worries. Releasing her lips, he ran his hand
through her hair and pulled her head against his chest.

"It's going to be okay, Nan. I am good at this, or I
wouldn't be trying. It's something I have to do. I must
do it. And I'll come back to you. You mean too much to
me to let anything else happen."

Nan couldn't find the words to express her feelings.
She pulled his mouth to hers and tried to show him with
her kiss.

"I know," she said softly under her breath as she got
into the car. She slipped the small vial of the Kiss at
Dawn perfume into the pocket of her jeans. She hoped
she would use it to get his attention again tomorrow.

As Nan drove through the mountain roads, Brad
studied the maps and gave directions. He was all busi-

ness, all concentration and directed effort. She hated to interrupt him.

"Brad, there's a gas station up ahead. How about stopping to see if they have a little girls' room?"

"Okay, lady. We've got time."

While Nan went inside, the attendant approached the car, but Brad waved him off. The old man hesitated, then leaned against the car and pointed into the backseat.

"You goin' huntin' with that thing?" the grizzled face asked.

Brad noticed that the old man was pointing to the customized rifle. The coat had slipped off of it.

"You got it. It's a customized deer rifle. Damned good gun."

The man nodded and shuffled back into the station. Nan appeared a few moments later with a puzzled look on her face.

"What went on out here? That old man wished us good hunting. What did you tell him?"

"I didn't. He saw the rifle and assumed we were hunting. Did he bother you?"

"No, nothing like that. He was making a phone call. I guess I'm just nervous and overreacting.

"Probably. Just relax and enjoy this while you can."

She got behind the wheel again and pulled out of the station back on the highway. Brad went back to scouring his maps. She felt shut out and wanted to participate in what was happening.

"What are you going to do when we get to the ranch?" she asked.

"We'll stop here, at the ranch's edge," he said, indicating a point on the map. "I'll go cross-country from there to the ranch headquarters and try to make contact with anyone I can find. I'll try to locate Lin and Mallard, and if possible, take them."

"And what should I do in the meantime?"

"I want you to drive around to the ranch entrance and wait. If I don't meet you there within four hours of the time we separate, go for the sheriff and get him out here. Here's the phone number." He handed her a slip of paper with several numbers written on it.

"I have to cool my heels for four hours while you're wandering around in there?"

"Neither Lin nor Mallard will be in any of the obvious places a sheriff would look. I've checked over the terrain and the layout of the ranch on the maps and photos. In that time, I should know whether I can handle this alone, or if we'll need the sheriff to help."

"But four hours! I don't know if I can sit still that long, knowing what you may be up against."

"I don't need to be worrying about your safety while I'm doing this. I have enough of a problem getting you out of my mind to concentrate on what I have to do."

She looked across to see his smiling face. He looked capable and confident, and more handsome than she could ever remember. As she drove on, a sensation of possessiveness moved deep within her, a feeling of wanting and having, of needing and being satisfied. He was hers.

"Okay, pull over up here. This is where I get out."

He said it evenly, without emotion, but the words pierced her heart with pain. The feeling of separation settled heavily upon her as she realized that in moments he would be gone, perhaps never to return.

"Brad, wait," she cried as he retrieved the pack from the back seat and put on the pistol belt. "Not yet!" She wanted desperately to be held by him.

Brad was around the car by the time she had opened her door. He clutched her tightly in his arms, his mouth seeking the warmth of her neck beneath her ear.

"Nan, honey, I wouldn't go without a proper good-bye." His kiss echoed the sentiment, a long, lingering, eloquent statement of his love. "I'll be back to finish that," he whispered as he drew his mouth away.

"Not soon enough, Brad, but I'll be waiting. Take special care, my love. I'll be in agony until I see you again."

Picking up the pack and the rifle, he started for the barbed wire fence beside the road. He was having trouble separating the reality of what was happening from what he wanted it to be. He had to get his concentration in line.

"We'll have that time together soon, love. Don't stay here much longer. Someone might spot you. Remember, four hours from now at the ranch gate. And have a kiss ready for me."

She watched him climb the fence, put on the pack, and pick up the rifle before he turned and waved. As she waved back, she remembered the last time someone she loved had waved goodbye like that, just days ago. The boiling clouds of black smoke churned in her mind, and she closed her eyes in fear that Brad would suddenly be struck down by a sniper's bullets as she watched.

She opened her eyes again to see Brad darting into the trees up the hill, moving alertly and cautiously, his camouflage-green clothing blending into the underbrush. She drove away slowly, watching the road through uncontrollable tears.

BRAD MOVED QUICKLY up and across the ridge that separated the highway below from the ranch house in the valley on the other side. The tree cover was broken and the underbrush spotty in places. He avoided the obvious paths and easy routes without allowing the rough terrain to slow his progress significantly.

He couldn't help comparing the parting from Nan with the many departures for battle in Southeast Asia. There was often a casual attitude by those going into battle, perhaps to ease the tension, or maybe to help the Knives convince themselves that they had things under control. But none of the departures over there came close to the heart-wrenching emotions he had just experienced. He had to get his thinking under control and forget about her for the moment.

He felt his instincts take over. The colors and tones of leaves became important. The smells of pine and mountain soil, the movement of birds, the sounds of breezes and branches were all a part of his surveillance of the territory. He remembered Lin's remark about having sensors as good as they had used in Southeast Asia, and he watched for signs of them as he moved through the brush. There was a lingering concern that he, too, was being watched.

Upon reaching the ridge line, he paused for a breather, and to sum up what he had seen so far. This was not a working ranch. A fence in bad repair told him that it was not being properly maintained. Nor was it needed, for there were no signs of livestock of any kind, nor was there any evidence that this area had been traveled by men on foot or on horseback. There were no new trails, and the old ones looked unused. Lin was not really a rancher on a scale to match the land available.

Through an opening in the trees, Brad could see the ranch house far below. He took his bearings on it and planned his route down the slope before moving along the ridge line to a dip in the elevation. It was a natural passage from one side of the ridge to the other, and was a place Lin would want to watch.

Approaching the notch from above and out of sight, he stopped to inspect the area, and then used his field glasses to check specific locations that could hide an observer. There was no evidence that anyone was there, or had been there. He checked the trail that crossed the gap below, and then searched the sides carefully with the glasses.

He found what he was searching for on the ranch house side of the gap, just off the trail. A casual observer would have ignored it as a spindly dead bush. However, having hauled and planted such bushes years ago, he recognized the coloring and the smooth, even surface and curvature of the metal branches. It was a trail sensor, an acoustical device installed to monitor movements on the route through the gap.

There was no way to tell how many of these he had passed in his climb up the ridge. But a long look through the glasses at the ranch house in the distance allowed him to pick out the right antenna from the many on the roof.

With a relay, Lin could easily monitor the entire ranch area through this electronic listening surveillance.

If all the equipment were this sophisticated, he wondered if it were combined with seismic or pressure monitors in the ground. There was no sign of activity around the ranch headquarters area, so there was no way to determine whether he had been spotted yet.

From this distance, Brad could not tell how many ranch hands Lin might have, so before starting down the slope to the ranch house, he checked his equipment again. He assured that it was immediately ready and yet would not be lost or make any noises that would give his position away.

The last item he checked was the combat knife at his belt. It was a foot long, sharpened on both sides of the blade, and tapered inward to a jagged, serrated edge midway to the hilt. It was a killing instrument, and the scars it carried told of much use. It was the weapon of last resort, for quiet use at close range.

He had just started down the slope, keeping to the cover of the low trees, when a movement on the edge of his vision alerted him. He crouched and rolled quickly into the brush as quietly as possible. Sighting over the rifle at the movement, he saw a large buck deer walk out into a nearby clearing.

Scanning the brush around the buck, he saw no other movement. Brad had to stifle a laugh as the deer started nosing at one of the acoustical sensors that he hadn't seen until now. Had the animal not appeared, he would have passed very near the device. To spook the deer would be as bad as making a noise the device would pick up, so he changed his direction slightly and eased down the hill downwind of the deer and out of range of the listening device.

Arriving at a rock outcropping near the ranch house, he took up a position he had chosen from above. It gave him a full view of the ranch headquarters area without exposing him. He had a rock in front of him and a rock face behind, and he could enter and leave the area without being seen from below. Removing the pack, he used the field glasses to check out the area beneath him, picking out other places for concealment. He looked around for movements, but saw none. The ranch house appeared deserted.

There was a fairly large cleared area between him and the house that would make an approach difficult. He puzzled for a moment at an arrangement of posts in the clearing that reminded him of a soccer goal without a net. An unruly tangle of ropes hung above a pile of hay at the base. His eyes were drawn over it to the other side of the house.

There was something in the rocks across from him that didn't look right. It was an equally good firing position to cover the ranch house, and one he would have chosen had he approached from that direction. Being careful not to allow a sun glint off his equipment, he removed a surveillance scope from its case and began to observe the area through various color filters.

With the deceptive colors removed, he identified the texture of camouflage netting that covered an area of rough rocks and brush. After watching for a few moments through the high-powered scope, he saw the careful movements and unmistakable profile of Denton Mallard.

If Lin were in the house, he must have been there for some time, and Rafe had said that the deputies had not found him. So Lin must be somewhere out on the ranch, and blocked away from his surveillance equipment. He couldn't have heard Brad coming in, but Lin must be aware of a threat in the area. He might be watching them even now, with his personal knowledge of the terrain to his advantage.

Brad thought back to the ambushes in Southeast Asia, to the hours of watching and waiting, to the constant attempts to take the advantage away from the enemy, if only for the brief time of attack. His mind dwelled upon the times he had followed Luke Bonner down narrow trails, avoiding enemy ambushes and setting others. He recalled the time a third group had passed them to take the ambush they had avoided. They were never sure just who the enemy was on any given day, or where they would come from.

Now Brad knew that he had two separate enemies to fight. One was located, but the other, the real threat in this locale, could be anywhere. He slowly turned to scan the rocks around him, to convince himself that Lin was not above or behind him. He saw no one.

The buzzing of a light plane engine at low altitude suddenly filled the valley, and an earth-colored aircraft with no markings appeared from beyond the ranch house, waggling its wings as it passed. A small parachute was ejected from the plane with a bundle swinging beneath it. The package landed in the clearing below. The plane quickly pulled up and circled the area, apparently for another pass.

This time, Brad saw a tail hook assembly drop from the rear of the aircraft as it approached. His eyes went immediately to the posts in the clearing below as he realized the purpose of the ropes stretched there. The tail hook neatly caught the rope between the posts and pulled a bundle from the hay piled in the area. The bundle was reeled into the plane as it climbed and departed. Brad suddenly realized that he had just observed a delivery and payoff, probably involving illegal drugs.

He was still leaning forward on the rock when a burst of slugs hammered the boulder near his hands. He jerked back quickly, his eyes going immediately to Mallard's position. He saw no movement or change there. Another hail of slugs slammed into the rock behind him, showering him with cutting fragments of rock. The slugs ricocheted off the rock wall behind him, making his position immediately untenable.

Grabbing his pack, he scrambled in a crouch to another rock nearby. Wiping away the blood from cuts on his face and neck, he extended the folding stock of the rifle and prepared to fire. All he needed was a clear target.

He used the rifle's telescopic sight to observe Mallard's position, and much to his amazement, saw him rise and take aim to his left. He heard the shots of the unsilenced rifle and saw the puffs of dirt as the slugs struck. Through the scope, he saw Lin rise and run quickly to another position, with a second burst of slugs right behind him.

Brad fired several shots at the rocks around Mallard, taking away his advantage of concealment. In return, he was driven back by the close impact of slugs from Lin's

silenced weapon. Brad looked up quickly to see Lin
climbing the slope behind him, darting from tree to rock
to tree, with Mallard's bullets striking close behind him.
It was a three-way shootout that was about to give way
to a three-way chase through rough country.

Brad ducked under a hail of fire from Mallard, and
returned the fire just as Mallard scrambled behind another nearby rock outcropping. Seeing that Mallard did
not appear, Brad slung his pack over his shoulders and
started out on a line that would let him cut Lin's trail up
the slope.

AFTER DROPPING Brad off, Nan drove slowly up the
highway that bordered Lin's ranch. The parting had
touched her deeply, and she struggled to regain her
composure as she drove. She kept telling herself that
what they were doing was right. They had to stop Mallard and Lin before they got away. And no one could do
that as well as Brad.

Checking the roadmap again, she decided to go on to
the gate at the entrance of the ranch now. It might be
locked, and she would have to find some way to open it
other than ramming it with the rental vehicle. But then,
that might be the easiest solution. She felt her impatience sitting heavy on her shoulders, and she was determined to help in some way.

She didn't notice the cluster of cars at the ranch gate
until she was almost there. A uniformed man stepped out
and held up his hand. She had no choice but to stop. Two
other men then stepped out from the cars, and Nan saw
that they were police cars. The men seemed to be young,
officious looking, and full of swaggering self-impor-

tance. As the first man stepped up to her side of the car, another stood behind, with the third positioned on the other side.

"What seems to be the problem, officer?" she asked in the best voice she could muster. She was feeling guilty already.

"I'm a deputy sheriff of this here county, ma'am. I'll have to ask you to pull over here off this highway and step out of your vehicle."

The look that went with the words was stern. The faces of the other two matched his, and their hands seemed ominously near their pistols.

"Of course. Right over here?" She kept her voice even, but just barely. She was afraid she would start trembling. She drove off the road to the place the deputy indicated and sat waiting.

"Now you just keep your hands on the wheel and step out of the car."

Grasping the wheel tightly, she asked, "How do I get the door open?"

As the absurdity of it hit her, the tension relaxed in her body. The deputy opened the door, and she stepped out, feeling more confident than nervous.

The deputy took the keys from the ignition and pitched them to another deputy who stood at the trunk of the car. The third deputy had opened the other car door and was searching the back seat. "Nothing in here, Asa," he said, slamming the car door.

"Anything in the trunk, Clem?" the deputy beside her asked.

"Yeah, Asa. A large suitcase."

"That your bag?" Asa asked of Nan.

"Yes," she lied in her most confident voice. She didn't like the lie, but it might give Brad some advantage. Still, she was surprised at how easy it came.

"Check it, Clem," Asa instructed.

To Nan's dismay, Brad had left the suitcase unlocked, and the deputy opened it and rummaged through the contents.

"Man's clothes, Asa. And some leather cases," Clem announced.

"Well, ma'am, it looks like we'll have to hold you here for a while," Asa said, taking a notebook from his pocket and jotting a note in it.

"Just what is this all about? I haven't done anything wrong!" Nan said testily. She was beginning to feel humiliation and growing anger replace her nervousness and guilt.

"The sheriff of this here county told us to detain any suspicious characters we see hereabouts. We got a call from a gas station up the road that said a man and a woman was driving through here in a car just like this one with a customized Mini-14 rifle with folding stock and telescope sight on the backseat. Seems the caller is a gun collector, and he knews a huntin' rifle when he sees it, and a killin' gun when it turns up. That makes you a suspicious character. Now where's the man who was with you?"

Nan hesitated, her mind reeling, not wanting to do anything to harm Brad.

"I'm gonna need some identification," the deputy continued.

She reached into the car for her purse. The sudden movement brought a series of snapping sounds as the deputies reached for their weapons and unsnapped their holsters. She stopped, halfway through the window, and held up her purse for them to see.

"Easy now. Let's have it."

The deputy called Clem stepped up to take the purse, his other hand replacing his pistol in its holster. Nan's fright at the sudden threat changed again to anger, and she fought to control her temper. These men were obviously on edge, and could be dangerous. Clem took her driver's license from the purse and gave it to Asa, throwing the purse back on the seat.

"From Chicago," Asa said, walking to a patrol car.

The harsh tone of the deputy's voice said that her current residence did not add to their confidence. Nan felt a quick pang of longing to be back in her dress design office in Chicago. It was quickly replaced by her concern that she had placed herself and Brad at odds with the law.

Clem stood beside her, looking her body up and down with appreciation while Asa talked on the radio. As Asa returned, he also looked at her with speculation, but apparently with new respect as he spoke with Clem.

"Her ID checks out. She came out here with a guy named Brad Gaelman. He's some kind of high-falutin' Washington security man. We're to find him and hold them both in protective custody for later questioning when a Sergeant Johnson gets here. He's with the Washington, D.C. police, and he'll be here this afternoon."

Nan relaxed somewhat and smiled at the thought of Rafe's arrival. Her change in mood apparently made the deputies uncomfortable, as they searched the ground with their eyes instead of staring at her blouse.

Clem looked at her and said patronizingly, "If you think you're protecting Mr. Gaelman or something, you better think again. They's been some mighty mysterious killings going on around here, and he could be the next one. Why don't you tell us where he is and what he's doing?'

Nan turned away from him, not wanting her face to reveal anything to the deputy.

"I guess you can sit in the car, ma'am, but don't try to go anywhere," Asa instructed.

As they walked away, Nan realized in irritation that she couldn't go anywhere because Asa still had the car keys. She looked at the gate to the ranch and saw that it was not only unlocked, but stood wide open. It was blocked by one of the patrol cars, which faced into the ranch. And somewhere out there, Brad was unaware of all this. She wanted to be with him, to warn him. But now she could only wait until he came to the gate.

NAN SAT in the rental car for some time listening to the deputies talking by radio with another deputy who was apparently parked up the gravel road to the ranch house. In between calls, they discussed the weather, the sheriff, the cattle market, and the girls at a nearby truck stop. She was growing increasingly tense and impatient with the inactivity. She felt she must get to Brad.

A loud, excited transmission by the deputy up the road brought the three deputies at the gate running to the patrol car nearest the highway.

"Yeah, Hank. Go ahead," Asa said into the microphone.

"It's that same small dirt-colored plane flying low over the ranch again. I just seen it go by real low over to the ranch house. Over."

"Damn! Does it look like it's gonna land?" Asa asked.

"Dunno. Hard to tell. Here it comes again. Over. Wait a minute! I heard shots!"

"Someone shootin' at the plane?" Asa yelled into the mike.

"Can't tell. It's flying off now. Wait! More shots! Down to the ranch house!"

Nan had come out of the car at the first mention of shots. She noted that the deputies were all away from the gate and looking the other way. In a few short steps she was climbing through the open door of the patrol car near the gate and turning the keys that had been left in the ignition. The engine caught immediately, and her rapid acceleration through the open gate caused the car door to slam. She instinctively snapped the seat belt.

"Are you sure they're at the ranch house?" Asa was asking when he heard the car start up and speed away. "Clem! Get after her! That bitch is gonna be more trouble than her cute ass is worth!"

Since Asa had not released the mike button, Nan heard his words on the radio in the car she had taken. The remark irritated her even more. Her heart was hammering, her mind was racing, and her whole body was taut and committed to keeping the speeding car on the gravel road. She looked in the rearview mirror to see another car approaching rapidly behind her. And she heard Asa still talking on the radio.

"Hank, they's a woman tearing down the road at you in one of our patrol cars. Just stop her, but don't hurt her none. She's some special treatment item for the Washington, D.C. police, and we've been told to cooperate with them."

"Gotcha, Asa. I'll just flag her down."

"You got a good block there, Hank?"

"Sure do. Got gullies on both sides. What about them shots?"

"Sheriff says to hold our position until we get some backup out here. Just hold your position and let Clem bring the woman back when he catches up."

"I'm right behind her, Asa. Damn, if she don't drive as good as she looks!"

Nan checked the mirror to see that the car following was right behind her. She was beginning to wonder if her actions were a good idea when she saw the patrol car blocking the road ahead. At the speed she was traveling, she wasn't sure she could get her car stopped in time without being hit from behind by the car almost on her bumper.

She saw that to the left of the blocking car was a steep bank, but the right side was practically level. She accelerated the car and steered for the clear area on the right.

Nan didn't see the gully until the patrol car launched out over it. Fortunately the roadblock was set up to stop traffic from the other direction, and the bank she left was higher than the bank that the car slammed down on across the gully. She wrestled the car back to the road quickly and looked into the mirror in time to see the deputy following her perform the same maneuver.

The radio came alive again.

"Whooooeee! That's a wild woman I'm chasing. She drives like a bat outta hell!"

"What's she done now?" came Asa's agitated voice.

"She's jumped the gully at the roadblock," Hank yelled into his radio.

"Well, stay after her, Clem! Pull her over before she gets into that shooting!" Asa directed.

"I'll do it, Asa. But I do admire her drivin'."

The road had curved into a narrowing of the valley out of sight of the road block when the windshield in front of Nan began to shatter, along with the right side window. She threw up her arm in front of her face instinctively while fighting for control of the car. The odd holes in the glass that she saw beneath her arm told her that someone was firing at the car, even as she felt more slugs strike the vehicle. She heard one of the tires blow out, and the car swerved off the road.

The sudden movement of the car caused Nan's head to strike the window beside her. Only her seat belt kept her from being slammed against the steering wheel when the car struck a rock beside the road. A kaleidoscope of stars filled her head, and she leaned back holding it with her hands, trying to clear her vision.

Through a haze, she saw Clem's car race past, run off the road, and roll over, crashing against some rocks. She saw him climb from his window and collapse on the ground. She heard Asa calling frantically on the radio as she slipped into blackness.

NAN AWAKENED to feel someone pulling her roughly from the car. Her head felt as though it were about to explode, and she felt a wave of dizziness as she was jerked to her feet. She swayed heavily against the arms that held her and struggled to clear her head to complain to the deputy about the rough handling. She opened her eyes and looked directly into the smiling face of General Tran Vinh Lin, the Golden Dragon.

He was wearing camouflage clothing like Brad's and was wearing a pack and carrying a strange-looking rifle. She tried to twist free, and opened her mouth to scream. Before she could make a sound, his strong, bony hand gripped her mouth cruelly, closing it and pinching her lips and cheeks painfully.

"It would be wise for you to realize that you are quite vulnerable and that any noise you cause will only make things worse for you. Now move! Quickly! That way!"

His voice was flat and bitter, and his expression was one of cruelty, if anything could be read in the hardened face. He pushed her up the hill into the trees, and she again felt a wave of dizziness and an excruciating pain in her head. She felt hurt and helpless, and could only do as he directed through the tight grasp of his powerful hand on her arm.

They crossed the low ridge above the road, and Lin pushed her against a rock in some underbrush. His eyes terrorized her, telling her to be still and silent. He kept the rifle pointed at her while he surveyed the scene on the road below and scanned the terrain around them. Nan could see over the rocks that Clem still lay beside his car, and she could still hear the chatter on the radio, though she could not make out the words. She wondered how long she had been unconscious.

Lin's hand pulled her roughly to her feet and he pointed up the hill behind them.

"Move quickly and remain quiet," he said threateningly.

She did her best to fight her dizziness and pain while struggling up the steep hillside. When they reached the top of the next ridge, she slumped to the ground, no longer able to keep up the pace.

"You are very soft and weak, Miss Donahue," he snarled. "But you should know that if I leave you here, it will not be in a condition that you or Gaelman will like. I doubt if he would ever look at you again, if you lived. If I am forced to leave you, you would want to die. Now get up!"

As she struggled to her feet, Lin grabbed her blouse, ripping it open. She drew back from him in a new terror, only to see him thrust at her with a knife. He deftly cut her bra between her full breasts, and pulled it from her, cutting the straps as she twisted away and fell to the ground.

"Don't you touch me!" she gasped, trying to pull the ragged tatters of the blouse together and to cover her breasts with her arms.

He stood holding the large knife in one hand and the bra in the other while he grinned down at her. "Get up," he said in a low voice.

She pulled up against a rock behind her, still trying to cover herself. She tried to show her determination in her voice.

"I mean it. I would rather die than let you do that to me!"

Lin threw his head back and laughed out loud, a low, harsh, guttural sound.

"You stupid cow! Do you think I would want your fat, bulging body? How ridiculous! Even if you were as slender as the beauty of the Orient, I would spit on your garish reddened hair, your outsized height and your spoiled and outrageous mannerisms! Don't make me laugh with your insults!"

Nan looked at him in shock and suspicion at his words. No one had ever talked to her like this. What did he mean by tearing her clothes? What did he want from her?

Holding up the bra, he explained with a grin. "This, you western slut, is for bait, just as those voluminous breasts will be. I have Denton Mallard and your capable Brad Gaelman chasing me back there," he said pointing across the last ridge. "This clothing will give them something to think about, something to worry over. Later you will be my decoy. That will give me all the advantage I need. You are a hostage to be proud of."

Nan groaned aloud as she realized the meaning of his plan. She tried to run, but he grabbed her hair and jerked her painfully to her knees in front of him, the bra draping from his hand. With his other hand, he held the knife in front of her, grazing her firm nipple. Then he plunged the blade through the bra.

"I intend to leave only this stupid apparel. If you do not cooperate with me, I will slice off your breasts and leave them for Gaelman to find. You'll be my decoy, living or dead. Take your choice."

Nan's head was spinning, and her stomach turned with his grisly words. The thought that he had killed others recently gave added meaning to his threats. As she hesitated, he leaned closer, speaking softly but precisely into her ear.

"Do you doubt my words, or merely find them distasteful? I feel quite comfortable with them and what they mean. You see, we are from different cultures, with different values."

She felt horrified and powerless. Even so, she had to find a way to warn Brad. Maybe going along with Lin would give her that chance, or at least let her live to try.

"All right," she muttered. "What do you want?"

"That's better. Now move. This way, and be quick about it. And very quiet." As he spoke, he draped the mutilated bra across the branches of a nearby bush.

Nan moved ahead of him, trying to protect herself from the branches. The day had warmed up, but she knew the night would be colder for her, if she lived that long. She was tired, and her head ached. And she wanted Brad. She wanted so much to be in his arms again. All this seemed so unreal.

BRAD CROUCHED in the brush just below the ridge line, looking down at the wrecked cars on the road beneath him. Two deputies searched the brush further down, and he listened with interest to what he could hear of their conversation. He couldn't get all the words, but he heard a mention of "that Donahue dame" several times, and some discussion of the gate. He assumed that Nan had gone to the gate to wait for him, and was now safely with the law officers.

He couldn't fully understand the meaning of the wreckage, but the tracks of Lin and Mallard had led to this spot, and he had found brass casings from rifle shells among the pine straw here. There had been another shooting, probably from Lin's silenced rifle. The trail leading away showed that Mallard had passed this way, and someone had joined Lin here, so now he had three opponents to worry about.

It was growing late in the day, coming close to the dangerous half-light of dusk. He knew Lin well enough to expect an ambush during those darkening hours, if he or Mallard didn't catch up with him and his companion first. Brad moved out at a faster rate, determined to close the distance between them, feeling more comfortable now that Nan was safe with the deputies.

THE LAST RAYS of the sun were peeking over the mountain when Lin grabbed Nan's hair and pulled her to a painful halt. She leaned over, hands on knees, winded and nearly exhausted from the rapid pace Lin had set.

"We will stop here for a while. Do not move from that spot."

Gasping for breath, she could not respond. She rubbed her hands soothingly over her body, sore now from a hundred scrapes by branches. She shivered, feeling the evening cold creep in now that they were no longer moving and staying warm.

"Come quickly," he said in a low voice. "Stand against this tree." He indicated a tree right off the narrow trail they had been following.

As she leaned back, he grabbed her wrists and tied them around the tree behind her. Before she could object, he stuffed a rag in her mouth and tied it there with another strip of cloth.

Running his hands roughly across her breasts, he snarled, "Now, look pretty for me." With those words, he disappeared into the gloomy brush beside the trail.

Nan realized that this was no rest break, but a trap for one of the men pursuing them. Would it be Brad? She struggled to move her mouth to loosen the gag, and peered with tired eyes down the darkening trail. But though a full moon was already rising, she could neither see nor hear anyone.

After struggling unsuccessfully with the gag again, she glanced at the trail in time to see a movement in the growing darkness. She realized that she now stood in the bright light of the rising moon. She stayed very still, listening, and was beginning to think she had been mistaken, when she saw the head and shoulders of a man emerge from the bushes near the trail. She began to squirm against the ropes, trying to yell through the gag in warning.

To her dismay, the shadowy man emerged from the brush and approached her slowly. He was but a few steps away and moving faster when another shadow leaped from the bushes and kicked the newcomer to the ground, sending his rifle flying into the brush. The two men grappled on the ground, and then came to their feet in the moonlight right in front of Nan.

She saw the glint of reflected light off one knife, then another. She could make out Lin's form from its size, but the shadows and the movements of the other man made it difficult for her to identify him. The knives slashed between them, as they silently circled about before her, each knowing there was another opponent out in the darkness. Then the larger man leaped at Lin with a vicious thrust of his long knife.

Lin adroitly dodged the man and parried his thrust, bringing his knife up under the larger man's extended body. There was a loud grunt, then a weak cry, followed by a gurgling as the man fell heavily to the ground.

Lin stood panting over the fallen victim. "Die, you foolish pig! No nation will suffer under your ambassadorship!"

Nan slumped against the tree in relief as she realized the fallen man was Mallard and not the man she adored. She was also panting for breath, and her pulse was racing with the fear she had held in her heart.

As Lin stepped up to her to remove the gag and the bindings on her wrists, Mallard moaned in his agony. As Nan stood rubbing her wrists and jaw, Lin turned and leaned over the fallen man, speaking to him quietly but harshly, and then rolling him over onto his back. Lin kicked him unconscious. He then grabbed his rifle and pack and pushed Nan onto the trail.

"Move, slut, and do it quietly," he said in a low tone.

"You're going to leave him to die?"

"He didn't come here to congratulate me, nor did your Brad Gaelman. Now, if you don't want him to see you in pieces, you'd better move out!" he growled.

Nan turned and picked her way up the trail through the broken moonlight and shadows. The thought that Brad was somewhere just behind them gave her encouragement and dread at the same time. She had to warn him somehow.

BRAD MOVED CAREFULLY along the narrow trail, ever alert to the night sounds, the odors along the trail, and the instincts within him. The moonlight was a help and a hindrance. He was able to see the outline of the trail and some detail of the brush. But he could no longer read the signs left on the trail by earlier travelers, and the shadow he threw across the landscape was often larger than his body and much easier to see.

At intervals, he reached into his pack to draw out the large infrared nightscope. In its passive mode, the enhanced moonlight was as bright as day. He could spot the coolness of overturned rocks, and see broken branches. By projecting its invisible infrared beam, he could illumine the countryside with light visible only through a nightscope, if the battery lasted.

Because of its bulkiness and limited battery time, he could not use it for constant viewing: He used it now with no infrared projection to scan the rocky terrain about him, to pick up only the infrared heat being emitted by the plants and rocks.

The nightscope showed a slight movement on the trail ahead. It was a form that looked out of place. Replacing the instrument in his pack, Brad crouched, staring into the darkness ahead, marking every detail as he proceeded up the trail from shadow to shadow. As he approached the area where the scope had shown the movement, he heard a low groan and a rustle of pine straw. He crouched again, waiting and watching, wary of an ambush.

The form on the trail was the body of a man, apparently injured, and moaning in agony. Even at this distance, Brad could smell the blood. Seeing no evidence of a trap, he approached the figure slowly. Eventually he was close enough to see the face in the bright moonlight. Denton Mallard. There was no gun in sight, and both of his hands were visible. It looked as though Mallard had caught up with Lin and his traveling companion.

Brad moved to Mallard's side and took his arms carefully.

"Denton, it's Brad. Where are you hurt?"

"Gaelman. Knew you'd come along. For God's sake, don't move me!"

"I'll be careful, Denton. Can you sit up and drink?"

"No! Don't! That yellow bastard left a live grenade under my back. Don't move me! Besides, he gutted me with that dragonhead knife of his."

Brad didn't know what to say to that. "Can I do anything for you?"

"Just listen. Here."

Mallard handed him some soft fabric that was unidentifiable in the dark. "What's this?" Brad asked.

"Found this on the trail. Brassiere . . . all cut up. Left the pieces for us to find. The Donahue woman was with him. Saw her . . . tied to a tree there. Was watching her . . . when I should've been looking . . . for Lin. He jumped me. Cut me up in a fight." Mallard was speaking and breathing with difficulty from the effort. A gurgling followed his words.

Brad's mind was reeling with the revelation that Nan was in danger. His heart was pumping, and he was fighting the urge to run up the trail in pursuit.

"Nan! Was Nan okay?"

"Looked okay." He coughed, in obvious pain.

"Easy, Mallard."

"Killed her dad. Dan...was getting too close. Would've screwed up the ambassador confirmation. Knew about my drug business. Tried to get you, too. Knew too much. And that dragoness bitch on the island. Was...trying for Windham, but...wanted to get both." He ended in a cough again.

"What about the others?" Brad asked.

"Musta...been Lin...got them. Came here to... finish him. That golden dragon bastard got me instead!"

Mallard shuddered and went rigid, then relaxed with a long sigh. Brad felt for a pulse and found none. He realized he was losing time, while Lin was moving ahead with Nan. He would have to leave Mallard's body. But he couldn't leave the grenade for some deputy to detonate.

From his pack, he took a small roll of wire, and quickly attached the end to Mallard's arm. As he moved up the trail, he strung the wire out behind him. At a safe distance, he stopped and pulled on the wire, rolling Mallard's body over. There was a brief pause, then an explosion ripped the night air.

Brad knew Lin would hear the noise and he would have to worry about it. After scanning the landscape ahead with the nightscope, he moved out as quickly as the darkness and his instincts would allow.

Nan stopped suddenly when she heard the explosion. She turned to see Lin looking back down the ridge in the direction of the sound. He quickly removed a nightscope from his pack and surveyed the terrain behind him. She wanted to run, to hide, but she realized that with this instrument he could easily find her in the dark.

"What was that?" she asked finally.

"It was either Mallard in search of a quicker death, or your Gaelman trying to move him." His tone reflected confusion and doubts. "The Cowboy is too smart. He wants to confuse me."

Nan felt a tightening in her chest beyond what the exertion had caused. She knew in her heart that Brad had to be okay. He was back there, coming for her. He had to be.

Scanning down the hillside again with the nightscope, Lin said evenly, "This is a good place. We will wait here to see if the Cowboy survived."

Pushing her roughly against a tree, he again tied her hands and gagged her. This time she was expecting it, and she tried to hold her jaw in a way to resist the tightness of the cloth he tied over her mouth and around her head. Though she was not entirely successful, she felt that she might be able to work the gag loose if he didn't watch her too closely.

As he moved away into the brush, she sat at the base of the tree and tried to focus her eyes on the shadows of the trail that ran along the ridge in front of her. She tried to concentrate, to reach out with her heart and mind to Brad and somehow warn him. She could feel that he was alive and close. She shivered as the cold crept into her.

"Please, oh please, Brad, be careful," she mumbled into the cloth that bound her mouth.

MOVING QUIETLY and carefully along the trail, Brad stopped to remove an insect that had landed in his eye.

He stood struggling to remember the maps and photos of this area that he had studied so diligently. If he remembered correctly, there was a flattened elevation ahead and above him. The slope of the land indicated that the trail probably went up the hill and across the side of the ridge.

Lin would have to stay with the trail to make good time and avoid loud noises in the underbrush. He would probably wonder by now about the significance of the grenade explosion. The edge of that level area would make a good place to stop and observe the trail behind. Brad took out the nightscope and set it on a tripod to steady the projected infrared light. He just might be able to catch Lin in the open and away from Nan.

He scanned the area above in the passive mode, and saw that he was right about the direction of the trail and the area above. He checked the battery and switched to the projection mode to get a look ahead under the invisible infrared rays. As he swept the area up the trail, his eye began to water from the irritation the insect had caused, blurring his vision.

He rolled over and took out a handkerchief to clear his eye, and the nightscope exploded beside him. The whining ricochet of another slug told him he was under fire. He rolled over and grabbed his rifle just as another burst hit the weapon, knocking it from his grasp into the darkness, and numbing his hands. A sudden, sharp pain in his side and the spreading warmth that followed told him he had been hit.

On hands and knees, he scooted backward, the pain in his side grabbing him like a giant fist. Hoping that Lin was too far away to hear the noise he was creating, he rolled through the leaves to a rock that was covered by shadows.

The storm of rage inside his head masked all external inputs. But soon the pain could not be ignored or resisted. It dragged him brutally from his personal order and discipline into panic and withdrawal from the events around him. Flashes of jungle trails and death and destruction ran through his chaotic mind. He lay still, fighting for control. Another burst of slugs slammed into the area, bringing back his need and demand for discipline.

Using the handkerchief he still held, he cleared blood away from the injury, which he told himself was just a flesh wound. From his pistol belt, he removed the first-aid kit, ripped open a sulfa-drug packet and poured it into the area of the wound.

Another nightscope! Brad realized suddenly that Lin had a nightscope, too. He had located Brad by observing the infrared projection of Brad's scope.

But Lin was just ahead on the trail. Now Brad had lost his weapon and his scope. But he still had his pistol and his knife, and if he moved quickly, perhaps he could catch Lin before he moved too far. Brad slapped a bandage over the wound and wrapped another around his body to hold the first in place. Struggling to his feet, he grabbed his pack and started quickly up the trail.

NAN HAD WATCHED in horror as Lin set his nightscope on a tripod and began to fire into the darkness. She felt as though each sputtering burst was hitting her. A desperate need to take some action was pounding in her head.

He stopped firing and leaned his rifle against a tree. Then he quickly folded the tripod and walked up to her, his scope under his arm. He leaned into her face.

"Your cowboy lover seems to have more lives than a cat, but that should slow him down. I've destroyed his nightscope, so I now have a decided advantage in the darkness."

As he reached and untied the rope that bound her wrists, she spun and lashed out with her foot, kicking the scope from his grasp. It flew into the darkness, and she heard glass breaking when it hit a rock below. As Lin turned to look in the direction the scope had fallen, she kicked out at the strange rifle, and the weapon tumbled over the edge of the rocks in a clatter.

She scrambled toward the brush for escape, but before she could duck away, he grabbed her and knocked her to the ground with his fist. He fell upon her immediately, his knee in her midsection painfully pressing her breath away. The dragonhead knife was in her face, its blade against her neck as she lay gasping for breath through the tightly-bound gag.

"You stupid slut! You think you've saved your lover? You think I need that toy to finish his mediocre life? I would kill you now, but I want him to see you die just before he does. You will both die slowly and painfully by morning, and to my great enjoyment. Now, get up and move out. We'll go to the killing ground."

Her jubilation fought with her fears as she stumbled along, breathing deeply against the gag. She had done something to even the odds against Brad. No matter what happened to her now, she had helped the man she loved.

BRAD HAD NOT GONE far up the trail when the sound of shattering glass pierced the quiet night air. He crouched suddenly, and then realized what the noise must be. Had Lin dropped his scope, or had Nan flung it away? If she did, what would Lin do?

He decided Lin would want a showdown on his terms. Probably at dawn, at a place he would choose. And he would want Nan to suffer through it.

He reassured himself that he had extra magazines for the automatic pistol in his belt and the extra canteen of water. Then he placed the pack on the side of the trail and moved ahead at a steady but cautious pace, watching for the place Lin would choose.

NAN FELT totally exhausted as Lin pushed her to the ground in a flat clearing just below the ridge line. The full moon was gone, and the darkness before dawn had grown deeper and colder. She was aching from the chill and the bruises on her body. She clasped her arms around her torso, shivering as the heat of movement faded away and the coldness seeped into her bones.

"Here, against this tree," Lin growled in a voice that showed exhaustion and anxiety. He sounded more dangerous than ever.

She slowly dragged herself to the tree and leaned heavily up against it. As he again tied her wrists, she held them further apart than before, fighting the tightness of the knots to find some slackness. Her spirits dropped when he removed the gag, for she had covertly loosened it on the trail. She moistened her mouth and spit to clear away the sour taste of the material. He prepared to gag her again.

"You killed my father, didn't you?" she said with difficulty into the cruel face before her.

"No, you useless bitch, but I wish I had. Mallard did that. He always was good with booby traps. That's why I enjoyed so much leaving him back there with that grenade."

"And the others?" she asked hoarsely.

He stopped his straightening of the cloth to look into her eyes as he spoke quietly.

"Mallard killed Alpha Three because he was about to learn of his drug dealings long ago. That would've ruined his chances at becoming an ambassador. I had nothing to do with that killing." He paused, looking down at the rags. "He also killed my daughter!" he said with bitterness.

Again he was silent. She heard him take a deep breath and continue.

"I eliminated Ed Richards to stop his persistent meddling. The Colombian I killed because he tried to sell out to Richards. Luke Bonner died because he had learned that I controlled the old drug routes through Xiang Province years ago, and he learned too much of my smuggling successes more recently. I did not enjoy eliminating such a good soldier. I told the helicopter how to do it, and it killed him."

"And Bum Shandy?"

"He broke into my house and found evidence of my smuggling. When my bodyguard found him, he killed the guard and took the evidence to Quincy Sennet. I caught him there and killed them both. And I would've killed Ralston and your cowboy lover at that restaurant if their reactions hadn't been so good!"

"He is good. And he's coming. I can feel him out there now," she said in a taunting voice.

He slapped her roughly and stuck the gag into her mouth.

"You won't sound so glad when you watch his life spilling out on the ground."

Despite the pain from the blow, she stretched her jaw as he tied the gag, creating some slack. Having secured her, he checked his pistol and knife and moved away into the dense brush. She immediately went to work to loosen the gag.

On the tree behind her was the short stump of a limb just above her head. This tree was smaller than the others he had used, and she had more leeway for movement with the slack she had created in the rope as he tied her. On tiptoes, she caught the binding of the gag on it, and after some effort, pulled it away from her mouth. She slumped against the tree, breathing hard from the effort, but looking for Lin in the brush. The first light of dawn was not yet showing, but she feared that Lin could see her already.

She shivered as the morning breeze washed over her with the strong pine smell. The pine smell. Lin was off to the side of her, and the breeze was blowing from behind her down the trail. Brad would approach from downwind, and Lin couldn't avoid it. Lin had chosen the wrong place for the killing ground.

She had to reach the pocket of her jeans. The tree was not thick, but the constriction of the rope would barely allow her to reach her pocket, even when she twisted her arm painfully. She could feel the small vial of perfume there, but she couldn't pull it out.

By using the tightness of her pocket to hold the bottle, she slowly unscrewed the cap. Sitting to raise her leg, she felt the sharp coolness of the liquid as it spilled into her pocket and across her belly and thigh. It wasn't much in the way of help, but maybe, just maybe, Brad would smell the strong, distinctive fragrance.

"It's up to you now, Cowboy," she murmured softly.

BRAD TRUDGED up the trail slowly and painfully in the almost absolute darkness before dawn. The darkness would slow Lin as well. But Lin would select an ambush spot and be waiting. Dawn would come very soon.

As the trail turned back up toward the ridge line, Brad halted abruptly. Something was different. He gave way to his senses. There was no sound, not even from morning birds. That was of some importance, but it didn't ease the nagging concern tugging at his subconscious. He breathed in deeply. A familiar spicy scent assaulted him, and a sudden flash of warm and precious lovemaking filled his mind, creating an overwhelming desire for Nan.

"Kiss at Dawn," he muttered quietly. Peering into the darkness up the hill, he said quietly, "Thank you, lady. You are something very special. And I'm coming to get you."

He sat against a tree at the side of the trail, easing the pain in his side, and breathing in the lush fragrance of the woman he would soon have again at his side. He thought of how cold she must be, and how he would warm her.

After a while, the first light of day began to appear. He could see the outline of a rock formation to his left that ran up the hillside and over the ridge line. It was free of brush, and would give him a quiet approach with some cover. He checked his pistol and pulled himself to his feet to begin the climb.

By the time he had reached a ledge just below the ridge line, the sky had lightened considerably with the reddish color of dawn. He raised himself painfully to peer over the rocks, and he saw Nan tied to a tree not far away. She was straining against the rope that bound her, her full breasts jutting out of the torn blouse.

A sudden movement beyond her caught Brad's eye, and he saw Lin crouched by a rock, shielded from the trail by dense brush. He had an automatic pistol in his hand, but there was no rifle in sight.

Brad slid his hands to the top of the rock and carefully took aim at Lin. It was a long shot for a pistol, and Nan was between them. It had to be one good shot. He took a deep breath and held it, ignoring the pain it caused. He squeezed the trigger slowly.

The explosion tore through the still morning air. Brad quickly brought the gun back in alignment for another shot, but he saw Lin thrown into the brush, his pistol tumbling away as if in slow motion.

Nan screamed when she heard the shot, looking in panic first to her right for the source, and then to her left to see Lin sprawl face down into the bushes and remain still.

"Brad! Brad!" she screamed. "Where are you?"

"Take it easy, Nan. I'm coming," he said, stepping from the rock so she could see him. He slowly made his way to the tree.

"I'm all right, Brad. Be careful, please!"

When he reached the tree, he pulled the gag down from her face and kissed her lips firmly.

"Oh, God, I'm so glad to see you! But you're hurt!" she said, seeing the blood and his awkward movement.

"Not too bad," he said. He put the pistol in his left hand, and with his knife in his right, he moved around the tree to cut her loose.

"Brad! Watch out!"

Her scream caught him in mid-stride. Something sharp struck the hand that held his gun, knocking it away. As Nan ducked, a vicious five-pointed metal star struck the tree where her head had been, pinning her long hair into the bark.

Shurikan! The deadly Oriental throwing weapons. Brad spun around to see Lin on his feet and moving slowly toward him. Lin's dragonhead knife was in his left hand, and his right hand was a bloody mess. Blood stained the side of his jacket. The shot that had knocked Lin into the brush had apparently hit his gun hand and had struck his side as well. But it was obvious that Lin was equally deadly with either hand, as his throwing had shown.

Brad moved away from Nan toward the advancing threat, now circling for advantage, watching his opponent's eyes. Brad moved to his right, away from Lin's left hand, and into the strength of his knife. He was obviously trying to draw Lin away from Nan.

"Brad, don't worry about me!" she screamed. "You can do it! You can stop him!"

"You are a worthy opponent, Bradford Gaelman, but now you must die, while the worthless bitch watches. I will kill her next."

Lin's words were slow and slurred, showing that the depth of his pain at least matched Brad's. Lin moved in and slashed at him quickly several times, and then followed with two vicious thrusts of the wicked knife. Brad moved with difficulty, but evaded and parried the moves, catching the dragonhead knife with the hilt of his own combat knife. Nan screamed in panic.

They continued to circle and weave, in and out, thrusting and slashing. Lin's movements became awkward as the pain and bleeding took their toll, but Brad could feel himself weakening as well. Lin was backing him up to the rocky edge of the hill.

In an intense effort, Lin made a rush with his body, trying to thrust through Brad's defenses. Brad dodged painfully and kicked at Lin as he went by. Lin's yell became a scream as his spinning body went over the edge of the rocks. The terrible sound ended with a muffled thump as his body hit the rocks below.

Brad turned to see Lin's body sprawled face-down on a ledge below. The bloody tip of the dragonhead knife protruded from his back, the handle still beneath him where he had fallen on it.

Hastening back to the tree, Brad cut Nan free and threw his jacket around her. Then he called upon his reserve strength to build a fire for them. When she had cleaned his wounds as well as she could, Nan tore off a strip of her blouse and bandaged his hand and put a new dressing on the wound in his side.

Brad awkwardly took her in his arms. They sat against a tree, clinging together for warmth.

He tried to think of a time like this in Southeast Asia, but he had difficulty remembering any of those battles.

He could only think of how good Nan felt now and what he wanted with her in the future.

Sitting there on the ground, she was sore and uncomfortable, but surprised by her calmness and happiness. She had no real idea of what lay ahead. But she had no dread or concern. Her inner spirit was content with the calm knowledge that whatever happened now, she and Brad were together. Not as strangers held together by chance, but as lovers joined at the soul.

The sudden whapping of helicopter blades nearby startled them, and they looked up to see a sheriff's copter pass low over the ridge. Brad found new strength to throw some green brush on the fire for a signal. Nan ran to the edge of the clearing, waving her arms frantically.

The helicopter soon touched down in a nearby clearing, and Brad and Nan were helped on board by two astounded deputies. As the chopper lifted off, Brad and Nan leaned close to talk.

"What will we do now?" she asked.

"Well, first we'll have to answer a lot of questions for Rafe and the sheriff."

"And then what?"

"We'll go set up house somewhere," he answered with a grin.

"Oh we will, will we?"

"Why not?"

"Yes, why not," she answered. "We'll do it."

"Do you really think we can have a future together?"

"Take a deep breath," she said.

He inhaled deeply, wincing from the wound.

"Smell it?" she asked.

"The mountain air? The Kiss at Dawn? The helicopter?"

"No, can't you smell it? The good food cooking? The fresh sheets? The clean clothes? The good life we'll have together?"

"The shampoo when we shower together."

"Oh, you! You're impossible, and I love it."

"And you're a hopeless romantic, and I love you. Don't you think one of us should move?"

"Why, is the wound hurting more?" she asked with concern.

"Yes, but I meant apartments."

She stroked his face lightly, feeling the rough beard and the warmth beneath it.

"With you to comfort me, I won't need Dad's apartment for support. Would you like a roommate?"

"Sure. Would you care to make that permanent?"

"I do," she said, embracing him carefully.

"See how easy that was to say?"

She raised her voice to be heard above the whapping helicopter blades above them.

"If you only knew, Cowboy. If you only knew."

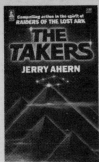

THE TAKERS

JERRY AHERN

£2.25

A gripping story in which the legends of the past could shape the future.

JACK ADRIAN

DEATH LANDS

Pilgrimage to Hell

£2.75

JAMES AXLER

DEATH LANDS

Ren Holocaust

£2.25

The aftermath of the nuclear holocaust – the fight for survival in a living hell stalked by fear.

VIETNAM: GROUND ZERO

ERIC HELM

£1.75

VIETNAM: GROUND ZERO

P.O.W.

ERIC HELM

£1.95

The saga of an American Special Forces Squad embroiled in the bloody violence of Vietnam.

Widely available from Boots, Martins, John Menzies, W. H. Smith and other paperback stockists.

GOLD EAGLE

MACK BOLAN, SUPERHERO